GW00642251

RUDOLPH BADER

WHAT HAPPENED IN THE FOREST

A NOVEL

Copyright @ 2023 Rudolph Bader

All rights reserved

ISBN # 978-1944156930

The right of Rudolph Bader to be identified as the author of this work has been asserted by him.

This is a work of fiction. Names, characters, places, incidents, and dialogues are the products of the author's imagination or are used fictitiously.

Where locations are used, all characters described herein are fictitious. Any resemblance to actual people, living or dead, events or locales is entirely coincidental.

Novels by Rudolph Bader

The Prison of Perspective **(2010)**

White Lies **(2018)**

What Happened in the Forest **(2023)**

PART ONE

ONE

She lifted the curtain. Carefully. So as not to be seen from the street. In the other room, she had no curtains, only a reasonably dirty windowpane. That was easier. But she preferred her comfortable armchair in this room. She wondered what distance she ought to keep from the windowpane. She would never stick her face so close to the window in the evening with the lights on. But now, in full daylight, with that grey weather?

Ah, there he was. He had been hidden behind those bushes, but now he was busy with something in his front garden. That hypocritically tended front garden! Everybody knew what a dirty old man he was. He couldn't fool her, not her. She knew what he was.

She lifted her left arm to scratch herself behind her left ear, a gesture which had become more and more habitual for her. However, she wasn't aware of this habit. Otherwise, she would have realised that it usually occurred when she was nervous. Perhaps she wouldn't admit to herself that she was nervous, even in the slightest degree.

How awkward! Her hand caught the thin fabric of the curtain and gave it a twitch that could be visible from the street. Luckily, there wasn't a soul in the street. That was only the sharp edge of her thumbnail, so sharp because she had been biting it. A bad habit, she knew, but one that gave her great comfort.

Should she go out and face him? After all, they were only neighbours and this was a free country. Every time she met him face to face it was the same thing. Great expectations before and nothing but disappointment after the physical confrontation. She knew he was a man with a dirty mind, the way she knew he would look at her, but then it always turned out a complete anticlimax. The way he greeted her, calling her "Miss Phee" in his high-pitched voice and giving her his false smile as if butter couldn't melt in his mouth...

John was the man who occupied her mind more than any other neighbour. That wasn't because of any positive quality of his but rather because she was a little afraid of him. She never knew why she should be afraid of such a quiet old man, but deep down in herself she had this strange feeling whenever he was looking at her.

What boring man was called John? Simply John? She considered John the most unimaginative name for a man. There were so many other names, more colourful names, names that reminded you of music and spurred your mind towards wonderful fantasies. But not John.

She preferred Alfred. There was an Alfred in the village. It was a pity he lived further down the street behind those poplars. She could only see the edge of his grey roof from her window and she could never see him as often as she saw John. People in the village called him Mr Winslow, but she knew his first name was Alfred. He was much better-looking than John even though he was probably older than John, who was always called John by everyone, never Mr Fletcher.

On the rare occasions when she saw Alfred walk down the street, she often wondered what his life must have been like before he came to the village and settled behind that row of poplars. She heard people say he was very educated and he had lived in exotic places. He was a tall man with a lean figure and beautifully combed, wavy white hair. It was the sort of hair you could sometimes see on elderly film stars. In contrast, John's hair – the little remaining hair that encircled his otherwise nearly bald head – was far less attractive. It always looked greasy, dirty and unkempt.

She suddenly felt ridiculous. What were those men to her? She stood up and walked to the kitchen. She remembered she still had to bake that chocolate cake. She had agreed to meet Robert later. She liked her brother, Robert. After all those years, ever since he was a little boy and she was a teenager, she had always felt responsible for him. She still had a slight feeling of responsibility whenever she met him these days, both of them being middle-aged by now. Robert was a teacher and he lived in town. He had won some money in a lottery a few years ago. She never knew how much. But she knew how fond of shopping Maggie was. Maggie was his wife. Well, she wasn't really his wife, but they let everyone believe that she was. In reality, they weren't married. Maggie was a snob and she occupied herself mainly with her own looks, her clothes and her allegedly important connections. She knew how to burn Robert's money. She was extremely gifted at it.

The cake was a long-standing tradition between brother and sister. Philomena knew how fond he was of her chocolate cakes. Given the sad fact that his so-called wife would never make one for him, she made it her special duty to bake a cake for him every time they met.

They had arranged to meet at the railway station in the nearby country town just after two-thirty. It was now ten o'clock, so she'd better start on the cake now.

She had just put the cake in the oven when her phone rang. She knew you could type your friends' names and phone numbers in your phone so that you could always tell who was calling. But she never bothered to learn the rather complicated procedure, so she wondered who it could be now.

9

"Hello, Philomena," sang Maggie's voice, making an aggravating show of her name by stressing every single one of the four syllables.

"Good morning, Maggie," she answered. She knew Maggie certainly wanted something from her. She would never call without wanting something specific from her. Philomena didn't mind the fact that Maggie obviously considered herself above her, entitled to make use of her whenever she needed her. Philomena considered herself to be a humbler person than Maggie. But she wondered what it was now.

"Oh, my dear, you're going to meet Robbie later, aren't you? Now, as it happens, I just remembered you are such a bookworm. You've got hundreds of books, haven't you?" She waited for a reaction from Philomena. But what was there to say?

"You see, I'm going to meet my ladies next Tuesday. You know, the group of high-class ladies I usually meet on Tuesday afternoon. We usually have tea and cucumber sandwiches at Mrs Miller-Pendleton's and there's also good old Trudy Saundersbury. You know she's the cousin of that member of Parliament, and also Judy Tunbridge, whose husband is a doctor, a consultant, in fact, and we were..."

" – Come on, Maggie," Philomena was getting impatient, "I know how important your social connections are. Just tell me what you want."

"My goodness, aren't you touchy this morning! I was just trying to tell you how important this was for me."

"I know, Maggie, but come to the point, please."

"Let me just give you a minimum of background. As it happened, we came to talk about literature, I mean serious literature, and one of the ladies mentioned a book called *To the Lighthouse* written by some woman called Wolf or such."

"You mean Virginia Woolf?"

"That's her, yes indeed. My! Aren't you clever! Well, I felt at sea, completely at sea. They all seemed to know what they were talking about. Now, since I fear they might return to the same topic next Tuesday, I see it my duty to update my already considerable literary knowledge and hoping you might have a copy of that book, I want you to bring it along when you meet Robbie later."

"You *want* me to do that, do you?"

"Yes. I mean, only if you've got it."

"As it happens, I do have a copy and it's a first edition."

"Well, it doesn't matter which edition, as long as it's the right book. I don't want to make myself appear like a fool when the conversation returns to it next Tuesday. I might even direct the conversation to it so I can show the ladies I'm as good as they are."

Philomena couldn't hold back her smile. But she agreed to let Maggie have the book.

"Also, if you don't mind," Maggie continued, "there's that thing about good books, you know, when people talk about them, they throw around all those big words. Plot, character, symbolism, even things like metaphor and narrative structure. Don't they?"

"Well, yes, if they want to have a more professional discussion. What about these words?"

"My dear, you know I have too much on my plate, you know, with all my important social engagements. I just haven't got the time – and indeed the patience – to make an effort to learn all those clever words, so I wondered..."

11

"But you just used them. So you must know them."

"I don't *know* them, my dear little thing, I just noted them down when I heard them in that literary programme on the BBC last week. Some of them I looked up on the Internet, but I just can't get my head around them. So I was wondering whether you could just let me have the ones that could apply to this Wolf book, so I can make a note and throw them in when it's being discussed next Tuesday."

Philomena hesitated before answering. "Just read the novel and then decide which of them might apply."

"But that's the problem. Can't you at least give me one of them?"

"All right, Maggie. What about symbols? Does the title of the novel strike you in any symbolic way?"

"Come on, this isn't a school lesson. Just tell me what you mean."

"Doesn't a lighthouse in a title of a novel raise any symbolic expectations in you?"

"I don't get you."

"Well, think about it then. I'm sorry, Maggie, I have to rush off. I'll get you the book. Have a nice day." And she rang off. She knew Maggie would be furious. She didn't like it at all when you terminated the conversation, she considered that her own prerogative. So it was a particular pleasure to do it whenever the opportunity arose.

Philomena had long since given up trying to understand Maggie's world and she never stopped wondering why Robert loved her. How could he not feel embarrassed when she behaved in such stupid ways? She had tried to get him to talk about his choice of partner, but over the years, she had given up. You just cannot understand other people's tastes, least of all in the love

12

department. Not that she often thought about such things. In her life, there wasn't a lot of room for erotic fantasies; in fact, her present-day life excluded the entire aspect.

However, she had to admit to herself that she sometimes wondered about certain men or women in the village. Her logical mind told her that two people, a man and a woman living together, must have a certain interest in that enigmatic aspect of life. Lucy and Don, her neighbours at the back, seemed quite preoccupied with the topic. At least, Lucy often talked about the physical side of relationships when they had a chat over the fence.

Was it all just fantasy or did they actually do it together? Philomena just couldn't imagine how it was done decently by all the couples she knew in the village. Her own experience in this department was not the best. She didn't particularly like to remember such things from her own past. Also, she was convinced that present-day society, at least in Britain, was far too obsessed with the topic of sex.

She deliberately dismissed such thoughts. They were too disgusting and depressing.

Sometimes such thoughts led to other forbidden corners in the deepest recesses of her mind. Typically, they cropped up at night, for example, when she couldn't go to sleep after an evening with a little too much red wine. She would toss and turn in her bed while dark memories would crowd her consciousness, memories that she had long banned from her life. They were too dangerous.

It was better to think of the chocolate cake at hand. She stretched her whole body, reaching up to the top of the kitchen cupboard with her fingertips. She took a deep breath and sighed. Like this, she arrived back in the real world, the world of facts.

There was a light rain, but it wasn't cold. While she was busy in her kitchen, she watched the birds in her back garden. She had a large window above her kitchen sink, which allowed her a good view of the whole back garden. She liked the sparrows. She didn't like the blackbirds and she hated the jays. Crows, ravens and magpies were all right. Her admiration of the crows had grown when she'd read that long article in a *GEO Magazine* that explained the birds' high intelligence. They must be the most intelligent birds.

The cake was nearly done in the oven. She took off her pink apron and put the kettle on. While she was leaning on the work surface waiting for the water to boil, she realised that the rain had stopped.

Enjoying her cup of tea was a ritual for her. It required her always to follow the same procedure. First, select her cup from the overhead cupboard, where she always selected the same cup, the one with the white and yellow stripes running diagonally around the side. It still looked clean despite the hundreds of times she had to rub off the tea-stain rings around the inside. Secondly, give the cup yet another warm rinse under the tap and dry it with her tea towel with the nine colourful pictures of English castles. Thirdly, carefully inspect the cup for its cleanliness and put it down on the exact spot between the kettle and the sink, take the old Tupperware box from the cupboard with her right hand and the cracked sugar-bowl with her left hand and place both items on the right of her cup; then take a tea bag from the plastic box and a spoonful of sugar from the bowl and put them in her cup. While she replaced the box and the bowl in the cupboard, the water had usually just come to a boil. So the hot water could be poured and the tea could be brewed. She knew, of course, how many people swore that the milk had to go in first, but in her experience, it was much more practical to add it at the end.

While she was slurping her tea, languidly looking out of the window, she lost herself in memories of her childhood. The silhouette of the trees reminded her of her feeling of loss and abandonment. She pushed it from her mind and tried to concentrate on the present, on the here and now. She had to leave the house in half an hour to catch the bus. So she steered her thoughts to the question of what to wear. The day was still rather cool, but spring was already in the air. She decided to keep on her brown jumper and her mauve skirt. Should she put on her fake pearl necklace? She knew Robert often called her plain.

"Why don't you do something for your appearance?" he had asked her on various occasions. "You could at least put some jewellery," he had suggested the last time. When she had protested that there was no need to improve her appearance, he had just laughed.

Philomena was no fool. Of course, she knew what she looked like, what sort of appearance she presented to the world. Of course, other women were much more beautiful, much more flashy, much more attractive to men. Those were strategies of attraction she could very well do without, thank you very much.

She finished her tea, rinsed her cup under the hot water tap and replaced it in its precise spot in the cupboard. Then she went to the toilet, pulled her hairbrush through her dark hair and checked herself in the mirror. Her face was clean without any touch of make-up or lipstick. She considered herself a healthy and natural girl. She pulled on a grey woollen coat, picked up her black handbag in which she had placed her copy of the Virginia Woolf novel, made sure that the dish for the cat wasn't empty, and stepped out.

On the bus, she sat by a window on the right side near the back. She liked to watch the landscape drifting past with its different shades of green, brown, grey and blue. On leaving her village behind, the bus wound its way along country lanes which used to be ever so quiet only a few years ago. Now, the bus was overtaken again and again by flashy cars driven by impatient maniacs and the oncoming traffic was too dense for such a small road.

Seeing all those new cars, she was glad she didn't have to drive one of them. She had her own car, a fifteen-year-old little Ford, which she kept in her small garage behind her cottage for most of the time. She didn't use it very often, seeing no need for it, but she couldn't convince herself to get rid of it. On the rare occasions when she did drive it, she was glad to have it. Just to own it and keep it meant a symbolic freedom, a vague possibility of things that might still come to her in her quiet life.

Getting off the bus in town, Philomena checked her watch. She still had time to go to the bookshop in High Street. It took her just two minutes to reach the bookshop, which she entered with a warm feeling of comfort. She loved the bookshop. Indeed, she loved all bookshops and libraries. Like most others, this bookshop oozed such a pleasant smell of paper and print, she virtually bathed in its soothing effect. The place was a real refuge from the awful materialism of the outside world. Of course, she was aware of the fact that it was also a business, a place that was trying to sell you books to make a profit. But the mere presence of all these books, giving off this fantastic smell, still represented the world of letters, knowledge, and the supremacy of the human mind over matter.

She found the letter W in the fiction section and extracted a Penguin edition of Virginia Woolf's novel *To the Lighthouse.* On the bus, she had already decided to get a new paperback edition. It would be foolish to let Maggie have the valuable first edition. It was better to keep that in her handbag and let the silly woman have this paperback instead, which was replaceable after all.

At the check-out desk, she decided to ask the young man who served her why she hadn't seen any author's events at the bookshop for quite some time.

"You used to have authors in your shop, usually on Saturdays, who signed copies of their books. It was always a highlight to meet such new authors and to get a signed copy from them. I haven't seen any recently. Don't you do such book-signing events any more, I wonder?"

"I'm afraid not anymore."

"But why? It wasn't only for customers like myself. It must have been a welcome opportunity for the authors themselves as well as the bookshop. Bookshops are partners of the authors, aren't they?"

"That's not how our management sees things. They think such events are only profitable if we can have a really big best-selling author in the shop, a big name which will attract lots of customers. All those new and upcoming authors we used to have didn't attract enough customers."

"But don't these upcoming authors need such events much more urgently than those that already have a big name? If you see yourselves as partners and supporters of the literary life of this country, you should offer such opportunities particularly to new and struggling young authors."

"It's the big names that sell books."

"And how do names ever get big, if not by getting their books taken notice of? By being exposed to their potential readers?" Of course, Philomena knew the answer to that. After all, she had her professional background.

"The marketing departments of the big publishing houses look after that side of things. I'm sorry, but would you please move on? There are people waiting to be served behind you."

Philomena took the receipt and placed the book in her handbag. She shook her head as she was leaving the shop. She knew her struggle was useless, but every time she came in contact with people involved in the business side of books, she couldn't hold back. She knew enough about the workings of the book trade to know how those "best-sellers" were made. They were created by marketing strategies based on the marketability of certain books or names of authors, not on the quality of the books themselves. It was the same thing as you could find in other art industries.

In the same way, for example, certain musicians or painters could be pushed to the top on the basis of their marketability, while hundreds of other equally good, or even better, artists were left aside and the doors to their opportunities were artificially closed on them. She put her thoughts away and resigned herself to the fact that those sad procedures were just another aspect of today's rampant neo-capitalism.

Greeting Robert in the café with a kiss on the cheek, she placed the bag with the cake on the table. Before they both sat down, he looked her up and down.

"Couldn't you find a more boring coat than this?" he mumbled between his teeth.

"How uplifting to meet you, dear brother, and to be the happy recipient of your charming compliments!" she answered with a broad smile.

Their bantering went on for a while. Then Robert thanked her for the cake. They ordered their cappuccinos and looked at each other over the small table.

"How's your job these days?" she wanted to know. She remembered his complaints from their last conversation. He was obviously getting a bit fed-up with his workload. And to tell the truth, he looked rather worn-out as he was sitting opposite her now.

"Oh, you know how it is," he replied with a sigh, rubbing his tired eyes with both hands. "We live in strange times. Parents say they love their children, but they haven't got the time to look after their emotional well-being or their healthy social development. All these important aspects of upbringing are delegated to the schools. Teachers are no longer the professionals who used to transmit knowledge to young people. No. They have become social workers, troubleshooters, babysitters, nurses, psychological and legal advisers – sometimes even psychoanalysts – and all sorts of other specialists. Jacks of all trades, if you know what I mean."

"That's quite a handful, I see."

"Yes, and do you know how perverse human intercourse has become within educational establishments? We aren't even allowed to touch the children. I mean when a boy or girl has a sad spell, he or she may be crying over some trouble at home or pressure in the peer-group, we are not allowed to put a comforting hand on the child's shoulder or touch his or her wrist in a soothing gesture. That would constitute a case of child-molesting."

"I'm sure that's only to protect children from real child-molesters, which you know are more numerous than we like to think," Philomena interjected.

19

"I know. But does the whole of society have to become so hysterical about it? By meaning to protect children, we are turning the whole of society into a prison. Like this, the molesters will have won. It's a similar thing as our reaction to terrorists. Just because a few maniacs want to destroy modern civilization, do we have to make public life so much more difficult and so much more alien for everybody with our crazy measures in the name of safety, safety, safety? I can't hear the phrase 'health and safety' anymore."

"What do you suggest instead?"

"Well, I'm not saying we shouldn't do anything to protect us and particularly our children. But do we have to accept all those stupid exaggerated and hysterical measures?"

"For example?"

"Talking about children and school, I would suggest discontinuing the stupid routine of mothers driving their children to school in their Chelsea Tractors, or in any car, for that matter."

"What are Chelsea Tractors?"

"That's a nickname for SUVs, which should be banned from urban roads anyway. But what I'm trying to say is this: by driving their children to school, the mothers, apart from clogging up the streets around the school, deprive their children of important life experience. Do you remember how we used to walk to school? Didn't we have a lot of fun with other children on the way? Didn't we learn a lot of things about the world, our environment, things we could see, dealing with other children and with adults in real life situations, rather than trying to learn about these things in staged situations in school lessons? It's as simple as that. Children should walk to school, except in rural situations where they live too far away from their school, where school buses can be of service. Besides, did you know that one third of the morning rush-hour traffic in and around Britain's towns and cities is caused by mums on the school run?"

This was such a heavy speech that they remained silent for a while, sipping their cappuccinos and looking around the café. Philomena had read about such facts before, but she had never connected them like her brother. Eventually, Robert resumed his lament.

"The other thing which makes our lives as teachers difficult is the relative position of schools and teachers within our society. Teachers in this country have such a low social prestige. The general public doesn't trust them. Parents either ignore the teachers' efforts or they believe they have to criticise them all the time. None of my colleagues are prepared to take a group of children on a school trip any more. If anything happens, even if it's the child's own fault or a case of *force majeure*, it's always the teacher who is blamed. The school will soon have to employ their own lawyers to deal with all the unfounded attacks on their staff."

"But isn't that a consequence of people's fears in the modern world?"

"It doesn't have to be. Look at the position of educational systems in other countries. It's often reflected in the level of teachers' salaries. The pay of a certain group within a society is a direct reflection of the value this society attributes to the group."

"This is becoming too theoretical for me. Let's change the subject, please."

"Okay, dear. Actually, I wanted to meet you today because there's something I want to discuss with you. It's a letter I got last week."

"Well, tell me about it." She was glad they could leave the other topic behind and she realised from her brother's manner that this was something more personal, something closer to his heart. She had suspected from the start that he would have something more personal to convey to her when he had suggested their meeting at this café without Maggie being with him.

"It's from a woman in Gloucestershire. She found my school and you know all our staff are listed on the school's website. So, she managed to send me this letter." He pulled out an envelope from the breast-pocket of his corduroy jacket. "Do you want to read it, or do you want me to tell you?"

"You tell me. Like this, I can get your opinion of it and if necessary, I can still read it afterwards," she suggested.

"Well, the woman we're talking about is not altogether unknown to me. About ten years ago, as you may remember, I taught at a large comprehensive school in the West Country. She was one of my pupils. Her name's Lizzie. The problem was, at the time, she firmly believed I was in love with her, which, of course, wasn't the case."

"So, you never gave her cause to believe that? Was she good-looking?"

"Oh, she was a real head-turner among the boys."

"You must have given her some encouragement. Normally, teenage girls may have erotic fantasies about their younger male teachers, but they would never let them know. They're far too embarrassed."

"Not Lizzie. She sneaked up to me whenever she had an opportunity in the carpark, behind the gym or wherever she could find me as if by accident. Then she

22

told me how much she loved me and asked why I wouldn't admit I loved her, too."

"And you really never touched her or told her you loved her?"

"Never ever, I swear."

"How long did this go on?"

"For almost a whole school year. Then, as you know, I left the school and moved down here."

"Okay then. What about this letter now?"

"She writes she still loves me and she wants to see me. But that's out of the question. I don't want to see her and I can't see her. She gets on my nerves."

Philomena reflected for a few moments. For her, it was impossible to imagine such a situation. As a woman, she would never throw herself at a man like that. She did trust Robert, but in this case, she was not a hundred per cent sure. His role as a man remained a secret to her. Though they'd grown up together as brother and sister, they had never discussed things like sexual attraction and they'd never told each other about their very personal things. So, she didn't know how a young man might react to the overt advances of a pretty young girl. It must have been very tempting for him at the time.

"Where does she live now and what's her life like now?" she asked.

"She lives in a small place in Gloucestershire and she is a teacher, too."

"What do you intend to do? And why are you telling me all this?"

"It bothers me so much. It's such an attack on my peace of mind and I can't tell Maggie. She would think I had an affair with Lizzie."

"Why would she think that? She lives with you and she says she loves you. Doesn't she trust you then?"

"She has always held a strong belief that all men are dirty pigs."

"Well, she may have a point there…"

Brother and sister were silent for a while, sipping their coffees.

"You haven't told me what you intend to do about it," she resumed the conversation.

"I don't intend anything in terms of action. I'm not going to answer her and just forget about the whole thing. I'm asking you as a woman what you think about it. You know, her letter is very explicit about what she wants us to do together."

"I can't give you any advice except what you just said yourself. Don't answer her letter and don't give her any other encouragement of any kind."

Then Philomena changed the subject. She gave him the book for Maggie and said she could keep it. Robert wanted to hear her news, but she didn't have any. She hardly ever had any news for her brother, but he always asked her. What did he know?

TWO

"I hate you, I hate you, I hate you!" she shouted. At moments like this, she could kill her mother. At least, that was how she felt. She was only six, but she knew how deep hatred felt. Her mother often treated her in such unfair ways. Only this morning, they had made a deal about tidying up her room. Dad had been present, too. The deal was that the room had to be in order by six in the evening. And now, just after lunch, Mum had told her she wouldn't get any pudding because her room wasn't tidied up. If only Dad was present now! Philomena argued with her mother, referring to the deal made earlier, but her mother remained adamant, denying that there had ever been such a thing as a deal. Their words grew in volume and while the mother stood with a stony expression, her little girl grew hotter and hotter. She glared at her mother with a flushed face and spat the most offensive words at her.

This was just one of several incidents that darkened Philomena's otherwise unspoilt young years. Even though she loved her mother, she had to learn that her mother could be the most painful impediment to her happiness. On the other hand, Mum could also be very nice and understanding. It was clear that the woman had to have several modes, several personalities, within herself. She could switch from one mode to another within seconds. Anything could trigger such a switch at any time. This was probably the harshest lesson that little Philomena had to learn before she was even old enough to go to school. It meant that life wasn't going to be a piece of cake. She would have to cope with adversities originating from the most unexpected sources.

About two weeks after the quarrel over her untidy room, she was sitting on her tree in the back garden when her mother called her. How awkward! She didn't want to leave her cosy branch just now because she was in the middle of a game with Lucy, her favourite doll. This was one of her best moments, sitting on her branch, telling Lucy her innermost secrets. Secrets about her life, her parents, her baby brother and, of course, Sandy next door.

"You are a dreamer, Philomena," her mother complained. "What's to become of you if you can't listen? I called you three times and you wouldn't listen."

Mother was waiting for her on the patio just in front of the French doors when Philomena reached her on her way to the house. She was holding Lucy in her arms.

"I'm sorry, Mum. I was having a nice chat with Lucy."

"When will you ever grow up, you stupid child? You are about to start proper school next week, but you still behave like a baby. It's time to wake up, kid! Real life is waiting for you."

Philomena knew her mother didn't really mean it when she called her names in situations like these. She was just nervous. She'd probably just had a row with Dad, which had made her jumpy. She would soon calm down. Nevertheless, Philomena would have to be on her guard in all dealings with her mother. She knew from experience that her mother could not always be trusted, being too moody, too fickle. Also, she suspected her of being a selfish and altogether too self-centred person.

"Listen, Philly, I want you to come in and wash your hands. Uncle Bertie is here. He wants to see you. I don't want him to be disappointed. He's such a fine uncle to you, isn't he?"

Philomena didn't know what to make of Uncle Bertie. He was always very good to her, but somehow, she had the impression he wasn't quite straight, which was her word for honest. She wondered why she had that impression, but it was probably because she often heard her parents talk about Bertie, who was her dad's older brother. They had a great deal of bad things to say about him, but whenever he was here, they treated him as though he was the emperor of China.

Only the other day, she had heard her mother complain to her father that Bertie was a dirty old man who ran after every skirt. She couldn't understand why a man would run after every skirt, particularly because she didn't know many good-looking women who wore skirts, most of them always wore jeans anyway. Another time, Mum had told Dad that Bertie knew how to undress a woman with his eyes. Now that was incomprehensible. How could anyone ever be able to do that? But Dad always reassured her that Bertie was a fine fellow and there was nothing wrong with him. Besides, there was the question of money. Philomena didn't know about such things. But her parents often talked about Bertie's money and how it might come to them one day.

One thing was clear. Bertie certainly liked her. He always brought chocolates and other sweets for her and he was genuinely interested in what she was doing, what games she played, the friends she had, and so on.

When she entered the lounge, she found Uncle Bertie sitting on the large sofa, smiling his broad smile. He always sat right in the middle like a Buddha or like a king holding court. He was smoking a cigarette, which neither her mother nor Philomena liked. They hated the smell of it, but Dad used to say it gave their lounge a homely atmosphere.

"Hello, Uncle Bertie," she said.

"Hello, my little princess. Come here and give your uncle a kiss and a hug."

She did as she was asked, but she considered it bad manners that he didn't even put down his cigarette while she gave him her quick hug. He kept it between the fingers of his left hand. And she loathed the cigarette smell on his cheeks that she had to kiss.

They had their usual chat about her games and her activities. After a while, her mother joined them with a tray on which she brought two cups of tea, a sugar bowl and a small pack of biscuits. Bertie loved his cup of tea and Mother found it easier to talk to him when she could hold onto her cup. Soon, the grown-up people were deep in conversation and Philomena found herself to be superfluous. She was about to leave the lounge when Uncle Bertie spotted her.

"Oh, come on, little princess! You're not going to leave us like that? Won't you play something on the piano for your poor old uncle?"

"No. I don't like to play," she replied.

"Don't be naughty, missy. Go and play something for Uncle. Is that your gratitude for the chocolates he brought you?"

There was no way out of this. So, she sat down at the old piano in the corner of the lounge and played a small piece she had learnt in her piano lessons. She was about seven bars into the piece when Bertie's voice could be heard.

"I say, Linda, your little girl is quite a stunner at the piano."

Philomena stopped immediately.

"Hey, why do you stop, little princess?"

"You're not listening. So why play?" was her answer.

"You naughty girl! You go straight up to your room and be ashamed of yourself!" Mother screamed and her face went red all over. Her eyes stared at her daughter as if she could kill her there and then. Philomena was not impressed. She knew the situation very well. She had done the same thing before. She wanted her parents to understand that she wasn't a music box they could just switch on. She wasn't an instrument they could make use of when they wanted to show off to visitors.

If someone was really interested in her playing, they would have the decency to listen and be quiet while she was playing. Like Sandy next door. Sandy was a little older than Philomena, but she was a real friend. She couldn't play the piano because she had only four fingers on her right hand, a physical handicap she shared with her aunt. When Philomena played for her, Sandy always listened attentively and praised her afterwards.

In her bedroom, she wondered what you do when you have to feel ashamed of yourself. Did you have to sit down and mumble "shame, shame, shame" for five minutes or so? She certainly didn't feel anything but annoyance. How did one feel ashamed? What was shame? She imagined what her doll Lucy would tell her. Lucy's opinions never made her angry but usually soothed her. This time, Lucy suggested she should just ignore Mum and Uncle Bertie when it came to musical appreciation. True, Mum had allowed her to take lessons because otherwise, as she said, the piano in the lounge would serve no purpose.

But neither Mum nor Dad were musical in the slightest degree. They couldn't even sing a song more or less in tune, although Dad seemed to have an inkling of what music meant to their little girl. Philomena's developments at the piano and in music generally were going far beyond anything her parents could have any idea of. So, they didn't know how humiliating it was when they used her piano-playing as a mere status symbol for visitors.

Philomena knew that her level at the piano was still a beginner's level, as she could hear when she heard Sandy's big brother, Henry, play. He could already play real pieces by really great composers, while she was still struggling with pieces written for her level by her music teacher. While Henry's pieces were printed in real music books, hers were hand-written on sheets. Nevertheless, she was confident that her ability at the piano was making good progress and one day she would also play really great pieces composed by famous composers. She was determined to take part in the cultural activities of the world.

Her confidence was not confined to the piano. She knew she was still a child. After all, this fact was hammered into her brain almost every day by her mother. But she had this warm feeling inside her, a feeling of future achievements, of great things she would do one day. She couldn't tell in which areas her talent would shine, but she knew it would do so when it was time. She knew her mother didn't expect great things from her. On the other hand, her father, despite his intellectual limitations, appeared to have some admiration for her piano-playing and was willing to support her in her more artistic or intellectual plans. This gave her a degree of confidence. So she had some hopes for the future.

When, a few weeks later, Philomena started her school career, things began to change for her. While she still confided in Lucy, she found she didn't need the doll as much as she had used to. Two very important things she kept up despite her new everyday timetable. Sandy's friendship and the piano. Sandy wasn't at the same school. She went to a Catholic school, which was in town, but the two friends always found time to be together after school. And though Philomena's school offered cheaper piano tuition, she managed to convince her parents that it was much better to stay with her private teacher.

At school, they had a male teacher, whereas her private teacher was a woman, Mrs Penfold, a really very agreeable person and a gifted musician, in Philomena's opinion. Her argument with her dad was that a change of teacher meant falling back and having to re-learn everything she had already learnt from Mrs Penfold, which meant that although tuition would appear to be cheaper, it was really a waste of money. That did the trick. That, and her father's belief in her talent. Dad agreed and Philomena was so happy that she actually made an effort to practise more regularly, which resulted in better progress with her instrument. She was very happy about this outcome. There was only one drawback. Since she now spent more time at the piano, there was more piano music in the house – not always played with perfection – which annoyed her mother considerably during her household chores. She sometimes lost her patience.

"Do you have to produce such a racket?" she would shout. "I can hardly hear myself think with this din. This piano is driving me up the wall!"

Of course, Philomena was perfectly aware of the fact that the piano was quite a loud instrument, especially in a small room. But when her mother called her music a racket and a din, her ego as a young musician was truly offended. She reminded herself to play more softly, not to exaggerate parts in her pieces which were marked *fortissimo*. But she realised this diminished her pleasure considerably, particularly in the final chords of a great piece. After all, there was such power in this instrument. It lay dormant and the pianist could awaken it when it was called for.

At school, Philomena didn't make many new friends. She considered most of the girls silly sissies. One couldn't have a good conversation about the world with any of them. They were not interested in the world. Philomena wondered why the weather was warm in summer and cold in winter, why the same birds came to feed in their back garden every day, why certain things like a wooden log or a rubber ball would float in the water, while a pickaxe or a knife would sink, why cats and dogs talked an animal language that we humans could never understand.

For her, the world was full of mysteries. Naturally, the greatest mystery was human behaviour. Why were some people so awful while others could be so charming? Why did some people move slowly and clumsily while others moved quickly and nimbly? Why were most girls so stupid while a few of them could say such clever things? Why could mothers and fathers behave in such strange ways? Why was there such a difference between males and females? – questions over questions.

All the other girls considered boys a nuisance. She knew that it was the same for boys, only the other way round. They considered the girls silly creatures. She had seen a short cartoon in a funny book in which one of the little boys called Charlie Brown said something about girls that Sandy's brother, Henry, read out to them. He said, "Girls are the thistles on the meadow of life."

So, it was probably a natural law that boys and girls disliked each other. She wondered if this would last through her whole life but came to the conclusion it was probably just a feature of childhood, since grown-up men and women liked each other most of the time. Of course, there were exceptions…

Uncle Bertie was a regular visitor in those days. Philomena sometimes wondered what her parents had to discuss with him all the time. They seemed to like his visits and they always had topics to talk about. Especially Dad. He admired his older brother.

Bertie was eight years older, which made him an authority on many things. One thing that he often explained to Mum and Dad was politics. He often mentioned a certain Mrs Thatcher and a certain Mr Reagan. Dad didn't seem to agree with him when the discussion came to those two public figures. He considered Mrs Thatcher an ugly and arrogant woman and he expressed his concern over what he called "the bad American influence."

They spent hours quarrelling over what was going to happen to something called the Iron Curtain. Philomena never knew where that curtain was supposed to be. A teacher had explained to them how certain theatre stages had iron curtains behind the fabric curtain, between the stage and the hall, for the audience to prevent a possible fire from spreading to both areas. But she got the impression that Bertie and Dad didn't mean that type of curtain because, in their discussions, it seemed to be a really bad and dangerous thing, that curtain.

Philomena wondered why they didn't discuss more personal matters more often. And what about TV? Mum and Dad watched TV every night, something that Philomena thought stupid. It wasn't for children anyway. On the rare occasions when she got a chance to watch something on TV which was meant for children, she considered it too childish and silly. So, she dismissed TV. But it was a different thing for her parents. Why didn't they discuss TV programmes with Uncle Bertie more often? Could it be, perhaps, that they were fed up with his superior knowledge, his clear-cut opinions about everything on TV?

One day, Uncle Bertie was just leaving their house when Philomena came home from school. Mum was about to close the door behind him when she spotted her daughter.

"Oh, there you are, Philly," she sighed, blushing. "Would you mind walking to Sainsbury's and get me a pound of flour? I've just realized I haven't got any left and I'd like to bake a cake."

She squeezed a five-pound note into Philomena's fist. The girl turned round and walked down the front garden path with Uncle Bertie. It wasn't very far to the supermarket, so she didn't mind Uncle Bertie walking at her side and talking to her. He placed his left hand on her shoulder and pulled her a bit closer.

"Do you know how much I admire you, my little princess?" he asked, squeezing her shoulder and pulling her even a bit closer.

She didn't know what to answer.

When they saw Mrs Henderson from down the road walking in their direction, he let go of her shoulder and continued walking at her side. They soon reached the shops, where Uncle Bertie took his leave and walked on to the bus-stop further along.

*   *   *

When, in September of the next year, Sandy's parents quarrelled with the headmaster of the Catholic school and as a result sent her to Philomena's school, both girls were very happy. Now the two friends could walk to school together. These walks to and from school proved to be among the most important moments in their young lives. On these walks, they could discover things together, they could talk about their parents, their siblings and their little problems.

A recurring topic covered all the aspects of their parents' behaviour. Sandy explained to her how her parents talked to each other. She imitated their voices, her mother's loud but insecure, high-pitched voice and her father's deep, warm voice which was oozing self-confidence at all times. But on the whole, it seemed to Philomena that Sandy's parents didn't discuss the same things as hers. Sandy's parents liked to discuss books they had read, pictures they had seen at exhibitions and concerts they had attended in town. Sometimes, they got very excited about what they called "a recently published best-seller" that everyone ought to have read.

When Philomena visited Sandy's home, she noticed that there were bookshelves laden with books in every room of their house. Even in their bathrooms. When she had to use one of their bathrooms, she liked to have a peep in one of the books she found there. It was usually a book full of black-and-white cartoons by an author called Gary Larson, which Philomena didn't quite understand but intrigued her a great deal, especially those depicting animals such as elephants and huge cockroaches. The women in the pictures all looked middle-aged and wore ugly glasses. She never asked Sandy if she had seen those cartoon books and if she understood them.

How could it be that a middle-aged couple would welcome a couple of cockroaches the size of humans and seemingly a man and a woman, too, the cockroach-woman also wearing the same glasses? That was really odd. Dogs, too, were rather strange box-like shapes and did all sorts of things dogs could never do. For example, they talked like humans. What little she understood in those books presented a rather gloomy and sinister world to her. And yet, she was always pulled towards those books whenever she was on the toilet in that house.

As she told Sandy, her own parents never read a book. There were a few volumes on a small shelf in the lounge. One of them was a Bible, another one was called *The Works of William Shakespeare*, the rest were all called something beginning with *The Reader's Digest Book of,* followed by more words. However, she never saw either Mum or Dad take one of those books from the shelf and actually read in it. Also, her parents never went to exhibitions or concerts. She remembered that one day, Dad was talking about an exhibition in town that everybody was talking about. She had learnt at school that exhibitions were places where artists showed their works – paintings, photographs or sculptures – to the general public. She asked Dad what sort of things were being shown at this exhibition.

His answer was short. "Some rubbish that nobody can make head nor tail of."

"But are they paintings or photographs?" she wanted to know.

"I don't know if you can call them paintings, they're just canvases splashed over with paint. Something every child could do better."

"But if people go and look at them, they must be special. Sandy's parents like to go and have a look, then they discuss the pictures over their meals."

"Oh yes, they would, wouldn't they?" Dad concluded the conversation with this cryptic remark.

The fact that her parents never read any books, whereas Sandy's parents did, was obvious. As Dad explained, he and Mum had better things to do than steal the Lord's time and stick their noses in useless books. It was all right for Sandy's parents, who had nothing better to do and probably thought they were better than "other folk". Such remarks surprised Philomena since she was quite confident that her dad seemed to support her in her ambitions in intellectual and artistic areas that were way beyond his sphere. Did he really believe that books and artistic endeavours only belonged to the upper classes? She knew that her parents considered Sandy's family "upper-class", whatever that could mean.

So, for the time being, Philomena just accepted the fact that even grown-up people could be very different in their likes and dislikes. She didn't criticise her mum and dad and didn't think that Sandy's parents were in any way better people. She just took things as they were without any value-judgement. Her world was still too simple at the time.

However, as time went by, she began to learn more about books and the arts. Especially books. Once her reading had become fluent enough, she started on her first proper book. It was an adventure story by Enid Blyton. In later life, she sometimes wondered how she had found her way into books with her parents so utterly distanced from the literary world and she always came to the conclusion that it must have been Sandy's home with that abundance of books.

Philomena knew about the difference between boys and girls. She was aware of the physical difference, having seen her baby brother, Robert, when Mum gave him his bath. But at school, she realised that boys were a lot more different from girls in other ways, too. Their behaviour often irritated her. She agreed with Sandy that boys couldn't really be taken seriously and Sandy had to know, having Henry as an older brother.

Eventually, she found out that Sandy's feelings about Henry were divided. On one hand, she considered him even more stupid than younger boys. On the other hand, she admired him. Henry was the pioneer in Sandy's world. He fought for more freedom in disagreements with their parents, later bed-time hours, a say when it came to wearing the right clothes, more up-to-date hairstyles and more pocket-money. As long as she could sail in his wake in disagreements with their parents, she was safe. And that was a good thing.

Because going to school also meant more observations in the street and in public generally, Philomena gradually found that not only boys but many grown-ups could also behave in the most peculiar ways. For example, why did people always talk about the weather? On some days, it rained and on other days there was more sunshine; on some days there was an early-morning fog and on other days, it cleared up very early and turned into a really hot day. What difference did it make if you talked about it or not? It happened anyway.

Another thing that she observed was the way people talked about one another. When Mrs Snowdon chatted with Mrs Perkins and Mrs Barber on the street-corner, Philomena could hear them mention Mrs Henderson, calling her "a sly one, that woman, if you ask me," whereas on days when Mrs Henderson formed part of the group and Mrs Perkins was absent, they would talk about Mrs Perkins, calling her "that busy body, always putting her nose in other people's affairs." The constellation of the group of women gossiping on the corner was a constant source of revelations.

One day, one of the women must have reported to Mrs Snowdon that Mrs Henderson had called her "a bloody bitch, if you know what I mean," which led to loud words and absurd accusations that Philomena couldn't understand. What remained the greatest mystery, however, was the fact that those four women in public – which meant in the company of people outside their inner circle – always referred to each other in the most charming terms, as if they were the best of friends.

"Oh yes, I had it from Mrs Henderson," Mrs Barber said to Philomena's mother as they happened to stop and have a quick chat on the pavement in front of the betting-office.

"Indeed?" Mum asked, "Now that's something! Quite a surprise."

"It is, isn't it? And dear Mrs Henderson, she's always so right about things. And isn't she just a dear? So charming."

Philomena seriously asked herself where Mrs Barber's loyalty lay. But that was only the first time such a conversation gave her such an impression. It happened many more times with all the other women of that group. In her mind, Philomena eventually came to call that group the Group of the Ugly Four. Thinking of her new name for them, she said to herself that the "ugly" in the nickname did not refer to their looks but to their characters. Once she had given them their well-deserved name, she could make her peace with them. She knew they couldn't be trusted or relied on and she just considered them a special feature of Woodbridge, which was the name of their area.

And what about the men? Whereas she heard women's gossip more often than she liked, she hardly ever heard men talking among themselves. Did they only talk with each other at their jobs or in the pub? She wasn't allowed in the Red Lion, so she couldn't tell. But she gradually came to be convinced of the fact that men had to gossip about one another in a similar way as the women did.

* * *

By the late 1980s, the two friends had become inseparable. They shared all their new discoveries, opinions and experiences. So, it was quite unexpected when, in early 1990 – Sandy was turning fifteen, while Philomena was nearly fourteen – Philomena felt that a sudden distance was beginning to grow between them. She couldn't put her finger to it, but all of a sudden, she had the impression that Sandy was keeping things back from her. She had no proof, but since they knew each other so well, she thought she could detect a new expression in her friend's face, a sort of evasive smile.

On some days, she said to herself she was over-interpreting things and there was nothing wrong with Sandy, but on other days, she could feel the new doubt creeping into her brain again. Gradually, this doubt assumed the mental shape of a hard conviction. Even though the two girls continued their heart-to-heart talks on most afternoons and sometimes into the evenings, the estrangement between them could no longer be denied when, about two weeks after Sandy's fifteenth birthday, Philomena asked her about one of the presents that Sandy had apparently dismissed and put away behind a pile of clothes in her wardrobe without opening it.

At the time, Philomena had hardly noticed it with all the excitement and all the festive activities during the birthday party, but later, when she was reviewing the events in her mind, it struck her as rather odd. Why would Sandy want to hide a birthday present from her best friend? So she collected all her courage and asked.

"Oh, that was nothing really," said Sandy and Philomena thought she could detect that evasive smile on her friend's face.

"Why are you doing this?" she asked.

"Doing what?"

"Hiding things from me and not being honest with me."

"I'm not hiding anything. Besides, who says we have to know everything?"

"I thought we were best friends?"

"Of course, we are. But please just forget it." With these words, she nervously dismissed the topic and began to talk about their homework for school.

Philomena was disappointed. She told herself that she was probably expecting too much from their friendship. Perhaps her expectations in life in general were too high. People had to keep certain things to themselves. It was Sandy's right to have her own secrets. Only in this case, Philomena suspected something fishy. Her friend's nervous reaction suggested something that wasn't right, something that was immoral or illegal. She wasn't sure, but she thought it wiser to forget the incident. She had just overreacted.

Besides, she had other things to worry about. Over the recent past, she had become increasingly aware of the uneven relationship between her parents. To her, it appeared to be one-sided, not based on mutual respect. Mother would fly off the handle at the slightest mishap or misunderstanding, seeing herself struggle alone against the world and especially against her husband, turning everything into a huge quarrel. Dad always tried to be supportive and understanding, listening to her rantings and trying to suggest solutions. She would just tell him off in a furious voice and with offensive vocabulary.

In such cases, Dad eventually withdrew, looking very sad. This pattern also became more and more common when it was a question of dealing with their children, Robert and Philomena, who were growing up and who started to be more critical about their parents. Throughout their childhood, the children could never get between them, their parents had always stood together. For example, when it was a question of going out, staying over with a friend or being home at a certain time, the parents' answers were always in harmony with each other. They always negotiated beforehand so as to appear to the children as a unit.

Of late, however, this system seemed to crumble with Mum opposing the children's ideas with vehemence and Dad taking their side. As the children were growing into their teens, their father seemed to understand their position much better than their mother. It wasn't a case of *laissez-faire* on the father's side – which Mum often accused him of – he really understood their situation because he listened to them and he managed to feel empathy for them.

It was about three weeks later when Philomena saw Sandy get out of Mr Sullivan's green Range Rover. It was on the edge of Weald Forest near Mrs Henderson's cottage. Mr Sullivan was their French teacher. Both girls often had a chat with him during school breaks or after school. He could talk so interestingly about French culture, French food and French literature. Usually, his explanations were far above the girls' heads, especially when he went on about what he called French symbolism, but they both admired his knowledge and the fascinating way he could talk about the world and France in particular. He called everything to do with France part of *la grande culture*.

He liked to tell them about the easier and more relaxed way the French handled everything to do with sexuality, relationships or public morals. He explained to them how most Frenchmen considered English women plain and unimaginative, whereas French women had a lot more practical wisdom, more sex-appeal, and they dressed in a far better style. After the last summer holidays, he had told them about his time in a place called St-Tropez, where – according to his experience – all women went to the beach topless. Neither Philomena nor Sandy could believe this.

When he explained to them how Baudelaire and Mallarmé were far superior to Proust, the girls were lost at sea. But they still admired him in an innocent way. Sometimes when they didn't understand his stories, he smiled at them with his narrow dark eyes in such a charming way that they didn't quite know how to react. One afternoon, Sandy had confessed to Philomena that Mr Sullivan's warm smile could give her soft knees. Philomena couldn't understand this, but she liked the way the man pronounced their names, Sandy became Sandra with a nasal "an" and Philomena became Philomène. That was really uplifting.

When she saw Sandy leaving his car now, she went up to her friend and asked her where she'd been with Mr Sullivan. Instead of answering her question, Sandy said, "He's told me to call him André." He was called Andrew, but André sounded much more sophisticated. While Philomena envied her friend just a little, she was not sure if she would like to call one of their teachers by his first name. It was not right.

Philomena liked to go for long walks through the countryside around their village, through forests, along wheat fields and following the paths that led along winding creeks. Now, in June, she liked the smell of the fields and green meadows. When she came to a pasture with sheep or cattle, she called to the animals. Sometimes they came up to her to stare at her in blank ignorance, the cows sometimes shaking their heads to chase away the flies, their small ears twitching. Then she stared back at them, wondering what might be going on in their brains. From her biology lessons, she knew what they were doing when they were chewing the cud, but she was still fascinated when she observed the regular movement of their jaws. One day, she suddenly felt disgusted when she imagined what it must be like to regurgitate what she'd eaten just to chew it again. Didn't it taste bitter?

It was towards the end of June when she followed a narrow track through the denser part of Weald Forest. Suddenly, she saw the green Range Rover, which was parked among the trees, right in the thick of the forest. She would have missed it if she hadn't happened to look into the dense foliage on her left, turning her head at ninety degrees. She stopped in her track, wondering if she ought to have a closer look. The car had tinted windows and there was very little light in the shady surroundings, but she managed to look through the rear window from a certain distance without being detected. She thought she could clearly distinguish the silhouettes of two people. They were sitting very close to each other. Philomena thought they might be kissing and nervously moving in various ways.

She lifted her left arm and scratched her neck behind her left ear.

After only a few seconds, she stepped back and walked away from the scene. She wondered if it could have been Mr Sullivan's car. She didn't know a lot about cars. However, she was sure it was a Range Rover, the same type as Mr Sullivan's. Unfortunately, she didn't know anything about registration numbers. For her, the number plates on cars were just a wild accumulation of digits, a mix of letters and numbers that didn't make sense. So, she couldn't be sure if that was really Mr Sullivan with someone else in his car.

On her walk home, she wondered if it could have been Mr Sullivan and her friend Sandy. She was convinced it must have been someone else, Sandy would never do such a thing. But as much as she tried to dismiss the idea, the more forcefully it crept back into her consciousness.

I must be crazy, she said to herself. Sandy would never allow that.

She decided to ask her father about cars and number plates.

"Why do you want to know about such things?" her father asked. "It's normally boys' stuff, not for girls."

"But Mrs Goodwin, our maths teacher, told us that there was no such thing as boys' or girls' knowledge. We have the same brains, the same intelligence and she explained how this was shown by IQ tests."

"All right, my dear. I didn't mean to be dismissive or rude. What do you want to know?"

"For one thing, how do you recognise a certain type of car? I mean, I know most of the different names, the different makes, because those are usually written somewhere at the back of the cars. Ford, Vauxhall, Peugeot and so on. But there are different types and they seem to change almost year by year. For example, how many different types of Range Rovers are there?"

"Oh, that's easy. There's only one Range Rover, the one and only. But as you say, the models may slightly change over the years."

Philomena realised that her father admired this particular type of car. Also, he seemed to welcome the opportunity to teach her things that girls were usually not interested in. It seemed to make him proud of his daughter.

"Okay, Dad. But what about the registration numbers? What's the system?"

"My dear girl, that is quite a long story. Our system is one of the most complicated in the world, mainly because of the stupid British idea that the number plate ought to show the year of a car's first registration. That's an absolutely unnecessary bit of information because it can be found out from the vehicle documents, the so-called V5. Do you want to know the whole history through the twentieth century? The system was changed several times, first in the early sixties, then in the early eighties, and now we'll have to think of a new system by the year 2000."

"Thanks, Dad, but I don't need the whole history. Just tell me how I can recognise a car registered within the last few years, say from about 1980 to now."

"If you buy a new car today, your number plate will start with the single letter G, followed by one, two or three numbers and three letters. If you wait another few weeks, until August, you'll get the year letter H."

Philomena thanked her father again and decided to learn Mr Sullivan's registration number by heart in order to recognise it whenever she might come across it.

When she was with Sandy, she was nearly bursting with curiosity. Should she ask her friend if it had been her in that Range Rover? She didn't have the courage, sensing that Sandy might want to keep it a secret if it had been her. *If* it had really been her…

THREE

On her way back from town, Philomena remembered her brother's story about that girl, Lizzie, and she turned it round and round in her mind. It reminded her of something that was buried deep in her memory. She had lived for many years without ever thinking of that story again. It had just been dismissed from her mind, crossed out from her mental record, discarded from her life. She wouldn't allow her brother's present situation to make her succumb to such a weakness as to open that forbidden drawer in her mind.

She drew a deep breath and scratched herself behind her left ear.

Back in her cottage, she brewed herself a refreshing cup of tea. She sipped it slowly, looking out of the back window, watching the birds. Then she sat down in her armchair and opened a book. It was *Quichotte*, a novel by Salman Rushdie which had been published not too long ago. She liked all his novels but still considered *Midnight's Children* and *The Satanic Verses* his best works. She was convinced that Rushdie would eventually get the Nobel Prize for Literature. In fact, she had openly expressed that opinion back in the early nineties, soon after the mad affair about his great novel dealing with the Muslim diaspora in England. People had not believed her. "Well, we shall see," she always said.

Philomena's taste in literature was varied and much wider than most people of her generation. For her, it was important that the plot of a good novel caught her attention. It didn't matter whether it was more traditional like a nineteenth-century three-decker novel or rather more modern like the works from the fifties and sixties, or even a so-called post-modernist example of magic realism such as Rushdie's work, which she truly admired. Apart from the plot, character was just as important to her. She wanted the various characters in a novel to be credible, somehow coherent in their actions and utterances.

She visually imagined what she read. While her eyes were travelling across the page, her brain was transforming the story into an inner film. An author may not have described the exact physical setting in every detail and still she could see exactly where the door was, where the protagonists were standing or sitting, how many yards from that woman the man was standing and what colour the picture on the wall behind that old man was. Every detail of each scene was clearly visible in front of her inner eye. She could see if the visitor was approaching from the left or the right side of the street and she could see the facial expressions of the characters engaged in discussion.

In music, her taste was not so varied, although she considered it very broad, from Renaissance madrigals to mid-twentieth-century pieces, music which was normally played by BBC Radio 3. But she never even considered popular music, jazz, beat, pop, rock or heavy metal. She didn't mind if she happened to hear a piece of pop music, say in a shop or at garden parties, but she would never ever sit down and deliberately listen to such music styles. She considered them organised noise and she absolutely hated pieces with heavy, regular and loud percussion parts which might as well have been produced by a machine. So, in a sense, she had missed out on some of the popular pleasures of her generation.

But Philomena was a happy woman. She did not want for more. Her life was quiet and uneventful. She was

49

content to be at home in her cottage, read a good book, listen to some beautiful classical music, sometimes leaf through a fascinating photo book with artful pictures of distant regions or exotic cultures and last but not least, play the piano herself. She regularly listened to the news on the radio and sometimes she watched TV.

She liked programmes about art and sometimes she enjoyed a good film. A good film was a film in which the actors could display their talents, not films based on weird technology and computer-generated scenes. Science-fiction films were a horrible ordeal for her. Some of the films she tried to avoid reminded her of some dark memories that she had been struggling hard to suppress for many years. She wasn't going to allow them to bother her – ever again.

A few days later, she had been reading for almost two hours when there was a knock on the window over the kitchen sink. It was Lucy Charlton. She waved, signalling to Philomena to let her in. Philomena reluctantly obliged her. Lucy stepped in and walked straight to Philomena's armchair, where she sat down and crossed her legs with an air of proprietorship as if the armchair, indeed, the entire cottage, belonged to her.

"Oh, my dear," she said with a loud sigh. "You have no idea what I have to go through. No, you can't have an idea. Your life is so protected, you don't know how mean people can be. In your world, there is no evil, you – "

"Hold your horses, Lucy," Philomena said. She was annoyed. Naturally. What a cheek to come in here like a snowplough and occupy such a position in her house! But she swallowed her anger and asked her neighbour what the problem was.

"Oh dear, oh dear, you have no idea! You have no husband who's cheating on you. Your life is so well-ordered. But let me tell you, the world is full of deceit and crime." Making this statement, Lucy bent forward and gesticulated in the air with her arms, a position which looked rather odd and extremely uncomfortable with her legs crossed.

"What's the matter then?" Philomena asked her nervous neighbour.

"It's that woman again," Lucy answered.

"What woman?"

"I've told you about her before, haven't I? Her name's Eva. She's Don's floozy, the bloody cheek!"

Philomena had heard Lucy complain about her husband's affairs before. It was a constant topic of hers. The problem was that Philomena believed that it was all pure imagination. Don was the type of man who was devoted to his wife and she couldn't imagine him having an affair with another woman.

For a few moments, Philomena just looked at her neighbour without responding. She wasn't sure about how to react, what to say.

"You see," she said at last, "it's not for me to judge, but Don doesn't appear to be the type, now does he? He's always so nice to you."

"Oh, my dear Philomena, you have no idea of what's going on in the world."

"But have you got any proof? How do you know her name at all?"

Lucy hesitated before she answered. "I've discovered her name in one of his books. I was dusting his study when I came across a book I'd never noticed before lying on his desk. I opened it and on one of the blank pages after the title page, I found her name. Now, there you are!"

"Was there a dedication or some form of greeting?"

51

"How do you mean?"

"Well, was it only her name, or was there something like 'with love' or 'for my darling Don' or a similar form of dedication?"

"No. All it said in a frightful scrawl of a handwriting was 'Eva Mayhew' and nothing else. But, of course, I knew it must have been a token of love."

"What makes you believe that?"

"Don never mentioned this book to me. So, he must have a bad conscience about it, can't you see that?"

Philomena just shook her head. "Oh Lucy, you do jump to hasty conclusions, if you ask me. I'd suggest you try to give Don the benefit of doubt." She sighed before she decided to change the subject. "I say, Lucy, did you see the drama on TV last night?"

Lucy was taken aback by this abrupt change of topic, but she quickly recovered. The two women continued their chat with a range of other topics and Philomena was glad to have got away from the futile question of Don's alleged affairs.

After Lucy had left, Philomena thought about what she had heard about Don. She still believed the man to be completely innocent. But it suddenly hit her that she had heard the name of the woman before. Eva Mayhew. Where was it? Where and in what context had she heard that name before? She just couldn't remember. But she was absolutely positive she'd heard it before.

Lucy's suspicions had opened up her mind and made her wonder about the phenomenon of love affairs between two people who shouldn't let themselves be drawn into such a complication of their lives. Philomena knew that her friends and neighbours considered her an old maid who had no understanding of the more problematic sides of life, especially illicit love, human passion and sexual relationships. After all, how was such an old maid to know about such things?

Thinking of illicit love affairs reminded her of things she'd written down in her diary all those years ago. She went to her study, a room which wasn't much bigger than a shoebox, the typical third bedroom in English bungalows or cottages like hers. It was where she kept her official documents and bank statements, photo albums, random samples and incidental scraps of paper. To herself, she sometimes thought of this small room as her 'paper room'.

Although there were usually two or three piles of unsorted papers on the floor next to her small writing-desk, she generally kept the room relatively neat and tidy. She dusted it every Saturday and she kept a general order on her bookshelves that lined three of the four walls, which made the room appear even smaller. The shelves contained a good selection of books, mostly paperbacks, but also many office files filled with papers of all sorts, small blue boxes from IKEA containing things that couldn't be left lying about such as photos, post-cards, old letters, tokens and souvenirs, a small wooden picture-frame with an old portrait of her parents, and her binoculars which she sometimes fetched to watch the birds in her back garden.

She knelt down on the carpet and pulled out a bunch of old and rather worn exercise books. They contained texts she had written as a child and as a young woman. These days she very rarely felt the urge to write down anything that happened in her relatively secluded and protected life. But in her younger years, she had often found she had to take notes to write down certain lessons which life had taught her.

She grasped a bunch of exercise books which she had pulled out from the shelf and sat down at her desk. Then she opened one of the books at random.

She read:

I just can't understand Sandy. How can she live like this? How can she sort her experiences in her mind and live on as if nothing has happened? Is she mentally handicapped perhaps? A. S. is such a dangerous idiot, a fake gigolo, a deceitful would-be casanova. All those seemingly continental habits aren't genuine. How can Sandy trust him?

Is it my duty to save her? But what can I do? She wouldn't listen to me. She thinks I'm just a silly baby who doesn't know about what she likes to call "the facts of life". She thinks that carrying on with A. S. like that will make her more grown-up.

Often enough, in good novels and in films, such situations can only lead to disaster and calamity.

Dad said that the new American president was going to be one of the best they've had since Kennedy and he would make peace in many dangerous regions of the world. I asked our form teacher and he explained to the whole class how politics mattered to all of us, and we shouldn't think that things which happen in other parts of the world have nothing to do with us here in our safe country. I imagine what it must be like to live in the Near East.

So that was what she'd written down when she was fifteen back in 1991 or thereabout. What did she know about the world in those days? What did she know about her friend Sandy? About big politics? And yet, those were topics she often mentioned in her diaries: her friends and their activities, her parents, her teachers, the news of the day on TV and what others had said about recent events in the world.

Now, sitting at her desk as a middle-aged woman – was she really middle-aged? – she asked herself if she ought to destroy her diaries. They were so simple, so badly informed about human behaviour and about world politics that they served no purpose.

And yet, the day might come when she would be glad to have those documents of her own views and her own interpretations of the world in the last decades of the last century and into the early years of this century. One could never know. She was convinced of the fact that our past would always shape us.

She sighed deeply and stood up, putting the exercise-books back where they belonged on the bottom shelf. As she was leaving the room, she suddenly remembered where she'd heard the name of Eva Mayhew before. She was one of Robert's colleagues teaching maths at the same school. Robert had mentioned her occasionally but she didn't seem to be a very special person in any way. At least in her brother's view. Otherwise, he would have mentioned her name more often. Philomena decided to ask him about that mysterious Eva when she saw him next time.

On the next day, it was time to go shopping in the middle of the day. It was a glorious day with a pure blue sky. Since she was planning to get some bottles of wine, which would be too heavy to carry in her shopping bag, she decided to take her little car. She walked round the cottage and opened her squeaky garage door. Slamming the door, she made herself comfortable behind the wheel of her small Ford. She backed out of the narrow garage, nearly scratching her rear wing on one of the bushes and headed off through the village.

The man appeared out of the blue. She'd just negotiated the speed hump and the sharp bend in the middle of the village when Mr Winslow stepped onto the street, gesticulating wildly and trying to get her attention. She was about to swerve round him but changed her mind and stopped. She wound her window down while the man approached her nervously and in great agitation.

"Can't you…?" she was going to ask him when he interrupted her.

"Please, can you help me?" he shouted.

Philomena lost her mode of reproach and she suddenly felt sorry for the man. He seemed so desperate. "What's the matter, Mr Winslow?"

"Oh, I just missed the bus and I have to get to town. I've got an important appointment and I can't be late. Oh dear, oh dear, can you give me a lift? I can pay you for your petrol, but please…"

After a moment of hesitation, she agreed to help the man. She opened the passenger door and he sat down beside her. She helped him buckle up, then she drove on, looking straight ahead.

"Are you comfortable, Mr Winslow?" she asked.

"Call me Alfred," he said.

"Okay, Alfred. I'm Philomena. Just calm down. We'll get to town in twenty minutes. Is it an important appointment then?"

"Oh yes, it's about my son, Norman," he said, stroking his white hair. "As I was saying, I'll pay you for your petrol."

"No need for that, Alfred," she replied. "What a world this would be if we didn't help each other as neighbours in the same village, I wonder!"

"You are very kind, Philomena." He looked at her face from the side.

They drove on in silence for the next three miles.

"Have you got a family?" he suddenly asked.

"I have no children. I never got married," she confessed, "but I have a brother. What about you?"

"I've only got Norman. I had a second son, but he's been dead for a long time. So now it's only Norman. My wife died ten years ago."

She dropped him near St. Mary's church. A tall man with a winning face was waiting for him. When Alfred had just got out and was about to close the door, the younger man bent down and peered through the open door. Alfred quickly told his son who she was.

"Hello, thank you for helping my father. That's very kind of you."

"Oh, that's nothing," she said and smiled. The man – obviously, Norman – smiled back and Philomena thought it was one of the most charming smiles she had ever seen.

She did her shopping and drove home in a light mood. The car radio was playing some festive music by Handel, with oboes and trumpets, which suited Philomena's mood to perfection.

After stowing all her groceries in the kitchen cupboard and the small portions of meat in the fridge, she allowed herself a relaxing cup of tea in her armchair in the lounge. Gradually she drifted off into a pleasant afternoon nap.

She was pulled out of her dreams by the telephone. It was her brother, Robert.

"Hiya, am I disturbing you in something?"

"No, I was just having my afternoon nap. You only killed off my nice dream about a good-looking man," she chuckled.

57

"Oh, my big sister is having dreams like a teenager!" he sang in his theatrical voice. "And who was the lucky guy, may I ask?"

"Nobody you know. Can't I have my own dreams? Am I too old for dreams like that? Just because I live on my own doesn't mean that I am not a human being. So, I think I am entitled to my share of romantic feelings. Have you never dreamt of a good-looking woman you had seen somewhere in the street?"

Robert was silent. Then he said, "I only dream of Maggie."

"Liar!"

"Let's be serious now. I'd like to tell you about that woman from Gloucestershire."

"Oh, yes. What about her, then?"

He told her that he had received another letter from the woman called Lizzie Benson. She wrote that she was planning to come to visit him. He was terrified about Maggie's reaction if Lizzie really turned up at his place. Philomena tried to convince her brother that he had nothing to worry about if he was innocent of such allegations.

During their conversation, it occurred to her that she might ask him about that Mayhew woman who had caused her neighbours such problems.

"Eva Mayhew?" Robert asked in surprise. "Why her? What's the matter with her?"

Philomena told him what Lucy had complained about. She asked her brother if he thought Eva capable of such an affair. He laughed, then he considered the possibility for a few moments. He hesitated before he gave his assessment of such a possibility suggested by her neighbour.

"I don't know what you think, but to me, it seems highly unlikely for a young man of – how old is your neighbour Don? – to have an affair with a woman in her sixties?"

"I'm not sure, but I think he's in his late twenties. If what you say is correct, I mean if she's really in her sixties, then Lucy's fears are quite unfounded. There has to be some simple explanation for the fact that her name appears in one of Don's books."

They continued their chat with a few further remarks about the problem with Maggie and the woman from Gloucestershire, but nothing gave them more insight. They drifted into small talk about other people they both knew. Finally, she told him she had other things to do and terminated the conversation. Just before she was going to press the off button, he stopped her with an exclamation and said he had just remembered what else he had called her about. It was about Maggie and her circle of ladies. Obviously, she hadn't managed to read the book Philomena had given her because she'd found it too demanding. But she'd picked out a few sentences and phrases at random, which she found very helpful when she casually dropped them in her polite conversation with her ladies.

"What sentences and phrases?" Philomena asked.

"Let me find them. Just a moment, hold on." He disappeared for thirty seconds, then he came back on the phone. "Here we are. She wrote them down to memorise them. Let me see. Here's one example. *He was really, Lily Briscoe thought, in spite of his eyes, but then look at his nose, look at his hands, the most uncharming human being she had ever met. Then why did she mind what he said?* Now, Maggie thought that was a fine example of good literature. I think it's just useless bullshit, just some phrases out of context. What do you think?"

"Well, let me remember the novel. I think it's Lily's reaction to Charles Tansley's arrogant behaviour. He realises the contrast between his more philosophical view of the world and the shallowness of the women's conversation around him. I think the exact phrase in the book was. *Everything about him had that meagre fixity, that bare unloveliness.* Do you think it possible that Maggie might have sensed the contrast between her expectations about her ladies and their true intellectual depth? Wouldn't that be a piece of irony?"

"I don't understand what you mean."

"Then let's just drop the subject."

"Oh, you are so deep, sister. Okay then." And they rang off.

Philomena was left thinking. Why was it that so many people misunderstood the meaning of literature, indeed the function of the arts in general? Maggie and her ladies weren't the only people she knew who considered the arts mainly a quarry for tools in the game of social arrogance. An especially sharp weapon was the quotation of phrases from famous books, most effectively a few lines from Shakespeare. But what a fantastic piece of irony that Maggie should quote from Virginia Woolf! She couldn't think of two worlds more apart than Woolf's views and Maggie's ambitions.

But then, on the other hand, even though Maggie was a silly, pretentious social upstart, it couldn't be denied that she had a certain charm, too. Philomena could clearly see that. Yes, she often criticised Robert for choosing such a shallow woman as his companion, but she had to admit that Maggie had great physical beauty to offer the world, particularly the men. She was warm-hearted and kind (unless she happened to be on one of her warpaths for a higher social position), she had a way of making herself well-liked in any group of people and one could see how male eyes often followed her buxom figure.

Philomena asked herself if she was jealous of the better-looking woman, but she could clearly admit to herself that that was not the case. Maggie's world was a different world. Philomena had absolutely no ambitions to shine in that world. Her own sphere was good enough for her.

This reminded her of other passages in her diaries. She picked up one of the exercise-books and looked for the passage.

Sandy is a dear girl. I like her very much. She knows so many things that I don't. She is a girl of the world. I am not. She can look at a boy and he will come to her. I can see the admiration in the boys' eyes when they look at her. But why does she want to shine like that? Does she need this admiration? Does she thrive on boys' leering eyes? I prefer to draw my energy from my own heart. I am utterly contented about myself and the things that give me pleasure. Of course, I have ambitions, too, but they have nothing to do with silly boys but rather with lessons I learn about the world. And I can learn my lessons from the pages of a good novel, a fine painting or an earth-rocking piece of music. I could never learn anything from a boy's eager glances.

Does this make me a prig?

Why does Sandy strive to please even A. S.? What does he have to offer her? I wonder. I fear for her safety.

So, looking back to her puberty and adolescence now, Philomena realised how her ambitions differed from her friend's. Sandy's world was a different world. So why did they become such good friends? This remained an enigma.

The next morning, Philomena found a small envelope among the catalogues and pamphlets on her hall floor. She rarely received any letters, so she wondered who this could be from.

The envelope, which carried no postmark, must have been delivered by hand. It contained a card. The card boasted a printed heading, "Alfred M. Winslow, Esq." She was curious what the old man had to say.

Dear Philomena, in gratitude for your kind services, I would like to invite you for afternoon tea on Saturday. Say 4.30 p.m.?

Sincerely yours,
Alfred Winslow.
R.S.V.P.

A clear and short note indeed. She liked that. But did she really want to visit Alfred Winslow? True, he seemed a very kind and respectable man, but wasn't this going a bit too far? Afternoon tea with a male neighbour, just the two of them?

It was only Tuesday. She could afford to sleep on this before giving an answer. She put the card on the mantelpiece in her lounge and devoted herself to her other things.

In bed that night, she remembered the invitation. She turned it round and round in her mind just as she physically turned round in her bed. Was it appropriate for her to accept the man's invitation? She came to the conclusion that it was the right thing to decline. Then she fell asleep.

When she woke up in the morning, she wrote a short note accepting the invitation. After her meagre breakfast, she walked down the village road and dropped the note through Alfred Winslow's letterbox. After returning to her home, she already began to doubt her decision.

On Saturday, she was walking up the garden path to the Winslow residence – which was just a slightly larger cottage than her own – when she took note of a large Jaguar saloon standing at the kerb. Alfred opened the door and welcomed her with a friendly face beaming with pleasure. She wasn't used to this new aspect of the man. Up to now, she had registered him as a rather grim and unhappy man. This new man took some getting used to.

He led her to the sunlounge at the back of his home where he had laid the small table for afternoon tea. Philomena saw the beautifully laid table before she realised that there was another man in the room. It was Norman.

She quickly recovered from the surprise and polite introductions were made.

"But we have met before," they both said at the same time.

"Don't you remember, Dad?" Norman added. "We exchanged a few words when she dropped you in town."

"Oh yes, silly me, I forgot that you'd actually spoken to each other," Alfred answered. "Please, Philomena, do sit down."

The following hour passed very quickly. Philomena was genuinely pleased and liked the men's conversation very much. They had so many topics that the three of them found interesting. They shared her views on the general situation in the world, her misgivings about British and American politics, her opinions on the role of the arts, and her assessment of the dangers in some of the European societies.

While Alfred tended to agree with things said by Norman or herself, it was mainly between the younger man and herself that new ideas were generated and assessed primarily. At one point, she realized how much she got entangled in Norman's arguments and he in hers. They grew more and more confident with each other as time passed. She completely forgot where she was and in her mind, she actually left this house, this village, this geographical reality, she got so engrossed in the ideas and opinions that were being thrown about between them.

It was Alfred who suddenly remarked. "Well, Philomena, this is a real pleasure. We've been neighbours in the same village for quite a few years, but we could never have realised how much we have to talk about. This has been a very pleasant afternoon indeed." This speech marked the end of their rewarding discussions and soon it was time to say goodbye. When she left the house, not only Alfred but also Norman gave her a hearty handshake. She felt a quick tremor shooting through her body when the warmth of Norman's large, self-confident hand ignited the skin of her hesitant pale hand.

When she went to bed that night, she was in a very positive mood. She was conscious of her good luck in life. She was grateful for her general happiness.

Hardly had she switched off the light and snuggled her body into a comfortable position under her duvet when her mind began to race through time and space. She was suddenly confronted by a spooky scene. She saw herself in a forest in autumn with great masses of brown leaves spread out on the ground. Why was she afraid? She was obviously working hard at something. Sweat was running down her face, her neck…

It took her a very long time to drop off into a troubled sleep.

FOUR

Philomena was not sure, but she suspected Mr Sullivan of having an illicit affair with Sandy. However, when she tried to speak to her about it, her friend changed the subject or just assured her that there was nothing of the kind going on.

In July and August, the weather was sunny and hot for several weeks. During their summer holidays, the girls often went swimming. They took the bus to town, then the train down to the coast and they spent most of the afternoon on the beach in Hastings.

The place was full of day-tourists who were enjoying the merry beach life, some of them spending considerable sums of money on the various attractions on offer, from merry-go-rounds to bouncy castles and from dotto train rides to ice cream kiosks. The beach near those attractions was quite crowded, whereas it was a lot quieter further to the west. After a few visits to the place, the two girls found that it was even more pleasant on the beach at St. Leonards, one of the western suburbs of Hastings. So, they began to make themselves comfortable on their bath-towels on this stretch of beach.

At first, Philomena was a bit embarrassed to strip when they changed into their swimming things in the small changing huts along the beach. Sandy had no problem and stripped down completely before putting on her swimsuit, while Philomena turned round, alternately covering parts of her body while pulling off her top or her jeans with complicated contortions. When Sandy noticed her friend's embarrassment the first time, she only smiled. The second time, she made a special effort and turned round several times in complete nakedness so Philomena had to see her. She couldn't miss her in such close quarters. Philomena blushed when she saw her and didn't know where to turn.

"Why are you doing this?" she asked.

"Don't you like my body?" Sandy asked back.

"My mum says it's indecent to show off your body. It's only the prostitutes who do such things."

"Rubbish! Don't you sometimes feel the urge to enjoy your own beauty? Besides, it's quite safe in this hut. Nobody can see me, only you. And we are best friends."

Philomena was lost for an answer. She threw a sidelong glance at her friend's cream-coloured body and realised that Sandy's breasts were already well-developed, while she still had a child's body. Sandy noticed her surprise and in a theatrical stance, straightened her back so that her fine breasts stood out even more.

"Don't you like my titties?" she asked in a provocative voice.

"Stop that!" Philomena shouted and turned round. She was ashamed for her friend. She quickly finished changing and stepped out of the hut. She walked down the beach to their chosen spot, where she spread her bath-towel and sat down. She looked out towards the sea trying to forget the little incident in the changing hut. After a few minutes, Sandy joined her and sat down beside her.

The two girls were silent for a while. Then Sandy broke the silence.

"I'm sorry, Philly. I shouldn't have done that. I wasn't aware of your feelings in such matters."

Philomena hesitated before answering. "It's okay. I'm a year younger than you and I'm not ready for such things."

"But you'll have to grow up, too. Quite soon, in fact. You'll see. Your breasts will grow, too."

"That's not the point, silly. I don't care whether your breasts are a Hollywood film-star's or my own size. Who cares?" Philomena paused before she slowly continued in a new tone. "Is it because of Mr Sullivan that you suddenly take such an interest in your own looks?"

At first, Sandy didn't answer, then she said, "At least he knows about women and he has a fine taste."

"Has he said anything about your figure? Has he admired your breasts?"

"Of course, he likes my breasts, you silly child."

"Don't call me that. Do you really think it's right for a teacher to admire or even to comment on one of his pupils' breasts? Is that right?"

"He doesn't admire me as a pupil but as a woman."

Another long silence. Philomena felt a strong urge to cry. Her best friend was about to destroy herself, destroy her reputation, destroy her future. Mother had often warned her of the dangers lurking behind men's admiration and had, on several occasions, lectured her about what she called her chastity. She didn't quite know what her mother meant by that, but she knew that as a girl, she couldn't let herself be drawn in by a man's praise of her physical beauty. It wasn't right. Such things were for grown-ups only.

"Such things are for grown-ups only," she blurted out.

"Oh please! Don't use such childish expressions. Of course, erotic attraction is one of the great creative powers in the adult world, but this starts right now, now that we are growing up, leaving our girlhood behind us and growing into adult women."

"I am not a woman, I'm still a girl. I like to think of myself as a girl."

"Well, I don't. I am sixteen, I'm a young woman. I have my period, I have a woman's breasts, and I enjoy being admired by men. I'm sorry if I'm leaving you behind, but in a few months, you will understand and you will feel the same."

After this bold statement, the two girls changed the subject. They talked about the attractions of Hastings. Philomena said she found this an exciting town. Sandy disagreed. She said that Hastings was a sleepy backwater, just a minor Eastbourne, and Eastbourne was just a minor Brighton. She found Brighton the real hotspot for young people. She declared her intention of going to live in Brighton when she was older.

"But," Philomena objected, "my dad says Brighton has a bad reputation. It has always been the place for businessmen's sleazy week-end affairs with their secretaries and these days it's full of homosexuals."

"So what? Have you got a problem with gay people?"

"I don't mind them. I just don't want to have anything to do with them."

"Are you afraid a lesbian woman could rape you when you meet one personally?"

"Well, not exactly. It's just, well, it makes me sick when I think of what they might be doing with each other."

"Do you feel the same with heterosexual people? Do you always think of their sexual practices when you meet one of them?"

"Of course not."

"You see. You are full of prejudice. I can tell you, at least three of my parents' close friends are homosexual and my mum told me that she had tried to be with a woman before she met my dad. So, it's nothing bad or unclean. They are just normal people and in many cases, they are even more sensitive than heteros. It's only their private sex life and their tender feelings that are different from ours."

Philomena voiced her father's opinion. "Well, that's clear, most arty people are queer. Otherwise, they would find some real work instead of stealing the Good Lord's time." But she had just uttered these phrases when she realised they were her father's views, not her own. So she added, "At least that's what my dad thinks."

"How narrow-minded and provincial can you be!" cried Sandy.

"I think I should give myself some time to think these things over. I haven't arrived at my own opinion on things like that. They are just not part of my world."

"Then you better hurry up with your growing-up." Sandy calmed down. "I'm sorry if I have been too brash for your feelings. But you see, once you come to my level of understanding, my more mature view of the world, you will see."

"Big mouth!" Philomena said.

"Yes, I'm sorry. I shouldn't have said that. But you've got to agree that you haven't got the same experience as I have."

"Agreed. Now let's go for a swim. The water looks refreshing and there aren't many big waves."

The girls stood up and ran down the beach until they reached the edge of the water. The surf was moderate and the water temperature was cool but agreeable. They swam in the refreshing sea for more than a quarter of an hour before they returned to their towels on the hot beach.

During the school holidays, Philomena didn't see Mr Sullivan, but she was certain that Sandy kept seeing him regularly. In late August, Sandy was different when they met for one of their walks in the woods. She appeared nervous and Philomena thought her friend might be angry. At first, she didn't say anything, thinking that her friend's mood might change when they relaxed and talked about the usual gossip on their walk. But when Sandy fell silent and only sighed a few times, Philomena broke the silence.

"Are you mad at me? Have I done something to upset you?"

"No, you silly."

"What is it then? I can see there's something that bothers you. You are not yourself. Has there been a row with your parents, Henry or Mr Sullivan?"

"Don't mention that monster's name, if you please."

Suddenly, Philomena felt sorry for Sandy. She realised that her friend's affair with the teacher might have come to an end and naturally, it must have been a disappointment for her. The question for her now was, what could she do to help her? How should she react to this? Probably the first thing would be to find out if her assumption was correct or not. Was the affair really over?

"So it is something to do with him, isn't it? Do you want to talk about it?"

"Oh Philly, my dear, you have no idea…"

"Has he lost interest in you? Or have you decided to terminate the affair?"

"Don't call it that! Affair! What a hypocritical word!" she snorted.

"What is it – what was it then, I'd like to know?"

Sandy didn't answer for a while. They walked on a bit more. Eventually they came to a large mossy log on the left of their footpath. They sat down on the cool surface.

"Oh, you see... I... I don't know what to do, I..." Sandy wailed and then broke down in tears.

Philomena placed her hand on her friend's back trying to calm her down. But Sandy needed her time to cry. Her body shook in convulsions and her tears ran down her face. Philomena gave her a handkerchief. She knew it wasn't the time for discussions right now. She had to let her friend cry freely for as long as she needed. It would come to an end eventually and then they could talk. Perhaps.

It took more than ten minutes.

"Listen, Sandy, you can trust me. You can tell me everything. We are best friends. Whatever you tell me will be safe with me."

"You don't understand," Sandy said with a wobbly voice before her body was shaken with pain again.

"But as your friend I can try to understand if you tell me."

After another long pause, Sandy began. "You were right, I did meet André in secret, all through the past few months. I only didn't dare to tell you because I knew it was a forbidden thing. But that was part of the fun, can't you see?"

"Did you love him?"

"Of course! And I still love him. But I also hate him now!"

"I don't understand." Philomena frowned.

"Okay, I'm going to tell you. But please, don't be shocked. You are so young, so innocent, dear Philly."

"I am growing up."

"Okay, okay. Well," she sniffed, "the fact is, André and I became lovers. He was so good to me, so considerate, he gave me such confidence, with him I could

71

be a real woman at last. It was the happiest time in my life. – Until three days ago!"

"What happened then?"

"He'd promised to take me out after the village games and we'd planned to go to Battle for ice cream. At least I believed we had an agreement and I was really looking forward to it. But when the sports activities were over, I went to our usual meeting point behind the King Harold Building between the large birch trees and the school carpark. He wasn't there and when I looked over the carpark, I just saw him getting in his car together with that awful Miss Mitford."

"The young science teacher?"

"Yes, that's the one. He was kissing her before opening the door for her and hopping in on the driver's side. They drove off before I could shout to them. They wouldn't have heard me."

"Would you have shouted at them if you'd been closer?"

"I was going to, then I realised it would be pointless."

"So what now?"

"Can't you see? He's left me for that ugly Miss Mitford!" Sandy cried.

Philomena reflected before she said, "They may have been friends. After all, they are colleagues, so they may very well be very close friends. And very close friends sometimes kiss without being lovers."

"You didn't see their kiss. It was so intimate and he had his left hand on her bottom, squeezing her through her thin summer dress. It was ever so sexy. Not the way a man kisses a woman who's just a 'friend', it was definitely a lover's kiss. Even though it only lasted two or three seconds. I saw them!"

"But that was three days ago. Why are you still so upset?"

"I was just reminded and telling you has made it come back to me, just like that, the whole shock."

"Oh dear, what can I say?"

Philomena knew there wasn't anything she could say to make her friend calm down. She saw that Sandy needed more time to digest the disappointment, to recover from the shock.

"In a way, you should be glad it's over."

"How do you mean that?" Sandy flared up.

"Sorry, I only meant…"

"You stupid bitch! Just because you have no lover, you think you can trample on my feelings like that."

"I didn't mean to upset you."

"But you don't understand. The man has destroyed my life."

"Oh, come on," Philomena still tried to calm her down.

"I could kill him," Sandy snarled.

"You're only saying that because you're hurt, disappointed, humiliated. In a few days, all this is going to be – "

"Oh, stop it! Of course, I'm going to kill him. I mean it. I really mean it!"

Philomena thought it best to leave her friend alone for a while. She turned and walked back in the direction of their village, leaving her angry friend behind. Sandy, sobbing, sat down under a tree and didn't even realise Philomena's absence for a few minutes. This was a huge breach and a terrible rupture between the two friends.

They did not meet again for a long time after that.

* * *

"You just have to be patient, my dear," the nurse said as she was arranging the bedding, careful not to hurt Philomena's left leg, which was encased in a thick plaster. "Things will get better, you will see. Once that plaster has come off, you're going to feel a lot better."

"And when is that going to be?" Philomena moaned.

"I think you might leave the hospital in two or three days, my dear. You heard the doctor this morning, didn't you."

Philomena felt bored today. She was sick of this hospital bed. Although the doctor had told her that patients with fractured legs used to remain in hospital a lot longer when he was younger, she still wished she could leave the hospital and get rid of this plaster soon.

It had been such a stupid little accident. All because of her silly old dolls. She'd decided to stow them away. Three dolls she used to play with throughout her childhood. Her childhood was over and she was going to be an adult woman soon. She wouldn't need her dolls anymore. She'd fetched a box from the attic, placed the dolls in the box and attempted to put the box on top of the wardrobe in her bedroom. She'd got a stool from the kitchen, climbed on it, and just as she was pushing the box onto the top of the wardrobe, she slipped and crashed to the floor. At first, things had seemed to be okay, only a slight awkwardness in her left leg. But then the sharp pain had hit her. She had broken her leg.

And now, she was imprisoned in this awful hospital bed. She wasn't worried about her leg, or about her health on the whole, but she was terribly bored. How could she kill her time? She'd read several books, but she was getting fed up with the girlie books her mother had brought her. Somewhere she'd read those books belonged to the category called "Chick Lit". Not a very character-building name for a literary category. But she didn't know enough about literature to know what else she could read and her mother was no help there.

What could she do?

All of a sudden, it hit her like happy lightning. She would write her own books. She had often played with the fantasy of becoming a serious writer herself. Like this, she would be able to forge her own plots and design her own fascinating characters. She was confident of her own powers. She would enthral her readers.

She fetched her exercise-book, in which she'd scribbled some texts they had to compose as homework for school and some minor maths calculations. She opened a new page. Chewing her pencil, she wondered how to begin her story.

One day, Anna Lisa Moore was walking home from her work. She wrote in her neat handwriting.

Now, how to continue?

Anna Lisa was an only child. She was twenty-five years old. She was not rich. But she was a happy person. She still did not know anything about the awful things that were going to happen later.

Oh no, this was too boring. And how can a writer who is still a child describe a woman of twenty-five? Philomena realised she would have to design her character in more detail before the actual writing process.

There was a knock on the door and a visitor entered. She looked at him and at first, she hardly recognised him. It was Henry, Sandy's older brother. Why did he look so different, so grown-up?

"Hello, Philomena," he said and she noted the deep manliness of his voice. In a flash, she remembered that he

75

had always called her by her full name, never by any of the short nicknames that his sister used.

"Hello, stranger," she replied. "Long time no see. How are you these days?" She looked him up and down. He was still a teenager as far as she knew, but he looked like a grown man. He sported a shadow of a moustache on his upper lip. He gave her a winning smile.

"I thought you might be bored and you'd welcome a chat with somebody who shares some of your interests."

"Oh, that's very nice of you." Philomena smiled.

"And how are you? Any pain?"

"No, that's no problem. It's just boring to be sitting here. I have no books worth reading. And I miss my piano."

He nodded. "Oh, I can understand. I would miss it too if I was in your situation."

"Of course, it would be a lot worse for you. You play so much better."

The two young people discussed several aspects of piano pieces they knew. While Philomena's experience didn't go beyond Clementi sonatas and easier Telemann pieces, Henry could tell her about the difficulties he was having with Haydn and Mozart sonatas. Eventually, they ended up with their opinions on Bach's *Italian Concerto* BWV 971. Whereas Philomena could only play the first page of the first movement, Henry told her about the grandeur of the entire work and especially praised the middle movement.

"I believe the slow movement is one of Bach's finest compositions for the keyboard. I wish I had a harpsichord to play the piece, but even on the piano, it's so beautiful. Do try to learn it, Philomena, and you won't be disappointed. You can play this movement in all your different moods. It will make you even happier when you're happy and it will give you great consolation when you're sad about things. The piece will be your most reliable companion through life."

After this great speech, he remained silent and watched her reaction. She was impressed and decided to learn the whole concerto, but she knew what a challenge this was.

"I have great respect for the concerto. There's the independence of the two hands and there's the exact fingering to get through the whole thing."

"I know," he said, but in his tone, there was great encouragement.

They spoke a bit more about other topics such as school, Sandy and the news of the day. Henry also told her about his driving test he was hoping to pass soon.

After he had said that they should continue their chat once she was out of hospital, he took his leave and quietly left the room. Philomena began to ruminate about what they had discussed. Naturally, she was determined to learn the Bach concerto as soon as she was back at home. It would take her months, if not years. But after going through the topics they had discussed, her mind led her to the basic question. Why had Henry paid her this visit? They had never been very close. He was just Sandy's older brother. She didn't find a satisfactory answer, but she found that the visit had made her feel better. She felt less annoyed about her situation.

She didn't feel like returning to her writing. She decided to change her daily routine back at home in order to have more time to practise the piano. She didn't know why, but she definitely wanted to show Henry that she was able to play the entire Bach concerto, all three movements.

However, she admitted to herself that she might have to be satisfied with a slower pace in the third movement. Even so, it was a great challenge she was ready to accept. Mrs Penfold had announced only recently that she might allow her to play Mozart's C-major Sonata K 545, which was often called *sonata facile*, but which was anything but easy. About her ambitions for the Bach concerto, Mrs Penfold didn't know yet. Philomena would have to tell her. She knew what the answer would be. "That's a bit beyond your level and you'd have to practise a lot more. Why don't you learn some of the easier pieces that I gave you?" But this time, she would stand up against the woman's reservations.

With these new plans on her mind, Philomena's time at the hospital flew by more quickly. Soon the day came when she was discharged to go home. Back at home, she still had to be careful about her left leg, but she was free at last! She had to stay at home for another week, but then they gave her a special walking plaster, a modern contraption which allowed her to walk – and even to step on her broken leg – without harming herself, while the fracture could continue its healing process. This allowed her to go back to school.

For the next three weeks, her father gave her a lift to school in his small car every morning and he met her again after school. She missed meeting her friends and classmates on her way to school, but she told herself it was only for a limited period. Soon, she would be back to normal.

Sandy helped her with the school work she had missed. It wasn't very much that she could have found difficult, especially not in maths and science, but she had apparently fallen behind in French. Several times per week, Sandy came to Philomena's home to do some

French exercises with her. The most difficult bits had to do with what the teacher called *la concordance des temps* and with verbs with two objects, *un pronom objet direct et un pronom objet indirect*.

The two girls spent many hours in Philomena's room to practise these special features of the French language. During these sessions, Philomena never asked her friend about Mr Sullivan, but his shadow was always present. It stood between them when they practised *me le, te le, le lui, nous le, vous le, le leur* and similar routines and it stood between them when they summarised a text they had just read.

Of course, Philomena remained true to her resolution and organised her time at home so that she could practise at least a whole hour at the piano every day. She plodded her way through the remaining six pages of the first movement of the Bach concerto. She spent hours upon hours just getting her fingers round the notes in bars 42 to 46 and 96 to 101. This concerto would remain a constant challenge for her throughout the rest of her life, she knew.

When she looked at the sheet music in her hand, she didn't know how long her tatty old edition of the concerto would hold together. She had found it among old stuff they kept in the garage. Apparently, one of her great-aunts had played the piano, so they still had some of her sheet music among the old stuff. That great-aunt must have been a very good pianist. But her parents had never told Philomena about her. Perhaps she might learn to play the piece so well that her parents would agree to buy her a new edition?

Meanwhile, her normal everyday life continued in regular grooves. The better her leg healed, the happier she felt. And the day came when she had no more plaster or bandage and could walk normally. No more limping, no more pain.

One day, Henry came to see her at her home. He seemed a bit more nervous than she remembered him from the hospital. She invited him to her room. As they were stepping up the narrow staircase, her mother looked round the corner from the kitchen.

"Are you going to introduce me to this young man?" she enquired in a forced singsong as if this was some formal occasion at Buckingham Palace.

"Oh, Mum, you know Henry, Sandy's brother."

"Good afternoon, Mrs Webster," Henry said politely.

"How do you do, young man," the mother replied in an attempt to appear upper-class. Philomena felt awful but decided to say nothing and let it pass.

When they reached her room, Henry asked, "Are you sure it's okay for your mother if you have a 'gentleman caller' in your room?" And they both laughed at the expression.

"Where did you get that from?" she asked.

"From *The Glass Menagerie*, a play by Tennessee Williams, a very good American playwright."

She was impressed by all the books he had obviously read. And she decided to read a lot more. She was already a happy reader, but she yearned for more. It dawned on her that one could learn ever so many things about the world from books.

FIVE

It was a beautiful spring afternoon when Norman came to see Philomena in her cottage. She was surprised to find that she wasn't surprised by his visit. She hadn't really expected him to call, but at the same time, she felt it to be completely normal.

"Do come in," she invited him.

They stood in the hall, looking at each other, not quite certain about what to do next. Philomena wrung her hands and realised that she wasn't dressed for a visitor. She was in her gardening things, her dungarees still a bit dirty, but at least she had washed her hands.

She pushed a small streak of hair from her forehead behind her ear and stammered, "Won't you come to the lounge?"

They sat down facing each other. Norman began to tell her about his father first. She was glad to learn there still existed an excellent relationship, mutual respect and even love between parent and son. It made her wonder why she hadn't kept a better relationship with her own parents. Of course, parents have to be prepared for the fact that their children will develop different interests, a different career and indeed a different world view. Her own parents had never understood how she could devote so much time to her reading and her music. They considered it a waste of time. And when she declared she was hoping to become a writer, they had finally given up on her.

Norman looked round the room, saw the piano and changed the subject. He asked her how good her piano-playing was. She answered that, unfortunately, she couldn't afford to spend enough time at the piano. She felt

81

she didn't know him well enough to talk about her difficulties with the more challenging pieces for this instrument. So, she just gave him some general comments about how the piano gave her a lot of hard moments but also a great deal of extreme pleasure.

"Have you ever had any higher ambitions for the instrument?"

"Perhaps sometimes when I was a teenager, but never seriously. I was honest enough to admit to myself that my talent was limited."

"You are very wise. It's not so easy to judge oneself accurately, especially to admit one's weaknesses or even defeat. I knew you were a very wise woman when we first met at my dad's. And to tell you the truth, I was impressed with your knowledge of world literature. Many people in this country know something about Shakespeare and Jane Austen. Shakespeare because his works are taught at school as national monuments. Everyone is called upon to have a few quotations ready for use in social talk, to claim a certain degree of education even though they might not understand the full meaning of such quotations.

"Jane Austen because people like to read her novels as romantic love stories, not because they admire her stance on the important social development at the turn of the century, from the eighteenth to the nineteenth century, with the changes which gradually took place, from the arranged marriage to the love match, and her exposure of the precarious position of women at her time. Apart from Shakespeare and Austen, however, they haven't read a great deal, certainly not foreign literature. But you, Philomena, seem to go deeper in your reading."

"Hold your horses. You are exaggerating. Although I agree with some of what you've just said, I think your view of English society is too arrogant. You would be surprised at how much people actually read."

"Yes, men read car maintenance books or biographies of footballers and women read cheap pulp fiction or cookery books."

"I think your view is too superficial, too negative, too distorted. I'm sorry, it's the view of an arrogant prig. Sorry for this! And incidentally, why should pulp fiction be cheap? You just called it cheap."

Her heated reaction surprised him. He was silent for a few moments while she wondered if they could still become friends. Despite his arrogant description of the reading habits of people in general, she still liked him as a person.

They changed the subject. She realised that he liked to talk about himself. He liked to talk about the narrow-mindedness of the village. She asked him how he could imagine himself to be a judge of that, living in London. It would rather be his father who could give an informed opinion on the village. He admitted that she was probably right. She liked men who could admit mistakes or false judgements.

"Can you tell me about London these days? Are people less narrow-minded there? Does the big city inoculate its inhabitants with deeper insight and with a wider understanding of the world?" She smiled at him questioningly.

He took up her challenge. "As far as I can tell – and I am far from perfect in my assessment – people in London may have a better understanding of the hardships of modern life. When it comes to the world at large, I would say that they believe they are on top of international affairs and they live up to the latest trends in

83

all kinds of fashions. But it's only their interpretations of those foreign fashions that they emulate.

"They also think they understand all the other nations, all the different cultures of the world, because they have all those cultures living in London. But they would never understand that their city may be as multicultural as you like but the people from other cultures in London are different from the people of the same cultures who live in their home countries. Can you see? A man from Pakistan or a woman from Brazil become different persons once they migrate to Britain. The process of migration transforms them, a transformation which lasts over several generations."

"You may have a point there," she conceded. "But I think you are oversimplifying things a little."

"I don't think I am. And do you know why? It's the English language. The English see the world through their English filter, missing out on many aspects. If they knew more foreign languages, things might be better. But knowing only one language limits your view of the world considerably, no matter what that only language is.

"Just take Europe, for example. We need not even talk about the whole world; Europe is complicated enough. I don't think you can say you understand Europe as a continent unless you have a fair knowledge of French, German, one southern European language and one eastern European language. And when it comes to the whole world, you can multiply this."

"I think that's a perfectionist's view."

"That may very well be. But don't you sometimes get a bit irritated when you watch a TV programme or read an article in the paper in which journalists give their interpretations of certain problems in other countries? Of course, there are a few very able journalists who actually speak several foreign languages, but the majority of them can just give you their interpretation which is narrowed down by their English perspective."

"Perhaps, yes. But don't forget that it is their task to help their English audience understand those foreign facts, which they can only achieve if things are served up to them within their own system of beliefs."

Norman looked at her, thinking. He realised that Philomena represented an equal challenge for him. With her, he would never get away with apodictical statements from his high horse.

They talked a bit more about everyday matters of the village and they also discussed Norman's father. Norman believed that the old man was getting a little forgetful. He wondered if Philomena might visit him from time to time to make sure he was all right. He was very happy for his father to have made friends with her. She would be a very good influence for him.

She promised she would check on Alfred Winslow from time to time. "I don't mind. He's such a friendly man. In fact, I quite like him."

This made Norman happy and he soon took his leave. Stepping out of the door, he shook her hand and looked at her with a friendly face. She noticed that his eyes were a deep brown and when he smiled, he was actually quite attractive.

*   *   *

Alfred Winslow was sitting in the corner of the saloon bar at the Fox and Hounds, sipping his pint of Bombardier. He had yesterday's paper in front of him and was scratching his stubbly chin when he was addressed by a man standing at the bar, holding his pint of London Pride.

"Hey Fred, how are things? Still unhappy about the world?"

Alfred looked up and recognized John Fletcher, the "dirty old man" who lived on the other side of the village. He called him a "dirty old man" in his mind because most people called him that.

"What makes you think I'm unhappy?" he replied to John's rhetorical question. If John was generally considered a dirty old man, Alfred was the permanently unhappy, grumpy old man in people's minds.

"Oh, you went on about Brexit and the PM in such a way when I last saw you."

Alfred was silent for a while, just looking at John and taking a sip from his pint from time to time. He thought of John's poor reputation in the village, his uneventful life and his lack of education and he wondered why he should take anything seriously that the man had to say. He didn't think John had ever been abroad and he'd ever read a good book. He could just imagine the dirty old man sitting in front of his TV, watching pornographic DVDs.

"I say, Fred," John began anew, "didn't I see your boy carrying on with the strange old girl next door? He won't get anywhere with her if you ask me."

Alfred remembered that John's cottage was next door to Philomena's. "First, he is no longer a boy but a grown man in his forties and second, he certainly isn't 'carrying on' with her, as you call it. He merely paid her a polite visit. Obviously, they seem to share a few interests."

"How could they? Your boy has been to university, hasn't he? And quiet old Miss Philly hasn't the slightest clue about the world. She hasn't travelled, she's as uneducated as an old bat, and she has certainly never had sex or even just kissed a bloke, for that matter. She's so ignorant, I'm telling you, she avoids any chats with me, afraid she might betray her ignorance. She just keeps to herself. A bloke would have a hard time cracking her shell and showing her what's what between humans. So hoity-toity, she wouldn't ever call a spade a spade."

"How do you know?"

"Oh, it's common knowledge. Everyone in the village considers her a dry old hag. She's probably a feminist or a lesbian. It's obvious she has no sex life. I'm telling you."

"So you are. You really seem to be well-informed." Alfred was so disgusted, he drained his glass and stood up, mumbling, "Gotta go, sorry."

As he was walking home from the pub, Alfred was thinking about what old John had said to him. The old chap was really senile. How could he think such things about Philomena? How could he believe such gossip, even if such gossip existed in the village? True, she was a quiet woman, mostly keeping to herself. How unfair to spread such rumours about a woman who lived on her own! And what did it concern other people whether she had a sex life or not? How vulgar!

As he was stepping up his garden path, he said to himself he had a duty to protect the poor woman. Next time anyone in the village should utter similar opinions about her, he was determined he would stand up for her. He would defend her good reputation. With this resolution, he entered his front door.

As it happened, he had his next opportunity two weeks later at the small village grocery store in Beech Lane. He did his regular shopping at the supermarket five miles away, but today he just needed some butter. He liked a buttered toast with his bacon and eggs in the morning and he'd run out of butter for the next morning, so he thought he might as well nip down to the grocery store in the village. He put on his shoes and grasped a paper bag from the bottom drawer in the kitchen before he left the house and leisurely walked through the village. He even felt like whistling an old tune, he felt so relaxed and happy.

As he entered, he mumbled a soft "good morning" to the three persons in the shop. They consisted of Emily, the young girl who served the customers when her parents were out – probably getting supplies from the market in town – the hyped-up Lucy Charlton from the other side of the village and a plain woman with greyish ginger hair in her sixties whose name he didn't know.

He realised at once that the three had been in a heated conversation when he entered and interrupted them.

The elderly woman seemed unwilling to sacrifice whatever she still had to say just because of the old man entering the shop. "I'm telling you, she's a sly one, that floozy with her mock-innocent face."

"No," Lucy couldn't resist the temptation to contradict, "I'm her next-door neighbour and I can tell you she's a dry old hag who has no idea of the world. Everyone knows she hasn't ever had you know what I mean…"

"Come on, old girls," Alfred said with a firm voice. "I think you'd better look after your own business rather than spread stupid rumours about your neighbours. You have absolutely no idea what you're talking about. So please, just shut your mouths!"

Three pairs of eyes stared at him as if they could kill him and three mouths remained gaping for another two seconds before they were shut. The women were too shocked and surprised at the nerve of this old man. How could he dare to criticise them! They were entitled to their share of innocent gossip. But neither of them said anything. Finally, young Emily asked in her musical voice. "What can I do for you, Mr Winslow?"

He got his butter and left. Hardly had he closed the shop-door behind him when he heard that the gossip had resumed inside. His admonishing words had obviously been without effect. Nevertheless, he was resolved to speak up whenever he encountered unfair gossip or false rumours.

Three days later, as he was sitting in his lounge reading the paper, he saw Philomena's car passing in the street. This reminded him of all the gossip about her. He wondered if any of those unfair allegations had any foundation in reality. Probably not. They just sprang out of people's fantasies if they couldn't place a person. Philomena did not fit any of their categories, so they invented all sorts of things about her. He did not know much about her either, but he would never invent stupid things about her. He had his high moral standards, always respecting the integrity of other people.

And even if the poor woman might have had a quiet life as a recluse, even if she never had a gentleman-friend or never had a very adventurous life, she still deserved his unmitigated respect. True, she kept things to herself as if she had to hide something and her dress-style signalled to the world that she wanted to be seen as a sexless person. But was that a reason to treat her in such an unfair and rude way?

He wondered about Philomena's life. How could she cope on her own? What source of income did she have? Not that he wanted to be too nosy, but she was far too young for a state pension. She was probably in her forties, possibly in her late forties. What was her job? He never saw her go to work and she hadn't mentioned any kind of employment or free-lance work when they had approached the subject a while ago. He didn't want to ask. Was it possible that she was a person of independent means?

In the following week, Philomena paid him another visit. They smiled at each other when she stepped through his front door.

"I hope I'm not disturbing you," she said.

"Not at all, I was merely preparing my next speech for the General Assembly at the United Nations," he replied with a twinkle in his eyes.

For a fraction of a second, she nearly believed him, but seeing his face made her realise his healthy sense of humour. "Oh, come on," she said, "let me give you some good ideas about how to promote world peace."

He shuffled to the kitchen and she followed him. "Tea or coffee?" he asked.

"Tea," she answered.

He took hold of the kettle and started the procedure. She asked him where the cups were and he showed her his collection of mugs in one of the cupboards. She was impressed. He had quite a collection, mugs from all over the world.

"You know, when I was travelling in my younger days, I often picked up a mug from a souvenir shop. You might as well get something useful, I told myself. Please, take your pick."

She selected two cups from Italy. Soon, the tea was ready and they settled down in the lounge.

"Have you often been to Italy?" she asked.

"Quite a few times. But don't get me wrong. I never went to those ghastly tourist spots. I liked the more remote places in Liguria, Emilia-Romagna, Campania, Puglia or Calabria, you know, those small towns on top of a hill or sticking to a steep slope, places where you could sit in a small street café and just enjoy normal Italian life unrolling around you. You could chat to the locals and forget the passage of time over a glass of red wine.

"Of course, you can never completely escape the tourists, but at least you can avoid the destinations of mass tourism. I think it's terrible how tourism has developed into a huge industry over the past few decades. Travelling was still a real adventure and a unique experience which taught you ever so many things when I was a young man."

"You are quite right," she said, taking another sip from her mug.

"And what about you?" he asked. "Have you travelled a lot?"

"Well, I have been to a few places, but it wasn't really as a tourist. I collected material."

"Oh, that's interesting. What is your work, may I ask?"

"I'm an author. You will be horrified when I admit to you that I write pulp fiction, or romance. You know, those novels where you soon find out who is going to fall in love with whom, who is a good person and who is a villain and everything in the plot is predictable, often embedded in beautiful landscapes where the sun always shines. No real conflicts, no violence, no sex, only occasionally implied or hinted at."

He was speechless.

"Are you shocked?" she asked.

"Well, I was just a bit surprised. Knowing you as a literary person and a woman who can talk intelligently about serious literature, someone who is familiar with some of the great works of world literature, it is quite an unexpected revelation. How can you keep these two conflicting interests apart?"

"They are quite separate areas of interest, two different existences of myself. When I read a good book, I don't compare it with my own writing and when I'm writing my novels, I exclude my experiences in the literary world."

"Isn't that very difficult sometimes?"

"Let me give you a comparison. It's like a woman who is happily married but who regularly works as a prostitute. When she is in bed with her husband, she has no recollection of her activities with her customers and when she has sex as a prostitute, it has nothing to do with the loving togetherness with her husband. These are two separate worlds for her. Does this make things clear?"

"A stark comparison. Really crass! I admire your courage."

Philomena smiled.

"But can you live from your royalties?" he asked. "I mean, does it really pay to write such novels? Or do you write them for pleasure?"

"The money is more than enough. More than I can spend. And pleasure? Well, when I was younger, I tried to write serious books, historical novels, plots about social problems, political thrillers and such stuff. The problem was I couldn't even find a literary agent who would represent me, let alone a publisher. I got one interview with an agent and he told me I would have to build up a big name. He asked me if I had a famous actor or politician as a father, or if I had a popular footballer as a brother. I said I didn't want my name to become famous, I just wanted my books to be published and enjoyed by readers because I believed they had real quality.

"That was wrong. The agent dismissed me, as did the publishers to whom I sent my manuscripts, unsolicited. It seemed no agent or publisher went so far as to read even just the first page. After all those disappointments, I realised I also wanted my books to sell and make money for me. So, I changed my tactics. I assumed a *nom de plume*, a literary pseudonym, I wrote my first romantic love story with a very superficial plot and a simple moral lesson and I approached a few publishers specialising in such books. The first publisher I approached with my manuscript took the bait and it has been a success story from then on."

"Well, I must say I'm impressed." Alfred didn't know what else to say.

"I'm sorry if I have shocked you," she remarked.

"Oh no, don't be sorry. If anybody has to be sorry, it's me. I wouldn't have expected you to have such an exciting career. Probably because your lifestyle rather suggests an uneventful life."

"Why should I adopt a flashy lifestyle? Should I wear fashionable clothes, drive expensive cars and live in a posh mansion? What for? I am perfectly happy with my life as it is now. I don't need a spectacular life anymore. I had my share of excitement when I was younger and I can tell you I can very well do without any more of that. It wasn't all so pretty and I'm glad I can go to sleep without nightmares these days."

Alfred began to admire her. He smiled when he thought of the irony of her reputation in the village. Everyone thought she was a boring woman with no

93

history behind her, a plain person not worth knowing. And here she was, a highly interesting writer with a great deal of life experience. What would people in the village say if they knew the truth?

As if she could read his thoughts, she added, "But please, Alfred, don't tell anyone what I've just told you. I don't know why I told you, really. It's probably because I trust you and I like you. Will you promise not to tell anyone without my permission?"

"Yes," he said, pleased about what she'd said about liking him. "I promise."

*   *   *

When he was in Maidstone two weeks later, he went into Waterstones' bookstore. He looked for the types of books that Philomena had described to him. What a pity he hadn't asked her for her *nom de plume*. He didn't even know if her pen name was a male or female one. He took a few books from the shelf and leafed through their pages, wondering which of them might have been written by her. They all had very romantic-looking covers and the names of their authors were embossed in gold. He hovered between books written by someone called Elizabeth-Jane Hardy and another by a certain Concetta Fiorentini. It might be one of these two names, or not. What about a book by an author calling himself Sam Samson? He couldn't make up his mind and decided to ask her next time.

On the next day, Norman came to see his father. After discussing some current affairs, they came to talk about Philomena. Alfred asked Norman if he knew about the woman's work. Norman answered he didn't want to know. He wanted to get to know her better before asking her. He believed too many people were defined by their work only.

"Well, not everyone," he admitted, "but certain people can never get away from their professional identity. Some teachers are always teachers, even in private life and it's the same with lawyers, plumbers, IT people, civil servants and many others, if you ask me." Norman looked at his father.

"But isn't that normal?" Alfred asked. "Considering that most of us spend eight hours per weekday in our jobs, some of us even more and that for forty-five or fifty years, we're bound to be influenced by the worldviews of our careers."

"Yes, I agree, but do we have to be blinded by our professional perspective? Can't we open up when we're off work? Can't we all learn to see other realities, other people's worlds?"

"I think, theoretically, we can. But it takes an extra effort, it takes courage and it takes a certain degree of intelligence."

"Okay, Dad. Let's say I'm going to ask you – or her personally – about her work after my next visit to her place."

"So you intend to see her again?"

"Yes, why not? I like her and we have a lot to talk about. Apart from you, she's the most interesting person in this village, believe me."

SIX

It was the second year of John Major as Prime Minister in Britain, the middle of the Bush administration in the United States, and Germany had been reunited for eighteen months. Philomena, fifteen, approaching sixteen, was beginning to take note of such important facts in the world. Whereas she had hardly known anything about public affairs, even in her own country, throughout her childhood and early puberty, it dawned on her that the politics of the world might have an impact on her life as well.

It had first entered her sphere when the former threat of the Russian power behind that legendary Iron Curtain began to crumble. Her parents watched on TV how the Berlin Wall lost its terrible significance with people climbing over it and soon starting to destroy it with hammers and pickaxes. And at school, the teachers told the classes how the entire system of communism had collapsed.

Philomena's father tried to explain how the so-called capitalist system was far superior to the communist solutions. And when she watched some documentaries that showed them how derelict the towns in the East looked and how desperate the people were to move to the West, it seemed obvious to her that she was a fortunate girl, having been born in the better part of the world.

Although it was now Mr Major, people still talked about Mrs Thatcher, calling her the Iron Lady. Sandy's parents often discussed the damage that she and her friend Mr Reagan had done to the world. They called it the introduction of a galloping neo-capitalism which was going to destroy the most cherished values of the Western world since the Age of Enlightenment. Now, those were obviously technical terms that were beyond Philomena's comprehension, but she gradually came to the conviction that she had to learn more about such matters in order to be fit for the adult world, to grow up and participate in things that concerned all the important spheres of life.

Philomena's life had taken several turns in the past two years. She still played the piano, but she devoted less time to her practice sessions. There were whole weeks that went by without a single hour at the instrument. Father had asked her on several occasions why they were paying all that money for her lessons if she never practised and he threatened to cancel them. So far, however, she was still allowed to attend her lessons and her parents paid the bills. It was clear that with her irregular and erratic playing, she did not make significant progress. But when she sat down to play, she liked to warm up the pieces she had learnt in earlier years.

The problem was that she simply didn't have so much time for her music with all the other activities and preoccupations filling her mind and demanding her attention during her spare time. Her mind was principally occupied with fantasies about falling in love with Henry, worrying over her friendship with Sandy and plans about her writing career.

The stories she had been writing about her teenage protagonist, Anna Lisa Moore, still existed on paper in her desk drawer, but the more distance in time she gained from them, the more insignificant they became. She was now planning new stories with different protagonists. Also, the plots were now becoming less childish. She tried to see things from an adult perspective or from what she considered to be an adult perspective.

When Henry asked her one day if her ambitions as an author had anything to do with a wish to change the world, to educate her readers in order to contribute to a better world in the future, she didn't quite know what to answer. She was more interested in human intrigues, love stories and the solution of puzzles.

She admired Henry. One day in June, when she was in his room chatting about music and literature, she suddenly thought she might ask him if he would like to be her boyfriend. But she didn't know how to approach the subject. She thought of film scenes she remembered. She would have to get him interested in her physically. Had he noticed how she had grown into a woman? She considered herself to be grown-up enough for a man to desire her. So she stood up and positioned herself near the window so that Henry couldn't miss her womanly shape. It was a warm day and her T-shirt and jeans showed up the contours of her slim body in the best possible way.

Henry didn't react. He kept talking about a book he had read recently and although he was looking at her, he didn't appear to register her sex appeal.

Why did it not work? It usually worked in films. The woman would stand near the window showing up her fine figure and the man would step up to her and take her in his arms, first kissing her cheek, then her mouth, and everything would be fine. He would breathe, "I have always loved you," and she would give him her sweetest smile.

Henry was utterly immune. Her womanly charms did not reach him. What a disappointment! She would have to learn more about sexual attraction between men and women. She had obviously missed out on some vital aspects.

Since it didn't work in real life, Philomena decided to make it work in the next story she intended to write. She was convinced her heroine could get the tall handsome stranger to approach her with amorous designs. He would embrace her and they would kiss for a very long time. They would both become very happy. But what then? Things had to go wrong at a certain point, otherwise there wouldn't be a serious plot. Probably the usual thing, the man would grow tired of her, he would see an equally beautiful woman and would temporarily fall in love with her, but after a few complications – which she still had to think about – she, that is the heroine, would forgive him and they would get together again, this time kissing even more passionately.

"Don't you think so?" Henry asked, tearing her out of her thoughts.

"Sorry, I was just dreaming a little. What was it you were asking?"

"I asked if you also believe *Mansfield Park* to be a far better novel than *Pride and Prejudice*. But never mind."

"Oh yes, I quite agree. Elizabeth Bennet is far too good to be true, whereas the Bertrams are more realistic."

"And what do you think was the financial background of the Bertrams? Where did their wealth come from?"

"Well, I think they were just a wealthy family."

"That may be, but Sir Thomas Bertram has to travel to the West Indies to look after his business interests there. And that could only be sugar plantations and slave trade. So, you see, it is the only novel of hers in which she allows a small slice of the harsh realities of her time to intrude in her plots. There's also the social contrast between the Bertrams and the family of Fanny Price, not to forget the backdrop of the Napoleonic Wars. Normally, for example in *Emma*, her plots evolve in a sheltered world, cut off from the political upheavals of her time."

"You are probably right. But I haven't read all her novels and I believe their main attraction for her readers lies in the development of relationships between men and women, eventually leading to a happy ending."

"Well, yes, but there's a lot more than meets the eye, I can tell you."

Philomena sat down again. She liked Henry's comments about books they had both read, but sometimes – like now – his theories went a bit beyond her understanding of literature. She still had a great deal to learn.

Three days later, she sat down in her room and began to write her new story. When she was going to tell Sandy, she hesitated, not quite sure how much of her new plot she could reveal to her best friend. But Sandy was very enthusiastic and encouraged her to go on writing.

"I believe in you. One day you're going to be a really great writer and I'm going to read all your books the moment they are published."

*   *   *

The relationship between the two girls slowly began to undergo a slight change, too. They had both become more critical about each other. But still, it was Sandy who played the leading part and Philomena usually followed her blindly.

On a particularly hot day in late June, Sandy confessed to her friend how much she was offended, how humiliated she felt about her relationship with Andrew Sullivan.

"I trusted him absolutely. I was so blind in my love for him. He showed me so many things, he took me to all sorts of places, he gave me such confidence... until..."

"You mean until your love for him diminished?" Philomena guessed.

"No. Much worse. Much more dramatic," Sandy admitted with a shaking voice.

"He was mean to you, wasn't he?"

"In a way, yes."

"What exactly happened?" Philomena wanted to know. "You can tell me, we're best friends, aren't we?"

After some hesitation, Sandy began to explain, "Do you remember when I saw him embracing that slut?"

"You mean Miss Mitford, the science teacher?"

"That's her, yes. When I met André last Friday after school, he told me he had to leave because he had to meet Christine Mitford. And when I asked him why she was more important for him than I was, he must have sensed my jealousy and decided to spill the beans. He told me he loved her and wanted to be with her more often. I asked him about our relationship. He explained he was still willing to go out with me and he used some very insulting language, insinuating that I was just a little girl. He said that my body was younger and sexier because – he seemed to insinuate – I was apparently trying to allure him with vulgar methods normally used only by prostitutes, but Christine was more mature, more stylish, and she was the woman he loved. What bullshit!"

She paused, looking down. Philomena got the impression her friend was inspecting her own body, trying to detect the physical attraction Sullivan must have meant with his awfully offending comments. In truth, Sandy was a very attractive young woman indeed. At least Philomena thought so.

101

"It's probably best to let him go. He wasn't worth your love. Just forget him, the sooner the better."

"Not before I have punished him and that Mitford woman. You don't know everything."

"What do you mean? Is there anything else you want to tell me?"

"Well, Philly, you see... I mean... I gave myself to that brute. I gave myself completely, body and soul."

"You mean you had sex with him?"

Sandy hesitated again before she answered, "I might be pregnant."

Philomena swallowed hard. Of course, she knew about the facts of life. But the idea of actually having sex with a man was still far removed from her world. It belonged to the generation of her parents.

Sandy interrupted her thoughts. "I'm going to punish them."

"How are you going to do that? What are your plans?"

"Just give me time. First, I want to know about my situation. If I'm pregnant... well, my punishment will be different... anyway, I'll let you know. I might need your help."

*   *   *

Her friend's experience with Mr Sullivan made Philomena think about her own situation. She wondered if she could ever have sex with Henry. Apart from the fact that Henry seemed to see her only as a good friend, not as a sexual object, the idea was also very farfetched in terms of her own desires.

She realised that she was yearning for pure love, emotional protection and a feeling of belonging, while the physical aspect of love – obviously far more important for Sandy – was still beyond her imagination, although she was just about one year younger than her friend. She was confident that physical desire in such a relationship would automatically grow once the time was ripe. No need to rush. She had lots of time to grow up.

Some of these thoughts were on her mind when she met Henry the next time. After seemingly ignoring her attractions, he had nevertheless surprised her with an obvious interest in her. He invited her for a walk along the river with the chance of an ice cream from the little kiosk near the bridge the following Saturday afternoon.

"And have you read any more Jane Austen?" he asked as they were strolling along.

"I'm afraid I haven't," she replied. "I've found that I'd like to read more modern literature."

"Which authors do you have in mind?"

"I don't really know any. But what I'm looking for is a piece of good literature that doesn't exclude certain important aspects of human life."

"What aspects are you thinking of?"

Philomena hesitated. "Well, you don't mean Mr Wickham or Frank Churchill – to mention just two examples – are never thinking of kissing the girls they admire, do you? Kissing, or even more…" Her voice trailed off. She was looking at him from the corners of her eyes.

"Ah, I see. You want to read more modern literature because you want to have more sexually explicit scenes. Why?"

"Well, it's obvious. When I look at the world around me, I can see that people's actions are often driven by their sexual desires, aren't they?"

"You have a very mature mind for your age. Of course, you are right. But I thought you were still too young to have an interest in that direction."

"I don't have 'an interest in that direction', as you put it. But is it not normal for me as a teenager to wonder about how the adult world functions? Sandy, for example, seems to know a lot more than I do. I feel at a disadvantage in comparison."

They walked on in silence for a while. When they reached the kiosk, he bought a vanilla ice cream for her and a chocolate one for himself and they sat down in the grass to enjoy their delights. Eventually, he spoke.

"I say, Philomena. Have you expected more forward actions from my part? Have you expected me to kiss you?"

"I don't really know. Only, I think we've become very good friends over the past few weeks and in a way, I think it would be normal for us to become lovers. Wouldn't it?"

"My dear Philomena! Of course, I have my desires and I like you very much. But I think it would be taking advantage of you if I kissed you, just like that. You are still under age and it would be unfair."

She believed she had already overstepped a mark and she almost felt embarrassed. The way she'd opened her innermost self to him. And his reaction? Was he still seeing her as a child? She decided to leave things as they were. After a few minutes, she stood up. "I think we ought to go back now."

He stood up, too, and they walked back the way they had come from.

In the evening, she thought about her discussion with Henry when she lay in bed. She didn't know whether to feel offended or pleased. His reaction was so unusual, so unexpected. She had practically offered herself to him on a silver tray and he had refused her.

She tried to go to sleep, but she couldn't relax enough. Her mind returned to the subject of love, passion, relationships, and human intercourse, again and again. It was clear to her that the whole topic encompassed much more than what was covered by the concept of romantic love. After all, even her relatively short life up to now had taught her that love stories could often go wrong. She was thinking of couples separating, newspaper reports of violent fights between married people, even men or women murdering their partners. Also, there were those Hollywood film stars committing suicide because of relationships going sour. Human passion could obviously produce more than tempestuous love scenes, it could also grow into terrible destructive violence.

So, possibly, Henry's stance might also be seen as a sign of respect for her. He might not wish to involve her in too much passion, perhaps leading them into situations that might be beyond them. Eventually, they might love each other so passionately that – like the relationships of those film stars – their love might suddenly turn into passionate hatred. And Henry wanted to spare her such an experience.

But wouldn't that somehow defeat the purpose of their relationship? Philomena realised that there was still an argumentative flaw in her ruminations. In the end, she lost her reasoning and drifted off into the land of her dreams.

When she woke up in the morning, she decided to let things take their own course. She would no longer try to attract Henry. If he was interested in her, she would let him take the first step.

Her education in the domain of human intercourse underwent another experience a few days later. On Thursday afternoon, she ran into Uncle Bertie at the supermarket. She had just taken a packet of salted potato crisps from the shelf when a voice behind her back took her out of her dreams.

"Well, this is a lovely surprise!"

She immediately recognized the voice and turned round.

"Good afternoon, Uncle Bertie."

He put his hand on her shoulder and approached her face with his eager expression, smelling of stale cigarette smoke. "It is so refreshing to see you."

She drew back from his unpleasant approach. "So, you're busy shopping, too?" She said this to lead the topic of conversation into a more banal and everyday territory.

He made a few more complimentary comments, which she didn't listen to, and they walked in the direction of the check-out queues. She wanted to get away from him as soon as possible. The last few times they had been together without anyone else present, he had made more and more comments on her beauty as a woman. That had been extremely unpleasant for her. So now she swiftly paid for her crisps and was going to turn round and say goodbye to him when he caught her sleeve and begged, "I say, don't run away. I can give you a lift home."

Now, this was a dilemma. As much as she wanted to get away from Uncle Bertie, he was still her uncle and if she refused his offer of a harmless lift home, he might complain about her lack of good manners to her parents, who had a very high opinion of him. She might be a rebellious teenager, yes, but it was still important for her to know that her parents had a good opinion of her. She still struggled to be seen as a good girl, a decent girl and a girl with good manners.

So, she waited for him to pack his shopping bag and to follow her out of the supermarket. They walked to his slightly rusty brown Jaguar XJ6. She sat in the passenger seat, keeping her hands in her lap, not to give him an opportunity to take hold of her right hand and stroke it, seemingly by accident.

After a few hundred yards along the main road, Uncle Bertie turned right.

"Where are you going?" she asked.

He didn't reply but continued driving along and after about five minutes, he turned into a deserted carpark on the edge of the forest.

He switched off the engine, turned to her and asked her, "Why do you always try to avoid me? Don't you like your own uncle?"

"I just don't like it when you come too close. You smell of cigarettes. Please, just take me home."

"Of course, I will take you home. But first I want you to realise how much you mean to me." With this, he put his left arm on her shoulders and began to stroke the back of her neck.

She tried to pull back, but he followed her movements with his whole body. He looked into her eyes as if he was going to devour her with desire.

When he started to reach for her with his right hand, she panicked. He put his hand on her small breasts and began to breathe heavily. "Aaah, lovely…"

She screamed and opened her door. Unfastening her seat belt, she jumped out of the Jaguar, yelling, "Leave me alone, you dirty pig!"

She didn't know where to go. She just ran into the forest, afraid he might follow her. But he was too slow, heaving his heavy body out of the car would take too long, so he remained where he was and merely followed her with his eyes until she disappeared among the trees.

She continued for another ten minutes or so, then she turned back. When she reached the carpark, his Jaguar was gone and there was a different car parked there. It was a blue Toyota. Its driver, a middle-aged woman, was standing next to it, smoking a cigarette.

"Oh, hello," she said when Philomena stepped out of the forest.

"Good afternoon," was Philomena's answer.

"Nice day, isn't it?" the woman said as she was exhaling the smoke from her cigarette.

"Yes, it is," the girl said, trying to hide her excitement, still breathing hard from her run through the forest.

"Are you lost?"

"Well, I… I was supposed to meet my uncle to take me home, but he seems to have forgotten me."

"That's unfortunate. Can I give you a lift? Where do you live?"

Philomena gave the kind woman her address.

"Let me just finish my fag," the woman said, smiling and taking another puff.

*   *   *

It was a gloomy afternoon after school when Sandy came up to Philomena with a smirk on her face, obviously full of something she had in mind.

"I've got a proposition for you," she announced.

Philomena just looked at her with a blank expression. Whatever it was, she was glad to occupy her mind with Sandy's concerns to get away from her troubled thoughts of Uncle Bertie. The truth was, she hadn't found the courage to tell her parents yet.

"I say, Philly, I got the impression you developed a crush for my brother. So, I thought we might make a deal. If you help me with my plan about you know who, I'm going to put in a good word for you with Henry. How's that?"

"No, I don't want you to do anything about Henry. If he's at all interested in me, he should come forward on his own without being urged by his little sister, if you know what I mean."

"Okay then. What else can I do for you to get you to support me?"

"You don't need to do anything for me. We are best friends, so I'll help you anyway. I don't need any kind of reward. No quid pro quo or compensation called for here."

Sandy gave her a big hug.

"My plan is to get at him and give him something to chew over for the near future, something he won't forget so quickly. All you'll have to do is come along with me and give me a hand where necessary. Will you be able to get away for the weekend after next?"

"You mean Saturday and Sunday?"

"Yes. We'll take our bikes and spend the night in a tent. But I'll tell you all the details later."

"Okay then." Philomena was glad to have a new project to occupy her mind. She began to look forward to whatever Sandy was planning.

PART TWO

SEVEN

New Labour had just won the general election. The new Prime Minister represented a new type of British politician and his party promised to introduce a new style into British politics. Despite the victory, the country was still full of sceptics. Was Labour falling into the trap of Thatcherism and forgetting the interests of its traditional electorate, the blue-collar workers in the Midlands and the North East?

Philomena was reading the paper while the train was rushing her along through the innocent green landscape of Lincolnshire. She was returning south after a long spell in Newcastle. Her parents, who now lived in a London suburb, were expecting her.

She was still undecided whether she should settle in or near the capital or rather follow her heart and settle in the North East with all those friendly people and with so many of her friends and former fellow students. She was twenty-one, nearly twenty-two. So, she really ought to make up her mind. Life after university was beckoning with its open spaces, its endless possibilities.

Philomena was a free woman. She had no ties, nothing that could restrict her or hold her back. There was no boyfriend and no financial liabilities. And ever since she had escaped from the influence of her former best friend, Sandy, which had been some five years ago, she had gradually developed a new form of self-esteem. As things stood now, she was a confident woman who didn't have to live up to any other person's standards.

In the old days, she had admired Sandy for her alleged superior beauty and her longer experience. That was gone. These days, Philomena knew that beauty wasn't only a matter of one's face or one's figure or even one's stylish clothes, but real beauty had to come from within. She was confident about herself and about what she knew of the world, even though she was modest enough to admit to herself that there was always more to learn in the world. She knew that, in the eyes of her peers, she was probably a woman of mediocre looks but respected for her compassion, open mind and strong power of judgement.

What were good looks anyway? When she looked at herself in the mirror these days, she saw a well-proportioned woman with dark brown hair of medium length with radiating dark brown eyes, a full figure that was just right around her midriff, fine legs and only a bit too heavy around her bust. In moments like these, she couldn't repress a smile when she remembered how Sandy used to taunt her about her childlike figure. What would Sandy say if she could see her now as a fully developed woman with such full breasts?

Although she sometimes found it irksome when men in the street turned their heads to admire her buxom figure, she nevertheless experienced a gush of satisfaction over her personal attraction. Yes, but that was not what she had in mind when she thought about beauty. What she rather wanted to be seen as, by men and women alike, more than anything else, more than the most stunning film star, was a person who was respected and liked on a level of equality, not on a pedestal erected by male fantasies. She didn't mind the fact that sometimes a man would first glance at her breasts as long as he also recognised her face and her personality. After all, she could never erase the conservation drive of the human species, but interpersonal intercourse had to go beyond that and leave all primitive drives behind. That was what made humanity differ from the other species.

She sometimes wondered what might have become of Sandy. And what about Henry? After what had happened that time, a time she liked to keep hidden in the deepest recesses of her mind, she had cut off all connections with them. That had been the right thing to do and she had never regretted it. But there were moments when the events of the past were pushing into her consciousness and threatening to disturb her well-designed and well-developed new self-confidence. These days, she had nothing to do with those events. Nothing at all.

It didn't always work. After all, your actions of the past never let you go completely. She had her odd moments when her memory tortured her through a sleepless night.

Only recently, she had remembered how Sandy had tried to get her to do things she didn't want. It had started during the period when Sandy was still friendly with Mr Sullivan.

*   *   *

Sandy had urged her to come along to a place in the woods suggesting that her friend André had some good ideas "for a spicy adventure," as she put it.

"What do you mean?" Philomena asked.

"You will see," was Sandy's answer. Philomena had her suspicions, but she went along to please her friend. They took their bikes.

When they got to the little shack in Bedgebury Forest, a hut that seemed to belong to Mr Sullivan, as Philomena assumed, he was already expecting the two girls. They entered the hut, which was furnished like a holiday cottage with a double bed, a sideboard and a small wardrobe. One corner of the hut was set up as a little kitchenette and another corner was walled off as a bathroom. Quite a cosy little hideaway, but very derelict.

He offered them a Coke. They sat down and began to chat. Gradually, it dawned on Philomena what the man wanted. At first, he was talking about their careers, their opportunities in the modelling industry based on their good looks. Then he asked them about their personal picture portfolio. While Sandy seemed to agree with his notions, Philomena gradually felt more and more uncomfortable. And when he finally came up with his intentions, she was disgusted. His idea, as it turned out, was to take nude photographs of the two girls to support them in their careers, as he explained. Philomena saw through his mind. He was only hoping to have his own erotic pleasure with them, exploiting their good trust as a teacher. Besides, she wasn't at all interested in a modelling career.

She jumped up, shouted at Mr Sullivan, calling him a dirty pig and left the hut, slamming the door behind her.

When, a few days later, she asked her friend what had happened at the hut after she'd left her with Sullivan, Sandy proudly explained that the man had taken a series of "really very fine pictures" of her. She laughed at her younger friend's reluctance.

"You never know when such pictures might come in handy. You might want them in your portfolio just in case."

"How naïve are you?" Philomena asked her friend. "Do you realise that Sullivan can blackmail you now, at least until he hands over the negatives of those pictures? You're in his hands now."

"Oh, André would never do that."

But as things turned out later when Sandy found him cheating on her and starting his affair with Christine Mitford, Sandy began to realise that she might find herself in a very precarious situation.

"Can't you talk reasonably to him, demanding the negatives from him?"

"I tried but he only laughed. He said that the Mitford whore's pictures were a lot better anyway. So, I slapped him in the face."

From there, things only went from bad to worse. Philomena tried to suppress her memory about what followed. The only positive thing she remembered was Sandy's information that she wasn't pregnant after all. But everything else now appeared in a sort of haze. Sometimes Philomena wondered if those awful things had really happened or not. Perhaps her memory was just playing bad tricks on her.

*   *   *

When she got off the train at King's Cross, she went to a phone booth to call her parents.

"Hello, Mum. I'm at King's Cross. Are you in later this afternoon?"

"Oh, how wonderful, Philly! Of course, you are welcome to come and stay here – "

" – I won't be staying. I just want to say hello and see your new flat."

"Whatever you say, dear. By all means, do come. We'd love to see you."

After ringing off, Philomena stepped out of the booth and went to the underground station. She took the southbound Piccadilly Line. On the train, there was a

117

young man sitting opposite who couldn't take his eyes off her figure, particularly her bust. Philomena was sure she wasn't dressed in a way that invited such glances from strangers. Her whole dress style was decent, even a little prim. After all, she was on her way to an interview. When she got off the train at Covent Garden, she was glad to leave the man's eyes behind.

She found the address she was looking for, entered the large glass door and took the lift up to the first floor, where she came to the reception desk.

"Good morning. What can we do for you?" a friendly young woman in a smart business suit asked her.

"Good morning. My name is Philomena Webster. I have an appointment with a Mr Langton. It's for half past eleven."

"Yes, Ms Webster. Please take a seat over there. Mr Langton will be with you shortly." The young woman pointed to a group of modern easy chairs across the room.

While she was waiting, Philomena glanced around the room. The reception area, which naturally was the face to the customer of this company, oozed an atmosphere of professionalism and easy-going activities. She had only rarely seen such a well-appointed room in English business premises. Usually there were lots of desks overladen with paperwork, overspilling files, used tea-mugs and the odd personal talisman, an atmosphere of chaos and slovenliness. Not here. This publishing company seemed to value a certain emphasis on well-being and professionalism without appearing too cold and impersonal. She liked the quiet voices in the background, the soft light and the colour scheme of the reception area.

"Here you are, Ms Webster," a tall, cleanshaven, middle-aged man in a grey business suit and a white shirt without a tie beamed at her, approaching her with outstretched hands to give her a warm greeting. "I am Brian Langton. We've been in touch by phone. It's a pleasure to meet you in person. Have you had a pleasant journey down from Geordieland? Please, do follow me to my office."

What followed was a professional but also very pleasant interview in Mr Langton's office. There were three other people present, two women and a man. Mr Langton headed the conversation, but the others also asked a number of questions.

After a full hour, Philomena walked out of the office and out of the building. Outside, on the pavement in front of the building, she breathed out and relaxed. She reviewed her chances for the job she had applied for and guessed she probably had a good chance of getting it. She knew – since Mr Langton had told her – that they had invited three other applicants for an interview, but she was confident of her own qualities. Her university qualifications, along with the references from her student's part-time jobs in Newcastle, were quite convincing. With this in mind, she went to get a train to her parents' address in Blackheath.

Her mother embraced her and her father cordially shook her hands. Despite their friendly welcome, Philomena couldn't shake off a certain feeling of embarrassment. Could it be that they still resented her role in the affair of Uncle Bertie? That would be absurd! Or was it about the other events? That couldn't be the case either. They had behaved in such a fine way that she was sure there were no resentments or regrets.

She had a cup of tea and a Victoria sponge cake in her parents' sitting room and she told them about the possibility of her new job with the publishers in Covent Garden. Her mother was proud of her, she could see that, and her father also grunted a few positive comments. Soon, it was time to say goodbye. Since she didn't want to stay at her parents' flat in Blackheath, she walked to the train station in Lee from where she travelled back to Waterloo.

She walked along the South Bank, thinking of her situation, and eventually checked into a hotel near Westminster Bridge. Later, she took a stroll across the bridge and up Whitehall. Crossing Trafalgar Square, she realised she hadn't been there for a number of years. Would she be able to get to know London better if and when she got this job? She would have to find an affordable flat.

She found an Indian restaurant in Soho where she enjoyed a lovely chicken vindaloo with a side portion of bhindi bhaji and some egg-fried rice. The meal filled her up more than she had expected. She remembered the various delicious Indian meals she'd had in Newcastle and she wondered why she'd had to get away from her parents before she even discovered how wonderful Indian food was. Her mother's cooking had been very traditional, bland and boring. She was glad she had discovered Indian restaurants, not only for the delicious meals but also for the fact that they belonged to the few categories of restaurants in English cities where a woman on her own could feel safe and comfortable without a male companion to protect her from unwelcome comments. Well, probably along with Italian and Chinese places. But she could never go and have a meal at a pub-like restaurant.

On her way back to her hotel, she picked up a paper from a newsagent's. Back in her room, she took a shower before she made herself comfortable in her pyjamas, lying on the bed and browsing through the paper. She read how

Tony Blair hypnotised his audiences and played on their frustrations, advancing his own agenda. Oh, those politicians! But, unfortunately, the system seemed to bring forward types like him. There were men – and women, too, thinking of Mrs Thatcher – who needed power over others in order to feel okay. But who could believe their high-flying words?

She fell asleep with the open paper over her legs. Later, she woke up and got into bed properly. She had a quick flashback about Mr Langton's pleasant smile before she dropped off to sleep again.

*   *   *

She had been told by Mr Langton to phone in after twelve the next day. He'd said he wished to speak to all the candidates personally on the phone, no matter whether they'd got the job or not.

So, she had to spend the morning in London, keeping herself busy somehow to avoid getting nervous about the outcome of her career opportunity. Really, it was a great opportunity and it was already a huge success for her to get as far as an interview. She ought to be grateful and content with what she had already achieved. But naturally, she couldn't help being nervous and desperately hoping for a positive decision, even though her inner voice told her not to be too unrealistic. Nobody got a job right after university and right on their first application. She had to be mad to expect anything more. She wouldn't get it. End of story. She would have to go through the job ads again and again for the next few months. And for that, she would have to go back to her digs in Newcastle.

After a pleasant breakfast at a small place near Leicester Square, during which she was browsing through the morning's *Independent*, she strolled up Charing Cross Road and continued into Tottenham Court Road, looking into some shop windows and even entering two bookstores. In Foyles, she browsed through the modern fiction section, discovering the emblem of "her" publisher on the spines of several paperbacks. In a second-hand bookshop, she let her eyes travel along the various spines of nineteenth-century books on history, recognising several titles and authors' names.

She turned off into Great Russell Street, passing the British Museum and eventually found a row of red phone booths. She dialled the number and was immediately connected to Mr Langton's office.

"Yes, my dear Ms Webster," he said after the customary greetings, "we have come to a decision regarding the advertised position as a junior editor." Then he paused. Philomena was biting her lips and she could feel a weakness in her knees.

"I can tell you, I'm glad to say that we would like to offer you the job. Your considerable experience given your young age, your excellent references and, of course, your personality, which we all felt good about in your interview… all these factors have resulted in a unanimous decision in your favour." He paused again. Philomena wondered what she was called upon to say now.

"Thank you, Mr Langton," was all she managed to stutter.

"Would it be possible for you to come here again as soon as possible? We would like to discuss the contract and a few other matters relating to your new employment. Also, we would like to introduce you to our team. When do you think you could come in again?"

"Oh, any time that suits you, Mr Langton – "

" – Call me Brian."

"Oh yes, of course, thank you very much. I could come in this afternoon if that would be okay for you?"

"Perfect. That would be splendid. See you, say, around half past three then?"

"Yes Mr – Brian, thank you."

She rang off and took a moment to catch her breath. What a fantastic piece of good luck! She got her first real job with a regular salary and she was going to live in London. She was a really lucky girl!

*   *   *

Philomena was sitting at her desk in the office together with five other people. She looked round the well-lit room, which was dominated by soft colours such as light grey and light beige with a few single colour spots near the door. Besides herself, there were two women – Denise and Janet – and three men – Tom, René and Charlie – at least that's how they were introduced to her. She'd already forgotten their family names, but that didn't seem to be a problem since everybody was on first name terms anyway.

This was only an introductory day for her. She was given her desk and a whole bunch of paperwork which informed her about the company's policies and processes. She was invited to study these and to get her bearings. She was then allowed to take a few days off until the end of the month before starting work properly. The thing was, she had to have some time off to go flat-hunting in London, which wasn't promising to be an easy task.

Of course, there were a lot more people working for this publisher. Apart from Brian Langton, who worked in a separate office behind a glass door and who was her immediate superior, there were people even higher up and people in different departments who worked in other offices on the same floor and also two more floors upstairs. On the ground floor, there were archives and storerooms. Philomena realised she would mainly work in the company of these five colleagues, all of whom were junior editors who got their orders from Brian. She was the youngest of them.

"You seem to be more efficient than Poppy," Denise remarked with a sidelong glance at her. "At least that's the impression you give with the way you go about things."

"Who is Poppy?" Philomena asked.

"Oh, sorry. Of course, you wouldn't know her. She's the woman who had your job before you. Your predecessor."

The others looked at Denise with what Philomena interpreted as a certain degree of criticism. Tom was shaking his head ever so slightly.

"Oh, Poppy was quite a handful," Denise continued. "Not at all like you…"

Philomena waited for further explanations for this odd comparison to come from Denise. But there wasn't any more. Denise bent her head over the papers she was busy with and continued with her work.

When lunchbreak came, she found herself in the lift with René. Standing next to him in the narrow space of the lift, she realised that he was almost a head taller than her. He smiled at her in a friendly way.

"Do you know where you can grab a decent snack for lunch?" he asked.

She was glad of his advice, being new to this part of the great city. So, she followed him to a small restaurant only just round the corner. They got some sandwiches and some mineral water from the counter, paid for their lunch and sat down at one of the tables. The place was simple but clean and there was even something of a cosy atmosphere if you were not too demanding.

René first took a few bites from his sandwich and a few sips of water before he said something. Philomena remained silently concentrated on her tuna sandwich.

"Don't mind Denise, that's how she is. She only misses Poppy. And she often gets into disagreements over our former colleague with Tom. This is office gossip, so you'd better get used to it."

"What was she like?" Philomena asked. "I mean that Poppy woman."

"Oh, she was quite a handful, I can tell you." René smiled in an enigmatic way and continued to munch his sandwich.

"In what way? How do you mean?"

"She was a man-eater if you ask me. That was also the reason for her getting fired."

Philomena was going to ask another question when she checked herself. She could still get all the gossip later and besides, she wanted to form her own opinion about Denise before joining in the general picture prevailing in the office. She wanted to start with a clean slate.

She got some papers that carried property ads and she spent the evening sitting in her hotel room studying the various ads. She didn't know London well enough to decide on a particular area. On one hand, she quite liked the area of her parents' flat, but she didn't intend to live too near them; on the other hand, she believed the western suburbs might be just as nice or even nicer. But they seemed quite a bit more expensive. Chelsea or Paddington would be out of her financial reach, but a bit further out, say Hammersmith, might be her ticket.

She decided to take the underground to Hammersmith in the morning. She would find some estate agents in the area and find out a bit more about available flats. She would have to rent. Her financial situation didn't allow her to buy, but if she could stay in this job for a few years, she might save enough money to buy her own place, perhaps, if she was thrifty and lucky enough.

In bed that night, she remembered what René had said about Poppy, a man-eater. What a strange label to attach to a woman! Philomena immediately remembered Sandy. Would the term have applied to her? In a way, perhaps. After all, what had originally led to her disaster was her belief in her own attraction for men. For Sandy, catching a man with her looks had been the primary motivation for her actions. Would that constitute a man-eater?

In the morning, she took the District Line to Hammersmith. Not far from the tube station, she found several estate agents. After discussing the available rental properties, she calculated that the maximum she could afford – if she wanted to be able to save some of her salary towards the purchase of her own place – was an older one-bedroom flat, perhaps on a lower ground floor or in an attic. She arranged with estate agents to see some of the flats in the afternoon and on the following two days. All in all, Brian Langton had allowed her five days to get settled, so she had to make haste to find the right place.

*   *   *

Philomena was happy to have a good friend and former fellow student in Newcastle who was ready to help her with the move to London. Her name was Emma and her father had a small construction business in Gateshead. Emma was allowed to borrow a small van from her father's firm and this was spacious enough to transport Philomena's belongings from Newcastle to London.

The two women stored everything in the van, which was still half empty when they had completed their loading. But that was all that Philomena owned. A good bed, small wardrobe, sideboard, kitchen table and two chairs. Plus her clothes and some books. They had to secure their stuff with several ratchet straps to prevent them from moving about during the trip. The loading work had made them so hungry that they stopped for a snack before they reached the motorway. But then they were ready for the long drive south.

Philomena did some of the driving, but Emma did the longest bits. The drive was extremely boring for them since they didn't dare to exceed sixty on the dual carriageways and motorways for fear that their load might shift. They stopped for petrol twice and about fifty miles short of London, they had a puncture and had to stop on the emergency lane in order to change the wheel. They were busy jacking the van up when another van stopped and a young man got out.

"Can I help you ladies?" he asked in a friendly tone.

Emma was just about to answer him in the negative – being proud of her practical skills – when Philomena urged her to accept the man's help. He stepped up to the faulty wheel, checked it and remarked, "Great, you certainly know what you're about when changing a wheel. Unlike most women, you know that you've got to loosen the wheel nuts before jacking the thing up."

Although Philomena considered that an admiring remark, Emma snarled at the man. "You obviously have no idea of women!"

"Come on," he replied. "I didn't mean to be unfriendly."

Emma just grumbled, but she allowed the man to do the wheel change. When they stowed the faulty wheel in the back where the furniture was, the man asked, "Moving house?"

"Yes," Philomena answered. "I'm moving from Newcastle to London."

The man, who said his name was Jeremy, took his leave and they all got in their vans. Very carefully, they eased their vehicles back onto the main carriageway and continued their southbound journey. Of course, Jeremy overtook them and disappeared on the faster lane. In a way, Philomena was sorry to let him go. She was touched by his personality, but she didn't say anything about her feelings to Emma.

"I say, you'll have to get the faulty tyre mended or replaced," was her only remark.

In the late afternoon, they arrived at the flat in Hammersmith. It was an attic flat in a quiet backstreet only a small distance from Ravenscourt Park. When the two women set about heaving the bed up the three flights of stairs, they struggled. Two young men who happened to pass in the street saw their efforts and offered to help them. This was a piece of good luck. With the help of the two men, they managed to carry all of Philomena's belongings up to the flat.

After just under one hour, it was all done. Finally, the four people stood in the flat and looked at what still appeared like an almost empty space, since her furniture couldn't fill up the place. If she wanted less open space, she would have to buy a few things. But she guessed that had time. For the time being, the flat was all right as it was.

Philomena invited the two men, whose names were Max and David, for a cup of coffee at a small café near the tube station. Emma only stayed with them for a short time, then she started on her drive back to Newcastle. She was hoping to get there soon after midnight.

Philomena stayed on at the café with Max and David. They seemed to be very close and she wondered if they were gay. While Max, who seemed a bit older, was a tall man with a bald patch on his head and was generally a quiet type, his friend David was a rather boisterous chap who had a small beard which didn't grow regularly between his mouth and his ears. Despite their differences in appearance, they seemed to harmonise extremely well in their views of the world. Especially David seemed to like to talk about politics and recent history. He grew very excited when they came to talk about the recent events in the Balkan region. One thing he even got quite angry about was Serbian aggression. The Serbian leaders of the day were still dreaming of a large Serbian Empire, which was why they opposed all other nations in the region who didn't welcome such megalomaniac designs.

Max, on the other hand, while respecting his friend's opinions and assessments, was much more relaxed about such questions. He said you couldn't change things anyway, so just learn to live with them. Of course, he agreed that greedy dictators no longer have a place in modern Europe, but at least there was the European Union who exercised a regulating influence on all European countries, its members as well as its non-members. Besides, the notion that territorial expansion could lead to more political power was no longer valid

129

these days. It certainly wouldn't have a place in the twenty-first century, which was only a few years ahead.

They discussed some more dictators in the world before the two men took their leave and Philomena walked back to her new flat. She was happy and satisfied.

*　*　*

On the following Monday, she started to work properly in her new job. Her first task was to read some manuscripts that had already been assessed by Denise with the idea that they could compare their assessments afterwards, which ought to give Philomena a taste of the company's standards. Denise explained to her how they followed a three-level procedure. The first level comprised manuscripts that were clearly of excellent quality and would be published successfully. They were usually manuscripts sent on from one of their established literary agents.

The second level were manuscripts that had a good chance of being published but needed some editing to become successful. They formed the most difficult group because they meant extra work and also because there was never a guarantee that they would actually work with the critics.

The third level consisted of manuscripts that didn't even deserve to be assessed all the way through because they were too bad for publishing. In this group there were some manuscripts that were sent in unsolicited by the authors themselves without having gone through an agent's assessment.

Philomena found her work challenging but very rewarding. She had done quite a bit of proof-reading for two publishers during her time as a student in Newcastle on a part-time basis. So, she already had a considerable portion of experience. After all, this publisher wouldn't have given her this job if she had been a complete newcomer to the industry.

Despite her positive attitude and her satisfaction over her work, she found that it was taking her a great effort to keep up with her colleagues. Some of them seemed to be a lot more efficient than her. For example, Janet would work through a 400-page manuscript over a period of two days and her assessments were always very accurate. On the other hand, she realised that she could be faster than Charlie, who took about three times as much time for the same job as Janet. Philomena was somewhere between them, but she had the constant feeling that she was not good enough. Perhaps it was the relaxed way they all spoke about their work as if it was a piece of cake. Philomena found she had to take work home over the weekend to keep up with them.

She wondered about her future. How long would she stay in this job? Would she get along with her colleagues over a longer period? Or would she start to loathe them once she'd known them long enough? The answer to that was clear. She would have to be tolerant. She couldn't criticise them in her mind and expect to keep her respect for them in the long run. Besides her colleagues and Brian, there was also the job itself. Would she grow tired of the work?

Deep down, she knew she was only happy to do this kind of work because what she really craved was to become a writer herself. Sometimes, when looking at a new manuscript in her hands, she imagined her own name to be printed on the front page. Not because she wanted her name to become famous, just as a confirmation of her authorship, but to prove to herself that she was actually able to write a full novel. Her books – if they ever came into existence – would probably be very philosophical, very intellectual.

However, for now, she was sitting at her desk doing exactly what was expected of her and getting paid for it.

So, this was the real world of employment. Now she knew.

EIGHT

Her first year on the job had been satisfactory, a bit challenging at first, but gradually becoming more and more like routine with occasional hiccups and finally balancing out into a more quiet and relaxed part of her life that she honestly cherished.

During this first year, she really concentrated on her work. She had practically no private life. This was about to change one day when she bumped into Max at Hammersmith tube station. He cheerfully greeted her, but she took a moment before she recognised him. Probably because he was stored in her memory as a minor encounter in the context of moving her furniture and only in combination with his friend David.

"Don't you remember?" he asked. "You know, your moving into your new flat up in the attic. It's Max."

"Of course, I'm sorry. Hiya, Max, how are you?"

"Fine, thanks. It's Philomena, isn't it?"

"Yes. It's unusual to see you without David."

"Is it? Well, we're good friends, but we don't always do things together. These days, he's very preoccupied with his girlfriend, Marilyn. She takes up most of his free time."

"Oh, I see." Philomena cleared her throat. Then she looked Max up and down. He wasn't such a bad-looking guy, after all. She blurted out. "Like to have a cup of coffee with me?"

She realised immediately that this might have been too forward and regretted it. But it had just come out like that.

He agreed, so they went to the same small café where they'd had their post-removal coffee with Emma and David. She had never been back there through the whole year, but now it seemed the obvious spot for them.

When they were sitting at a table in the corner, slowly sipping their coffees, she felt that something was happening to her. She felt two conflicting emotions struggling in her breast and she felt her whole frame in limbo.

Her thoughts did not often stray into memories of her past. Not the section of her past with that horrible thing with Sandy and not her experience with her own sexuality. While, as a teenager, she had seen herself as a sexless human being, uninterested in the topic of sex and eroticism, unlike her friend Sandy, she now saw herself as a tainted woman, damaged goods. This had made her careful and wary of situations that could make her lose control.

*   *   *

It had been in Newcastle in autumn. Philomena had been in her first term at university. She had not stored all the details in her memory. It was too unpleasant. But she remembered the first time her tutor, Dr Robson – Colin – had invited her to his small office to discuss her reading list. She had immediately fallen under his spell. Only two weeks later, he invited her to his flat in Jesmond, where he kissed her.

From there on, she let herself be led on by him and after another fortnight, she lost her virginity to him. Over the following two or three months, through most of the winter, they were almost inseparable. She lived in a trance-like world, utterly dependent on him and his whims.

Reluctantly looking back later, she felt ashamed of herself. She knew perfectly well that she hadn't really loved Colin. It had been the sex and the sex only. As their relationship continued, he became ever more demanding, asking her to do things that she didn't really feel comfortable about but that she only did to please him and in the hope of increasing her own erotic pleasure. There was no way she could deny him anything. One thing he particularly loved was having sex in unusual places. So they had sex in the toilets of their institute, in his office and in one of the empty classrooms, whereby the tantalising thing was that they always stripped completely naked in all those places to heighten the excitement. It seemed to give him extra pleasure to do it in places or situations where they might be discovered at any time.

When the warmer season came, they often found exciting spots outdoors. One warm afternoon, for example, they stripped in a small patch of grass that was only visible from the adjacent railway line. They had wild sex in that patch while no fewer than three trains passed from which passengers could get a good view before they gave up, got dressed again and disappeared from the spot, careful not to get caught by the police. The train passengers might have reported them. One never knew…

The affair ended abruptly. They were having sex in his office when one of the older professors gave a quick rap on the door and immediately entered. The old man was so shocked to find them both naked on that desk that he had a heart-attack and the ambulance had to be called.

Of course, there was quite a scandal. Colin Robson was dismissed and she was asked if she wanted to press charges, which she declined. She decided to keep it all as quiet as possible. She woke up as if from a bad dream and she thought herself lucky to get off so lightly. The inquiry that was set up believed her that she had become completely dependent on Robson. They gave her an official caution and allowed her to continue her studies. But the whole affair had been the shock of her life. She felt so ashamed of herself. How could she let herself become such a slave under the rule of a man?

The result was that she was now much more careful. She still did not know how much she could trust herself. She believed she had the potential of a sex maniac, a dormant lion, so to speak, within her and it was always in danger of being reawakened.

*   *   *

Sitting across from Max in that little café, she felt her entire shame over her sexual experience overwhelming her like a giant ocean wave drowning her. How she would love to let herself go and fall in love with this man as if she were still a virgin about to discover the world of a sexual relationship for the first time! How wonderful it would be to be untainted and unencumbered by her heavy memories!

She held back her feelings. Max, being some eight years older than her, seemed to like her a great deal. When he looked into her eyes, she felt a sort of click inside her. She never really liked older men, especially after her experience with Uncle Bertie.

She had tried to tell her mother how Uncle Bertie had touched her body in intimate places, how she had tried to reject him unmistakably and how she was in such a dilemma with Uncle Bertie being so liked by her parents. But her mother had dismissed any allegations, turned away any hints at such a thing and overruled Philomena's view of Bertie. Her mother even ordered her to be more friendly and accommodating with her uncle. But Philomena was stubborn and henceforth avoided any contact with him. She didn't mind her parents' reprimands. They couldn't touch her. She just had to learn to avoid meeting the dirty old man. In time, her parents accepted her dislike of her uncle and just added it to their daughter's other strange moods. For them, it was probably just a sign of revolt so typical for teenagers.

But this was different. Max was not an old man for her, just a man in the same age group, only a bit more experienced than her.

Since Philomena had only recently acquired a mobile phone – now that nearly everyone seemed to have one – she was ready to exchange phone numbers with him. But because of the turmoil within herself, she decided to break off this chat at the café as soon as possible. She wanted to sort out her feelings before meeting him again. So they soon said goodbye, but she could see the same disappointment that she felt in his eyes too.

Over the following days, she banned the topic from her mind. She went to work, had lunch with one of her colleagues and came back to her flat in Hammersmith, where she usually sat down with a good book and a light supper, such as a piece of brown bread with a tomato or a gherkin, perhaps some salad, some smoked salmon or a slice of cooked ham. When she felt generous, she even went for some French and Italian cheeses, which she found rather an expensive luxury. She had a small TV set, so she sometimes watched the news or a film, but on most evenings, she continued to improve her knowledge of English and world literature.

She read the works of the great French and Russian masters, but in English translation, though her French wasn't so bad, but she had neglected her foreign languages after leaving university. She even dabbled in Spanish, German and Scandinavian literature. In truth, she read books from all over the world if they were available in English translation. She also liked a lot of good novels from other English-speaking countries, such as Canada, Australia, New Zealand or the United States. She found that the nationalities of the authors were becoming less relevant the more she was reading.

What mattered was their humanity, common – albeit different – concerns about people, conflicts, dreams, ways of dealing with each other and yearning for peace and understanding. Of course, she admired authors who were struggling for more democracy in their societies and she felt awful about writers and journalists who suffered under the rule of dictators or would-be dictators like the Chinese or Russian leaders.

When she read texts from African authors – like Chinua Achebe, Wole Soyinka, Ayi Kwei Amah or Ngugi wa Thiong'o – or even Indian writers – like Raja Rao, Mulk Raj Anand, R. K. Narayan or Vikram Seth – she found she was really venturing into unknown territory in terms of familiarity with the underlying cultural context. On the whole, however, she felt enriched by her widespread reading. So her evenings were filled with intellectual pleasure.

After a few months, she got herself a CD player and some CDs, mostly of the great classical works. Since the floors of her flat were wooden – this being an older building – she knew she couldn't listen to this music at full volume, but she was grateful for having the music at all.

This was the life she liked. Quiet, uneventful, reasonably happy and connected with the world through her intellectual pursuits.

So why complicate it by falling in love with a man? With someone like Max? She felt she didn't need wild sex again. She'd had her share of that. But emotional closeness, a person to love, to hold, to trust…? And to be loved back, perhaps, if things went well?

During her intensive reading phase, she remembered her own ambition to write books, which she had developed and cherished during her teenage years, but which she had abandoned later. Suddenly it dawned upon her that she might give it another try. In contrast to her teenage years, she could say that she had quite a lot more experience now, both intellectually and practically. She knew more about life and she knew a lot more about good literature.

Times had moved on, also in technology. She got herself a personal computer and soon learned how to use it. She discovered the WORD programme, which opened up endless possibilities for her writing ambition. One grey Saturday in her small flat, she sat down and began to plan her first serious novel. She wanted this first book of hers to include so many ideas of hers. She drew up a list. It began with very big topics: war and peace in the world, the evils of human greed, the dictators of the world, inhuman systems, global warming and what we ought to do to stop it…

After those big topics, she realized that they couldn't make up a story that her potential readers would like. She needed something more personal, more individual, to construct a credible plot. Now what were the ingredients for a good plot? What made people tick, really? Probably love, hate, envy, jealousy, personal gain, loss, hope, disappointments, loneliness, yearning for fulfillment… She couldn't think of any more such driving forces for a good plot. She was confident that she could still add items to both her lists later, but for the moment, she was quite satisfied.

With these lists in front of her, she just jumped into a human situation that sounded credible and began to write. She began with a man and a woman meeting on the bus. They begin to talk. They meet again later. He falls in love with her, but she doesn't fall in love with him although she quite likes him. So far so good. What next? Her problem is that she has her eyes on another man. So here's the first conflict. Should she find out what to do by talking to both men? Or should she just let things take care of themselves? Situations can develop, people can change…

But somehow their conflict should reflect some of the great problems of the world. How to connect the woman's dilemma with the problem of the bad political systems and the evil dictators of the world and possibly include an aspect of global warming? Perhaps a bit too early in the novel. Those topics could still be connected later. First, the personal plot ought to continue.

Philomena was quite content when she stood up from her computer and prepared to go to bed. While trying to fall asleep, she thought of her plots and turned them round and round in her mind until she dropped off.

In the morning – a Sunday – she jumped back into the world of her story. But now, she suddenly found it banal and stupid. The exuberance of the previous day had evaporated completely. How could she be so naive? How could she hope to connect such an everyday plot with the really big issues of the world? She deleted everything she had written and decided to make a new start.

She put her writer's ambition on hold and decided to meet Max again. They went out to art exhibitions together and Philomena convinced him to accompany her to an occasional classical concert at the Royal Festival Hall or at the Barbican. Although he came along quite happily, she sensed that he wasn't really so keen on classical music.

One evening walking home across the footbridge between the Festival Hall and the Embankment tube station, they stopped in the middle of the bridge and looked down on the river. They were quiet. He put his arm across her shoulder, bent his head to hers and began to kiss her on her lips ever so gently. And she fully enjoyed this. The kiss was very slow and full of tenderness. It shot through her head that she might let herself go. But then she checked herself.

"I'm sorry," she breathed. "It just… well, I'm just not ready for this."

"Oh, then it's me who should be sorry. I shouldn't have been so forward. I apologise, really, I do." His face was full of regret. "I misjudged the situation. I thought you had similar feelings for me, but obviously you – "

"My dear Max! I promise you, I like you. I like you a lot. But I'm just not ready for this."

"So, you like me a lot, but you don't like me to kiss you. Is that it?"

She hesitated. "It's hard to explain. You see, the kiss was wonderful, very delightful… you kiss in such a wonderful way, you are so good to me… but…"

"But what?"

"But I've had such awful experiences in my life. They seem to set up some sort of blockade or barrier, they put a stop to all such tender acts. I know it's awkward, but please don't take it personally."

141

She could see in his eyes that he was disappointed, possibly even a bit offended, but he said, "I understand. It's all right."

Very slowly, they resumed their stroll across the bridge. After a few moments, he asked, "Do you want to talk about it?"

Philomena didn't answer, but she just walked on in silence. He seemed to understand that this was a "no" and just walked along with her. Eventually, they reached the tube station and took the District Line to Hammersmith.

After that, she didn't see Max for a while. It was after about three weeks that he called her again and asked if she still wanted to see him.

She said yes and they met at the old café again. Sitting over their half-empty cups they talked about many different topics: the politics of the day, computers – she even told him about her new PC – and the new exhibition at the Royal Academy. But her erotic problem was the white elephant in the room.

This state of things between them remained for about three months before he confronted her one day at the Tate Modern while they were walking towards the exit.

"I say, my dear, don't you think it's about time we decided on our relationship?"

She walked on in silence. After another minute or two, she answered, "Let's sit in one of the pubs or restaurants along the South Bank and talk."

They found a table for two and sat down. After ordering their drinks, she took his hand and cleared her throat.

"You see, my dear Max, this is all my problem. The story of my sexual life is quite a bumpy one to say the least. I don't trust myself. I have an awful fear of what I

142

know I'm capable of. I've done some really bad things. I can't explain all of them. It's ever so difficult. I don't know why." She scratched her head behind her left ear.

"You were treated badly by a man then?" he asked.

"Not really, or not only. I've done bad things myself. And... well, I... I've come to the conclusion that I must really be hooked on sex."

"You don't give me that impression, not at all! Rather the opposite."

"You don't understand. My prim exterior and my prudish behaviour are a sort of shield, a shield to protect myself."

"You mean, you want to protect yourself from yourself? That doesn't make sense to me."

"To me it makes sense. But it's not only that. At the same time, I am protecting myself from my own past."

"What do you mean?"

"Well, I don't know how to put it really. Let me say, everything I experienced in the field of more personal relationships between men and women misfired. In the end, there was always disappointment, pain and chaos. I've come to the conclusion that sexuality is a proper minefield. Things can go so wrong. There can be so much pain. And that's even without taking into account all the other bad things I've done."

"I don't agree. There's no need for pain. Things – I mean a healthy sex life – can also enrich you, give you fulfilment, unlimited happiness..."

"Not in my experience. I will be safer if I don't let myself go too far in this department." Philomena paused before she continued, "Perhaps I should take things more carefully, be better prepared for the worst so that whatever happens won't kill me."

"But the process of letting yourself go, of abandoning your precautions is the very essence of finding fulfilment in sexual love. You must have gone through some really bad patches in your younger days. Has a man been awful to you?"

"All the men I allowed to come close. And even men I didn't invite."

"Oh, you must've had a rough time of it."

"Yes, you could say that again. It started when I was a young girl. I had an uncle – my father's elder brother; in fact, he's still alive – who constantly tried to get in my pants. That was my first contact with male interest in my person. It still makes me sick just to remember it."

"But, oh, I mean… Did he abuse you?" Max was shocked.

"No, he didn't get so far. I avoided him. At first, when I was little, I felt pleased by the way he praised me and he gave me little presents, a toy or a piece of chocolate. Plus, it was all sanctioned by my parents. But then he began to touch me too much, too often. It came to the situation when I was already in my teens that he tried to fondle my teenager's titties. That was the moment I decided to tell my mother. But what did she do, the stupid cow? She didn't believe me. She said it was all in my teenager's fantasy."

"What did you do?"

"I just told my parents I no longer wanted to see the monster. At first, there was a huge row, but eventually they had to accept my decision. I never met my uncle again and I hope I will never see him again."

"So, what about us now?"

"Just give me more time. I might come round eventually. I really like you very much. But please, don't rush me."

This conversation put a damper on their tender feelings, dissipating all aspects of eroticism. Although they still found each other very attractive, it was not the time for kisses or other endearments. They changed the topic and discussed aspects of their working life.

In the evening, Philomena sat down in front of her computer. The events of the day had two effects on her. First, in her endeavour to come to terms with the events of her past, she was confident she could write her first successful novel now. And secondly, she realised it couldn't be another serious novel competing with the great works of world literature, as she had tried and failed, but rather something to help us get away from the harsh realities, something that allowed one to escape from the sadness of human intercourse.

There would have to be a happy ending, the good characters would find happiness while the evil figures would end unhappily or even be punished. She was confident she would find enough imagination in herself to fill in the middle field, the characters who were neither completely good nor downright bad. She realised this was called escapist literature and she knew it was not in very high esteem among the literary critics, indeed within the whole of academia dealing with literature.

On the following weekend, she sat down at the computer again and began to plan a new plot. A completely new plot. Nothing to do with her former ideas. A few men and a few women on holiday in Italy, one of the women owning this house in Tuscany. Two of the men would like to win the woman's love, but one day a stranger arrives who could be the woman's ex-lover fighting to get her back. At the same time, two of the women are rivals who want to get the same man who is one of the two men competing for the hostess. However, the hostess harbours a dark secret. All this should make up enough complications to serve a thrilling novel, something between a thriller and a love romance.

Once she had typed a few sentences into her WORD file, the text gradually began to flow. The characters began to take clearer shape; she could almost see them physically in front of her. Two of the men were absolutely gorgeous, while only one of the women was a person of notable beauty, most of the female characters being rather plain. She didn't know why this had to be the case. It just felt right. Besides, she could still change that later in the writing process. That was the good thing about modern computer technology. The programme allowed her to shape and re-shape her story as often as she liked.

After a few weeks, when she found she'd already written some fifty pages, she realised she was in danger of losing control of her numerous characters. She read through the text again, taking notes of all the characters and their looks, their various professions, their individual peculiarities. She found she had used certain words too often, for example "really" or "absolutely", so she replaced or deleted them.

Writing a fictional text wasn't so easy after all. After taking down all her characters' properties in her list, she decided to plan ahead a bit more carefully. Then she found she had to change some of the names. Two women had names that could easily be mixed up. She also decided to spice the list of the names with some more flowery names. A female character admired by several men was Jenny Chapman. Philomena now changed it to Miranda de Havilland. Much more musical, she found.

All men were tall and handsome. This, too, had to be changed. There had to be at least one boringly normal man and one quite sinister or ugly man. This would also add spice to her story.

For the rest, she trusted in the future writing process. Things would fall into place in time. She was confident now that she had actually begun her writing career.

When she went to bed in the evening, her thoughts circled around her plot and she wondered how far she could go in her planning of an evil character. Could she include any criminal acts? Or would that render her novel unsuitable for a certain type of readership? She arrived at a fundamental question. What constituted evil and what constituted a crime? The more she thought of such an enigma, the colder she felt. All of a sudden, she felt she was falling into an abyss of horror. The pain in her body and mind became so extreme that she found it hard to breathe.

Images from her past crowded around her, horrible images threatening to crush her. Images of a dark forest and being forced into things she didn't want to know about. Distorted faces. Awful images. She felt she had to fight them, so she struggled with her arms and legs, endeavouring to free herself, regain the upper hand, rise above those evil forces and get away from her bad memories.

As suddenly as it had overwhelmed her, it came to an abrupt end. She sat up in her bed drenched in sweat, feeling exhausted, breathing hard.

She got up and went to the kitchenette to pour herself a glass of cold water. She gulped it down in one go and went back to bed.

It took her a long time to relax and fall asleep.

NINE

Philomena was dodging through her cottage, trying to get to her phone in time. She had left it in the kitchen and she suspected the call to come from her brother.

"Hiya, Philly, have you got time? I need to tell you about things."

She didn't answer this rhetorical question, knowing full well that he would go on with whatever he had to tell her anyway. She was right.

"It's Lizzie from Gloucestershire. You know, I told you about her, didn't I? Well, the thing is, she'd threatened to come down south and confront me. I was ever so scared, you know, about Maggie. But listen! It's off. I got a letter from her to my address at school in which she writes that she has abandoned the plan. She thinks we'll meet up some time in the future anyway. I'm extremely relieved, I can tell you."

"Why should you have been scared in the first place? You had nothing to fear. You said you'd never had anything to do with her. So why the excitement?"

"Well, you know what Maggie is like."

"It's about time you spoke to that wife of yours. This relationship seems to be in shallow waters. How is she anyway?" Philomena thought it better to change the subject.

"Poor dear! She is always on the lookout for more serious books to read, you know, books she can talk about with her elegant ladies. Would you know of any more suitable ones?"

"How can I give her advice if I don't know what interests her or her so-called elegant ladies?"

"Don't be so hoity-toity. Can't you be a bit more helpful?"

"Okay, can you get her on the phone so I can get an idea of what sort of book she's looking for?"

"She's out, but I can tell her to call you back."

They chatted a bit more about the news of the day and also about Robert's school before terminating their conversation.

Philomena wondered how much longer her brother's relationship with Maggie would last. She could clearly see what a silly woman Maggie was. But Maggie wasn't evil or spiteful, basically she meant well. Her main problem – apart from her limited intellect – was her mother Rachel, or more specifically, the fact that she was completely dependent on her mother. How many times had her mother crossed the plans that Robert and Maggie had made?

For example, just the year before, when they had been planning a really great summer holiday, driving round Spain and seeing some friends who had holiday homes in the country – a former colleague of Robert's living in an old *finca* in the Estremadura and a former neighbour renting a great seaside villa near Alicante – hoping to have the holiday of their lives, they were suddenly ordered by Maggie's mother to cancel the whole trip.

They had already booked some of the hotels between England and the south of Spain, but those had to be cancelled. The reason, Rachel had suddenly remembered that she might give a birthday party in the middle of August, nothing grand, but still a party that would be unthinkable without Maggie and Robert. They argued that she could still have the party after their return from Spain, but Rachel remained adamant. The party had to happen on the 15th of August to celebrate her 75th birthday, which fell on the 5th of August. That was how it had to be. No discussion.

And the year before, things had been even more dramatic. Robert had won a scholarship to spend six months in Massachusetts, living in a nice house in a Boston suburb and working as a teacher in one of the renowned schools of the area. The idea was a cultural exchange between English and American teachers. He would be free to teach as much or as little as he liked. The main thing was experiencing a good cultural immersion and getting to know as many colleagues as possible.

Maggie had been as thrilled as Robert, looking forward to some of the more glamorous spots of the American East Coast, which they would have the opportunity to visit. They had both been in the middle of their preparations when Rachel announced that she'd always wanted to visit the United States and she would join them for this stint. They tried to dissuade her, but to no avail. So, she came along. On their second day in Boston, Rachel tripped over a kerb and broke her left leg. The result was a leg in a plaster.

Robert had to look after Rachel practically the whole time. He had to organise a wheelchair wherever they were going and push her around and he hardly had any time left to do what he was in Massachusetts for. He was only able to appear at his school on two days. This didn't allow him to meet any of his American colleagues or to participate in any of the projects that had been planned beforehand. He had to disappoint everybody – except Rachel, who sat in her wheelchair directing everyone about. She was holding court. And Maggie took her side when Robert tried to protest.

When one day recently, Robert was telling Philomena the full story of all the disappointments he'd had to suffer because of Maggie's dependency on Rachel, including the American scholarship and the Spanish fiasco, she told him to let her go. "Just forget about Maggie if she can't even stand up to her mother and support you in such important things." Both stories had been glossed over at the time, but they both rankled in Robert's heart. He just had to tell Philomena eventually.

So, she believed the question she asked herself was justified. How long would their relationship last? She gave them another year, maximum.

*   *   *

That night, Philomena couldn't go to sleep. She tossed and turned in her bed, trying to find some sleep. She was generally a good sleeper, but once in a while, say about three or four times per year, she was oppressed by unpleasant thoughts. They were vague fears that she couldn't pinpoint exactly but which always seemed to have something to do with relationships or with the wide range of human behaviour. Sometimes her thoughts took the form of memories, mostly memories from her teenage years, often to do with her childhood friend Sandy and sometimes memories about her sexual experiences of which she often felt ashamed. Then, also, there were the really horrible memories of an unspecified feeling of guilt. She was convinced she was guilty of some awful crime and it was only a matter of time before she would be found out and punished.

On this particular night, she was tormented by memories of Sandy. More particularly, Sandy's expectations of their friendship and her demands on her.

It had to be admitted. Sandy was simply asking for too much! When she had asked her to give her a hand in a delicate job, Philomena hesitated, but Sandy was so full of entreaties, she seemed so desperate and she lectured her on what it meant to be a woman, calling her an inexperienced girl and seeking justification behind her veil of womanhood. Philomena was even a bit afraid of her older friend.

Sandy lectured her on what it meant to desire a man, what grown-up men and women were doing when they loved each other and the emotional extremes that relationships could get into. When Philomena asked her what the problem was, she wasn't given a concrete answer but only sweeping theories on humanity and romantic glory in true relationships.

Again and again, Sandy returned to her topic of some great action needed in order to set certain things right. Eventually she became more specific about her plans and swore her younger friend to absolute secrecy. Eventually, albeit *contre coeur*, Philomena agreed to help her friend. And that turned out to be the greatest mistake of her life, a mistake she could never hope to atone for, even though she might live up to a hundred or more. Sandy didn't appear to be moved to the same depth. For her, it seemed almost like routine.

Despite her friend's promises, what followed didn't strengthen their friendship but rather burdened it. Finally, it led to a complete estrangement between the two women.

Thankfully, for the outside world, the thing didn't have a dangerous impact but just blew over in time. But for Philomena, it kept cropping up in her memory, always oppressing her. Mostly at night when she was trying to find her sleep. Was it a feeling of guilt? Yes, of course, that was what guilt could do to you.

Perhaps that might have been one of the reasons for her writing of romantic novels. The writing process offered her a kind of escape into a more clearly ordered world of her own creation. A thoroughly fictional world. A reality she could decide on. A series of actions and events she could conjure up and control, unencumbered by the harsh realities of the actual world.

*   *   *

Philomena's career as a writer – after the abandonment of her youthful stories – had taken off quite unexpectedly.

These days, she was satisfied that nobody in her village knew about it. No one even from her family. Her parents, who didn't keep in very close contact, had no idea and Robert would never have suspected it either. That's why she was surprised at her own openness with Alfred, who had informed Norman. A good thing she had sworn him to secrecy.

She sometimes found it quite ironic that people in the village considered her an old hag of no importance while so many readers were familiar with her novels. That was the advantage of protecting her private life by using a pseudonym, a so-called pen name or *nom de plume*. Sometimes it occurred to her that several people in the village – probably several women – might very well belong to her readership without realising the identity of the author.

It had started one afternoon when she was sitting in her attic flat in Hammersmith. Suddenly, a simple plot of intrigue and thwarted love came to her mind. She took a sheet of paper and drew up a diagram of a possible plot. After a week's work mostly in the evening and well into the night, she had a manuscript of some fifty pages and the continuation of the story was clearly visible to her. She could see it would all be plain sailing ahead.

After six weeks, her manuscript was complete. She bought a yearbook of British publishers and literary agents. With the data contained in that yearbook, she contacted several agents and publishers by phone to find out which of them catered to her type of novel. That process took the best of two months. Then, all of a sudden, an agent asked for her manuscript. She sent it in and within two weeks, she was invited by the agency to meet.

At their small office in Edgware, she was met by Hilda Cunningham, who, after an exciting interview, became her literary agent at once. Hilda was very confident. She promised Philomena that she would find a suitable publisher in no time. The novel was just right and it would sell very well if the right publishers got it under their wings. Together they tried to find a suitable literary pseudonym for Philomena. Eventually, they decided on Giulia Montepulciano, a beautifully suitable Italian name with the right sound even when pronounced incorrectly, but credible enough for an English authoress. Philomena also liked the association with that Italian wine of the same name.

When her first novel – *Deceit behind the Castle Walls* – was published, it was an immediate success. Hilda and the publishers considered it a disadvantage that they couldn't have a proper book launch with the authoress present because Philomena wanted to remain incognito, but their excellent marketing strategies led to this great success. Besides her privacy, Philomena also valued the fact that she didn't have to be exposed to the general public – including friends and relatives – with what she considered such a shallow novel. But obviously, there were many people who liked her romantic story and they asked for more.

Her success continued. Her novel sold by the tens of thousands, particularly at airport bookstalls and, quite unexpectedly, at small country bookstores. Even British expats in Italy bought her book. Soon enough, it became clear to her that she would have to write another novel in the same vein. So, after an initial phase of hesitation and procrastination, she sat down at her computer to start her second novel.

Within two years, she had published three novels and her royalties had earned her more than a million pounds. With Hilda, she had arranged the management of her financial affairs, so it was only the tax people who knew of her riches.

Even now, she didn't tell anyone. Somehow, she couldn't believe her success herself; in a way, she even felt a bit ashamed. She felt she was cheating people. But then, after her success had lasted for over a year, she gradually accepted it. And when, after two more years, her success didn't diminish but kept growing, she could make her peace with it. She admitted to herself that she was now a bestselling authoress in the department of romantic pulp fiction.

By the time she moved into her village cottage away from the noise and hassle of the big metropolis, she owned a considerable fortune, which meant she would never really have to work again but could easily live on her independent means up to the end of her life. Her money was carefully invested by her financial manager, who was very discreet and kept her informed regularly. She donated a great deal of her money to various charities but had instructed her financial manager to keep her name out of the transactions, telling the recipients that the donations came from "a concerned individual".

So, she was quite surprised at her own openness with Alfred and Norman. But although she admitted to them that she was writing such romantic novels, she refused to reveal her *nom de plume* to them.

* * *

Philomena was sitting in her lounge, ruminating on her situation. She found that her life really pleased her. If she had the occasional pang of guilt, she managed to put it away in her mind and if she felt she was probably falling in love with Norman, she felt she was strong enough to cope with it by now.

Both considerations – her occasional guilt feelings and her misgivings about falling in love – had become part of her existence, the guilt question already for several decades and the enigma of love for the past few weeks. She had learned to live with such disturbances. Yes, they constituted a degree of disturbance in her mental and emotional life, but they were really no great trouble. She was old enough and experienced enough to accept the fact that no one's life was one hundred per cent trouble-free. She knew the metaphor of the backpack of one's experience that one was carrying through life and she knew that it was getting heavier by the years, probably too heavy by the time one reached old age. Emotional burden was a fact of life.

When she met Norman the next time, she was determined to let herself go. She wouldn't hold back but go with the flow of their developing relationship. If he was really interested in her – even though she was his senior by a few years – who was she to stop him from falling in love with her, too? She admitted to herself that it was quite flattering to be the object of his desire after all, considering his good looks and his well-educated personality. This made her wonder why he had no girlfriend already. She decided to question him if and when they were going to take things any further.

The situation arose on the following weekend. Norman had asked her out again. They were driving through the lovely English country lanes heading for a day out at Hever Castle. As agreed between them, she had prepared a picnic while he had got them two bottles of wine, one white and one red.

During the drive, they talked about many interesting subjects, books they had read, music they both loved, places they had visited and opinions on the world in general. When it came to politics, they both agreed that the world was going through an extremely problematic phase. Norman suggested that globalisation and digitalisation made the world more complex.

"When we were young, our lives were a lot simpler. We didn't have to check our mobile phones and our email accounts all the time. In our jobs and when it came to dealing with businesses in ever so many ways, we were helped, things were arranged for us. There was a thing called service. Nowadays, however, we have to do everything ourselves. We can no longer walk into a shop and ask about something within their field. We are told to find out ourselves on their website.

"We can no longer phone a garage and arrange our car to be serviced. We have to book a time slot on the website. When we bought a new appliance, we got an instruction manual. Today we are told to find out everything on the respective website. These days, we spend a lot of time looking for things on our computers or, more recently, on our smartphones. What a waste of time! Thus, the amount of quality time in our lives is being reduced continually."

"Yes, that's why I'm trying to spend as little time as possible with these electronic devices."

"You are a wise woman. But most people just lose their bearings. They lose sight of what's important in life and what isn't. They have the illusion that they're very important persons when they have a great number of followers or 'likes' on one of the social media channels. What poor blindness!"

"Do you think they suffer from certain shortcomings eventually?"

"Indeed, I do. I believe their distorted sense of what's what in the world leads to a limited understanding of history and politics. They suffer from an unspecified fear, a fear of their own responsibilities, the future and all the dangers in the world. So, they follow some right-wing populist ratcatcher hoping to be led into a safe haven by those empty promises. The evils behind people's fears are quickly identified by those populists. The migrants, the foreigners, the intellectuals, the critical thinkers…"

"Are you sure?" Philomena asked.

"Yes, I am positive. Just look at the number of such populist liars oppressing their people or even just trying to undermine the foundations of democracy, usually beginning by suppressing a free press. Take Putin from Russia, Lukashenko from Belarus, the Chinese leader, the North Korean leader, the Egyptian leader and many more. Even certain democratically elected leaders are trying to develop into such oppressors. And we haven't even mentioned the various dictators in Africa or South East Asia. I'm telling you…"

"All right, all right, I think I got your drift. And I think you're right." Their conversation had become too much like a lecture for Philomena, so she tried to steer Norman away from his political views. Nevertheless, she fully agreed with his opinions.

Their mood was now more factual, more sober. Philomena realised that if Norman had any romantic designs on her, this was not the time.

They walked back to Norman's car and started on their homeward drive. They drove through some really beautiful parts of Kent. When they were travelling on the A21 between Bewl Water and Bedgebury Forest, Philomena was shaken by an attack of cold panic. She froze stiff, her hands and legs began to shake and she lost her voice. Norman, though concentrated on the traffic, soon saw that something was amiss with her. He turned off the main road and stopped at a suitable spot.

"What's the matter with you?" he asked, full of concern. "Should I call an ambulance or drive you to a hospital in Hastings?"

She stared at his face with big eyes. Gradually, she regained her composure and shook her head. "No ambulance, no hospital, please."

Reluctantly, he complied and waited for her recovery.

"It's just one of those attacks," she mumbled. "Don't worry. It's okay."

"Do you often get such attacks?" he wanted to know.

She didn't know what to tell him. This was too private for her. Besides, she wasn't even quite sure about such attacks herself. She only knew they had something to do with her past, but what exactly she didn't know.

"They are very rare, but they don't mean anything," she said.

"But I'm worried. Are you sure you're not an epileptic?"

"Oh yes, one hundred per cent sure," she replied with such confidence that he believed her.

All the same, she felt she had to give him some sort of explanation, so she came up with a stupid comment. "I think it was just the area we were travelling through, you know, Bedgebury Forest. I never liked that area. I don't want to go there."

He looked at her, frowning.

They drove on in silence. She felt that he wanted to ask her more about her panic attacks, but she appreciated his tactful silence.

After he had dropped her at her cottage, they said goodbye. She stepped through the door and felt safer in her own four walls.

She made herself a cup of tea, following her routine procedure and sat down in her lounge. She tried to come to terms with her own feelings. Also, she decided to put those attacks – which weren't very frequent anyway – behind her. Maybe they would explain themselves one day. They were certainly no concern of Norman's.

The telephone rang. It was Robert.

"I just wanted to let you know that things between Maggie and myself have improved a lot. You know, we've had our occasional differences over the last few months."

"The last few years, I would say," Philomena corrected.

"Well, yes, in a way, but not all the time."

"My dear brother, of course it's your own life, and it isn't for me to tell you what to do, but I've been watching this – what shall I say? – this odd relationship between you and your wife for a number of years now, and I must admit that I've been worried. I often wondered if you were really happy."

"Well, we have turned a new page in our lives."

"How is that?"

"We had a really long heart-to-heart talk about our life together. I managed to get a few ideas across to her. And she had quite a lot to drop at my doorstep. Apparently, she has felt unhappy for years. She says I never take her seriously enough. She wants to be respected as a woman of a certain class but I find it hard to go along with this would-be class thing. For me, she's just my charming wife, my Maggie. I don't need to style her as a great lady."

"I see." Philomena wondered what she was expected to say to that. "I agree with you in so far as I also consider social prestige a pointless endeavour."

"Yes, but when she is with the other ladies, she feels beneath them, so she wants to make a better impression. Now, what should I tell her? What can she do? She seems caught in a social dilemma."

"I think there would be a very simple solution."

"What would that be, I wonder?"

"Tell her to give up seeing those women. Let her find a new circle of friends. Those bitches aren't her friends. She'd be better to just drop them."

"Oh, I could never ask her to do that."

"Why not? Just explain to her how those so-called ladies have snubbed her over the past few months. Give her some examples of humiliations she has endured in her dealings with them. I'm sure she'll understand."

Robert was silent for a few moments. She decided to change the subject.

"Any news about that former pupil of yours?"

"Oh, she seems to have given up on me. The last I heard of her was that she'd decided to forget the past and return to her old job near Manchester. I haven't heard from her since. And that's over a year now."

Philomena was glad of this solution. Now she hoped for her brother that he would succeed with his wife. He should really manage to make her give up those awful "friends".

"About Maggie now, I don't know if she'll listen to me when I tell her to drop those ladies. Can't you talk to her? You are so much more convincing and you are an educated woman."

"No, Robbie, that is your job. And it seems very important that it is YOU telling her, not me."

"Well, I can try…"

They continued with some minor comments on the political situation before they rang off.

What her brother had just told her – especially his strange story about his former pupil Lizzie and the seemingly unspectacular ending of her stalking activities – made her think of the enigma of relationships between males and females that were not right, such as close relationships between older males in power and dependent girls. This whole affair – if it could really be called an affair – between Robbie and Lizzie represented yet another facet of this pattern. She remembered her own experiences with Uncle Bertie and Sandy's affair with Mr Sullivan. Were all these examples different variations of the same pattern, no matter if the initiative had started from an older man or from a teenage girl? She couldn't answer the question. But it seemed like a common pattern to her.

She returned to the lounge and sat down. She relaxed and dropped off into a sort of trance. She re-lived those moments of her nervous attack. She knew it wasn't a case of epilepsy, but rather some kind of nervous breakdown. She had those breakdowns perhaps twice a year, hardly more often. So, she wasn't worried too much about them. Perhaps she was just demanding too much of her nervous system. All that writing… She might have to cut back on her long hours of sitting at her computer writing her romantic novels.

As she was nearly dropping off into a pleasant nap, she suddenly remembered what Robert had told her about his former pupil from Gloucestershire. The phrase "she'd decided to forget the past" rang in her ears. How could anyone do such a thing? She never thought of her own past. It was just at odd moments, such as in dreams, when certain ghosts from her past cropped up and showed their ugly heads.

TEN

Philomena and Norman were walking along the seafront in Hastings. They were spending the pleasant autumn day on the coast. Norman turned to her as they were waiting to cross the street at the traffic lights.

"You know, Philly, I have often been thinking of that attack you had, you know, on our way home from Hever Castle."

"Oh, that was nothing."

"It didn't look like nothing to me."

Since she didn't react to this comment and he didn't want to pry into her more private life, he remained silent.

They did not mention the subject again for two weeks.

*   *   *

It was a windy autumn evening. Philomena sat down in her lounge. She noted the fact that the days were now really getting shorter. Only six o'clock and already quite dark outside! After she'd arranged the small side-table from her old nest of tables, she grabbed the remote control and switched on her TV set. The six o'clock news had only just begun. The various news items were the usual sad stories. Wars triggered by crazy dictators, people being exploited, right-wing maniacs trying to undermine democracies and so on. She wondered why she was still watching the news. She couldn't do anything about it. She couldn't even stop the liars and right-wing populists in her own country. While she endeavoured to keep abreast of the politics of the day, she felt that it threatened to make her depressed.

The last section of the programme switched to regional news. Within this section, the first item concerned a new plan for wind turbines on Thanet. But the second news item gave her a cold shock. As it appeared, police had found the remains of a dead body in Bedgebury Forest. A reporter was standing on the edge of the forest which was so familiar to her. And yet she dreaded it for some mysterious reason unknown to her.

"Sixty year-old Mark Thompson was walking his dog along the edge of Bedgebury Forest, here right behind me," the reporter told the TV-viewers and the camera moved to a puzzled man in a dark green anorak, "when the animal suddenly rushed off into the deep forest. Mr Thompson followed the barking noises and came to a spot where his dog was digging up the ground beneath a thick layer of brambles and brown autumn leaves. He tried to stop the dog, but the animal had obviously found the scent of something interesting. When Mr Thompson saw that the dog had unearthed a bone, he had his suspicions and when a second bone turned up, he decided to call the police."

"And have you got any information from the police?" the anchor-woman asked.

"Indeed, I have here with me Detective Inspector Jamie Harrison from the Maidstone Police Department. Can you tell us anything more about the remains found? Are they human?"

"We cannot make a definitive statement at this point in time, but the remains appear to be of human origin. We should have more specific information once the coroner has come to investigate."

When the anchor-woman changed to the next news item, Philomena switched the TV off. She heaved a deep sigh and scratched herself behind her left ear. She didn't

165

know what was happening to her, but somehow this story from Bedgebury Forest had upset her more than she could explain.

She decided to call Norman. He picked up the phone on the second ring and knew at once what she wanted to talk to him about.

"It's the TV news, isn't it?" he began. "When they showed the pictures of Bedgebury Forest, I knew immediately that that had been the spot which had upset you so much that day. You know, your attack or nervous breakdown which we couldn't explain. So, naturally, I realised that such a news item was bound to upset you again. Am I right?"

"Yes, I feel awful. Really awful. But I couldn't tell you why exactly. It's just that the story caused me so much pain, such an awful feeling of guilt and deprivation. I felt I needed some sort of emotional anchor, you see." Her voice was shaky and betrayed her inner turmoil. Norman could tell that she really was in a very bad way.

"Do you want me to come over?" he asked.

"Would you mind?" she hesitated.

"Of course not. I'll be right over."

Fifteen minutes later, he rang her doorbell. When she opened the door for him, he entered with a bottle of red wine in his hand.

"I thought you might welcome a soothing drink."

She ushered him to the lounge, where they sat down. Philomena sat in her armchair while Norman sat on her small sofa opposite.

At first, neither of them knew what to say. To begin with, pointless small talk or silly comments about the autumn weather would be as inappropriate as rushing straight to the topic at hand. It was a delicate situation.

Eventually, she said, "I'm sorry for my stupid moods, but I'm grateful you could come."

Norman stood up and fetched two glasses from her kitchen. He opened the bottle and poured two glasses of the lovely wine. "Let's relax first," he suggested.

They sipped their wine for a few minutes. Then he asked, "Can you identify the nature of your shock?"

"I don't really know," she answered. "It's only, well, those pictures of the forest on TV triggered some hidden memory in my mind and the effect was pure panic. I thought I knew the spot in the forest, but I don't know why. It was what they call a *déjà vu* effect."

"I see. Have you had this before?"

"Not that I know. Perhaps only in dreams." She looked down into her glass.

"Do you know of any connection with that section of the forest? Perhaps from your younger days?"

"Well, we used to go there as teenagers from time to time."

"Who is *we*?"

"My friend Sandy and myself. We used to go there with our bikes."

"You've never mentioned a friend called Sandy, have you? At least I can't remember."

"Well, you don't know everything, do you?"

"Sorry, I don't mean to pry."

"Oh, it's all right. You're probably right. I dismissed Sandy from my life."

"How can you dismiss a friend from your life?" he asked with a frown on his face. "Did you quarrel?"

"No, she just disappeared. I don't remember any details. There seem to be a few bits and pieces missing from my memory. I just can't remember how we parted.

All I know is that she has definitely disappeared from my world."

"That's rather strange, don't you think?"

"Now you mention it, indeed, it appears rather strange. But it never occurred to me in this light. It has been part of my emotional setting for more than two decades, so I never questioned it."

Norman was quiet for a few minutes and they both sipped some more red wine.

"Can't you remember anything about your friend?"

"Of course, I remember many details from our younger days... her good looks, her voice, the missing finger on her right hand, her superior ways... things like that. And I believe I was in love with her older brother. Henry was his name."

"Would you like to tell me everything that you can remember about her? Like this, we might eventually come to the bottom of the whole enigma."

Philomena hesitated. "You know, this is all very personal, not to say very intimate. I have to sleep on it. If we go into this amateur psychoanalysis, I'll have to trust you one hundred per cent. Are we close enough? Let's first find out how we feel for each other, what we see in each other."

"That's a good idea," Norman said. "It shows how much this situation – and by implication our relationship – really means to you."

After another pause, Philomena took the first step. "You know, Norman, you mean a lot to me, really, you do. But you have to understand that I have a very varied past. I am not the person that I appear to be to the people in the village."

"I know. The mere fact that you are the author of several romantic novels speaks volumes. I'm sure your life has been very exciting. And because I like you very much – which you must have guessed – I am very eager to know more about you. Everything about you is of the greatest interest to me and I promise any secrets you tell me shall be as safe as the crown jewels with me."

"You say you like me. But we're not having a love affair, are we? I'm older that you and a man never falls in love with an older woman."

"I'm not sure about that. There are only a few years between us. I'd say we belong to the same generation. And about a love affair, I don't know what it is, all I know is that I like you very much and I am concerned about your happiness. You mean more to me than any other person I know, except my father. Now, does this convince you that you can trust me?"

Philomena looked at him and their eyes met. She was conscious of the fact that she had promised herself never to fall in love again after that disaster in Newcastle all those years ago. She'd had her share of eroticism and sex. However, she realised she really liked Norman, too. She liked him very much to be honest. Yes, they were not lovers in the traditional sense, but there was something like love between them.

"I like you very much, too," she said in a plain voice. Then she stood up from her armchair and sat down next to him on the sofa. She turned to him. Then she leaned to him, put her right arm across his shoulders and moved her face closer. She remained like this for several seconds before she said, "I'll sleep on it. Can you come back tomorrow?"

He nodded silently.

She kissed him on his lips, tenderly, for something like three seconds. Then she stood up and her entire body language indicated that she wanted him to leave.

He stood up, too, and quietly left her cottage with a soft "good night, my dear."

Later in bed, trying to find some sleep, she made a huge effort to remember some of the events that happened in her teenage years during a period from which she had no recollection at all. Somehow, she could remember that her friend Sandy was beginning to get on her nerves with her constant focus on sex and erotic experience. Sandy could get quite vulgar in her expressions when it came to the topic of sexual attraction. Sometimes it got so irksome that Philomena wondered how long they could remain best friends. Also, she had a clear memory of Sandy's affair with Mr Sullivan, their French teacher.

How did the close friendship between Sandy and her end? Philomena could only remember that she was furious with her friend. Obviously, Sandy must have hurt her very badly emotionally. There was a hazy memory of the two of them getting their bikes and setting out to ride to Bedgebury Forest, but what they were going there for or what happened there, she just couldn't remember. It all disappeared behind a veil of ignorance.

Whenever she tried to recapture those events in her mind, she felt she was falling into a dark abyss. It was an experience that – in her imagination – was like being snatched away from reality by the spectre of death. Probably she had been scared, fully believing she was about to die. Otherwise, she couldn't explain her terrible fear she felt whenever she approached those events in her mind. It was this deadly fear that was at the bottom of her nervous attacks that she suffered when she was confronted with that dark period in her life. That was what had happened when they passed Bedgebury Forest.

But how could she ever explain this to Norman? He would never be able to understand because she could never explain what had happened so long ago, more than twenty years ago.

There was the memory of their plan to ride to the forest for some purpose. Then nothing for quite some time. Then, later, the next memory was Philomena at school without Sandy. She clearly remembered that Sandy was still in her class, but they no longer talked to each other. Indeed, they were like strangers to each other. And Philomena remembered that she felt like a sick person. There was no concrete memory of any real illness, but only that feeling of no longer belonging in the world, of being an outsider, a pariah who had no right to happiness, no right to any of the pleasures that life normally offered to her peer group.

Her parents took her to see a doctor, but he only diagnosed a typical case of teenage sadness, a light depression, nothing to worry about, and he gave her some yellow pills, which she didn't take.

The next morning, she decided to consult Robert. After all, her brother must have known at the time what was going on with her. She phoned him and asked him to meet her in town. They arranged to meet at the same café where they often met to chat about Maggie and her antics or to discuss Robert's marriage in general.

After some introductory exchanges about the weather and the latest blunders of the government, she came to her point. "Listen, Robbie, I'd like to tap your memory. I'd like to talk about the time when I was about fifteen or sixteen."

"Oh, you know, that's rather awkward. It was a strange time. I was still a young boy and didn't quite realise what was going on and when I asked you about those events sometime later, you refused to go into those things. You told me unmistakably that it was none of my

171

business. You were even quite angry when I tried to open the topic. So, you see, I'm hardly in a position to help you now."

"But can't you really remember anything at all? What was I like? How long did my bad period last? Did I suffer a lot? Were our parents involved at all? Just some of the questions for which I'm looking for answers." She looked her brother in his eyes, urging him to help her.

"The only thing I can remember is your tales about your friend Sandy. She seemed to have been a great role model for you. When you talked about your activities outside our home, it was always Sandy this and Sandy that. Then, all of a sudden, one day, you stopped mentioning her and you spent most of your free time locked in your bedroom. When you emerged from your room, you didn't answer any questions that Mum or Dad asked you. Eventually, they gave up.

"I don't remember how long that phase lasted – your hibernation, as it were – but apparently, you never fully recovered. Over time, however, we all forgot about it and went about our own business. It's strange that you mention your teenage years now. In my memory, you were never a teenager. Of course, I'm not objective, being your younger brother, but somehow you seemed to have moved from childhood straight to adulthood. You skipped your teenage years."

"And you never wondered?"

"Why should I? I didn't have another sibling for comparison, so I accepted your ways as the ways of an older sister."

They were silent for a few moments, letting this sink in.

Robert cleared his throat and asked, "Why are you trying to unearth all that now? Can't you accept the fact that you seemed to have had a strange teenage phase? Or has anything happened to trigger your sudden interest now?"

"I don't know, it has only started to bother me recently. Certain things give me panic attacks and I don't know why. Besides, I really do wonder what might have happened that time. I have shut out part of my memory. Why? Why does an adult woman blot out a certain period of her life? I just fear there must be some sort of trauma behind it and I'm too scared to face it."

"That's very deep. If I were you, I'd consult a psychologist to analyse you."

"You mean I should see a shrink?"

"Yes. If the whole thing really bothers you."

"Thanks, my little brother, you're really a great help." Philomena felt angry. She had expected her brother to give her some better advice.

They changed the subject and spoke of Maggie. Robert was eager to tell his sister about the way his wife controlled him. He explained how he had lost his sense of spontaneity. Whenever he wanted to do something on his own that couldn't be explained by his work or by the needs of their household, she checked him and killed his impulse. Every step of his daily life was under scrutiny. She decided what was good for him and what she didn't approve of. When he got an email message, she asked him, "Who's that from?" And when he was sitting at his computer, she asked, "What are you looking for?"

Thus, a relaxed browsing through the Internet was an impossible thing for him. He had to get her approval before he started an Internet search. He had long given up any spontaneous visit to any of his former friends. For example, there were a few of his old classmates who had businesses in the area and he used to drop in on them occasionally, just for a chat and possibly a cup of coffee. Those spontaneous sprees were things of the past. Before leaving the house these days, he had to explain and justify his intentions before she'd let him go.

"But why do you accept such a situation?" Philomena asked.

"I don't accept such things, I just slipped into them over the years because I love her. And now, there's no way out unless I leave her, which I don't want to do."

Robert looked at his watch. "I'll have to be off."

"Wait," she checked him. "We've just had a long chat. Will she ask you about it when you get home?"

"Of course. I'll have to give her a report."

"But please, don't tell her any details of my problems. I wouldn't want her to gloat over my problems. Promise?"

"I promise. I'll only give her a general summary of our chat, focusing on my work at school and on the political situation. Your secret is safe with me. Promise!"

"But she knows I phoned you and asked you to meet me."

"Oh, I'll just tell her you wanted to ask me about certain details, you know, uncomplicated things from our childhood. That will do."

They parted and Philomena walked to the bookstore.

She was just browsing through some Indian and African authors when a voice at her back spoke to her. "Fancy seeing you in here! Of course, I knew you liked books, but I thought you had enough of them at home. Do you still buy new books? I thought a woman like you might prefer to re-read her old books from time to time…"

Philomena turned round and greeted her neighbour Lucy. "Well, what about this? Do you often come here?

Are you looking for any particular book or are you just browsing like me?"

"Oh, I only come here when I need a new book by one of my favourite authors. You know, romance fiction. I like a good book that gives you something to chew over... or something to cry over."

"Oh, I see," Philomena said, trying to get away from Lucy.

But Lucy was so full of her own world. She wanted to convince Philomena of what she considered good books. "You see," she continued, "at the moment I find this an excellent author. This is my favourite at the moment. She's called Giulia Montepulciano." And she picked up the book she'd left on the counter before her, proudly showing it to Philomena.

For a short moment, Philomena was at a loss for words. She didn't know what to say to this. But there was no need for a comment from her. Lucy went on without being asked.

"Oh, you have no idea! The wonderful stories she writes. She can really move you. And she can make you cry, too. I don't know a lot about her. She seems to be Italian, but her English is excellent. I'm telling you, she's a real discovery, a real gem. Would you like me to lend you one of her books so you can read it, too? I have at least five of her novels at home, but this one is new to me."

Philomena was nearly crushed by the weight of the irony of the situation. She only wanted to get away from Lucy. She murmured something about being pressed for time and gave her a quick goodbye. She left the bookstore in a hurry.

* * *

When Norman appeared at her door later, she received him with a serious expression. "I'm sorry, Norman, but I haven't had time to make up my mind about how much I can trust you. Please, don't take offence. It's not personal, but you see, I've been through so many disappointments in my life that I find it hard to trust another individual, no matter how much I like him or how nice he is to me. Please, do understand. I promise I'll let you know soon. I'll give you a call when I'm ready."

Norman shrugged his shoulders, gave her a weak smile and left.

For the next few days, Philomena hardly ever left her house. She hesitated about what she might do about her terrible attacks. She hesitated to meet Norman too soon. She didn't know how to face him.

After another week, she found time and leisure enough to sit down with a cup of tea and relax in the late afternoon. It was very quiet about the house and the street was empty. She began to think about her situation. She knew she had to come to a decision about Norman. It was unfair to keep him waiting too long. He was so good to her and by now she was quite confident that he was actually in love with her. But was she in love with him, too?

Philomena told herself she was really a very lucky woman. At her age, it wasn't so easy to find a male companion, even someone who loved her. Norman knew she had a varied past and yet he loved her and he was willing to support her in her emotional difficulties, her weird mental attacks and her mysterious fears. Also, she had to admit to herself that she found him very attractive, too. But was this love? She rephrased the question in her mind. Did this have to be love as it was described in her own novels? All pink and jubilant with butterflies in her stomach? Was she meant to lose her head and be ready to do all sorts of stupid things with him? – No, she decided that was not what this feeling was. That thing about losing her head belonged to her past, her past in Newcastle. What she could let herself in for at this point in her life was something more mature.

Yes, it was love, only love of a different kind. Love based much more on trust and common respect. This was what she was ready to accept now. And she felt that Norman was probably ready to accept it, too.

Norman was a man, a man in his prime. And such men had needs. Was she ready to enter into a sexual relationship with him? She couldn't answer that. She thought about it for a while and came to the conclusion that she didn't have to decide right now. She could let things develop and everything would fall into place if they really accepted the principle of trust and common respect.

She picked up her phone and called him.

This time, she didn't send him away from her doorstep but invited him in with a winning smile. He seemed a little hesitant at first, but when he registered the true nature of her smile, he followed her to her lounge, where they sat down to another bottle of red wine. Whereas last time it had been a heavy Spanish Tempranillo, this time she offered him a lighter, more fruity wine from Austria.

She had lit a candle on her sideboard, which gave the room a very pleasant and relaxed atmosphere. The candlelight was reflected in the beautiful ruby hue of the liquid in their glasses. It was a very soothing moment indeed and it had its effect on Norman.

177

This time, they didn't beat about the bush with comments about the weather or other superficial topics. They came straight to the point.

"I'm grateful, dear Norman, indeed I am. Thank you for your patience with me and my irksome ways. As I told you, I just needed to come to terms with myself before I could open myself completely for you. I have been injured too many times. But I've come to the conclusion that our relationship has indeed become very important to me. So, my dear, tell me what you want us to be. Just good friends? Lovers? And if lovers, what type of lovers?"

He smiled and answered, "Yes, I would like us to be lovers. I know how difficult it can be for people like us, but I am ready to take the plunge with you."

"What do you mean by 'taking the plunge'? I hope you don't mean marriage."

"Oh no, my dear Philomena. What I mean is a trustful relationship. I don't even think we should move in together but remain living where we are. But I want us to trust each other one hundred per cent and to respect each other through all eventual ups and downs, if you can follow my drift. But first, my dear, don't you want to know more about my past? Don't you want to know how many women I've had?"

"You don't know about all the men in my life. So why should I ask you to tell me about the women in yours?"

"This is a very wise attitude. Naturally, with time spent together over the years, we might find the need to tell each other a bit more about our previous lives. But as for now…"

She hesitated, but then she took courage. "And what about sex?"

"I don't think we should set any hard and fast rules about sex or no sex. I believe that our wishes and needs in that respect will automatically develop as we share a constant relationship based on mature love and common trust. I, for one, don't wish to press you. Having said that, of course, I find you extremely attractive and I… well… I can imagine falling in love with you physically, too."

Philomena was satisfied with his answer. They would see in time.

She took another sip of wine. Then she stood up and sat down next to him on the sofa. She turned to him and kissed him very tenderly on his lips. He responded with a relaxed pleasure and a controlled eagerness. They began to forget the time.

ELEVEN

One morning, Philomena opened the paper. On page two, she read about the human remains that had been found in Bedgebury Forest about ten days earlier. Of course, the article attracted her very much, although it frightened her at the same time. It made her scratch her head behind her left ear and she felt her pulse race.

She read that they had found the remains of a human body. Forensic investigations showed that they were the heavily decomposed remains of a young woman. She must have been between thirty and forty years of age when she died and she must have lain in the ground for more than twenty years.

Whether the woman had died in an accident or whether she was the victim of a crime was still an open question. A detective from Maidstone was interviewed by a newspaper journalist and the information he could give was still rather vague. The detective and his team needed more time. But the fact that the body was found buried in a forest indicated a crime rather than an accident. In the police records, there was no report of a car accident on or around the A21 or any other smaller road around the forest.

When the journalist asked the investigating detective about the cause of death, the answer was again quite vague. The skull seemed to be fractured and there might have been some internal injuries. But the decomposed state of the body didn't allow any definite conclusions on this point.

Philomena put the paper away and she looked out of the window. The trees had already shed most of their foliage. This created a melancholy atmosphere, but it also helped her to relax and order her thoughts.

Why did the location – Bedgebury Forest – produce such a frightful reaction in her? What was it that had happened there and had something to do with her all those years ago? Did it have anything to do with that dead woman? She tried to focus on her memory, but whenever she approached that place and time, her mind went blank and she panicked.

It was obvious that whatever had happened must have given her a very bad trauma. By now she was certain that she wouldn't be able to solve the puzzle on her own. She needed help. Could she see a psychologist? She didn't like the idea.

What about Norman? What about Robbie? Whom could she trust most of all in such a delicate matter? She was at a loss. She knew that there were women who would turn to their mothers in such emergencies. But that was out of the question!

Although she was still in touch with her parents, there was no intimacy between them. In fact, there had never been any closeness or trust between them. The distance between their opinions, their interests and their political views was too big. Nowadays, this distance was even more pronounced than in the old days. She would never even think of consulting her mother on any problem, even a small one. She came to the point where she doubted if she was willing to consult anyone at all.

But the thoughts about her trauma and its connection with what had happened in Bedgebury Forest were with her all day. Finally, in the evening, she found she could no longer wait, she really needed some help soon.

When she considered the fact that Robbie already had quite a lot on his plate, she came to the decision to ask Norman. Would he help her? Would he be shocked at whatever they found out together? Would her real past – whatever it was – chase him away? These considerations meant that she was ready to risk her close friendship with Norman, if only he could help her to get rid of her panic attacks.

* * *

The next day, she was strolling through the supermarket, looking for coffee, biscuits and tea bags, when a man nearly bumped into her. Her mind was so preoccupied with her uncertainty over what to do about her trauma and the events around Bedgebury Forest that she didn't bother to look at the man. But the man stopped and looked her up and down.

"I say," he asked, "don't I know you? Aren't you Philomena Webster?"

She stopped and forced herself out of her ruminations. Looking at the man's face, she realised it looked familiar and after a moment's hesitation, she recognised him.

"Henry? Is it really you?" she cried.

"Yes, it is. Well, well! Long time no see! How wonderful to bump into you just like this after all those years! How are you?"

She looked at him properly now. She studied his face, noted his greying hair, his dashing moustache and his positive mood. Inspecting his figure, she found that he still looked athletic despite his small paunch.

His deep blue eyes looked into hers and he smiled uncertainly. She became aware of the fact that she had been in love with him all those years ago, madly in love, in fact. Something that seemed quite unthinkable now. But those had been the days… She knew that they had never admitted their love to each other and they had never even kissed or exchanged other forms of endearment. But they had both been conscious of their love whenever they were together.

For a few moments, they both didn't know what to say next; there were too many heavy memories between them.

"Would you like to stop somewhere for a cup of coffee? I'd really like to catch up with you. It's all so long ago…," asked Henry.

Philomena hesitated. "I don't know. I've got to do my shopping first." But then she admitted to herself that she was also very eager to catch up with him. There was such a lot that they could talk about. There was their own relationship, there was Sandy and there was her honest curiosity about his present state in life.

"Can I help you with your shopping?" he offered. "I'm nearly done myself."

"Okay, thank you very much," she relented. So, they moved along the long aisles of the supermarket together, Henry helping her to pull the items from the top shelves and Philomena ticking them off on her shopping list while dropping them into her trolley. On the way, he also picked out a few things for himself, which he put in his shopping basket. The procedure was almost business-like. They concentrated on the job at hand and saved any more private matters for their proposed chat later on. Eventually, they passed through the check-out and stepped out into the grey street.

In the café, they found a table near the window and sat down to their cups of coffee. They both took a few sips before Henry began.

"I often wondered what became of you. Do you live around here? Or are you just visiting?"

She gave him her honest answers and asked back, "And what about you? What's your job these days? Are you married? Have you got a family?"

"Quite a lot of questions at once," he answered. "But to give you my precise answers, I've got a job in the city, quite a demanding job, in fact, with a big company in international trade. I used to be in journalism after my university degree, but after a while, I realised it wasn't for me. So, I changed my career. Am I married? Well, I was. I'm divorced now and there are two children."

"How old are they?"

"Sixteen and fourteen. And what about you? Any family?"

"No. I live on my own," she explained, but she didn't tell him about her relationships with men. It was too early. They'd only just met again. She needed to get to know him a bit better again before she would trust him with her more private matters.

Their conversation continued for a while, touching on everyday matters such as the demands of his job, both their musical activities and their reading. She neither told him about her fiction writing nor asked about his sister. However, after exhausting those more mundane topics, they both seemed to become aware of the white elephant in the room, which was Sandy.

After an awkward silence, she decided to drop the bomb.

"What about Sandy?"

He looked down into his empty coffee cup. "I haven't heard from her in over ten years. Twenty years, to tell you the truth."

"But do you know where she lives? Has she got a family?"

"I don't know exactly."

"What do you mean?"

"Well, it's hard to explain. After what had happened that time, she just disappeared. Our parents were shattered with grief. They employed a detective agency, hoping to locate her, but it took a long time before they got their answers. As it turned out, she had moved to India to an ashram in Tamil Nadu, somewhere near Pondicherry. You know, that's on the east coast, south of Chennai – or Madras, as it used to be called – but we don't know any details. Apparently, she doesn't want to be in touch. Father sent a registered letter to the address revealed by the detective agency, but there was no answer from her although the letter wasn't returned, so she must've got it and decided to remain cut off."

Philomena didn't know what to say to this. She stared into his eyes, at first, in disbelief, then in amazement. Trying to remember her old friend, she came to the conclusion that the story just related by Henry – that's Sandy's actual career in life – somehow suited her. It suddenly appeared to be quite compatible with Sandy's character or with her character as Philomena believed she recalled. She remembered how Sandy had always struggled to reach out into the world. She'd always yearned for greater things, for a more meaningful life than the one they had where they grew up together. The petit-bourgeois thing wasn't enough for her.

But India of all places! It would've been more appropriate – or more expected – to be a place like

185

Hollywood or Monaco or any other glamorous place, but India? And even given that she was attracted by India, one could have seen her in the film studios of Mumbai, having a career in the film industry, rather than in an esoteric ashram, probably full of old hippies who'd escaped from their responsibilities in Europe.

"A penny for your thoughts," Henry suggested.

"Well, I don't know what to say. Did she ever mention anything that could've betrayed her penchant for meditation, for Buddhist philosophy or any other similar sphere in life? As for myself, I never expected her to go for something like that."

"It came as a big surprise to all of us. But then, considering what had happened…" His voice trailed off.

"What do you mean?"

"Why are you asking? You were in it with her, weren't you?" he said, looking at her carefully.

"No, really! I have no idea. In fact, I've been suffering from some kind of post-traumatic retrograde amnesia since then, trying to come to terms with what had really happened. There's only a blackout in my memory. All I can remember is that Sandy and I had planned to cycle to Bedgebury Forest for some particular reason. I think Sandy was pregnant, but everything else is lost to me."

Now he looked at her in disbelief. "I always assumed that you were with her and you were part of the scandal. I'm sorry if I misjudged you. So, you really don't know?"

"What is it that you know and I don't?"

"You say the last thing you remember was your plan to cycle to Bedgebury Forest with my sister? You can't remember why, what for?"

"Yes, that is the truth. That's all I can remember."

186

He sighed deeply. "So, you can't remember the big scandal at your school after your outing to Bedgebury Forest?"

They were interrupted by the young girl from the coffee counter who wanted to know if there was anything else they desired. They ordered another cup of coffee each and waited for her to disappear before they returned to their delicate conversation.

"What scandal are you talking about?"

"Well, it was after your outing, but it was connected to it later on."

"Why don't you tell me everything you know."

"Okay. And you really can't remember anything at all?"

"It's too important for me, so I wouldn't dream of lying to you."

"I see." He hesitated for a few moments. Then he began. "So, where to start? I think I'd better tell you about the events in chronological order."

"That's a good idea," she agreed, sitting up on her chair and giving him her full attention. What would he tell her? She felt a certain nervousness but kept herself under control.

The waitress brought their coffees before he could go on.

"Sandy returned from her outing to Bedgebury Forest. If anything, she appeared somewhat agitated and we all assumed it had to be because of her exhaustion after her bike ride. But after a few days, it became known that two teachers from her school – your school, I should say – were missing. At first, it was believed they were both on sick leave, but then it became a certainty that they had disappeared. They hadn't taken anything with them; both their apartments didn't give the impression of an ordered

187

departure. Unwashed dishes were in the kitchen sink and there was some washing in the washing machine. The police were at the school and interviewed everyone, especially those colleagues and pupils who had been known to be in touch with them when they were still at the school. It concerned a young science teacher and a French teacher."

"That must've been Miss Mitford and Mr Sullivan," Philomena contributed.

"Yes, you're right. Those were their names. The investigations found out that the two of you, Sandy and you, had been seen in the company of Mr Sullivan, but never with Miss Mitford. So, you were questioned more often and more intensively. It was so bad that Sandy had a nervous breakdown and from what we understood, it was the same thing with you. The long and the short of it was, it was an established fact that the two teachers must have disappeared on the same day when you girls had been to Bedgebury Forest. Whether the two teachers had been there at the same time as you or not, that remained a question. There were no witnesses who could confirm the time of either your or their visits to the forest.

"Mr Sullivan's car was found in a carpark nearby, while Miss Mitford's car was found in the school carpark. But it wasn't even clear if they had been to the same forest. They could've driven to a place nearby in two cars, dropped his car and returned to the school in her car before slipping away unobserved from there. That was as much as the police had found and what the press reported. The case was eventually dropped. The two of you, as well as other people who had been in frequent contact with the two missing teachers, were left alone. No wrongdoing on your part could be proved."

"That was all?"

"Yes. There were no charges and it was assumed the two teachers – who had been known to be secret lovers – must have eloped. That is, they were thought to have left together, probably to France, since especially Mr Sullivan was known for his admiration of France and knew the language very well. The French police were contacted, but nothing came of it. Nothing was ever heard from them."

They remained silent, Philomena digesting what she had just learnt from Henry. She stood up, murmuring, "I've got to go to the loo," and disappeared for about five minutes. Henry was patient enough to wait for her return.

"All right?" he asked when she was seated opposite him again.

"Yes, at least I think so."

"But tell me," he took up their conversation again, "do you have any recollection at all about what might have happened in or around that forest?"

"None whatsoever. It's all lost in my memory. But the recent news about that forest makes me extremely nervous."

"Can you at least try to explain what makes you so nervous about it?"

"That is the whole problem! I am sure there must be a connection between the events at that time and the police findings now. Did you hear they found the remains of a female body which must have been buried in the forest for over twenty years? That can't be a coincidence! There has to be a connection."

"But you have no idea what that connection might be, I understand. Why does the news frighten you then?"

"I can't tell you. I don't even know myself. It's just some deep-rooted horror, some absurd fear of what might come out in the end."

Henry was lost in thought for a short while before he had another question for her. "What I can't understand is why you're so convinced there had to be some horrible involvement on your part?"

"I don't know."

"So, it's all in your mind. There's no factual connection with the disappearance of the two teachers?"

"That's the point," Philomena sighed. "There just has to be a connection. There just has to be."

"Why?"

"Because, for one thing, I have this strong gut feeling. I can literally feel my own involvement with some terrible event. Besides, it must have something to do with Bedgebury Forest."

"I see."

"Yes, so you will understand why the latest news from Bedgebury Forest must upset me. I'm sure I killed that young woman who was found dead."

Henry was horrified. He nearly shouted, "Hey, that's really taking things too far! How absurd to blame yourself for some crime that just happened to be committed in a place that has nothing to do with you but just gives you the shivers whenever you pass it!"

They both realised they had become too loud in the little café. At least three other patrons were staring at them. They sent some apologetic glances round the place and remained silent for a while just sipping their coffees.

One of the men stood up from his table and prepared to leave the café. As he was passing Henry and Philomena's table, he stopped and murmured his comment, "You must be talking about the dead body from Bedgebury Forest. I have to say, that place has always given me the shivers, too. It's a haunted place if you ask me. So just don't worry too much!"

190

With that, the man left the café, while Henry was looking at Philomena with a puzzled expression. "What was that?" he asked.

"Do you know the guy?" she asked back.

"No, do you?"

"No idea who he could be. But the story was quite big in the news. Many people must have their own theories about the case."

"That's it. And that's also why you shouldn't let it bother you too much. When something like that about a familiar place is reported, it's quite natural to think you have something to do with it."

"You may be right there," she said.

Soon, they left the café and parted. They exchanged phone numbers and email addresses, promising each other to stay in touch.

*   *   *

When Philomena met Norman about a week later, she wasn't sure if she ought to tell him about her trauma, too. She knew she had already told him part of her problem, but not the full story. He knew that she hated to go near Bedgebury Forest and he was aware of the fact that there had been some bad experience in her life, but he didn't know the details. Now that she had already told Henry, it seemed logical to tell Norman too. After all, while Henry was an old friend from her younger days with whom she hadn't been in touch for decades, Norman was a friend of the here and how. But there was the problem of confidentiality. Would it be a good idea to involve too many people? Would she regret having told more than one person at some point in the future?

The answer to her question came naturally. When she was with Norman in his house, smiling at her and sitting on the sofa, holding a cup of tea in his hands, her heart seemed to melt and she told him everything about her trauma that he hadn't known already. He must have guessed some aspects, but he was full of concern for her dilemma.

"I understand how awful that must be for you," he said.

"But you can't help me either, can you? You can't tell me what I can do to find out what happened all those years ago. Or do you think I ought to see a shrink? They say things that lie buried deep in your memory can actually be retrieved by psychoanalysis or similar treatments."

"Would you like to try something like that?"

"I'm not sure," she said. "In a way, I'm a bit afraid. Afraid of what might come to the surface."

"Why should you be afraid?" he asked, full of concern. He placed his hand on her right knee, which was just a few inches from his left knee. She didn't move away and firmly sat next to him on the sofa.

She hesitated. Then, after a heavy sigh, she confessed. "Please, don't laugh at me, but I'm sure I must have murdered someone in Bedgebury Forest. There's no other logical explanation."

Norman was horrified. He looked at his friend with a painful expression. "Why would you have murdered anyone? Whatever the results of the forensic investigations will be, I'm sure you have nothing to do with any of the persons connected with the case. Or was there anybody that you hated so much that you wanted to murder him or her?"

"Of course not. Apart from my Uncle Bertie, there was no living soul that I hated and as far as I know, he is still alive."

"I'd suggest we wait for the outcome of the investigations. Once the dead body is identified, we'll see more clearly."

With this, they dropped the topic and began to discuss other matters. But Philomena was still nervous, not at all convinced that she had nothing to do with the case.

She was still feeling a little uneasy when she arrived back at her cottage. She watched the BBC news at six and was horrified over the nationalistic and racist slogans that some of the conservative MPs used in their speeches. Were those people blind? Couldn't they see that Britain was no longer the world power that it used to be a hundred years ago? She wasn't terribly keen on politics, but she believed she had a clear head on her shoulders.

So, although she knew the European Union wasn't perfect by a long chalk, she could clearly see how leaving it had done such irreparable damage to the country. What the politicians called Brexit – what an awful expression! – was one of the worst mistakes the government had ever committed. No wonder, since it was decided on the basis of a set of lies propagated by the UKIP party and other blind nationalists, people who still saw themselves in the nineteenth century. She wondered why she was still watching the news. She knew a number of people who no longer watched any TV news or read the political articles in the paper. What a dangerous development! What a terrible danger for democracy!

The next day she was on the phone with Robert again. She found that these days she was glad to hear his voice more than ever. She wondered why. She'd never been a family person and her relationship with her brother had been friendly but never intimate up to now. Perhaps it was because some awful memories from her own past were creeping up on her, torturing her conscience. She might be in need of emotional support.

However, she felt she couldn't tell him everything she had discussed with Henry and Norman. She wondered why. When Robert mentioned his problems with Maggie, she knew why. She couldn't trust him not to tell his wife. Even though he seemed to suffer in his pseudo-marriage, he was still so dependent on Maggie. He suffered from her various intellectual shortcomings, but he was very much in love with her.

So, she decided to say nothing of what occupied her mind so much. But he jumped to the topic at once.

"Did you hear about the news from Bedgebury Forest?" he asked. "Didn't you used to go there quite a lot with your friend Sandy? You've got to know the place quite well. Have you got any idea about what might have happened there?"

"No, I have absolutely no idea. And just to set things straight, I didn't go there so often. Not as often as you might think."

"Are you sure? Well, I bumped into Uncle Bertie the other day. He's a really old man now, did you know? But he recognised me immediately. We had a chat about the past and naturally we also came to talk about the case of the murder in Bedgebury Forest. Bertie said you used to like the place very much. He seemed to know quite a lot about you, although he maintained he hadn't seen you in ages. When I asked him why, he only said there were old misunderstandings between you. Have you got any idea what he might mean?"

"No, he's just a dirty old man and I don't want to hear about him!" Philomena shouted.

"Hey, sister! What's the matter? Why such strong words?"

"It's got nothing to do with you, Robbie, but Bertie treated me very badly when I was a young girl. I don't want to go into any details, but please, just accept that I never ever want to see him again and never want to hear about him again. Is that clear?"

Robert hesitated. He was going to say something to the effect that she might have misjudged the old boy, but the vehemence of her statement made him swallow his words. So, after a pause, he changed the subject back to Bedgebury Forest.

"But it's true that Sandy and you visited the place several times?"

"Yes, we liked to cycle there and we liked the atmosphere of the small forest. But these days the place rather gives me the shivers. I think it's haunted or something and I'm not the only person to think so."

"Well, what a strange story! In the papers, it says that the dead body hasn't been identified yet. Have you got any idea who it could have been?"

"No idea. But I assume they'll soon find out. You know, they are very clever about such things these days with DNA and other modern methods…"

At this point, she nearly spilled the beans. They were in the middle of the topic that upset her so much that she was about to tell him of her fears and her conviction that she had murdered someone in that forest. But she only just managed to hold back.

So, they chatted about other things and soon rang off.

*　*　*

It was about one week later when the big news came. It was in all the papers and on all the TV channels.

They had identified the dead body. It was a certain Christine Jane Mitford, originally from East Grinstead, lately from Maidstone, a woman of thirty-two years of age at the time of her death, a science teacher and a gifted guitar player.

"This is it," Philomena thought when she heard the news. "They'll come for me now, I'm sure."

After digesting the news, she phoned Norman and told him about her expectation to be charged with murder. But Norman only tried to calm her down. He didn't believe she would be charged since she had obviously never committed such a crime. It was only in her head. She remained convinced of her guilt and they needed quite a long time on the phone for him to calm her down eventually.

"Please, promise me not to do anything stupid. Don't be rash and go to the police to confess a crime you haven't committed. Shall I come over and be with you?"

Despite her uncertainty about her own behaviour, she was glad to have him over. He gave her such a lot of security. This was one of those moments when she really needed a good friend.

"Yes, please. Do come," she said in a low voice.

PART THREE

TWELVE

The light in the cabin had been dimmed for about three hours. Philomena had managed to catch a few winks. But she still felt a bit groggy when the full light came on again. Obviously, they wanted to serve breakfast before preparing for the approach to their destination. She wondered what breakfast would look like. Of course, she could check in the little folder provided in her seat pocket. But she didn't feel up to it. Ever since boarding at Heathrow, she had been in a sort of trance. Several times through the short night, she had asked herself if this was reality or just a bad dream.

They asked her to choose her breakfast, English or Indian. She chose English although she wasn't hungry and certainly not in the mood for bacon, sausage and scrambled eggs. The alternative – poori chole with idli – would be even more difficult to face now.

She looked out of her window but could only see darkness. It had been dark during a long section of her flight and she hoped it would be dawn by the time they disembarked. She suddenly felt freezing cold and was glad when her breakfast arrived. At least it would warm her up. Ridiculous! Why did they have to turn down the temperature on these long-distance flights through the night? She had only ever been on long-distance flights twice in her life, once to the States and once to Canada. On both occasions, she had been freezing, just as on this flight now.

While she was doing her best to chew her English sausages, she remembered what she had experienced in the early stages of the flight. The woman in the seat on her right had been fully immersed in her book, which happened to be one of the novels by Giulia Montepulciano. What an irony! Philomena hadn't kept up a long conversation with the woman, who had introduced herself as Jane Hutchinson from Bath. But she had also introduced herself and built up the courage to ask her neighbour what she thought of the book. Did she like the story?

"Oh, it's absolutely wonderful!" she had answered. "I've read all her other books. This is the only one I've missed so far. How fortunate that I managed to pick it up from the bookstall at Heathrow. Have you read any of her books, too?"

Philomena hesitated. For a few seconds, she was at a loss as to what to say. Then she said, "I've heard of her, but I've never read any of her books, I'm afraid. But I'm glad you like what you're reading."

What a daft thing to say! Why couldn't she admit the truth? She was a bit angry with herself.

The two women didn't exchange any further information. Eventually, Philomena took out one of her books, a novel by Rohinton Mistry. *A good introduction to the culture ahead,* she thought. However, she didn't get very far. Her mind was preoccupied with her fear and anxiety over what she was going to find out on this journey. Was it a journey into her own past, she wondered. No, she had never been to India before and the entire cultural context was a bit daunting for her.

Yes, she had read a lot of novels and short stories by Indian writers, so she had some theoretical knowledge about the country. She'd also read into some of the old texts like *The Upanishads, The Bhagavad Gita* and – the book she liked best of all – *The Ramayana*, which was the story of Prince Rama, the charming Sita and the great ape

Hanuman. Quite impressive how a story from the 2nd century was still so much alive in Indian culture today. But somehow all this remained a tradition which excluded her. So, she was anxiously looking ahead to what she might find in reality. Now, on the plane, the thoughts of Rama and Hanuman could at least take her away from other, more sombre thoughts, thoughts of her own past, of her guilt…

Hardly had the cabin crew cleared away the breakfast things when they distributed some forms to be filled in by the passengers for Indian customs and immigration. This kept people busy for another half hour or so before they could feel the plane's slow descent.

Arriving at the terminal of Chennai airport was quite a shock. Philomena's first impression was that the world was really overpopulated indeed. The crowds were absolutely overpowering. People in great numbers swarmed around her like bees around their hive. Many young men were holding up their cardboard placards with names written on them. Obviously, the names of people they were expecting to meet from this flight or other flights. As it appeared, these early-morning hours saw many flights arriving from all parts of the world. Her ears were ringing with the din of voices all around her, shouting and babbling, a mixture of sounds that were all utterly incomprehensible to her.

At last, she found the right counter to show her passport, the right baggage carousel to pick up her suitcase and the exit to the taxis and carparks. She had a slip of paper in her pocket on which Norman had written down the name and address of a reliable taxi company. She dug it out, switched on her mobile phone and called the number. There was an immediate answer in a charming Indian song-song voice. She mentioned her business and the voice promised to pick her up in about ten minutes from where she was waiting in front of the terminal.

She had to call the number again two more times because the taxi didn't show up for quite some time. Meanwhile, the early dawn had turned into a beautiful sunny morning. Every time she had the same friendly voice on the line and was assured, "Yes madam, of course, our taxi will be right there in ten minutes." In the end, after an hour and a half, the taxi did arrive. It was a white Toyota minibus.

The driver was so young that Philomena wondered if he was old enough to have a driving licence. When she mentioned her destination again, he asked for a ridiculously big fare. So, she negotiated with him and eventually managed to reduce it to a realistic sum. The driver, who said his name was Ganesh, seemed happy with the outcome and loaded her luggage into the rear compartment. "You will be very satisfied, dear lady, everybody say I very good driver."

She did not answer or comment on this statement, but just climbed into one of the rear seats. Ganesh made himself comfortable behind the wheel. He dug in his shirt pockets to retrieve a chewing gum that he slipped between his lips with a loud smacking noise before he started the engine.

"You know, dear lady, the journey take about three hours, but if you can pay me an extra two hundred rupees, we can do it in two hours. What do you think?"

She was horrified. She would certainly not give the man any extra money so he would drive more recklessly. But she didn't let him see her fears and she only answered, "Oh, don't worry, I've got plenty of time. We're not in a hurry, not at all!"

"But," he began, looking at her through the rearview mirror, "English people always in a hurry, so they pay me extra for speedy service."

"Other people may be," she replied, "but not me."

They were winding their way through the early morning traffic of Chennai, squeezed in between dozens of tuk-tuks, her driver skilfully avoiding any collisions, especially with black Mercedes limousines, but sometimes throwing his hands up in the air, murmuring some Tamil swearwords. She was relieved when the traffic eased a little once they had left the city behind them and Ganesh's hands were mostly on the steering wheel. During the early stages of the drive, he didn't say much. He just chewed his gum, smacking his lips. She understood that, despite his apparent easy-going attitude, he must have been highly concentrating during their dangerous drive out of the city. But she was as relieved as he seemed now in the open country. They were on their way south, still more than two hours to go to Pondicherry.

"So, you a philosopher, my dear lady?" he asked her suddenly.

"What makes you think that?"

"You say you have plenty of time. That is what philosophers say. In India, lots of very important philosophers, so we know. They not talk very much. Their business is to think. They think of all the important things in the world. We are lucky to have all these philosophers in our country."

"Is that so?" she only managed to answer.

"Yes," he said. "Our philosophers mostly holy men. If I may ask, are you a holy woman in your country?"

"Not that I know. What constitutes a holy person?"

"It different if you talk of holy men or holy women."

"Oh, there's a big difference, is there?"

"Of course. A holy woman we never look in her eyes. That would bring bad luck. But holy man we are allowed to look in his eyes if we ask him very politely."

"I see."

Philomena was trying to give the man only brief answers, not to lead him on. She felt slightly uncomfortable and wanted him to stop asking her questions.

They continued in silence for some fifty kilometres. She felt a bit drowsy after her short night's sleep on the plane. Also, the day was getting quite hot. She wondered if the taxi had air conditioning.

In the mirror, she could see that Ganesh had been reading her thoughts.

"Would you like me to switch on A/C?"

"Yes please, if it's okay for you."

"No problem for me. I very tough man, freeze or heat, no big difference. But my passengers normally pay a little extra for A/C. But you very nice lady, so I say, no extra charge. You happy now?"

"Yes. Thank you very much." She was glad about the cool air wafting in her face and leaned back in her seat. But after about ten minutes, the temperature was getting too cold for her taste and she began to shiver.

"Do you mind turning it down, please?" she asked.

"No problem. You just say what you like. I'm your driver, so I do what you say. I know women always want men to do what they say. We men just obey."

"I take this as a joke," she said.

This quietened him again for a while.

Suddenly, he slowed down. "We stop for a cup of tea. I need a break. Okay for you?"

There was a road-side stall of wooden posts and corrugated iron sheets on top. A man was obviously in charge of a ramshackle food-and-drinks counter. He beamed at them. They walked up to the counter, both of them stretching their backs. Ganesh rattled something in their language and the man answered with a happy grin. In the background, a woman in a colourful sari was busy cutting vegetables. She didn't look up and didn't say anything.

"Tea for you, too?" Ganesh asked her.

"Oh, yes please. Could I have something to nibble with it, I wonder?"

"You mean you want food?"

"No big deal. Just a snack if that's possible."

"No problem."

The man in charge of the business prepared the tea with large gestures, pouring the light brown, milky liquid from the top of his outstretched arm into a small tin-like container. After several procedures like that, Philomena was handed over a tin cup full of steaming tea. It was masala chai, sweetened black tea with milk and spices. She could see some cardamom pods floating in it. It tasted delicious.

"Thank you," she said and began to slurp her tea. Then Ganesh handed her a small plate with a chapati folded in halves.

"Good for you. Indian chapati best food in the world; it feeds millions of people every day. Good flour and expert preparation. I often stopping here for snack."

The Indians kept up a light conversation while Philomena was enjoying her snack and glad to stretch her legs after the long flight and the drive from Chennai.

At one point, the tea-man pointed at her while he was obviously asking the driver a question. He probably wanted to know where she was from. But when Ganesh explained, she was surprised.

"He ask why you a lady on your own. Not married?" he asked while he was putting the outstretched digits of both hands together, rubbing them against each other, probably signifying a man and a woman lying together. She was still wondering what to answer when he added, "You no children, no family?"

She decided to give only brief replies. "No, I'm not married and I have no children."

"But a woman need protection. Who protect you? And we need family, children, many children very good."

"Not in my country. I am happy as I am," she added, hoping to stop this inquiry.

Both Indian men shook their heads. Ganesh said, "No wonder England many problems. Not enough families, not enough children. Not good."

She decided not to comment on this. They all remained silent, obviously digesting what had been said. After another five minutes, she paid the tea-man and they walked back to the Toyota.

During the continuation of their drive south, never very far from the coast of the Bengal Sea but hardly ever in full view of the sea, Philomena looked at the landscape and at the few villages they were passing. Already on their way out of the big city, she wondered at the shocking poverty she could see everywhere. Now she tried to integrate this discovery in her picture of India, of this ancient culture, which was so full of history, art and spiritualism. India was one of the world's largest democracies and its history was full of glory, especially in the 17th century, when the Mughal emperors reigned, the Taj Mahal was built and many great cities were constructed, as she had read in her guidebook.

Also, she was surprised to see the number of people even in the country between the villages and the greatest surprise was to see the colourful saris that the women wore everywhere. The families might live in dire poverty, but the women were always beautiful in their lovely saris. In one spot, they had to slow down for road works and she saw women carrying large baskets full of heavy stones on their heads while the men were seated along the curb, hammering the corner stones into position.

A culture full of contrasts! She asked herself if the European hippies found it easy to cope with such poverty. Probably they made sure they didn't have to suffer from the same deprivation as the native people. She also remembered that more than seventy per cent of the population of the district of Villupuram – the district of their destination – were, in fact, illiterate. Their main industry was rice farming. Along the road, she could already see a number of rice fields with farm workers – mostly women – bent over and standing in the water up to their hips. *That must be hard work*, she thought.

How did democracy work with such a high rate of illiteracy? A question that remained to be answered.

Eventually, they arrived in Pondicherry. The city was surrounded by Villupuram but formed its own district. Some people called it Pondicherry, others preferred the name Puducherry. She had read that it was originally colonised by the French but taken over by the English. She wondered how much French influence was still visible these days. The traffic in the city was not quite as murderous as it had been in Chennai, but it was chaotic enough. The most striking sight was the number of full buses with people sitting on the roof and more people hanging onto the doors and windows.

Also, there were lots of small motorcycles with whole families perched on them, everyone holding onto the person in front. When she opened the window, she was hit by the din of the traffic. Most motor vehicles were emitting some form of an ear-splitting noise as well as clouds of stinking smoke. How could anyone live in streets with a lot of traffic in this place?

When Ganesh stopped the taxi in front of her hotel, he helped her with her luggage. Then he smiled at her, seeming to be waiting for something.

"What is it?" she asked.

"We got here without accident."

"Yes and I am grateful."

"When my passengers happy to reach their destination safely, they normally give little tip."

"Listen, Mr Ganesh! To arrive without an accident is the least one can expect from a taxi-driver. It isn't an extra, but the essence of the basic service." In spite of her words, she handed him a twenty rupee note.

Ganesh smiled and returned to his taxi. After he had driven off, she entered the lobby of the Hotel Richelieu. It only struck her now that it was a French name. So here was the first proof of the French element of the city's history. Philomena was beginning to hope that perhaps the food would also reflect something of the French influence. She stepped up to the reception desk and checked in.

Settled in her room, she was glad there was a window which faced a backyard and overlooked the roofs of the neighbouring buildings. There was only a very remote traffic noise. She stored her clothes in the wardrobe, which looked clean enough, as indeed did the entire room. A lot cleaner than she had expected when she booked the hotel on the Internet. In fact, the hotel proved to be the ideal spot for her proposed investigation.

She lay down on the bed and tried to relax. Her thoughts led her to her task at hand. She was here to find her old friend, Sandy, whom she hadn't seen for over twenty years. Since Sandy never answered any letters addressed to her, Philomena felt she had to talk to her personally. Perhaps Sandy was feeling ashamed of whatever had happened at Bedgebury Forest. Perhaps she just wanted to escape from her overpowering family or from some other limiting factor in England.

Why an ashram? Philomena was sure her friend hadn't suddenly turned religious. She had always ridiculed the power of the church and she had always made fun of clergymen. But perhaps she had been looking for some other form of spirituality, a spirituality she'd always kept from others, even from her best friend. Or was the whole thing just an escape from the law, Sandy perhaps guilty of murder?

Philomena went over the facts in her mind.

One. More than twenty years ago, their science teacher, Christine Mitford, had gone missing in Bedgebury Forest.

Two. Christine Mitford had been their French teacher, Andrew Sullivan's, secret girlfriend.

Three. Sandy had carried on a secret love affair with Andrew Sullivan.

Four. Sandy was probably pregnant when she disappeared shortly after the murder at Bedgebury Forest.

Five. Sandy and Philomena had planned to cycle to Bedgebury Forest around the time of the murder. But Philomena couldn't remember anything. Ever since that time, she had been suffering from post-traumatic retrograde amnesia and she felt scared or disturbed whenever she passed the forest.

Six. Not only Christine Mitford but also Andrew Sullivan had been missing more or less from that day on. It was supposed by the police that they were living in France now, but no-one was sure. Christine Mitford's whereabouts had been cleared up recently when her dead body had been found in the forest.

Seven. Philomena was convinced that she had murdered Christine Mitford. However, there was no proof and there would be no motive. Still, she had this gut feeling.

So what now?

Her plan was to find the ashram where Sandy could be found. She had to talk to her in order to find out what had happened at Bedgebury Forest, thereby hoping to be cured of her trauma. Sandy must know the facts, Philomena was confident.

On her first day in Pondicherry, she spent the afternoon strolling through the city, window-shopping and walking along the sea promenade with the bronze statue of Gandhi on that pedestal. She had a glass of beer on the balcony of the only sea-front pub overlooking the rocky beach and was enjoying the view of the Bengal Sea.

She was just imagining that somewhere out there, far away in the distance, there was Burma and there was Thailand, when she realised that a man from a table near hers was staring at her. When she stared back, he averted his face. She didn't know the man. He was middle-aged, stout, had a bald patch on his head and wore dark-rimmed glasses. A European rather than an Indian? Or just an Indian from the north with much lighter skin than most people's skins here in Tamil Nadu? He didn't look back again, so she dismissed him from her thoughts.

Later, she walked back to her hotel to take a shower. Then she went out again to find a restaurant where she could have a nice evening meal. She found a suitable roof-top restaurant, which served quite good food, she was happy to note eventually.

In the morning, after a good night's sleep, she walked to the police station. It was only a ten-minute walk from her hotel. When she arrived, there was already a crowd of people waiting to be let in. She joined the queue, realising that it would take her hours to get to someone in charge. But what else could she do?

After about an hour and a half, she could see a uniformed police officer walking along the waiting queue, throwing each person a quick glance, sometimes giving a short nod, sometimes touching the hands of another person and sometimes stopping for a quick chat. Some persons – especially those whose hands he had touched – he took out of the queue and gave them instructions after which they walked in the direction of the door of the building where they disappeared.

She realised this was what was called a triage. A French expression, she knew. The officer was deciding whose business deserved immediate attention and who would have to wait a lot longer.

She saw that he became aware of her standing there in the queue long before he came to her in his slow routine. At last, standing before her, he looked her up and down. It wasn't in impertinent or impolite gesture, it was just his way of saying, "So you are a foreigner!"

He asked her in reasonably good English. "And what is your business, madam?"

"I am looking for a certain ashram in this region and I'm hoping to find an old friend of mine who seems to live there. I hope the police might have the address."

"Come with me, madam."

He led her along the queue in the direction of the police station. She felt a bit uneasy. Though she was glad of this preferment, she wondered if the other people in the queue were not thinking, 'What a typical English snob, getting the de-luxe treatment!'

In the building, the officer led her straight to a desk with a plain-clothes policeman sitting behind. He exchanged a few words in Tamil with him before he disappeared. The officer behind the desk introduced himself as Mr Gupta. Then he came straight to the point.

"You are looking for an old friend? And this friend is supposed to be living in an ashram in this region? Am I right?"

"Yes, officer."

"Have you got any information that might help us find your friend?"

"I'm afraid not. The only thing I have is an address of the ashram where she was said to live, but I don't know if she still lives there. I haven't seen her in over twenty years."

She handed him the slip of paper on which she had noted the address.

"I see. This ashram is easy to find. It's located between this city and the spiritual colony of Auroville, which has been attracting many Europeans, mostly hippies. Let me ask you. Is your friend a hippy?"

"Not that I know. Why do you ask?"

"We generally don't like hippies. Many of them are escaped criminals from France, Germany and even from your country. Also, they create a lot of uneasiness among the native population with their drugs, unkempt looks, long hair and whole lifestyle. They swarm around this area quite a lot. As the police force, we have to keep an eye on them. Sometimes we can help the police in Europe to catch an escaped criminal. That's why I'm asking the question."

"Oh, please, Officer, my friend Sandy is certainly no hippy and no escaped criminal. She just went to live in India because she was attracted by the spirituality of your culture."

"All right, madam. I just had to ask the question. Please forgive me."

"That's quite all right, Officer. Now, can you tell me how to get to this ashram? Is it far?"

"Not that far, only about ten kilometres. Best to take a taxi. Any taxi driver will know the address."

"I see. Thank you very much," she said before she walked away. Stepping out of the building, feeling sorry for all those people still waiting in the queue, she realised Mr Gupta had not asked for any bribe. A good man, she decided.

Not far from the police station, she found a waiting taxi, a brand-new white Tata saloon car. She got in and was hit by the freezing temperature of the air conditioning. She asked the driver to switch it off or at least turn it down while she handed him the slip of paper with the address.

"But, madam, when I saw you coming to my taxi, I switched it on. Europeans always want A/C."

"Well, not me."

She sat back in the cool upholstery and let herself be driven out of the city. They were obviously driving in the opposite direction of the way she'd come. They were heading back towards Chennai. But it was only for a few kilometres before the taxi turned left, away from the sea.

"This area was very badly destroyed by the Tsunami back in 2004. It was on Boxing Day and the

213

water flooded everything around here. We lost a great number of victims. We all remember."

"I am sorry to hear this. Yes, I remember now. It was on our news, too. Many tourists from my country were killed. But, of course, it must have been a lot worse for you. Did you live here at the time?"

"No, I was a small boy then and we lived further inland in a city called Tiruvannamalai, the city of the most beautiful temples in the area."

They remained silent. After another five minutes, they came to a settlement of several simple huts.

"Here we are," said the driver.

"Thank you," she said, "can you tell me how to find a certain person?"

"Oh, you just see the Guru. His house is the largest and next to the temple. It also houses the meeting room and can't be missed once you walk along this path."

She thanked him again and paid the reasonable fare. Then she got out of the taxi and walked along the path ahead. The driver had called it a path, all right. It wasn't really a street, although it would have been broad enough for a small car, but the surface was very rugged. Too rugged for a motor vehicle.

The vegetation all around was extremely lush, full of colourful blossoms, large green leaves, sweet-smelling plants and it was full of colourful birds with screeching parrots flying from one tall tree to another. A tropical paradise, Philomena thought.

Walking along, she met several individuals. None of them looked like hippies, but rather like very ordinary persons, some Asian, some European. They all greeted her politely and she greeted back. At last, she arrived in front of what had to be the Guru's house. She wondered how to address the Guru politely, given the fact that he seemed to be the head of this community.

A youngish woman emerged from the building and approached her.

"Namaste! Good morning and welcome! Can we help you in any way?"

Philomena said good morning, too, before she stated her business. While she was explaining her wish to find her old friend, the woman raised her eyebrows in a worried expression.

"You must mean our Sita."

"Sita? No, her name is Sandra, Sandy for short."

"Our sister dropped her English name many years ago. She adopted her new name. Sita, after the most beautiful woman in our mythology. We all accepted this risky step since she was the most beautiful Englishwoman we had ever seen."

The woman hesitated.

"I'm afraid you have come at the wrong time," she continued. "Sita is in big trouble. You better see Narendrapradesh, our great Guru."

Philomena's heart sank as she was led into the presence of the great Guru.

THIRTEEN

"So, you have been in His presence. You are very fortunate and you must be deeply impressed!" said the youngish woman who had received her, full of awe.

Philomena didn't know what to reply. The truth was that she wasn't impressed in the slightest degree. The Guru was an overweight man who looked like a boring solicitor in England with the only distinguishing asset of an Indian gown that was supposed to give him a special aura but didn't.

"Oh, he was friendly enough," she finally managed to say.

"Narendrapradesh is a good communicator. Did you get the information you were looking for?"

"Yes, Ms..." Philomena wondered what to call the woman.

"My name is Parvati, after the wife of Shiva," the woman answered. Philomena remembered that the members of this ashram community had given themselves fancy names borrowed from Hindu mythology.

"Okay, Parvati. Your Guru told me I should ask Begum, obviously someone special in your community. Someone, as he said, who normally deals 'with such cases'. Why is Sandy – sorry. Sita – such a special case?"

Parvati looked at her with big eyes, ignoring her question. "Then Begum is the person to see. She is out this morning, I'm afraid. She has some business in town. But she will be back tomorrow. So you just come back tomorrow. But tell me, can we offer you some tea or fruit juice?"

Philomena was disappointed, but she was touched by Parvati's friendly ways and her hospitality. The woman had something very soft about her. One had the impression she couldn't hurt a fly. She wondered how men would react to such a gentle woman.

"Do you have any men in your community? I mean, apart from your Guru?" she asked without thinking.

"Oh yes, we do have a few men, but we make sure we have more than twice as many women. We believe that men have to be kept under control; otherwise, they can turn into a danger for us."

Philomena was impressed. In a way, this wasn't such a bad idea, but still she felt strange about it. "Can I ask you another question?" she added. "Do you have sexual relationships within the community?"

Parvati hesitated before she answered. "Yes, we do. But they are carefully regulated. If they were not regulated, they would disturb our peaceful togetherness too much."

"I see."

They were silent for a moment before Philomena asked, "But what about my friend? Do you know anything about her?"

"I'm afraid that's really Begum's business. She is our woman for all practical matters. She's only an associate member of our community but she's extremely useful. For example, she looks after our finances, dealings with the authorities, food supply and medical needs. Only Begum is entitled to give you the true picture of your friend's predicament."

"Sandy is in a predicament? How?"

"I'm not entitled to comment on this. I'm sorry, my dear sister."

Philomena felt she would get angry if she didn't stop here. Whether she liked it or not, she would have to come back the next morning.

Parvati brought her a nice cup of masala chai, which she gratefully accepted. It helped her calm down. It was really no use blaming this charming woman, so she sat down, said thank you and began to sip her tea.

While the two women were sitting in this kind of anteroom, there were several other women who passed through the room. At one point, a young woman stopped near Parvati and addressed her. While they had a very soft conversation, Philomena peeled her ears and tried to get as much as possible of what they were talking about. Apparently, the young woman – hardly older than a teenage girl – asked the more senior woman if she was allowed to start a special relationship with one of the men whose name was Vikram.

So, the men aren't given famous mythological names, Philomena thought, *probably not until they also obtain some senior position.*

She was quite surprised when she believed she heard the girl ask Parvati if she had permission to have sex with Vikram, to which Parvati referred her to the Guru. She picked up the phrase, "Only he can decide."

The young woman – whose name appeared to be Aditi – cast her eyes down in submission and politely thanked Parvati. Then she turned round on her heels and left the room. Philomena tried to catch a glimpse of her expression, curious how such dependence in such personal matters affected the girl. *How sad!* she thought. And the girl was so friendly and extremely beautiful. She decided it wasn't her business. But still, it made her wonder how Sandy could stand such customs. She used to be so self-confident, Philomena could not imagine her submitting herself like Aditi.

She soon asked Parvati to get her a taxi and when the taxi arrived, she noted that it was the same taxi with the same driver who had brought her here.

Back in Pondicherry, she went for a walk along the seafront and through the less busy streets of the city. She wanted to get a glimpse of ordinary life and avoided the typical tourist places such as souvenir shops. Whereas she had been a bit concerned about her safety as a woman on her own in an Indian city, she felt quite safe now that she was actually strolling through these streets.

It was only when she returned to the hotel in the early afternoon that someone addressed her. The hotel boasted a small bar for its guests. She sat down at the bar, hoping to get a cool drink, and ordered a Coke. When it was served, she realised it was far too sweet to be a real Coke.

"What's that?" she murmured to herself.

"That's not a Coke," a voice at her back said. "It's what they call a *Thums Up*, the Indian version of a Coke."

A young white man was sitting in one of the lounge chairs at the back of the room. She hadn't noticed him when she came in.

"They can't even spell it right," he continued. "These Indians think they can ape the Europeans, but they are still way behind."

She didn't like this arrogant statement and took an immediate dislike towards this man. Who did he think he was?

"I think if it is their own product, they're entitled to spell it as they like," she said.

"Well, you may have a point there, but they mean to suggest a delicious taste by calling it Thums Up, meaning thumbs up, you know, spelt t-h-u-m-b-s up with a B, very funny!" He laughed out loud, apparently convinced of the stupidity of all Indians.

Philomena wondered if she should say anything to that. She couldn't hold back, so she said, "The Indians are wonderful people, aren't they? I mean, just look at their ancient culture. They were way ahead of us in Europe."

"Do you mean to say the chaos you see everywhere out there is the sign of a superior civilisation?"

All she could think of at this moment was, "*Sic transit gloria mundi.*"

"What?"

"Never mind," she said and turned round again, devoting herself to her sticky sweet drink.

But the young man wasn't prepared to give up. He was apparently looking for company, hoping to get some admiration from a European woman. Not aware of the obvious fact that he'd never get it from this woman, he tried to keep up a conversation with her.

"I say, I haven't seen you round here before. Are you on your own?"

"I don't think that's any of your business," she calmly replied.

"Oh, her royal highness is getting all hoity-toity?"

Philomena just ignored this. She took a few more sips of her drink – she didn't manage to drink it all, it was too sweet for her – and stood up to leave the bar.

"And a good day to you," she said to the man and left the hotel. She went to the seafront café where she had a glass of Cobra beer. This cooled her down.

She asked herself what a man like that was doing in a place like Pondicherry. He wasn't a tourist and he wasn't a local either. A sort of globetrotter perhaps? No, too well-dressed for that, but not good enough to pass as a businessman. Well, what was it to her? He was too insignificant.

When she returned to the hotel later, she saw him still sitting in the bar, this time chatting to another young man. When he saw her passing through the lobby, he winked at her as if he was a good friend of hers, which made the other man turn round and look at her, too. She quickly disappeared in the lift and was relieved to reach her room.

In the evening, when she went out to go to a nice restaurant she had discovered on her daytime stroll, the bar was empty. She reached the restaurant unmolested and had a very good Indian meal.

The next morning, she took a taxi to the ashram again. This time the driver remained silent the whole way.

She was again received by Parvati, who greeted her with the palms of her flat hands pressed together and murmured, "Namaste!" Then she led her to another room of the large building, where she was greeted in the same way by a rather stout middle-aged woman who was introduced to her simply as Begum. From what Philomena had read, she'd expected Begum to be some sort of title rather than a proper name, but she didn't say anything. She only responded with a soft, "Namaste!"

"I understand you are Sita's friend from England," Begum said.

"Yes, I am. And I've come all the way from England to find her. We used to be very best friends when we were young."

"I see. Well, dear sister, I'm sorry to tell you your friend is seriously ill."

"What's the matter? Is she in hospital?"

"It started with a headache and a fever before it turned worse and made her really sick. She couldn't take

221

any food and her fever got so bad she sometimes lost consciousness. At first, we treated her at the ashram using traditional natural herbs and potions, but eventually, we had to send her to a special hospital near the city."

"To Pondicherry or to Chennai?" Philomena asked in panic.

"A special hospital in the outskirts of Pondicherry."

"Has her illness been diagnosed by doctors there?"

"Yes, dear sister. She was diagnosed with Covid-19."

Philomena had to sit down. She knew that the awful virus infection had lost its life-threatening aspect after a series of pandemics which had caused general lockdowns in many countries all over the world, but she thought it was defeated by now. She wondered whether these Indian doctors really diagnosed her friend correctly.

"Are you sure?" she asked.

As if Begum could read her mind, she answered, "You know, the virus can never be fully defeated, neither by Western medicine nor by our traditional remedies."

"So, can I go and visit her at the hospital? Can you give me the address?"

"I can give you the address of the hospital, but you can't visit your poor friend there."

"Why not?"

"For several reasons. First, because they don't allow any visitors for hygienic reasons, her state is highly contagious, she is in an intensive care unit, and besides, she wouldn't be able to communicate with you because she is in a coma."

Philomena had to recover for several minutes. They brought her some fruit juice and a cup of masala chai. Begum and her sisters were all sympathetic and extremely concerned for her welfare. They offered her hospitality if she wanted to stay at the ashram as long as Sandy was in hospital.

"We also hope and pray with you that your friend Sita will recover from her awful disease."

"Thank you very much. I am grateful for your kind offer, but I want to go back to my hotel first. I may change my mind after a while. May I come back on your offer later?"

"Of course, you can. We respect your wishes, as we respect the love you must have for Sita, a love that has given you the energy to travel all this way from England to India just to visit your friend."

Philomena knew it wasn't love that had driven her, but curiosity and fear. However, she didn't contradict Begum. She stayed at the ashram for another half hour before she ordered a taxi – she had, meanwhile, found out the taxi company's phone number – and left on her way back to her hotel in Pondicherry.

Back in her hotel room, she lay down on the bed and began to think. What should she do now? Should she go to the hospital at once and try to see Sandy, or was it better to follow the advice of the women at the ashram?

While she was still trying to come to a decision, suddenly her phone beeped. There was a text message. She opened it and read what Norman had written.

"Dearest Philomena, my thoughts are with you. I hope you can find out what you're looking for. I am convinced you didn't commit any crimes when you were at Bedgebury Forest all those years ago. But whatever the outcome of your quest, you can always count on me as your friend. And don't worry about your cat; I feed her regularly for as long as it takes. Love, Norman."

Of course, she was happy about the lovely tone in Norman's message. But most of all, the message gave her confidence to continue with her quest. She would remain in Pondicherry for as long as it would take for Sandy to wake up from her coma, even if it took a month or more.

*   *   *

Philomena was sitting in her favourite café in Pondicherry, sipping a cool fruit drink and looking out towards the Bay of Bengal. She had grown accustomed to the place, to its still slightly French atmosphere mixed with an English colonial flair. She had also accepted the fact of the enormous social differences in Indian society. In a way, Pondicherry had almost become a second home for her. She reflected that she had now been in this city for more than three weeks, in which she had strolled down to the seafront to look at the statue of Gandhi every day. Twice during this long waiting period, she had visited the ashram out of town, but always without success, despite the sisters' charming ways.

Her phone rang. It wasn't a call from England, but a local number. She picked it up with a misgiving.

The call was from Parvati. She greeted Philomena with flowery words before she told her that there was good news from the hospital. Sita/Sandy was showing signs of regaining her consciousness. Although she couldn't speak or understand, it appeared she might regain full consciousness soon, perhaps in a day or two, the doctor hoped.

After the call, Philomena felt excited. Her heartbeat went up by several degrees and she fell back into her old fear, her vague apprehension about what might come to the surface once she could speak to Sandy. She ordered a gin and tonic to calm down.

Back at the Hotel Richelieu, she couldn't hold back. She was so full of the news that she dropped a remark to the receptionist, with whom she had become quite familiar over the past few weeks. His name was Vernushan and he often liked to have a small chat with her. He never handed her the room key without at least one friendly comment.

"I just had a piece of good news," she blurted out, realising too late that the second gin and tonic must have gone to her head a little.

"Oh, I am very glad for you. Any family news perhaps?" His curiosity was apparent, but she didn't mind.

"No, it's just about my best friend. She's in hospital here in town and it seems she is on her way to recovery."

"An accident?"

"No, she fell ill with Covid-19 and dropped off into a coma over four weeks ago," she admitted.

"Oh, but that is so dangerous. Don't go near your friend or you might catch the disease, too!"

"I know it's a very dangerous disease. Millions of people died of it all over the world."

"Indeed, we had a large number of victims in this country alone. Of course, it was a lot more dangerous in the big cities like Kolkata or Chennai, but we had lots of dead people here, too. Some journalists said it was fake, there was no pandemic, but who can we believe?"

"Terrible!" murmured Philomena. "We had far too many people like that, too, in Britain and indeed in Europe. People who believed it was only a conspiracy concocted by some liberal politicians and journalists. They never believed the facts of the international medical community. They denied all proven scientific facts. The term *fake news* was circulated by the American ex-president Trump, trying to destroy democracy. Well, I'm sure you've heard about that guy's other crimes, for example, when he stirred up his followers to storm the Capitol in Washington. Wasn't that one of the most terrible moments in modern history? Or perhaps the second-worst moment, the worst moment being the criminal attack on the Ukrainian people by the Russian dictator."

"Yes, madam. We live in bad times. My uncle always says it's the fault of the Internet. But I say it is what the Internet made possible, the phenomenon called globalisation. You know, everybody thinks they can do what they like and they can always blame others. You can commit crimes and remain anonymous. Nobody says what is right and wrong. I think the Internet is only a tool. It's the people behind all the crimes. We can't blame a technical tool."

"How wise you are," she said. "You must have read a lot. Did you have any higher schooling, may I ask?"

"Not education. Good education would have been a very good thing, but for me, it is my uncle. He knows everything and he tells me everything."

"You are a lucky man."

"But you are very lucky too. You grew up in Britain, a very fine country. My uncle says there's better democracy in France than in Britain, but I think most countries in Europe have very good democracy. Except Hungary, perhaps."

"Well, my dear Vernushan, this is getting a bit too specific for me at the moment. I'm so concerned for my friend in hospital." She sighed. "Perhaps I should just go up to my room and try to relax. Can you give me a bottle of Cobra to take to my room?"

"Of course," he answered with a very sympathetic smile. He fetched a bottle from the bar and handed it to her. "Here you are."

Philomena took the lift up to her room. She got the water glass from the bathroom and filled it with cool beer. This helped her to relax even better. She pondered over some of the things she had discussed with the receptionist. It wasn't only the awful egomaniacs like Trump and Putin, it was also the people who made it possible for such criminals to get into such powerful positions. It was the lack of democracy. That was the problem...

Before she was aware of her fatigue, she fell asleep.

In the morning, she tried to get some details from the hospital. Vernushan got the number for her and she dialled it on her mobile phone. It rang a very long time before someone answered. It was a woman's stern voice. Philomena stated her business, asking about her friend's condition.

"I am sorry, madam," the voice answered. "But we cannot give such confidential information over the telephone. You will have to come here personally."

Disappointed, Philomena sat down in the bar area. Vernushan asked if anything was wrong, but she only shook her head, unwilling to tell him everything.

She asked him to order a taxi for her.

This time the taxi took quite some time to turn up at the hotel. But when it came, she was glad to sit back and let herself be driven through this fascinating city. The car was an older model. As she had found out earlier, this was a Hindustan Ambassador. As one of the drivers had explained to her, that was a licensed Indian product based on the 1955 Morris Oxford. She wondered if they were still in production these days, but she didn't care enough to ask the driver, who would most certainly know.

Arriving at the hospital, she found the reception area. There were several dozen people in the queue. Philomena joined the end of the queue. While waiting, she allowed her gaze to roam. She looked at the different people waiting, the various employees of the hospital, the occasional doctor or nurse rushing by, and the two policemen at the main gate. The hall was full of noises, but it all looked very well-organised. She didn't mind the long waiting period ahead of her. She liked to lose herself in her thoughts.

After waiting for about half an hour, she realised that one of the policemen near the door was studying her. At the same time, she became aware of the fact that she seemed to be the only non-Indian person in the queue. As if he had read her mind, one of the policemen approached her.

"Good morning, madam," the officer politely began. "Can I help you?"

She thanked him and replied that she was just waiting like everyone else. She was hoping to visit her best friend who was a patient in this hospital.

The officer made some strange fiddling movements with his left hand and winked at her, adding in a low voice. "Not good for fine English lady. I might help you to shorten your waiting period if you could find yourself to, you know what I mean…" His voice trailing off, again he winked at her and repeated the fiddling movements with the fingers of his left hand. At first, Philomena didn't understand, but then the penny dropped. He was offering to move her forward in the queue if she was willing to bribe him.

She hesitated, looking the officer in the eyes. He was still relatively young, quite good-looking, and he didn't seem to find their conversation in any way unusual.

"Okay," she murmured. "How much?"

"A hundred rupees, madam. That's the normal rate for Europeans." He didn't even blink but just looked her square in the eyes.

She took out a hundred rupee note and handed it to him. Nobody around them seemed to take any notice.

The officer took her by her left arm and guided her through the crowds up to the reception desk, where he nodded to the lady behind the glass counter, who just gave him a slight nod back before she asked Philomena what her business was.

Philomena explained her wish to see her good friend from England, who was a patient here. The receptionist checked on her computer screen and told her to go to the intensive care unit on the second floor, warning her she might not be able to see her friend. Not everyone was admitted there, but the medical staff on the second floor would be able to help her. Then she was dismissed and someone else was pushing to the front of the queue.

When Philomena reached the barrier to the intensive care unit, she had to wait quite some time until someone appeared behind the counter there. A middle-aged nurse, a large sour-looking woman who sat down on a stool behind the counter, looked through some papers in front of her and finally gave her a critical look.

"My name is Philomena Webster. I've come especially from England to see my old friend in India." Her voice nearly failed her. When she pronounced Sandy's name, she suddenly realised the seriousness of the situation. This was no longer child's play but very grave adult business, possibly a matter of life and death.

"I'm afraid, madam," the nurse replied, "your friend is in a very critical condition. We are glad to report she has regained consciousness at last. But at this stage, it would be too much of a health risk for someone like you to visit her. I understand you are no relation of hers, are you?"

"No, I'm not. But I'm her best friend."

"I am very sorry indeed, madam. There's no chance until the patient is in a better condition." With these words, Philomena was dismissed and the nurse turned her attention to the paperwork in front of her.

This was a great disappointment! Philomena slowly turned away from the counter and began to walk in the direction of the staircase when she heard the nurse's voice behind her.

"Since you are her best friend and since you've travelled especially all the way from England to see her, you might try the vice chairman of the hospital. Write a letter of application for such a visit, giving him your arguments. He might make an exception in your case. He sometimes does. But I can't promise anything."

Philomena turned back and took the slip of paper that the nurse handed her. It had the name and address of the vice chairman of the hospital printed on it. It looked important. The man's name was too long for her to try to pronounce and it had lots of important-looking letters behind it, but she was extremely grateful for this gesture. So, the big nurse wasn't such a gorgon after all. She had a heart!

Back at her hotel, Philomena reviewed her situation. She admitted to herself that she would still need a lot of patience. Things in this country took their time. But she checked herself. Was it so much better in Britain, given the lack of efficiency in the NHS?

She was glad about the good news. Sandy seemed to be on her way to recovery. She decided to stay on in

Pondicherry until she would be admitted as a visitor at the hospital. She went out to buy some writing paper and an envelope. Then she sat down to write her letter of application to the powerful vice chairman of the hospital. She gave him all her best arguments – her relationship with the patient, her special trip from England and a few other facts that might help – and made sure the letter was respectful enough.

Then she walked to the post office and personally posted the letter.

Her hopes were up.

FOURTEEN

Philomena submitted to the lengthy procedure of getting dressed up – or rather disguised – in the special protective clothing required for a visit to a patient in this unit. It was made of semi-transparent plastic material and covered the entire upper part of her body. Lower down, it was like a long coat, but she also got a pair of over pants in the same material. Round her head, everything was covered. Only her eyes were clearly visible, albeit through some oversize plastic eyeglasses. Her hands were stuck in light blue rubber gloves. The fact that her garb was semi-transparent allowed her normal street-clothes to shine through: her dark green T-shirt and her blue denim jeans. The overall impression – it seemed to her as she was looking at herself in a large wall mirror – was somewhere between a man of the Apollo Mission on the moon and a medieval nun from some obscure monastery.

But this was a precautionary measure because the type of virus infection that Sandy was suffering from was highly contagious. They told her that the really virulent phase was past, but it was better to be on the safe side. It could still be contagious.

Given this grave assessment of her friend's condition, Philomena was surprised – despite all her personal efforts to gain access, even her bribe for some of the officials in charge – that she was at last admitted to the intensive care unit dressed up like this and allowed to see the patient.

Inside Sandy's room, it was very quiet. There was only a hissing noise emerging from one of the machines that kept her alive. Sandy was lying flat on her belly and her body was showing the rhythmic movements of her heavy breathing. Philomena saw that she was wearing an oxygen mask, so she was being supported with her breathing.

In her position, it was not easy for Sandy to look her visitor in the eyes. But she turned her head to one side while Philomena sat down on a stool beside the bed and bent the upper part of her body so as to be able to establish eye contact with her friend.

"You?" was her first word, hardly comprehensible through the mask.

"Yes, it's me, Philomena, your old friend!"

"Are you…? Do you really want to see me?" Sandy asked in a weak voice. It obviously cost her quite an effort to speak so that she could be understood.

"Well, I am here. I've come to India especially to see you."

"That's nice."

Philomena wondered what to say next. Then she decided to wait with the more complicated topics that she really wanted to speak about with her friend that had been torturing her for years and were connected with such hopeful expectations. She realised she would have to hold back her really brutal questions until Sandy was a lot better.

"We deserve what we got," Sandy murmured through her teeth. Then she turned her head to the other side so that Philomena couldn't communicate with her any longer.

The nurse in the room told Philomena that her time with the patient was over. She left the room, but not without glancing back at her friend in the bed, who was looking extremely miserable. She felt that leaving the room was like leaving her in the lurch. She was abandoning her, betraying her. Sandy might die before she had a chance to talk to her again.

"What are my friend's chances?" she asked the nurse once they were out of the room.

"It's hard to tell for sure," the nurse answered. "But the consultant says there's a fifty-fifty chance at this stage."

Philomena assured the nurse she would be back soon. Then she got rid of the protective clothing, washed her face and her hands, and left the hospital.

Back at her hotel, she checked her watch and compared the times between Pondicherry and London before she picked up her phone to call Norman.

He was overjoyed to hear her voice. "I miss you," he said with an emotional sigh. "Are you coming home soon?"

"I don't know. Sandy is slowly getting better, but it's too difficult to talk to her about delicate matters at this stage. She seems to have difficulties breathing. They positioned her lying flat on her belly and she's got one of those breathing masks on her nose and mouth. I've got to wait for her to get better than this. They say she's got a fifty-fifty chance of survival. I know Sandy is a fighter, she won't give up. But still, I'm worried."

"That's natural. Who wouldn't be, in your situation?"

"Yes, but it means I'm not coming home for a while yet. I'd like to ask you to check on my cottage from time to time. Can you do that for me, please?"

"Do you want me to open any official-looking letters?"

"Well, you need not open them. The important services are all on direct debit. Please just tell me what letters there are. Then I'll know if there's anything I need to do from here."

"I'll do that. Well, I can tell you that everything's okay so far. You may extend your Indian holiday, Miss Montepulciano…"

"How do you know? I never told you my literary pseudonym!"

"When I checked on your cottage last week, naturally I walked through all the rooms, so I couldn't miss the books on your shelves. Those by Giulia Montepulciano were the only ones I could classify under 'romance' or 'pulp fiction' if you don't mind me calling your books bad names…"

"You cheeky devil! At least promise not to tell anyone."

"My lips are sealed. But I must say your books look pretty impressive. You must have written over a dozen. Is that right?"

"Yes, fifteen so far."

"And they paid well?"

"Far too much, in fact."

There was a fraught silence between them.

"To return to the serious matter at hand," he said, "have you found out anything about what happened at Bedgebury Forest all those years ago?"

She hesitated before she answered. She asked herself if it was appropriate to discuss such intimate business over the phone. "I only remembered a small bit of the events. That's all. It's probably seeing Sandy and hearing her voice which may have triggered my memory."

"What was it?"

"When Sandy and I arrived at the forest, Sullivan received us in a small hut. These days that hut is only a ruin of wooden planks overgrown with thick brambles.

That's probably why the police didn't think it was important in any way. But at that time, the hut was still habitable, if you expected no comfort. It was Sullivan's hide-away. It's where he took pictures of women and girls in the nude. When we met him there, he wanted us to pose for his camera, too. I refused and ran away, but Sandy stayed on. That seems to be the last time I saw Sullivan, but I don't know about Sandy. That's one of the things that I want to find out as soon as I can talk to her properly."

"I see. So you were not involved in what happened after that?"

"I really don't know. That's my problem. I'm convinced I must have been involved and in a bad way."

"Don't torture yourself! I'm sure you never committed a crime. Just relax, it must be Sandy's problem."

She sighed again. "It's easy for you to say that. But thanks for your understanding and your positive attitude."

After that, they soon rang off and Philomena went down to the bar area.

* * *

It was two weeks later when Philomena registered a marked improvement in her friend's condition. When she entered the room, she was glad to see Sandy lying there on her back like a normal patient. She couldn't sit up yet, but she looked so much better and she only needed her oxygen mask intermittently. The two women could talk at last.

"Why do you want to dig up all that old trash?" Sandy asked.

"It's because I don't know what happened. I suffer from what they call retrograde amnesia."

"But you were there."

"Yes, I know. But all I can remember is our quarrel with Mr Sullivan in that old shack in the forest. The rest is only a blur and then nothing."

"What's the next thing you can remember?"

"Someone must have picked me up with my bike along the road and given me a lift home. I was so shaken, they must have thought I was drunk. Anyway, that's what my parents believed, too. They left me alone in my room and only asked a few questions, which I found myself unable to answer."

"That's really all you can remember?"

"Yes – well, of course, I remember how most of us who'd had anything to do with Sullivan were later questioned by the police, but since I couldn't remember anything of importance for them, they left me alone. It was then assumed that Sullivan had absconded to France. Oh yes, and then there was Miss Mitford's disappearance. As you might know, they recently found her body. It was buried under thick brambles in the same forest and it was heavily decomposed after all this time, but with modern forensic methods, they managed to identify her."

"What?" Sandy was shocked. "The Mitford woman was found dead?"

"Yes, only a few weeks ago. They say she was murdered."

"That's bullshit! Absolute bullshit!"

Philomena was surprised. Why this violent reaction? Why couldn't Sandy just tell her the truth about those events in her own words? If she wasn't guilty of any crime, she should feel free to tell her old friend.

237

"Tell me, please," Philomena insisted, "what exactly happened?"

Sandy took her time. She arranged her seating position in her bed and pulled down her thin hospital shirt before she began.

"Well, when André wanted us to strip for his camera, you went berserk. At the time, I thought you were nuts. I mean, such a photo shoot could have been the beginning of a great model career for us. – No, don't interrupt! – I know, I know. I've become more mature since then.

"You were right. He was just trying to get his own pleasure. After you left, he persuaded me to strip. I was stupid enough to oblige him. I was just about half-undressed and he was clicking around with his camera when the door opened with a bang. I was frantic, trying to cover myself before I realised who was there.

"Then I saw it was the Mitford woman. She was yelling and shouting abuse at André, calling him awful names and accusing him of child-molesting. Of course, I felt offended. I wasn't a child anymore and if André preferred me to her... Well, what followed was a general shouting match between the three of us. Then he and she went at each other with their fists and whatever they could find in that hut. I think he hit her with an old saucepan and she had a wooden stick to defend herself and to attack him. I can't remember all the details, but I do remember that at one point the woman hit me with her stick and I lost consciousness."

With shaking hands, Sandy took a sip of mineral water from the bottle she had on her bedside table. Philomena waited eagerly for the continuation of the horrible report. After a short pause to recover from her exhaustion, Sandy continued.

"So I don't have the full truth either. I don't know how long I must've been unconscious. But when I recovered, I was alone. Both of them were gone. It was dark in the hut. I felt the pain on my head and I remembered the blow I had got from the Mitford woman with her stick. After recovering for a few minutes, I stood, rearranged my clothes and tried to find out what had happened to the two fighters. But no success! They had simply vanished.

"At one point, I imagined I had seen three people fighting, but they were all gone by now. I finally found my wristwatch – which I had taken off for the photo shoot – and saw that it was nearly seven in the evening. I must've been unconscious for several hours, which was confirmed by the heavy pain in my head. I wondered if my skull was still intact and found that my left arm also hurt. Nothing was broken, it seemed, but I was really in a bad way."

"What did you do? Did you find Sullivan and Miss Mitford?"

"No, they were gone. It was pitch dark in that forest. I opened the door carefully in case they were right outside, but there was only darkness outside as well as in the hut. I took all my courage and called their names, but there was no answer. Then the idea hit me that I might have injured the woman, too. I mean, it wasn't only her hitting me. I gave as much as I got from her. I could've hit her very hard."

"What about Sullivan? Did you hit him too?"

"I don't think so."

"Did you find one of them eventually?"

"No. I found my bike – which wasn't easy in that darkness – and returned home. When I sat down to think, I realised I might have killed the woman. She might still be lying there near the hut in the forest. Also, I felt I couldn't face André or her ever again. And even if the whole thing turned out to be a mere fight between the two of them, the truth of my photo shoot would come out and I would be humiliated at school and all over…"

"So?"

"So, I decided to get away. I collected all the money I could find in the house and left a few days later after we had been interviewed by the police."

"Where did you go?"

"I hitchhiked across Europe. Eventually, I reached Turkey. I spent a few days in Istanbul, sorting my thoughts and considering my options. It dawned on me that I had no intention of becoming a model anymore. I was much more worried about my potential guilt. I became more and more convinced that I had killed the Mitford woman. I even made my inner peace with the woman. I stopped calling her a bitch and a slut in my mind. She might have been a bad character, but she hadn't deserved to be killed by me. In a way, with time, I even began to feel sorry for her."

Philomena was impressed. For several minutes there was silence between the two women. Sandy seemed to be exhausted. She needed her oxygen more frequently and her breathing seemed to become more difficult. Philomena felt sorry for her old friend.

"Perhaps you should have a rest now," she suggested. "I can come back tomorrow. You'll feel stronger by then and we can go on with our heart-to-heart talk."

Sandy agreed and lay back in her bed. At that moment, a nurse entered and asked Philomena to leave.

She walked back to the busy main road near the hospital. She needed this walk before she would hail a taxi. She had to digest what Sandy had told her. In a way, she admired her friend's courage. She admitted to herself that she would never have summoned such determination and courage to tramp across Europe all the way to India. Also, even though Philomena didn't really love her parents and though she never had a great circle of friends, she wouldn't have wanted to be separated from her family and friends like that, to be declared a missing person back home. What a terrible situation! But she admired Sandy.

Then she thought about her own role. It seemed she'd disappeared before things got out of hand at the forest hut. But still, she had no recollection of how she got home. Could she have stayed on outside the hut and waited for Sandy, then saw Miss Mitford, got involved again and ended up murdering the woman? It was possible. But she had to admit that it was a highly improbable scenario.

At least she had more factual material – if it was true what Sandy had told her – to continue her quest. She had very high hopes about getting more details from Sandy once her friend was fully recovered.

Philomena hailed a taxi – another Hindustan Ambassador, this time one in a more derelict condition – and travelled back to her hotel. When she arrived at the lobby, the obnoxious young man was sitting at the bar. He called hello to her, which she tried to ignore. But the man stood up and confronted her. She couldn't get past him, so she had to acknowledge his presence and show a friendly face.

"Good afternoon, sir," she said in an even voice.

"Why so stiff, young lady?" he said with a teasing undertone. "My name's Benny, all my friends call me Benny. What's yours?"

"I don't think that's any of your business!"

"Hey, hey, young lady. Why so unfriendly? There's no harm in the two of us getting introduced. You would be surprised how much you can profit from my acquaintance…"

This time she managed to get past the man and she quickly disappeared in the lift. Back in her room, she wondered what that awful man had in mind. She was too old to be of any interest for him. Was he trying to cheat her out of some money? She only hoped she wouldn't see him again.

She spent the rest of the day reading on her bed and in the evening, she went to the same restaurant as on most days. Later, she went to bed and took a long time until she finally dropped off to sleep. She was still worried about her role at Bedgebury Forest.

In the morning, when she saw Vernushan behind the reception desk. She decided to drop a word about that awful Benny type.

"He's one of our regular guests," Vernushan explained. "He's from Chennai. He's a businessman dealing in jewellery. When he's in town, he always stays here."

"Have you never had any complaints about his behaviour towards female guests?"

Vernushan seemed to think of what to say for a long moment. Then he waved his hands in the air and said, "Indian women like being admired."

"I don't think his behaviour can be classified under 'admiration', but rather 'molestation', if you ask me."

"I'm so sorry, dear lady. Do you want to report him to the police?"

"Oh no, I don't think it's as serious as that, but it might be a good idea to watch that guy a bit better when he's getting drunk at the bar."

"Of course, we will do that. We are a very decent hotel here."

With that, Philomena was satisfied. She had a cup of coffee and a delicious French croissant at her favourite café at the seafront. She read *The Times of India*, which she had obtained from a kiosk on her way. The main headlines were about India's relationship with Russia and her role between Russia and China. This was really big politics, too big for Philomena at this moment. So, she just browsed through some of the regional news. It was easy reading. Nothing spectacular.

Later in the morning, when she arrived at the hospital, she was told she couldn't visit her friend again. At first, they were reluctant to give her any reasons, but when she bribed one of the doctors with two hundred rupees, she was shocked to learn that Sandy had had a relapse. She was much worse than the day before. There was nothing she could do for her. Dejected and disappointed, she left the hospital and took a taxi back to her hotel again.

In the afternoon, to calm down and to kill time, she took a taxi to the ashram. Parvati received her with a friendly "Namaste" and offered her a cup of masala chai. They sat down together. Philomena felt that this quiet and unspectacular woman had almost become a friend to her. She trusted her and enjoyed listening to her voice.

"I'm sorry to report," she began, "that Sita's condition isn't good. Though she seemed reasonably well only yesterday, they say she relapsed into another coma this morning." She felt some tears in her eyes as she was looking into Parvati's peaceful eyes.

"Yes, we understand that this disease is a very terrible punishment for us humans. It is so tricky. One moment it seems quite harmless and the next moment, it can be a brutal killer. We know it is a real scourge. Even here in our community, we've had several cases and we lost three of our sisters."

"That's not very comforting," Philomena murmured.

"If you want to find consolation, our Guru says you can only find it in deep meditation and prayer."

Philomena didn't know if such practices would help her. She was just worried about her friend in hospital and there was only one power that might help her and that was the power of modern medical science. She didn't believe in all that mumbo jumbo that they were on about in this ashram.

"Thank you for your kind words," she told Parvati. "I don't think your kind of meditation is for me, but I'd be glad if I might relax a bit here. Do you have somewhere quiet where I could spend a few hours?"

Parvati took her by her hand and led her to a room at the back of the building. It was a whitewashed room with a little shrine in one corner, otherwise nearly undecorated except for a portrait of the Guru on one of the walls. This was the so-called quiet room where people could meditate on their own when they didn't feel like joining the community for such practices. Philomena was happy to lie down on the soft mat that was spread out along the wall opposite the one with the Guru's portrait. Parvati left her alone with the words, "Spend as much time here as you need."

Lying down helped to calm her troubled mind. She tried to meditate – something she had never really bothered to learn – but she was so tired she soon fell asleep.

FIFTEEN

It was a dull morning. There was rain in the air. After weeks of blue skies and pleasant temperatures, this made the city of Pondicherry look quite different. One had the impression that some big change was about to take place in the universe.

Philomena immediately became aware of this new atmosphere. Entering the hotel lobby, she asked Vernushan what he thought of the weather.

"This is the monsoon season beginning," he explained.

"So, it's going to rain the next few months?"

"Not all the time, but often," he replied.

Hardly had she left the hotel when it really began to rain. She went back to the hotel, asking Vernushan if he could lend her an umbrella. "I'm going to buy some weather equipment, but to get to the shops, I need an umbrella."

"No problem, dear lady," he said and handed her a black umbrella, the type normally carried by men in England. But this was India.

At one of the shops in what appeared to be the main shopping street in town, she bought herself a good raincoat and a stylish umbrella. The raincoat was thin enough. It looked something like a trench coat and it suited the mild climate. Despite the rain, which had now become a heavy downpour, the temperature was still pleasant.

She walked back to her hotel and returned the black umbrella. Vernushan was glad to get it back because an Indian couple was already waiting for it. He handed it to them and they thanked her politely.

The rain now being too hard, she decided to call a taxi from the hotel. Probably because of the heavy rain, the taxi took over an hour to arrive. But when it came, she was glad enough and jumped in, trying not to get too soaked between the hotel front door and the taxi. She gave the address of the hospital.

"Traffic may be a bit difficult," the driver warned her. "Too much water in the street," he explained.

"Well, as long as we get there sometime today," she said jokingly. The driver looked back at her through the rearview mirror. His face looked puzzled. She wondered if she had made an inappropriate comment. She realised that difficult road conditions might mean a more dangerous job for him and decided to keep her forward mouth shut for the rest of the trip.

At the hospital, she was told by the duty nurse that Sandy's condition had become worse. Apparently, she had fallen back into a coma and the readings on her monitoring equipment didn't look very promising.

Philomena asked if she could still see the patient. The nurse's answer was a strict no. The patient's condition was too serious.

So, full of disappointment and apprehension, Philomena left the hospital and travelled back to town. She was so worried that she didn't fancy a pleasant reading session in her hotel room, so she told the taxi driver to drop her in the town centre. She had to do something to take her mind off the fears for her old friend.

She went from shop to shop, sometimes spending some time looking at new saris, golden bracelets, Indian guide books and other goods offered for sale. Some shop owners tried to get her interested in their ware. One of them got quite angry when he realised that she was just browsing, not really interested to buy anything.

At one of the narrow street corners, she ran into the rude man from the hotel lobby. She tried to get past him, but he stopped her, gripping her elbow and pretending to be offended.

"Hey, dear lady!" he cried in a hurt voice. "Are you trying to ignore me? Aren't we old friends?"

"No, sir! We are certainly no friends!"

He protested in mock-surprise. "But we're staying at the same hotel. That makes us friends."

"Acquaintances at most," she said with determination. She tried to get away from him, but he held her elbow again.

"Will you please let me go?"

"Why not stop here for a moment? I'm not going to hurt you. I just want to be friendly with you. And you look very sad and worried. Can't I be of any assistance to you? Won't you let me help?"

Philomena suddenly realised how desperate she was. She was alone in the whole world. Norman was so far away and Henry was also far. Nobody could help her. She might be losing her best friend from her young days. She had no one to turn to in her sadness and her loneliness hit her like a bomb. Why not lean on this man, awful as he was?

"All right," she said, "if you keep your distance, I might listen to what you've got to tell me. But don't try any tricks with me."

"I'll be as polite as a diplomat," he said.

"For a start," she demanded, "tell me your name. We haven't been properly introduced."

"My name is Bill Rochester. I'm an English businessman from Chennai dealing with several companies here in Pondicherry. I understand your name is Mrs Webster."

"Yes, Philomena Webster. Have you been staying at our hotel for long?"

"I've been staying here on and off over the past two months and on every stay, I noticed your presence. If I may ask, have you been staying here all the time these past two months?"

"Yes, I'm here because my best friend is sick in hospital here. She's suffering from Covid-19 and she might be about to die."

"Is your friend from England, too?"

"Yes, she is," she answered, realising that they were both getting very wet. So she suggested going back to their hotel and continuing their conversation in the lobby there. He agreed and they were soon back at the hotel. They ordered some tea and sat down in the easy chairs provided near the reception desk.

In the street, she had decided to give the man just a few minutes, but now she was beginning to feel a bit more relaxed and told herself that this guy's company was still better than no company at all. Despite his shortcomings, he might help her to cope with her sense of loneliness. She found him unpleasant enough to be safe from any sort of intimacy or any attempt of his to take advantage of her desperate situation. Naturally, she tried not to let him see her sadness and her worries. She knew she could put up a neutral face.

"May I ask how long you intend to stay on?" he wanted to know.

"Oh, that will depend on my friend's medical condition," she replied.

Then their conversation turned to more general topics: India in general, British colonial history in India, British politics and tourism. Eventually, they came to some of Philomena's favourite topics such as democracies and dictatorships in the world. And while he was trying to steer the talk towards her private life, she managed to lead him away from it. She didn't want to reveal any more about her life. When he asked her about her work, she just told him she was a person of independent means, which deeply impressed him.

"So you need not get permission from an employer to extend your stay in India?"

"No, I'm totally my own mistress. And I'm glad I am. I'm not dependent on any other person, neither man nor woman. I am a free woman," she declared with a certain pride.

It suddenly occurred to her that it might have been a mistake to tell him about her independence. He might get the wrong idea. He might think he could get some money from her.

"Listen, Mr Rochester – "

"Call me Bill," he protested.

"All right, Bill," she said, deciding to make an end to this conversation. "I think I'm getting a bit tired, so I think I've got to retire to my room."

"Of course. I'm sorry to keep you so long."

She stood up and walked to the lift. In her room, she lay down on her bed and tried to order her conflicting thoughts. Bill seemed not as bad a character as she had thought at first. But then, to be honest, he had been far too forward and downright rude to her in the beginning, when they'd first met at the hotel.

Now, however, she had to admit she had been glad of his company. She had enjoyed their half hour of general conversation. It seemed clear. It wasn't the man as a person, it was just because he'd relieved her of her loneliness. Any person would have done. She asked herself if she was an honest person. She had used this man to help her out of her desperate sense of abandonment. She only hoped she hadn't given him any false hopes.

With thoughts like these, she eventually fell asleep on top of her bedspread.

When she woke up, it was dark outside. The rain was still pouring down and making quite a noise on the window pane.

She took her phone and called Henry's number. She felt she had to tell him about Sandy's condition. He picked up the phone nearly on the first ring.

"I'm sorry," she said after their greetings, "but it appears Sandy is in grave condition."

He wanted to know more details, but she could only give him the information she'd got herself. Before they ended their call, she said 'sorry' again and he answered that he distanced himself from his little sister many years ago, so there was no need for Philomena to feel sorry for him.

"If there's really a big change, either for the better or for the worse, you can let me know again, but there's no need to call me every day. I don't want to be reminded of her too often after what she's done to our family."

"I see."

"Don't take offence, Philomena. I like to hear your voice, but I don't always fancy talking about Sandy."

"I understand."

She punched the off key and put down her phone. Then she went out to have a light evening meal at the nearest restaurant.

*   *   *

The next morning, she woke up to the rattle of the heavy rain on her window. She had a feeling that it might have rained all night. She hoped the bad weather wouldn't prevent her from travelling to the ashram. She got ready and took the lift down to the reception area.

Vernushan was behind the reception desk. "Good morning, dear lady," he said. "If you are planning to travel somewhere by taxi, it might be a bit difficult. It rained all night. Most roads are very bad this morning."

"You said it would only rain occasionally in the monsoon, on and off. What about this now?"

"I'm sorry, madam. This is also a possibility. In this country, you never know…"

She walked through the rain to the café where she usually had her breakfast. It was a journey through water, both from above and below. Her umbrella could hardly take all the water pouring down from the dark sky and her shoes weren't high enough for the pools she had to walk through. She would need a pair of wellingtons. But she got there eventually.

After breakfast, she rang the taxi company and ordered a taxi to pick her up from the café. She didn't fancy walking back to the hotel first. The taxi didn't arrive for quite some time. She had to call the number twice again to remind the woman on duty that she was still waiting for her taxi. When it arrived and she got in, the driver made a sour face. She wasn't sure if she had been in his taxi before, but he looked familiar.

When she mentioned her destination, he sighed. "Sorry madam, but water is very bad this morning. Some places actually flooded. We may not make it to your ashram." But he started the engine and drove off.

When they came to the intersection of Anna Salai and Mahatma Gandhi Road on the corner of the Hotel Atithi, the road leading out of town was so flooded that the police were erecting some barriers.

One of the officers waved the taxi down. He stepped to the driver's window. The driver wound it down halfway and the officer looked inside.

"Where do you want to go?" he asked.

The driver mentioned their destination and the policeman explained, "Impossible to travel on this road, too much water. You'd get stuck." He added something in Tamil, then changed back to English. "Why don't you just follow Anna Salai until you come to Kamaraj Salai, where you turn right, follow the road until you come to the big roundabout at the Rajiv Gandhi Statue. That's where you can turn right and follow number 332A highway north. I'd say that's your best bet."

The driver grumbled but followed the officer's directions. It took them about three quarters of an hour for a distance that could normally be covered in ten minutes maximum, but they got to the big roundabout where they joined the highway.

But when they had travelled on the highway for about ten minutes, the traffic came to a halt. The highway seemed to be closed further along and there was a long queue of cars. Meanwhile, the rain kept pelting down on the taxi's tin roof with a roaring noise.

"No use," the driver mumbled. "We have to turn back. No driving to your ashram today. Sorry."

So, she returned to her hotel after another two hours of traffic jams and heavy rain. Once she was in the dry hotel, she realised that she had, in fact, been quite lucky. After all, she had seen several cars that were stuck in the high water and there had been three accidents along their way.

After a troubled night full of threatening dreams, she woke up to a morning that was surprisingly quiet. The pelting rain on her window had stopped. She got ready for the day with high hopes. If the rain had stopped, this meant that a car might finally get through to Sandy's ashram.

Once in the street outside her hotel, she realised that there was still a lot of water on the ground. She went to one of the big shops in town and bought a pair of wellingtons. She knew she was presenting a funny picture to the world with denim jeans and wellies, but she didn't mind. Back in the hotel lobby, Bill was sitting in one of the easy chairs. When he saw her, he couldn't avoid a smile on his lips, but he immediately apologised to her.

"I'm sorry, I shouldn't have laughed. But you really look… special."

"Don't concern yourself. I can cope with the high water." With these words she ordered a taxi.

Again, the taxi took an eternity to arrive, but once she was inside and the driver had put the car in gear, she felt a lot better. They had no problem travelling to where they had to turn away the day before in front of the Hotel Atithi, but there was still a lot of water and their taxi could only travel slowly.

The driveway to the ashram was only a stretch of reddish-brown mud. Philomena admired the driver's skill. He managed to negotiate the most slippery patches and they only got stuck a few times. Every time, the driver put the car in reverse, then quickly back in third gear forward, which wriggled them out of the slimy patches. When they reached the ashram, she was so glad she gave the driver an extra big tip.

"Why have you come here?" Parvati asked her when they sat down together.

"They wouldn't let me near Sandy – sorry, Sita. They say I'm not family. So, I hope they may have been in touch with you. She must have given them your address, your community as the nearest of kin."

Parvati was thinking. Philomena didn't know what could be done in this situation. She couldn't order Parvati around. But she was desperate for news about her friend.

Parvati must have seen her desperation. She said, "Listen, I'm going to beg the Guru to speak to the hospital people."

She left her sitting where she was. A young girl brought her a cup of masala chai. The time ticked away for what seemed an eternity.

When Parvati returned, her face looked very stern. She sat down opposite Philomena and ordered her sari.

"I am really sorry, dear sister. Your good friend, Sita, passed away early this morning."

Philomena couldn't believe what she heard. Sandy dead? No, that was impossible! Only a few days ago, she had talked to her and Sandy had seemed to improve. She had to swallow hard and she tried to hold back her tears.

"Are you absolutely sure? Is there no misunderstanding?"

"I am sorry to say it is true. Can we be of any help to you?" Parvati offered.

"Can I lie down and recover for a while?" Philomena asked.

Parvati nodded and led her to another room where Philomena could lie down on a divan of some sort. Once Parvati had left her and closed the door behind her, Philomena broke down in a fit of tears.

*　*　*

The monsoon was still on, although it had never rained so hard again as on the day before Sandy's death.

To Philomena, looking back two weeks later, it seemed as if the sky had wanted to protest against the disease threatening Sandy's imminent death. The Hindu gods could've prevented this if they'd provided the rain with more power over life and death.

She knew, of course, that such ideas were pointless. Sandy was gone. She was burnt and buried and Philomena had received her friend's meagre possessions from the ashram. They consisted of some clothing, her passport, a purse with some rupees, a few pounds and three American dollars. There was also a small gold chain and a golden ring. Nothing valuable, but still these things had been Sandy's and Philomena was duty bound to return them to Sandy's family. She had now brought all her personal affairs to an end, she had taken her farewell from Sandy, and she considered herself fit for her return to Britain.

It was another rainy day when she took the long-distance taxi from Pondicherry to Chennai airport. This time, the driver remained silent for the entire trip. For his silence, which was a very good thing for her, she tipped him generously when she got out of the taxi at the terminal.

It was nearly midnight when the flight took off and Philomena looked down at the receding lights of Chennai.

"It's down there. That's where I really lost my friend Sandy. I hope she's happy where she is now." These were her last thoughts before she devoted herself to her own well-being, crammed in her seat and hoping to survive the flight with fortitude.

PART FOUR

SIXTEEN

Tom Mitchell was a man of many talents. Unfortunately, no one recognised his qualities. His parents never believed in his potential. When he was at school, his teachers usually put him down as a nonentity, so not a great deal was expected of him. He would never be a great artist, a great scientist, or a professional of any description whatsoever. His life – in other words – would never really amount to anything.

Such a reputation and such expectations were bound to affect a young man's life.

When he left school, he started to work for Tesco's supermarket chain, filling up the shelves in their Eastbourne branch. In the evenings and on weekends, he sometimes went out to a pub or a club, hoping to find friends or even a girlfriend. But his self-esteem was too low. He didn't have the courage to talk to someone he didn't know, least of all a girl. All these girls were too good-looking and they were not meant for him. Besides, when he visited his parents and tried to explain his embarrassment to them, they just laughed at him.

"You stupid loser," his father smirked. "Did you think a decent girl would even look at you?"

And his mother remarked, "You wouldn't even know what to do with a girl, would you?" With the rhetorical question, she expressed a more accurate truth than she imagined.

Thus, his parents weren't any great help for him. Tom began to be a lonely wolf, a shy young man with no prospects.

As he was growing tired of his pointless outings to pubs and clubs, he gradually drifted into the world of more theoretical interests. This led him to books, especially books on mathematics. He liked maths very much, but he went on searching for other interests, which eventually led him to the discovery of the game of chess.

A good thing, he thought, *that there are these magazines, too.* This took him to regular visits to WHSmith's on the lookout for interesting magazines on mathematics or chess.

At first, he discovered many interesting magazines dealing with mathematics. He had been passionately interested in the subject when he was at school, but the math teacher had never taken him seriously. Sometimes he knew that the teacher had made a mistake on the blackboard, but he didn't have the courage to tell him because he knew he would be ridiculed in front of the class.

Then he went on to chess. He was delighted. Such a fantastic game, such a game of endless possibilities. He soon learnt the different moves of the different chessmen. One day, he bought himself a real wooden chessboard from one of the shops in the Arndale Centre in town. When he placed the board on the table in his room, he set up the game by positioning all the pieces in their correct squares. One thing he found very important was the rule of the basic position of the board. He was proud he knew that in the bottom right corner there had always got to be a white square. Also, he told himself that probably not many people knew that at the beginning of a game the white queen had to be on a white square while the black queen went on a black square. So, both players didn't get exactly the same starting positions.

He began to play games against himself, after every move turning the board, first playing as White, then as Black, then back again. Like this, he found he could imagine himself in two different personalities, confronting each other. This was a lot more fascinating than going out to pubs and clubs!

Eventually, he found the ads in the magazines in which chess players were looking for partners to play against. He responded to the first such ad that appealed to him by calling the phone number in the ad. Like this, he got to know a man who called himself Chessnerd. He didn't learn his real name, not for a long time. Tom, however, used his normal name. Once the two men had exchanged a few basic bits of information about themselves, they began to play a game by distance. Every few days, one of them sent his next move to his opponent by phone. This state of things occupied Tom for many months and it made him reasonably satisfied, if not really happy. Like this, at least Tom had something to keep him interested.

His parents criticised his habit of sitting at home, reading maths books or trying out different chess strategies. "What are you doing in your room all the time? Why don't you go out like every other normal young man?"

These disagreements got worse and worse until the day came when they fought an open quarrel, shouting abuse at each other. Tom called his mother a stupid bitch and his father a blind idiot. This was a major rupture in his family. His father told him to leave the house and never come back. He was a disgrace to his family. The parents didn't want to have anything to do with him from now on.

Once the first wrath had calmed down a little in his father's attitude, Tom negotiated with him. He was allowed to stay on for a few more days until he found a place to start a new life away from home.

He found a one-bedroom flat in Brighton which he liked and that he could afford on his meagre wages. It was near Preston Park railway station, which meant he could get to work in Eastbourne by train. In fact, the rent was so low, he could still afford to save some money for future projects. But what those future projects might be, he had no clue.

Like this, he started out on his real life as an adult, fully responsible for everything in his life. He learnt to cook simple meals, do his own laundry, and the ins and outs of all the simple, mundane and practical tasks at hand, such as paying the rent, the council tax, the gas and electricity bills and so on. He considered himself quite an able man. However, this didn't help to improve his low self-esteem.

For the following two years, he continued in the same groove, doing maths and playing chess. But sometimes at night, he found himself dreaming of one of the girls or young women he had seen at the supermarket during the day. He began to suffer from a strange urge in his body and mind. What would he do if he got himself such an attractive woman?

He dismissed such ideas as quickly as he'd conceived them, knowing full well that any woman he might approach would just laugh at him. She would see through him, recognising his shortcomings and his ignorance.

To kill such unhealthy notions, he concentrated even more on his chess games. His partner, Chessnerd, was willing to exchange a new move with him every day.

One day, he found he had saved up enough money to learn to drive a car. He didn't have a car, but he thought it may be a good idea to learn before even thinking of getting himself some old banger. He registered with one of the driving schools in town. As it turned out, he was assigned to a female instructor, which shocked him a little at first.

He wondered how he would cope with the proximity of a woman. He was used to working with female colleagues at Tesco's, but this was going to be different. He was going to sit next to a woman in the close quarters of a car's interior. How would he manage to talk to her? Would she be wearing any perfume? Would she be dressed in an alluring way? Would he be attracted to her? He was full of apprehension when his first practical lesson was imminent.

The instructor introduced herself as Susan Knight. She was standing by the door of her car, smiling at him. "You must be Tom Mitchell?" she croaked. Her face was nothing extraordinary, but she had an extremely attractive figure. Tom's knees were shaking as he walked up to her. He tried very hard not to look at her pointed breasts. He made an extra effort to look her in the eyes and to give her a friendly smile, meant to give her a relaxed impression.

"Don't be nervous, Tom," she said, adding, "I may call you Tom? Is that okay for you?"

"That's okay," he answered, blushing.

"You will see. It isn't such a difficult skill, but it is a serious business when you're learning to drive a car." She gave him these explanations while they were taking their seats, he behind the wheel and she in the passenger's seat.

So, she was a serious person, after all, he thought. He wondered. Did she find him attractive? Did she see through him, discovering all his bad qualities?

While she was explaining the gears and how to change them with your feet on the clutch and the gas pedal, he could smell her scent. It was ever so faint, but soft and very alluring. He didn't dare to look her in the eyes. Her smiling face was too close to his worried face. Her proximity caused him a feeling of panic. At the same time, he was struggling hard not to let her see his nervousness.

"And this is your gearstick," she said. She took his hand and placed it on the knob at the top of the gearstick. When he felt her touch on the back of his left hand, it electrified him. This was the first time in his life that a woman who wasn't his mother had touched him, skin to skin. He concentrated not to let her see his emotions. He pressed his lips together, hoping to weather this onslaught on his most intimate feelings.

They were on a large space of asphalt where he was supposed to make his first move with the instructor's car. After she explained things to him while they were standing still in the middle of the practice space, she told him to turn the ignition key to start the engine. Then, under her watchful eyes, he followed her commands and put the car in first gear. Naturally, he stalled the engine several times, but on the fourth attempt, he actually managed to drive off. They drove round the square several times before she made him change into second gear. Like this, his first practical driving lesson passed in no time.

He was relieved when they parted and he walked to the bus-stop. The feeling of her hand still burned on the back of his hand. What a dangerous feeling! But what a wonderful feeling! He was still puzzled. How was it possible that he could have those feelings? She was just his driving instructor, but she was a woman. That was what it was!

That night, he had an erotic dream about Susan Knight and himself in the car. She was showing him not only the various switches and knobs on the dashboard of the car but asked him if he wanted to see some more of her. When he said yes, she began to undress, but when she got to her underwear, the dream faded away. He tried to recapture the dream, but he couldn't. He had woken up. He tried to go to sleep again to continue with his dream, but it didn't work. In the following nights, he had the same dream again and again, but it always stopped when she was about to take off her underwear.

For him, this was a sign. It showed how the erotic delights that a woman could offer a man were not meant for him. He was excluded from this aspect of humanity. He would never know what it felt like to be intimate with a woman.

Every driving lesson was a torture for him. The worst moment came when she was explaining a few things under the bonnet to him. She bent down to reach the little stick to check the oil level of the engine. She was in a position opposite him and he could hardly believe his eyes when he could see down her front, inside her shirt, part of her breasts – only the top parts unfortunately – exposed to his gaze. Her soft, pale flesh was wobbling while she was talking. Of course, he didn't grasp one single bit of the information she was giving him. His head turned in a turmoil of erotic pleasure. He felt his sexual organ getting stiff.

Back at his flat, he felt ashamed. He was sure the woman hadn't been aware of the fantastic show she had offered him. True, it had been beautiful and so exciting for him, but he knew it was forbidden territory. He decided to apologise to her.

In one of the following driving lessons, therefore, he was preparing an apologetic speech for her, but he couldn't get up the courage to say what he had prepared in his troubled mind. Just as he thought he was ready for his speech, she started with a long explanation of how to negotiate the traffic in a big roundabout. They were approaching the big roundabout at the intersection of the A23 and the A27. Naturally, this killed his impulse.

He decided to wait until he passed his driving test. But this was still several weeks away. Meanwhile, he would have to cope with the difficult situation. At one point, he thought that maybe he should discontinue the driving lessons with her and register with a different motoring school. But then again, he would miss her too much. The fact was, although he was suffering with Susan in the same car, on one hand desiring her and bathing in her aura at such close proximity, on the other hand, he felt the pangs of brutal torture because of her inaccessibility, the forbidden territory that she represented.

Despite all the suffering, it was still a gift from heaven to be able to be in her company, to enjoy her looks and to feel her charms. It was better to suffer with pleasure than to be cut off from one of the most fundamental joys in life. That was how Tom saw things. Besides, there was always the possibility that he might see more of her. She might show him more things in the engine compartment that would require her to bend down and allow him another exciting peep.

However, nothing of the kind happened again. He feared she might have realised his forbidden gaze that time. It must have been embarrassing for her. He believed he remembered her gathering the top of her shirt front with her hand as she had stood up straight again. So, she might know about his eagerness. He wasn't sure if it was a positive or a negative sign.

The time passed without incident and soon he had to take his driving test. At the test, a middle-aged male expert was sitting next to Tom and Susan came along with them, sitting in the back. In the first few minutes, it made him a bit nervous to know she was sitting at his back. He imagined he could feel her breath behind his neck. But he had to concentrate so much that he forgot about the feeling and he managed to do everything right. In the end, he passed the test and the expert took his leave. Susan asked him if he wanted to have a cup of coffee with her to celebrate. She didn't have another driving student for another two hours.

Tom was happy to accompany her to a nearby café. They sat down at one of the window tables and ordered cappuccinos. He knew this was the moment when he should apologise to her. In his mind, he prepared the speech required for this apology, but he never managed to pronounce it. She was sitting opposite him, smiling in such a friendly way that he didn't find the courage. When he realised it was probably the last time he would ever see her again, he decided to discard the apology and enjoy the moment instead.

*　　*　　*

The years passed without great incidents in Tom's life. He kept his routine, working at Tesco's and playing chess with Chessnerd in the evening. A few months after Tom's successful driving test, Chessnerd suddenly changed his routine. He explained to Tom that he was hoping to get together with a girl, which would mean less time for chess. Tom considered this a form of betrayal, but he didn't tell him. In reality, he envied him a little. How did the man find the time and opportunity to meet a girl who would be willing to come and live with him? This new situation between the two chess players gave Tom the courage to break their unspoken rule and ask Chessnerd his real name.

"I'm Steve and I live in Scotland," was the answer. Tom gave him his own address, so Steve would know. But this didn't change a great deal between them. They still only met by telephone, playing about once a week from now on.

When, about seven months later, Steve told him he was getting married, Tom felt extremely uncomfortable. Steve was about to experience something from which he himself was excluded in this life. Steve would know the joys of being with a woman. Tom wondered if he should ask him about the details of the sexual aspect of marriage, because he still couldn't imagine how a woman could ever consent to what a man wanted to do with her. But he didn't ask because he didn't want to risk Steve's distant friendship and his chess partnership.

His life continued more or less the same with the only difference that he could play chess with Steve less frequently.

One day, he got to work with another young man. They were assigned to help unload and then to unpack several pallets of goods. It was a huge new delivery of canned food and packs of pasta. The branch manager explained to them how he wanted them to work efficiently because he expected a rush of shoppers before the coming bank holiday weekend. So, they got down to work. His colleague's name was Bill Mason and he was about the same age as Tom. They soon found that they had a lot in common. Bill was also very shy about women, but he was better trained on the small fork-lift truck which they used to unload the full pallets from the large articulated lorry that was parked in reverse outside their delivery gates.

Bill drove the forklift truck and placed the pallets in a position that allowed them to unload the cardboard boxes of goods. He deposited six pallets stacked with large boxes in the correct spot before he got down from his forklift truck and joined Tom in the job of unpacking.

The big cardboard boxes normally contained between one and two dozen smaller boxes. The men stacked these on a smaller trolley which they could push along through the door into the actual shopping area, trying hard to dodge the ambling shoppers, to where they had to stack the contents of these boxes – cans, small cardboard packs and plastic packs of pasta – on the shelves.

When their boss saw that they weren't getting on fast enough, he assigned two of the female employees to the task at the shelves so the two men could concentrate on the transfer from the lorry to the shelves more efficiently.

The work went on with better efficiency. Tom saw that Bill was eyeing the two women who helped them at the shelves whenever they brought in another full trolley and so got in touch with them very briefly. Tom had actually decided not to look at them too carefully. He didn't want his suffering mind to get into trouble again as it had that time with Susan. He was through with the question of women. But once they were in the storage hall, just the two of them, it was Bill who opened the dangerous subject.

"I say," he began, "did you see that bird with the big boobs? Isn't she a real knocker?"

"Do you mean the one with the black hair and the dark eyes?"

"Yeah! I wouldn't mind getting into her pants. Wouldn't you, too?"

Tom was puzzled. The kind of language that Bill was using seemed to indicate that he was what was called a womaniser or even a lady-killer. So he wasn't such a shy young man as himself.

"Hey, what do you think?" Bill asked because Tom didn't know what to reply.

Bill turned away from him and pushed another loaded trolley. Tom looked after him, wondering if he should perhaps make an effort and give the two women working with them a better look. One never knew…

So, when he was near them in front of a shelf full of cans again, he made a real effort and glanced at the dark woman only to check if her breasts were really as Bill had said, then he turned his eyes to the other woman. She was considerably slimmer and had fair hair with a hue of green on one side. He couldn't really note her figure because he was a bit too close to her and he didn't have the courage to step back in order to inspect her more carefully. But the next time he approached her, pushing a full trolley, he saw that she seemed to have a really beautiful figure as far as he could judge. After all, she was in her Tesco outfit, which wasn't very sexy.

At the end of their working day, Bill and Tom went for a drink at a pub in town. Tom decided to take a later train home. They got their pints and stood in a corner of the pub. Bill wanted to talk about the two women from Tesco's. He realised that Tom was reluctant to join him in his erotic descriptions of the two women. He called them girls, sometimes birds and sometimes knockers, never women. Tom considered this vulgar, but he didn't have the courage to tell Bill. While they were getting through their pints and soon ordered two more, Bill ranting on and on over his fantasies about sex with the dark-haired woman, Tom went into an inner emigration, thinking about his own chances with the fair-haired woman. She was attractive, that was clear. But how could he approach her?

As it happened, about a week later, they had to work with the same two women again. This time Bill took the initiative. He introduced them to the women. The dark-haired one answered that her name was Mandy and her fair-haired colleague was Karen. Both women gave them very friendly smiles. Tom believed he could detect an extra shine in Karen's smile for him.

During their work through the day, they only exchanged some meaningful glances but had to concentrate on their jobs at hand. At the end of the day, Mandy asked them if they wanted to come for a drink with them. She said she had a small car and they could go to a pub in Pevensey Bay. The two men were happy to say yes. While they were changing from their Tesco outfit into their street clothes, Bill winked at Tom and made a meaningful face.

Tom was uncertain. Even though he was looking forward to what might become his initiation into the world of sexual experience, he was also afraid of what he was expected to do. "Do you think the two women are going to let us kiss them?" he asked his new friend.

"Hey, partner! They didn't invite us out to play noughts and crosses, did they?"

"Are you sure?"

Bill only laughed, adding, "You'll see."

They all met in the carpark. Mandy opened the door of her small Ford Fiesta and they all crammed in, Mandy behind the wheel and Bill on the seat next to her, while Tom and Karen were told to sit in the back. Mandy started the car, revved up the engine and sounded the horn for sheer pleasure. Then they were off.

As they were travelling towards Pevensey Bay, Tom felt a hard lump in his stomach. Karen was leaning towards him and when they went round a roundabout, she was thrown at him for a moment. After this sudden body contact, she seemed to like it and leaned in more closely.

Tom was glad to get out of the car when they had reached the pub they had in mind. He still didn't know what was expected of him.

The men ordered pints of ale, while the women went for gin and tonic. With Bill's and Mandy's festive moods, all four of them were soon engaged in lively conversation. This made Tom forget his uncertainties.

After their third round, Tom felt a call of nature. "Sorry, I think I need to go to the loo. Excuse me, please." He left the three of them standing near the bar and went out to the toilet, where he was relieved to empty his bladder. "All that beer," he murmured to himself, as he was buttoning up his pants.

When he stepped out of the toilet, he saw Karen waiting for him in the semi-darkness of the passage. She flung herself at him and began to kiss him on his mouth. He had never kissed a woman like this before. When she pushed her tongue inside his mouth, he was shocked. He didn't know that such things were actually done when two people were kissing. He thought it was just the lips. But despite his surprise, he began to like it, really, really like it! At the same time, he felt her body being pushed at his own, especially her abdomen pressing very hard. This started to turn his mind into a turmoil of emotions.

They went on like this for several minutes. Then she breathed into his ear. "Let's go to my place after we got rid of the others."

"If you'd like that," was the only answer he was capable of.

They went back into the bar area and rejoined the others, who were busy kissing too, but stopped when they saw them. The four of them continued with their earlier discussion, but their hearts weren't in it. It was clear that all of them had the same thing in mind. So they soon left the pub and drove back to Eastbourne, where Mandy dropped them near the railway station, where Karen said she lived.

Karen took him to her tiny one-bedroom flat somewhere behind the Arndale Centre. It was on the lower ground floor of one of those terraced houses converted into flats.

As soon as they were in her flat, Tom felt such an urge that he could no longer hold back. He tore off her clothes and stripped himself, all in such haste that she was a bit shocked. "Hey man, take it easy," she said. But he didn't listen. All he wanted was – at last in his poor life – to experience what it felt like to be with a woman. When both of them were naked, he threw her on her bed and jumped on top of her. He was so wild, he even forgot to look at her properly. He had always wondered what women really looked like, but now that he could actually enjoy this, he completely forgot about it and only went for his own satisfaction.

She yelled at him, but he stopped her by pressing his hand on her mouth and then he nearly strangled her.

It was all over in just five minutes. He was exhausted, breathing very hard and slipped off her sweaty body. She was choking and crying. "You stupid idiot! What do you think I am?"

He recovered and stood up. She yelled at him. She told him she'd go to the police and make him go to jail for rape. But he didn't listen to her. He quickly got dressed and left her. He managed to mumble, "Sorry," when he slipped out of the door. But then he was gone.

When he finally reached his own home later, he felt terrible. He knew he'd done a bad thing. He knew he'd raped Karen. But another voice in his brain told him to deny it in case she really went to the police. He knew they hardly ever believed women in such cases. They couldn't prove anything. He was safe.

SEVENTEEN

Back at work, Tom handed in his notice. The Tesco branch manager gave him a good reference, which allowed him to find a new job, this time in Brighton. This not only meant a shorter distance from his flat, but it also meant he wouldn't run into Karen unexpectedly. He didn't want to take any risks.

But the more days elapsed between his sexual attack on Karen, the more painful his sense of guilt became. Gradually it grew into an awful obsession. He sometimes believed he would have to tell someone in order to be able to cope with his bad conscience.

About four weeks later, he happened to run into Bill. They were both ambling through the Churchill Square Shopping Centre when they saw each other. At first, Tom had an impulse to run away and ignore Bill, but they were already too close for that. He expected his former workmate to accuse him of rape. After all, Karen must have told her friend Mandy, who must have told Bill. All the more surprising was Bill's friendly greeting now.

"Hiya, old chap, long time no see!" he said in a cheerful mood. "What have you been up to? Are you still seeing that bitch? What was her name?"

"She was called Karen."

"Yes, Karen, that was her name. Are you still seeing her, then?"

"No, we never met again after that first night."

"But you had great fun with her, didn't you? That night, Mandy and I also got along like a house on fire. We still see each other from time to time and I can tell you, the sex is simply earth-rocking!"

Tom felt disgusted, but he didn't let on. He knew he had to be careful. "Have you heard about Karen? Or has Mandy?" he asked.

"No, she seems to have disappeared. She no longer works at Tesco's and Mandy never mentions her either."

"I see. So, Mandy and you are an item now? Are you going steady, you know, boyfriend and girlfriend, like?"

"Hey, old man! No need to get tied down. She's just available sometimes. But I'm seeing other bitches, too."

Tom realised that Bill's life was still different from his. He seemed to try to get as many girls laid as he could. No feelings, no steady relationship. But what about himself, then? Was he really so different from his former workmate? He didn't have any tender feelings for Karen that night. It was just pure sexual instinct, male instinct, lust. The fact that Bill's language about women was so much more vulgar didn't mean he was morally his inferior. What he had done to Karen was at least as bad as Bill's attitude.

After they parted, Tom felt relieved. So she didn't go to the police and she didn't report a rape. He was safe. But for how long? She might still change her mind.

He had lost his interest in the shopping centre. He couldn't remember what he'd come here for.

*   *   *

It was late in summer when Tom had at last saved enough money to buy himself a small car. He got a grey second-hand Toyota Yaris for a thousand pounds. It had over 120,000 miles on the clock, but it came with a fresh MoT, looked decent enough and would do for him. He just wanted his own wheels, nothing posh.

Over the following few weeks, he often went for a drive in the country. He loved the soothing beauty of the Sussex and Kent countryside. He was particularly fond of those narrow country lanes that ran between thick hedges. He was aware of the fact that he was sometimes driving too fast along those lanes with the danger of oncoming vehicles, but he didn't care. He felt free.

One day he was driving along the A21 between Tunbridge Wells and Hastings, listening to some heavy metal music on the radio, when he was looking for a turning into a small country road. He wondered if he'd better turn right and drive round Bewl Water or turn left and drive to Cranbrook.

He wasn't too familiar with the area and hesitated for a moment. Then, on an impulse, he turned left. After about one mile, he stopped at a small carpark on his right. He got out of the car and stretched his back. The beauty of the surrounding scenery nearly overwhelmed him. He knew that people often said how dull the English landscape was in comparison to, say, a countryside in Mediterranean or Latin American countries. But he found this here extremely beautiful. Although he'd never travelled to any of those distant countries – he'd never actually been out of Britain – he was satisfied and happy with what he'd got here. This was his home and this was what would do for him.

Once he'd come out of his dreams, he began to walk into the nearby forest.

The forest contained some areas that were not very dense, but in other areas it was extremely dense; in fact, it was so thick with undergrowth and brush that one couldn't even see the ground beneath it. To make it even more impenetrable, there were large patches of brambles spread out. It was clear that this forest wasn't being looked after or tended by a forester. It was probably too small to make it worthwhile.

He stomped through the rotten leaves and mulch on the ground, enjoying the swishing noise he produced. The entire place gave him the impression that it was one of the most remote spots on Earth, or at least in the South of England. And yet he knew it was only a few miles from civilisation, from villages and busy towns.

As he was pushing more daringly into the denser part, he suddenly discovered a wooden structure which was not natural but clearly man-made. Was it a woodman's hut? He pushed through the brush and came to something that was a very decrepit shack or hut.

Tom pushed through the dense branches around the shack and found what looked like a door. Its hinges had almost collapsed with rust and when he carefully opened the door, there was a creaking noise.

Inside, it was relatively gloomy in a kind of semi-darkness that required one's eyes to get accustomed to the sparse light before one could distinguish anything. There was a musty smell.

He pushed back through the forest and fetched a torch from his car. When he re-entered the hut, he switched it on so he could really see what it was like. He saw a small bed with a bare mattress, a small wobbly table and chair, and a bucket of stale water placed near a camping gas stove. There was a small assortment of glasses, cups, plates and cutlery and there were two saucepans and a skillet. Also, he found a pile of old newspapers and a few candles. No running water, no electricity and no luxuries of any kind.

He wondered who owned this hut or who owned the forest. Was it owned by the county? By the Crown? Or was it privately owned? Whoever owned it or whoever had appropriated this hut, got himself a cozy little hideaway despite its rotten condition. What was it used for? It could be a hiding place for a criminal. Or it could be a love nest for a couple that was engaged in a secret affair. A criminal could escape from the arm of the law and survive here for quite some time. And a couple that wanted secret sex could enjoy it here without detection. The hut was so hard to find in the density of this forest.

Tom was impressed. He began to indulge in daydreams about taking some girl or other to this place. If he got himself a girlfriend, he could take her here to have uninterrupted sex with her.

After a while, he left the hut and walked back to his car. On the way home, it began to rain. He found that the windscreen wipers were broken, so it was quite a stressful drive home. He was relieved when he reached Brighton.

Through the following days, he often remembered the secret forest hut. He made a note in his small pocket-diary so he would be able to find that forest and its hidden hut again. He didn't know the name of the forest. Probably it didn't even have a name.

One night, he dreamt he was taking a girl to that hut. Of course, she was very sexy looking, as were all the girls in his dreams. She was wearing a tight yellow summer dress that clearly outlined her beautiful figure. Tom liked women with round bottoms and big breasts, but he knew he might only ever get a girl that didn't quite measure up to his unrealistic expectations.

In this dream, she was willing enough to come to the forest hut with him and once they were settled on the mattress in the hut, he could eagerly take off her clothes. But then again, as so often, his dream dissolved at this point. As usual, he was deprived of the pleasure he'd expected. He woke up with a swear word on his lips.

279

Several months elapsed before he had the opportunity to get together with a girl again. He just never had the chance. All through the autumn and winter, he never got near a girl that he fancied. All the girls in the pubs and clubs he frequented were either too ugly for him or they sent messages of "don't touch me" when he tried to approach them. He was aware that his self-confidence was somewhat wanting, but he was still hoping to get himself a nice girlfriend.

At his job, there was another young man who was as shy of girls as he was. His name was Oscar and he was about the same age as Tom. One day, as they were sitting at the back of the storage hall of the supermarket, Oscar drew a sad face. When Tom asked him what was going on, Oscar replied that no girls ever wanted him. He would probably die without ever having had sex. Tom tried to console him with the usual general phrases, but Oscar was still depressed as he'd tried to take out a girl only the night before and she'd dumped him when he'd tried to kiss her. What a bitch! Tom knew only too well what Oscar felt. He told him about some of his own failures. But he took great care not to mention Karen and what he'd done to her.

Over the following few months, the two young men gradually realised that they were not very good for each other. Instead of giving Oscar support and encouraging him to be more self-confident with women, Tom only pulled him down more deeply into his depression with his tales of failure. He suffered the same effect from Oscar's vulgar speeches. This state of affairs lasted well into the summer of the following year. Tom had reached a stage in which he had to admit to himself that he was, in fact, afraid of women.

One of the girls at work had a very special effect on him. Her name was Valerie. She was quite good-looking and had the sort of figure that Tom liked. The only drawback was that she was almost two inches taller than he was. But wasn't she a real beauty! Tom often caught a peep at her whenever he could. He didn't dare to address her, except when they had to deal with each other professionally. She didn't seem to take note of him. He had the impression that he was nobody to her, that he didn't even exist in her perception of the world around her.

So, it came as a surprise one evening after work when she accosted him in the corridor to the changing rooms.

"You're Tom, aren't you?" she demanded, standing in the middle of the passage, blocking his way.

"Y-yes, I'm Tom," he carefully answered. "Hello, Valerie!"

"Why do you keep watching me?"

"I'm not watching you."

"Yes, you are. I've seen you on several occasions."

"Oh, that?"

She looked him up and down. The fact that she was taller than he was meant that her large breasts, which Tom was very conscious of, stood even closer to his eyes. He had the impression that they were right in front of his eyes. He couldn't escape them and he felt a slight feeling of panic creeping up on him.

"Are you fancying sex with me then?" she asked, looking down from her height right into his eyes.

"I don't know," he stammered.

"You don't know?" she shouted. "What a pussy of a man are you, then?"

"I'm sorry! But yes, of course, I'd like to have sex with you," he said and regretted it at the same time. He was afraid of her, her size, her hard voice, and her general brashness.

What an impudent woman! What a brazen question of hers and what a weak answer of his! He decided not to let her see his fears but took all his courage to repeat his willingness. She only nodded.

"Let's meet outside after we get changed," she suggested.

"Okay," he only managed to reply.

While he was changing from his work-clothes into his everyday outfit, he felt his heart pounding. Valerie really meant business! Would he have to be her slave? Would he be able to perform? He felt his knees wobbling. His mind was divided between his desire to have sex with her and his terrible fear of her, her boldness and impudence, and her as a strong woman.

He took longer than usual to change, because he really had to build up enough courage to face Valerie again. What a pity Oscar wasn't here. His work shift had ended at midday. So, he couldn't have any moral support from him.

Eventually, he left the changing room and walked through the door to the platform outside. Valerie was already waiting for him, leaning against the wall and smoking a cigarette.

He didn't know what to do. So, she took the initiative and put her arm across his shoulders, gently pushing him to the carpark. It was a mild evening and they were both clothed in their summer things. While they were walking along together, he realised she was not wearing a bra, as he could see her breasts dangling a little with the rhythm of their steps. This aroused him tremendously and it gave him enough confidence to face what was coming.

*   *   *

Tom was sitting in his easy chair in his small flat, reviewing his situation. He wasn't happy with what had happened in the past few weeks. True, he'd had sex with Valerie, always in her flat, but he had to admit to himself that it hadn't been very satisfying for him. Valerie was so overwhelming in every sense that he felt crushed by her. He felt that their relationship had become a burden for him. He wanted to dump her. But she would never allow that. He had really become her slave and she obviously wanted to keep him.

He suddenly remembered the forest hut that he had discovered several months earlier. Would it still be there? He wondered if she'd agree to go there with him. He could explain to her that they might have even wilder sex there, hidden away from the world.

When he suggested such a thing to her, she was doubtful. "Perhaps," she only answered.

He decided to go and check the ground again before taking her to the forest. So, on one of his free days, he drove to the forest with the wooden hut. He parked his car and pushed through the thick undergrowth.

Suddenly he heard noises. He realised there had to be some people in the hut. He proceeded with care, avoiding any noises. That was quite difficult with all the bushes and leaves around him, but he managed to reach the back of the shack without detection. There were probably two people inside because Tom registered two voices, a man's and a woman's.

He tried very hard not to produce any noises, no rustling or cracking of twigs on the ground. He even kept his breathing very low. He didn't want to be detected while creeping up to the wall of the hut.

When he was close enough to place his right ear against the wall, he heard that it was a man and a woman who were talking inside. She was obviously telling him off.

"You poor womaniser," she said. "Can't you even keep your hands off young girls? I saw you with that Sandy girl. She seems to have a crush on you and you seem to have taken a fancy to her."

"That's not true, that's unfair!" he replied in an angry voice. "I only helped her with her French grammar and she likes my teaching style."

"Well, be careful she won't misinterpret your efforts. Or even better, just let her do her own schoolwork and you just keep away from her. Is that agreed, then?"

"Yes, my dear. I'm sorry if I gave you the wrong impression. Can you forgive me? For me, it's only you."

Then it was quiet for some time. Tom thought he heard some soft swishing noises. Were they kissing? Were they cuddling on the mattress? He looked around, hoping to find a crack between the wooden planks or some other small hole that might allow him to peep inside. At the same time, he felt ashamed. He realised there was nothing more shameful than playing peeping Tom on an innocent couple. The expression made him laugh. At least he had the right name for it.

He found a small crack that allowed him to look inside. He could see the two of them on the mattress. There was a candle burning near the gas stove. They were kissing and cuddling. The man was trying to take her dress off, but the woman gently stopped him. "Not today," she said.

The man was obviously disappointed but he complied. Tom watched for a few minutes longer until he realised there wasn't much more to be seen. Also, his shame came over him, so he took his face away from the wooden wall and carefully crept away from the scene. Soon he was back in his car and drove home.

Over the following days, he tried to forget his excursion to that forest hut and his eavesdropping on that couple. But it kept coming back, pushing into his consciousness. He often wondered what the couple had been arguing about. What about that Sandy girl? He was at a loss as to the exact nature of the conversation he'd overheard.

He concentrated on his work and he had occasional chats with Oscar. But he tried to avoid Valerie because she had definitely become a burden for him. He couldn't keep his misgivings from her. She told him off for not paying her enough respect and one day she asked him point-blank, "Are you still interested in me? Or do you want to pick up another girl?"

His answer was evasive. He tried to get away with a compromise, having his cake and eating it, which meant having occasional sex with her but at the same time not having any more to do with her than necessary. But this proved to be an illusion.

She told him either he was her proper boyfriend and they were going steady, or it was all over. If his heart wasn't in it, she wouldn't have him any longer. It was for him to choose.

Tom had to sleep on it, but on the next day he told her it was all over. They were no longer an item. She took it with equanimity and when he got home that night, he felt truly relieved.

He didn't have any more girls on his mind and he tried to exclude all thoughts of sexual activity from his dreams, plans, and activities. He remembered his old passion for chess and contacted Steve in Scotland, who was willing enough to take up their old routine of playing chess together.

Tom was occupied enough to help him over the following few weeks. But one night, the old urge raised its head again. He dreamt of enjoying his peeping Tom role and he thought he'd been a stupid idiot to give up that fine vantage point in the forest. What a fool he had been! Why couldn't he enjoy a bit of fun like that?

He drove to the forest again as soon as he could. He found the old hut again, but it was unoccupied. He decided to come back every day after work until he'd find the same couple again.

However, it was not the couple that he'd found there when he returned one late afternoon. It was the same man, but the woman was a different person. She was a teenage girl. The man had obviously installed extra lighting from a series of torches and he was busy taking pictures of the young girl, who – Tom had to admit – was extremely good-looking. He couldn't understand every detail of their conversation, but it was apparently about modelling and a photo shoot. He suddenly found that there was a third person in the hut, another young girl, but she was sitting on a stool in a corner so that Tom couldn't really see her. He only heard her voice.

After a few more pictures – obviously, they had been busy taking pictures for quite some time before Tom's arrival – the man suggested she should remove her

T-shirt. The girl smiled and began to take it off. But the other girl in the corner began to protest.

"Are you mad?" she shouted. "He's our teacher. This is wrong!"

"Oh, come on," the girl without her top now reassured her friend. "It's a good start for our modelling career. Don't be so prudish!"

But the other girl stood up and became visible in Tom's field of vision. She was furious. The two girls started to argue, while the first one continued taking off her clothes, all the while being photographed by the man. But suddenly, Tom heard a swishing noise from the other side of the hut. Before he could think what it could be, the door was torn open and a third woman was standing in the doorframe. She was the woman Tom had seen in the hut with the man before. She was older than the two girls, more the man's age. She was furious, too.

"So, this is what you've been up to all this time?!" she shouted at the man. "You child molester! You criminal! You're taking advantage of young girls! These girls should be protected by you. You're their teacher!" She was absolutely livid with anger. There was no stopping her.

She began to hit the man and the half-undressed girl, at first with her fists, then with a wooden stick and finally with one of the saucepans. At one point, the man had enough and started to fight back and the girls were caught up in the general mess. It was awful.

Tom wondered what to do while the whole drama was going on in the hut. He carefully walked around the hut to get a better view of the ensuing fight. Just as he was approaching the doorframe, he felt a tickle in his nostrils and he had to sneeze with a loud noise.

He desperately hoped that the shouting noises from the inside would cover up his sneezing explosion. But he was wrong.

Suddenly, they were silent for a few seconds, wondering what that noise was at the door.

They opened the door and looked out. All eyes were on Tom. He panicked. Then he was attacked and the whole fight became even more complicated.

Who was fighting whom? That was the question now.

EIGHTEEN

Tom woke up with a terrible headache. He was lying on the sofa in his small lounge. His mind was befuddled and he found it hard to concentrate. What had happened?

When he stood up from the sofa, he nearly fell back because everything in his body ached and everything in his mind was chaotic. He wondered if he'd had too much to drink the previous evening.

Then he saw the man sitting in the armchair opposite. He was observing Tom.

Gradually, his mind began to clear and bit by bit, everything came back to him. Slowly he remembered the events of last night.

He had driven home with a splitting headache. It had been hard to keep awake and he knew it was dangerous to drive in his state.

Where had he come from? Oh yes, the hut in that forest! There had been a terrible fight. There were several people involved.

There had been the young woman or girl who dropped on the forest floor and remained in what looked like a state of unconsciousness. She had been hit hard by someone with a skillet or a saucepan.

Another young girl was also hit on the head, but instead of dropping unconscious, she seemed to be in a sort of trance. She swayed and just walked off into the depth of the forest. Tom had lost sight of her. After all, it was almost pitch dark in that forest in the evening.

The worst fight had happened between the man who was now sitting in his lounge and the oldest of the three women. Yes, it was the woman who had appeared at the hut in a great rage and accused the man of molesting the young girls.

Tom couldn't remember every detail, but he did remember the fact that the woman fought both him and the man, whose name – he gathered – was Andrew. She'd got hold of a skillet and was trying to hit at them. Tom assumed that she must have thought he was part of the whole set-up, also involved in sleazy dealings with the girls, and she was obviously furious at the man.

And then, suddenly, the woman was lying on the forest floor, too. Tom could see she was in a bad way.

Andrew, still breathing hard from exhaustion, bent down and checked on her. He took her pulse and looked at her head injuries. Then he stood up.

"She is dead," he'd said.

Things happened very fast after that. Andrew told him they were both responsible and if they didn't want to be arrested for murder, they'd better be careful.

They sat down on the ground and began to plan their actions. After some arguing, Andrew told him to go home, but he warned him.

"I'll follow you in my car," he'd said, "so I know where you live. We'll both clean up, then we'll go to the B&Q store in St. Leonards to buy some pickaxes and shovels. Then we'll go back to the forest and we'll dig a grave for Christine."

So, that was the woman's name, Tom thought, before he was willing to agree to Andrew's plan.

And now they were here in his flat in Brighton. Tom almost panicked when he remembered the events of last night, particularly his own involvement, his own guilt. Was he a murderer? It wasn't quite clear who had dealt the fatal blow. Was she killed by a saucepan or by a wooden stick? Tom couldn't see clearly. It had been such a muddle and it had been so dark.

Once he was fully awake, he heard Andrew stand up. Tom looked up into his face, hoping to hear from him that it had all been his own fault. Tom wasn't to blame.

"Listen," he said in a quiet, controlled voice. "What's your name?"

"Tom," he slowly replied. "Tom Mitchell."

"Okay, Tom. My name's Andrew, Andrew Sullivan. We may as well get to know each other now that we're both wanted for murder."

Tom swallowed hard.

"Okay then," Andrew continued, "we're going to get those pickaxes and shovels and we'll drive back to Bedgebury Forest. I think my plan is pretty safe if you do what I tell you. We can't afford to make any mistakes. That forest is hardly ever visited by any living human being and the hut is so well-hidden that it can't be found easily. If we bury her right in the thick of it under lots of brush and brambles, her body won't be found. She'll rot there forever."

"Are you sure?"

"Yes, absolutely positive. I've used that hut for quite some time, several years, in fact. And I've never ever seen a living soul near it. There's no footpath through the forest and the undergrowth is too dense."

"What did you do there all those years, as you say?"

Andrew hesitated before he answered, "I usually took young girls to that hut. I took pictures of them. They all loved it, I can tell you."

Tom doubted this. The man was just showing off. Why would a young girl agree to go to that hut with him to take pictures? He could see that Andrew was very fond of himself. He probably believed himself to be irresistible.

"How did you trick them into following you there?"

"No trick. Just my charming personality. You are still very inexperienced, Tom, aren't you?"

Tom thought perhaps the man was right. He could never imagine doing anything like that. In a way, he began to admire Andrew for his dealings with girls; on the other hand, he was a bit disgusted at his callousness. But then he remembered his own cold-bloodedness over Karen. He was different in degree, but not in kind. They were a truly well-matched pair of criminals.

"Do you want us to leave soon?" he asked.

"Yes, if possible. Digging that grave will keep us busy for most of the day. But we might have a cup of coffee first. Have you got any?"

The two criminals spent the next half hour making coffee and enjoying it with a bite from the old loaf of bread that Tom sill had in the flat. Then they set out on their special mission.

They travelled in Andrew's Range Rover. They had no problems getting the tools they required and eventually returned to the crime scene. Christine's dead body was still where they'd left it in the night. Andrew entered the hut. He said he wanted to remove everything that could incriminate them in any way. He came out with a wooden box full of stuff: articles of clothing, photographic equipment, torches, and some personal items. He said he'd also wiped the saucepans and the skillet clean to remove any fingerprints.

Meanwhile, Tom had started to clear the ground around some brambles where they had marked the grave to be dug with some sticks. It was a good thing they'd thought to bring two pairs of thick garden gloves or they would hurt their hands very badly with the brambles. When they started to dig the grave itself, Tom checked his watch and saw that it was half past eleven. He thought they'd better hurry up if they wanted to complete the grave before the end of the day.

The job was extremely difficult. Not only was the ground quite hard, but there were also other difficulties. The forest floor was full of tree roots and it was not so easy to keep the prickly brambles out of the way. It would have made things a lot easier if they had cut away all those branches and brambles, but they knew they couldn't do that because it would have affected the density of the undergrowth, which was an important asset of their hiding place for the body.

So, they had to toil on in the midst of all that prickly and stingy environment. While they were digging, they got scratched along their arms and backs despite their thick gloves. From time to time, Tom let out a heavy swearword and Andrew's oaths weren't any less vulgar although they were in French.

"I say," Andrew breathed between two heavy shovelfuls, "I read that dead bodies are normally buried six feet under the ground. If we keep digging like this, it'll take us more than a few hours."

"That's bullshit! We're certainly not going to dig so deep. I reckon one or two feet ought to be enough."

"Well, let's not argue. Let's save our breath for the job at hand."

They continued with their hard work. Shovelful after shovelful was thrown on a spot between the hut and their projected grave. It was growing into a small mound of earth and roots. But it was growing slowly, very slowly.

When it grew dark, they stopped. They agreed that it wouldn't be a good idea to light a torch. They didn't want to be found out, both of them being conscious of the fact that they could both be accused of murder. So, they gave up and called it a day.

They drove back to Tom's flat in Brighton, where they had a few cans of beer and a sandwich concocted with leftovers from Tom's fridge. After that, they were so exhausted that they settled for the night right away, fully clothed, Tom on his bedcover and Andrew on the lounge sofa. They tried to keep up a light conversation; however, not only their exhaustion but also their guilty feelings prevented that.

One would have expected them to fall into a troubled sleep, but, in fact, they were so worn out from their heavy work that they dropped off into a deep sleep. Andrew could already hear Tom snoring through the open bedroom door while he was still trying to make a contribution to their fragmentary chat, so he dropped off, too.

In the morning, they made an early start. On the way, travelling in two cars, they stopped at a service station near Eastbourne where they had a cup of coffee and a sandwich. Having parked Andrew's car next to Tom's, they examined the surroundings for any stray joggers or people going for an early morning walk in the country. They couldn't detect anyone. So, the air was clear and they could slip into the forest without being seen.

They found the burying site as they had left it. Wordlessly, they began to hack and shovel again. In the early morning, the earth seemed harder than on the day before, but they knew that was only an illusion. They only imagined things because they found their job such an irking task. They were so reluctant to continue with the grave-digging.

Tom's main concern was that he didn't want to be detected and arrested for murder, so he wanted the body out of the way as quickly as possible. He would have been satisfied with a grave only two feet deep.

Andrew, on the other hand, found it difficult to bury his former girlfriend. He wondered if he'd be able to cover her body with shovelfuls of earth once the grave was deep enough. After all, he had loved her in a way. He had desired her. How could he do this to her now?

The body lay on the ground near the hut covered in flies and beginning to smell.

It turned out to be quite a sunny day. Though it was a cool autumn day in the morning, the temperature rose quite high in the afternoon. The two diggers were covered in sweat by the time they completed the grave to Andrew's satisfaction. It was not quite six feet deep, but still quite a good depth. About two feet, perhaps? They both agreed it was deep enough. The body couldn't be found once it was buried in this grave.

The time was five in the afternoon when they lifted the body from the ground. It seemed a lot heavier than they had expected.

Tom asked if they shouldn't search the body. In her pockets, she might have things that could incriminate them, at least Andrew. But Andrew refused to do that. He said he couldn't do it because it would constitute a sacrilege to invade her privacy.

"You think that?" Tom asked. "And what does killing her constitute?"

"Oh, come on, man! You can search her if you like, but I won't."

"No, she was your girlfriend, wasn't she?"

They argued for a few minutes. In the end, Andrew bent down and went through her pockets. Apart from a used handkerchief, he only found a small purse with a few pounds and twenty pence. But there was also a small slip of paper with a phone number written in her neat handwriting. It was Andrew's private number. He took both items and stuffed them in his own pockets.

"That's all," he confirmed.

Then they lifted the body again and carried it over the top of the grave.

"How do we lower her into the grave?" Tom asked.

"I'm afraid we haven't got any ropes. We can only drop her."

This was what they did. The impact of the body at the bottom of the grave made a dry thumping noise. It sounded like dumping a rolled-up carpet on an attic floor. The body came to lie in a somewhat twisted position, a position which wouldn't be comfortable for a living person. They both had the same thought. Tom uttered it.

"She can't feel a thing. Let's leave her like this."

As Andrew grabbed the shovel, Tom stopped him. "Shouldn't we say a prayer or something? I mean, we can't just leave her without some decent words, can we?"

"Okay, you say what you would like to say."

"No, you're the educated one here and you were her friend."

In the end, it was Andrew who said a few things. He quoted a phrase from the Bible that he could remember, then added something in French. They were both standing by the grave with their hands folded in prayer.

After a pause, Tom asked, "What was that in a foreign language?"

"It was French, something from Marcel Proust."

"I hope it wasn't anything filthy. One never knows with the French."

Andrew was going to protest, but he decided to shut his mouth.

They began to cover the body with earth taken from the mound they had heaped up when they'd dug the grave. This was another bit of hard labour, but it was easier than digging. After two hours, they had covered the whole grave. They made sure there were enough leaves and branches on top of the earth. The entire ground had to look the same as the ground in the whole area. The forest floor had to be as thickly covered in undergrowth as they had found it. It had to be in such a state that nobody would ever attempt to scramble through the dense jungle created by the brambles and branches. It had to be a forbidding, impenetrable thicket.

When they were satisfied with the job completed, they didn't know what to do next. They had the feeling that their job was not finished. They hesitated.

Finally, Tom said, "Let's go home. There's nothing left to do."

"Yes," Andrew agreed, "but before we part, let us promise never to contact each other. We must not know each other. We could both be accused of murder, so we'd better stay apart. We have never met and we don't even know of each other's existence. This is very important."

"You are right. Of course, you're right. But what will happen once she's been missed by her people?"

"Nothing. Nothing whatsoever that could incriminate us. I may be questioned because some people might have seen me with her at our school, but I'll simply say I don't know where she might have gone. And you have nothing to fear because nobody knows of any connection between you and her. We'll be quite safe."

Once they were both satisfied that they would be safe, they left the crime scene. Andrew stowed the tools in his car, promising to dump them somewhere and Tom walked to his car. Then they both drove away in different directions.

They never saw each other again.

*　　*　　*

Tom did not fancy going straight home. He drove into Hastings and parked his car near the seafront. He had to cool his head after such an emotional and physical stress over the past two days. It was a pleasant autumn evening, ideal for a stroll along the beach.

Suddenly, he saw a group of young women walking in the opposite direction, one of whom turned out to be Karen, the girl he least of all wanted to meet. He looked out towards the blue horizon, hoping she wouldn't recognise him.

"Hey there!" came her angry voice. "Aren't you Tom? Tom the criminal?"

Of course, she had recognised him immediately. She stopped in her track while her friends kept on walking.

Tom turned round and stared at her. At first, he didn't know what to say, but then he managed to utter a weak, "Sorry," which sounded absolutely ridiculous, out of context, there on the beach in Hastings.

"Is that all you've got to say?" she asked. She stood there on the pebble beach, her legs apart and her arms akimbo. She looked threatening.

"Look here, Karen," he tried to reason with her. "We were both drunk and I just got carried away."

"You know I could get you arrested for rape, don't you? What do you have to say to that, I wonder?"

His mind was racing through his possibilities. Under the impression of the events of the past two days, he felt a real criminal and he panicked. His heart was racing like mad and his mind was so confused, that all he could do was stand there and stare at her with big eyes. Tears were gushing into his eyes. He made himself believe it was the light breeze on the beach, but he knew it was his shame and horror about himself, his rotten character and his wasted life.

Karen waited for him to say something and when nothing came from him, she just spat on the ground and ran off, catching up with her friends.

Tom looked after her. Despite his awful condition, he found himself admire her figure. After all, she was such a gorgeous-looking woman. Hardly had he conceived this notion when he checked himself. He told himself he had to forget such ideas. Women were just not for him. Every time he found he admired a woman's beauty, things went wrong. He obviously couldn't be trusted with women. Their presence made him go mad. He was in danger of losing his grip on reality, his grip on life, whenever he came close to a woman, whenever he found a woman attractive.

He walked on. After a while, he revised his former insight. It could only be the way he saw women, he thought. The way he saw them at close quarters was too full of erotic desire. He would have to learn to see women as mere human beings, as friendly companions, before he allowed himself to see them as sexual objects. That would be his task for the future. He resolved not to approach another woman again until he'd be ready to recognise them as sexless human beings.

That would not be easy, he was sure. But it could be done if he concentrated on all the other things in his life first, such as his work and his games of chess.

With this in mind, he walked back to his car and drove home to Brighton.

He spent a troubled night. He dreamed he was killing the woman in the forest again – Christine her name was? – killing her while wanting to have sex with her. While he was dreaming this, he knew at the same time that he would have to go to prison. Then his dream switched to a prison cell, the kind of prison cell that he imagined. It was narrow and dark and there were vulgar drawings on the wall. He was hungry and thirsty and he could hear other prisoners crying and swearing. It was awfully cold and he felt ever so lonely. He began to cry, too. Then he thought of his mother.

He woke up drenched in sweat.

*　　*　　*

It was September 2001. Tom was sitting over a pint of lager in a Brighton pub. Looking into the glass on the small table in front of him, he was getting a bit moody. Melancholy was gradually taking hold of him.

Looking back over his life so far, he found that he was a lot more mature now. He was confident he could never do to a girl what he'd done in his younger days. He had been a cruel teenager, an irresponsible youngster. Ever since that affair in the forest, he had never allowed himself to enter into a close relationship with a woman. Yes, he'd had a few erotic encounters, but only when he was absolutely certain that the woman concerned also wanted it. This was not so often, but still, he'd had a few pleasurable encounters.

How could a man ever let himself be tied down by one woman? They called it love. What was love? The only way to be attracted by a woman, in his experience, was sex. He sometimes wondered when he saw a film with a couple falling in love. How did they really feel? Was it only put on? Of course, it would be with the actors, but what about such situations in real life? How does one fall in love? From films, he gathered it had to be something that really touched you, something that ran deep. And what about older couples? Why did they stick together, pretending they still loved each other, even though they'd lost their physical attractions? It was an enigma for Tom. He didn't even know if he wanted to experience such love. Obviously, it was not for him.

He took another sip from his pint. The beer, as always, made him even more moody. He looked round the pub, observing some of the other patrons. They seemed so carefree. Most probably, he thought, they had never murdered anyone.

Then it hit him suddenly. This new digital age could be his undoing. Everything was changing. Photography was becoming digital, typewriters were being replaced by computers, telephones were now mostly portable... everything was different now and had become more threatening. Nobody knew what all those new technologies would do to us. How would they make our lives different? And how would the new technologies help forensic research? Would they find the body in the forest more easily now? Would they find out it had been him?

He felt his heart beating faster. Then he calmed himself, telling himself there was no need to be alarmed. They hadn't found the body over many years, so why should they suddenly find it now?

But there again, they had new methods these days, all these digital methods. He'd seen on TV how they found people and animals by flying over the countryside with special cameras that showed everything in a green light and any bodies would stand out in white shapes. Or were these only the living bodies? Was it their temperature? He did not know. His education had never included science or physics.

Then there was the question of the condition of the body. How much was left of the woman? Could she still be recognised? Or was she just a skeleton? Even then, they say, modern forensics could identify a body. He would never be safe.

Looking up from his drink, he saw a man who slightly resembled that chap Andrew, the other murderer. It might just be because of his moody thoughts, his shyness. But there he was, that man with the narrow face and the thin hair, standing at the bar just about to take a sip of ale. Of course, Tom knew it couldn't be him, but he had to admit he really looked like Andrew, or as he remembered Andrew. He had never heard from him again and he had never tried to contact him. After all, he had no address. The man had said he was going abroad. So there was no way of finding him. And what for, anyway? No need to stir up things!

However, he had his moments when he longed for a chat with Andrew. He wanted to exchange their experiences. How was *he* coping with his role as a murderer? Did he have the same remorse, the same pangs of conscience? If he was at all human, he had to have similar moments. Or was it even more dangerous? Did Andrew still believe that they'd killed the woman together? Or had he changed his mind? If they caught him now, after all those years, would he accuse him alone, trying to extricate himself?

He suddenly remembered a phrase he'd read somewhere and had also heard from a character in a difficult situation in a film. It was like the Sword of Damocles. He didn't really understand it and he had no idea who this Damocles chap might have been, but he had this feeling that it would suit his present predicament. Andrew had him in his hands. He never knew when the man was going to betray him. This sounded like the Sword of Damocles to him.

But then, what about the other way round? He could equally accuse Andrew of having committed the murder alone, couldn't he? But for that, he would have to know his address.

Andrew knew his former address only. Tom had moved twice since then. He still lived in Brighton, but in a different flat. And he no longer worked for Tesco's but for a different supermarket chain, Waitrose in Eastbourne.

Once he'd drained his glass, he left the pub. The fresh air cleared his mind. All of a sudden, all his fears and misgivings were blown away. He felt a lot better now.

Strolling down to the seafront, his mind returned to the question of women. Trying to come to a conclusion about his dealings with women, he decided to find a new level, to discover a new way of understanding women. He believed that, if he let himself in for this, he might even discover what they called true love.

NINETEEN

As the first two decades of the 21st century were rolling by, Tom Mitchell was becoming more civilised. Year after year, he took courses, he learnt new skills and he read a great deal. His employers supported him in his further development and he even enrolled for courses with the Open University. He learned a lot about information and communication technologies and he found he had a real interest in history. He was also climbing the social ladder. By 2015, he was a manager of a regional distributor of high-class commodities.

His interest in history, along with his general education which taught him a great deal about political systems, human rights and democracy eventually led to a better understanding of what was going on in the world. He also learned to express himself, even using big words sometimes, though he never learned another language. English was good enough for him. All that filled him with greater self-respect. And that, in turn, led to a more confident demeanor. His shyness was a thing of the past and when he was in the company of others now, they registered his more marked presence. He was someone now. His word was listened to and he saw in other people's faces that they treated him with respect.

There was only one sore spot in his life... women! Although he had learned to deal with them without being tongue-tied or otherwise incapacitated by a woman's presence or even a woman's apparent interest in him, he still couldn't understand them. They still appeared to him like some alien race. And most of all, he didn't know what to do with his sexuality.

Whenever he felt aroused by a woman's charms, he lost his sense of direction. These days this no longer meant that he couldn't talk to them in a coherent way – as had been the case in his younger years – but he still felt handicapped, at a disadvantage. One of his problems was that whenever he was involved in a conversation with a woman he felt attracted to, he imagined how she must see him. He always wondered if she wanted to have sex with him and if she was waiting for him to make the first move for them to become lovers. How did she see him? That was the big question.

Then there was the problem of love. He still hadn't experienced anything approaching a fulfilling love for a woman. He couldn't imagine how a man could lose himself, lose his sense of reality, over his relationship with a woman. He admitted to himself that it had always been very pleasurable when he had intimate dealings with a woman, but it had never affected his emotions in any significant way. A sexual encounter with a woman – in his case, mostly in the form of a one-night-stand – never produced an emotion like love in him, never made him yearn for her after that one encounter.

Was he at all normal? he wondered. In any case, he knew he was much better in control of his actions than most men. He could never be persuaded to do anything he might regret later. Well, almost. There was still that nauseating feeling whenever he remembered his part in that murder all those years ago.

Tom was not interested in politics, but one day, when he saw that red bus with the caption "£350 million a week", suggesting that Britain was paying all that money to the EU administration in Brussels, he knew that things were going wrong for his country. He could see with his own eyes how much Britain was profiting from

305

the European Union. He could see how many people from Poland or other Eastern European countries were in the jobs that British people considered beneath themselves as bus drivers, delivery men, hairdressers, waitresses and other jobs in the service industry.

He had also heard on the radio many times how wonderful it was for young people to move freely throughout Europe and get jobs wherever they wished. And he had even read how much Britain could profit from its membership in European institutions. Furthermore, he had read in the paper that the EU was Britain's most important trade partner, most imports came from there and most exports went there.

One day an Irish colleague had been in the pub with him telling him how grateful everyone in Northern Ireland was that both Britain and Ireland were in the EU together. How important that was for peace in the region. Because of their common membership in the EU, they were all confident that the Troubles were a thing of the past.

And now, those populist liars were trying to get people to vote for an exit from the EU? They called it Brexit. It was only blind nationalism. So far, Tom's schooling was enough to understand that it was a cheap ploy of some selfish politicians to capitalise from the common sport of Brussels-bashing. They even forgot the British government was part of the Brussels administration. Britain was the third most powerful nation within the EU. Why cut off your own influence and opportunities, throwing your own power and wealth out of the window? It was like a man trying to cut off his own hand because he was told it was of no use.

Many months later, when the vote actually was cast in favour of Brexit, Tom and his colleagues could not understand their own people. The decision, if it could ever be implemented at all, would mean an economic depression for the country. It would aggravate so many problems. There would be insurmountable problems in Northern Ireland and ever so many problems in international trade.

Exports and imports would be affected in dimensions never experienced before. The British economy was bound to suffer. So many businesses would be killed, so many opportunities for Britain's population and so many positive effects of the EU membership would be discontinued and even everyday life would be affected in unprecedented ways. And all that because of those selfish liars, those rat-catchers misleading their people? It was so sad that the young generation mostly abstained from the vote, confident that the British public would never vote for such a nationalist stupidity.

The disaster announced itself soon after the vote, even before the rupture with the EU was complete. Road transports between Britain and the EU became more difficult because of the waiting times for customs at ferry ports and the Channel Tunnel, which meant road congestions between Dover, Folkestone and Ashford. New huge carparks for heavy goods vehicles were built in the area, which were filled up quickly. The entire area suffered from the traffic chaos. Then, shelves in supermarkets began to show empty spaces because the goods could not be delivered in time or in the required quantity.

Next, lots of EU citizens employed in Britain were dismissed and left the country. Shortages began to become apparent in many branches, most severely in the health care sector. Only a few years after Brexit, the NHS practically collapsed. The entire British economy dropped into a deep recession. Opinion polls and statistical surveys

307

showed how more than half the population of Great Britain would wish to be back in the EU again, even more so in Scotland. In addition to the whole disaster, there was the unsolved problem of the border between Ulster and the Irish Republic. It was now an outside border of the EU. This stirred up old animosities and none of the following British Prime Ministers managed to solve the problem to everyone's satisfaction.

In any case, the following Prime Ministers were very questionable politicians. They were so fixed on Brexit that they couldn't see how they were deceiving their people. This was partly because they were not elected in a democratic process but chosen by a handful of Tories. The people had no say in this.

That was what Tom could clearly see. Because he had only recently acquired his knowledge and understanding of history and politics, he often wondered if he was wrong in his assessment. But then he told himself he only had to read the papers or to watch the news on TV and it all became clear.

In discussions with some other people who could see the same dangers, he learned that it was probably just a national or regional representation of a big international phenomenon. The time elapsed since the Second World War had become too long for people to remember where rabid nationalism could lead. They had forgotten what a wonderful asset a peaceful democratic system was for the people of a country.

All over the world, new nationalist politicians with seemingly simple answers for complex problems were hijacking people's opinions and winning more and more elections before distorting their own democratic systems, for example, in countries like Hungary and Poland, even in the United States.

Then there were the new dictators who just killed off any democratic elements in their countries, step by step, until it was too late for their people to realise what had happened and to set up any form of opposition, such as in Russia and in China. Not to speak of the permanent dictatorships in several Arab countries or the religious fanatics in Iran and Afghanistan. Tom was very sad when he looked at the world of today.

*   *   *

Tom's life evolved along simple grooves over the following years. The older he grew, the less he was troubled by the sins of his younger days, particularly that mishap in the forest. He became more self-confident and with time, he made his peace with the way his life had developed. He became convinced of the fact that he had really shaped his life very well. He attributed all the good things that happened to him to his own ingenuity.

When he happened to browse through a paper one day, not really believing in what he could read there, he discovered a small paragraph about a dead body found in a forest near Hastings. His heart missed a beat and he nearly lost his balance. Could this be the body that he'd helped to bury all those years ago? He was impatient to read more about it in the paper over the next few days.

When, a few weeks after that first article, a longer piece about the case appeared in the paper, he was surprised that modern forensic methods could still identify the dead body even though it had to be reduced to its bones after all those years. It said that it was identified as the body of a woman called Christine Mitford, who had gone missing in the early nineties. Also, it was discovered that the woman had been murdered and now the police were looking for her murderer.

While he was extremely agitated with something like a panic attack, he managed to calm down after the initial shock. He told himself that there was no connection between the murder and himself. The other chap – what was his name? Andrew? – had never been in touch with him again. Didn't he say he was planning to emigrate? So it was clear that the police had nothing to go by, nothing that could lead to Tom or the other chap. They were quite safe.

Still…

He wondered if he ought to do something that would give him even more distance between himself and the events in that forest. He tried to summon all the facts in his memory. Was there any witness? No. Were there any other persons who might have suspected him at the time? No. Had they left any evidence that might betray them? No.

But what about the girls he had met at the time? Did he give one of them any reason to hate him and to point at him when questioned by the police? Of course not. And why would the police question one of his girlfriends of that time? Then there was the question of the location. Who knew of the existence of that hut in Bedgebury Forest? That was the name of the forest, according to the news bulletins. At least Tom knew the name of the location of his crime now.

He decided to lie low. He only had to be careful not to draw anyone's attention to himself in connection with the Bedgebury Forest Murder Case, as it was called in the media now. For example, when people in the pub happened to gossip about the case, he would have to be extra careful not to say too much or too little about the topic. If he said too much, the others might ask him why he had this special interest in the case and if he said too little, they might ask him why he was so silent. Wasn't he interested or did he have something to hide? This meant that he had to make sure he would never drink too much. He had to stay in full control. Didn't they say that liars needed an excellent memory? The same probably applied to murderers.

One thing was really hard to digest for him. It was his view of himself. Over the years, he had built up all this self-respect, seeing himself as an honest and hard-working citizen, a decent man with a lot of qualities. This image had now been undermined by the news. His self-esteem suffered quite a bit when he stood in front of the mirror in his bedroom and looked at himself with the label around his neck that read *murderer*.

Tom's life became more secretive. He became some sort of a recluse. He didn't go to the pub as often as he used to and he avoided women. He knew it was too dangerous. Once he would get involved with a woman, especially when he was losing his mind in the ecstasy of sex, he might spill too much of his secret.

Like this, he struggled through the following months until the Covid pandemic took hold of the country. When the lockdowns came, he was glad to stay at home and he was convinced that police investigations would also be a lot more difficult in times of such a general limitation to all activities. So, in a way, the pandemic was a blessing and the lockdowns were a relief for him.

He wondered if things might become more dangerous for him again after the whole pandemic was over. He had good hopes.

*   *   *

By the beginning of the year 2023, Tom and his pub acquaintances agreed that things had turned out exactly as they had feared and predicted when the country was abducted into what was still called Brexit. They all knew that there had been a referendum, but the voters had been informed in such a one-sided way that the referendum itself was not really a democratic step. The government ought to have informed the people in a neutral way about the pros and cons of both outcomes. By now, nearly half the British population lived below the poverty line and wished Brexit had never come. But it was too late.

Of course, Tom had to admit, there had been the Covid pandemic with its lockdowns and more recently, one of the worst dictators in the world had attacked an Eastern European country. The Russian dictator was trying to save his neck within his own system of corruption and political oppression by trying to turn the wheel of history backwards, trying to re-establish the old colonial empire of the Soviet Union. He had terribly miscalculated his chances. Believing he could eradicate Ukraine within a few weeks and thereby frighten the whole of Western Europe into disharmony, discord and division, he had achieved the exact opposite. Europe had never been so united as it was now in its support of Ukraine.

Despite a few spoilsports like Turkey or Hungary, the European nations were united in their common stance against the aggression of that megalomaniac from the Kremlin. But the economic problems caused by the Russian attack – directed less against military targets and more against the civilian population – affected the entire world. Even people in the poorest regions, such as East

Africa, were suffering from the lack of wheat exports from Ukraine.

So, on the whole, Tom was often falling into a depressive mood whenever he remembered the situation of the world today.

One day, he was looking forward to a good meal at a restaurant called Rules – apparently the oldest restaurant in London – with a woman he had met only three hours earlier. He was beginning to doubt why she had suggested a meal together. After all, he didn't know her very well yet. They had met in Trafalgar Square, waiting for the traffic lights to turn green for the pedestrians. She had stepped out into the street before the green light came on, nearly killing herself in the oncoming traffic, when Tom jumped forward and pulled her back to safety.

She was a bit puzzled but soon realised her mistake. She thanked him, inviting him for lunch. She had some business in a shop in Covent Garden, which she wanted to complete before lunch, so she suggested this restaurant after that. It was now half past one and Tom was still waiting, on the point of walking away, when she approached him on the pavement in Maiden Lane.

They said hello and entered the restaurant.

When they had settled down at a table, they looked at each other properly for the first time. Tom realised they hadn't even introduced themselves. "Sorry," he said, "my name is Tom, Tom Mitchell." And he stretched out his hand.

"Maggie, Maggie Webster," she answered, taking his hand.

They kept looking at each other for another few moments before she started to apologise. "I'm so sorry. I shouldn't have stepped out into the street like that."

"No big deal. It could happen to anyone. Don't worry. The main thing is you're not hurt."

"Yes, thanks to your heroic action. Thank you again."

"Okay, let's move on from there now. Do you want to suggest a topic for our conversation while we're waiting for the food?"

"Let me think. – Oh yes, why don't you tell me where you're from and what your business is in London? To make a start."

Tom cleared his throat and told her about Brighton, his job and his impressions of London. "I don't really like London. It's too crowded and too polluted for my taste."

"Oh, but Tom! London offers you anything you might wish for. The best shops, the best restaurants, the most interesting diversity of people, doesn't it?"

"Do you really think so?"

"Yes and it is also a very fashionable place. For a woman with style, I mean a woman with a certain social standing, it is an absolute must. I like to come here at least every three months to get away from the provincial atmosphere of where I come from. You have no idea how provincial eastern Kent can be!"

Tom began to suspect that Maggie might be a social climber like himself, with the only difference being that she had something else in mind. Her target was a fashionable social standing, while his aim was to make enough money to live and to find happiness in life. Hardly admitting this to himself, he was also hoping to find true love, but he was no longer so confident that he might find it one day.

While they were enjoying their starters, he told her he was still unbound and single, and she told him about her marriage to a teacher. They were so free to tell each other about their situations in life because there was no danger of feeling attracted to each other. They had just met by accident and now they were just having a good meal together.

Over their main course – they had both ordered roast beef with Yorkshire pudding and roast potatoes – they learned more details about each other. Tom told her about his hobby of chess and about his interest in politics and history. Maggie admitted that she had no idea of either history or politics. "I don't even know the names of the government ministers," she added.

Eventually, over their desserts, they came to talk about books and the joys of reading. He told her how late in life he'd come to literature. He'd come from a humble background, had been educated by the rules of the street, and had only developed into a decent human being when he was approaching his middle life. He revealed some of his favourite authors' names. Dickens, Thackeray and other great names.

"Don't you like any contemporary writers?" she asked.

"Oh yes, many of them. For example – "

"I can't compete with you," she cut in. "My favourites are very good authors, in my opinion, but my sister-in-law seems to look down on them and she is well-read. She would know those big names you just mentioned. So, I feel a bit embarrassed to mention my own favourites to you now."

"Oh, don't be embarrassed. There is no such thing as a wrong taste, neither in food nor in literature. Taste is something individual. We can't control it."

Having said this, he doubted if he really believed what he was saying. Was he just trying to console the woman?

They continued in silence. Soon, they were sitting over their coffees and Tom was wondering if he should call for the bill or if she really meant to invite him for having rescued her. Since she didn't seem to be aware of the approaching end of their tête-à-tête, he asked her if she cared to give him any names of her favourite authors.

"There's my absolute favourite. It's a female writer called Giulia Montepulciano. She has written more than a dozen novels and they are all so true to life, so gripping and so romantic, I can tell you…"

She stopped, breathing hard. "You wouldn't know her books, would you?"

"No, I'm afraid I don't." He didn't know what else to say to her. It would be intellectual arrogance to tell her what type of writer he expected this Montepulciano woman to be. He decided to look out for her books next time in a bookshop.

She called the waiter and ordered the bill. "It's my call. You saved my life and I pay."

He didn't protest. She paid by credit card and they stood up.

Outside on the pavement in Maiden Lane, they exchanged addresses and said goodbye to each other. "We never know. We might meet again," she added.

Then they walked off in different directions.

Strolling through the streets of this rather fashionable part of London always full of tourists, he went over their conversation in his mind. She was obviously someone who was struggling for recognition in life. Probably her husband – Robert, or what was his name? – couldn't give her what she needed. From what she explained, she was hoping to find access to higher circles or what she considered higher circles. In most cases, when she mentioned a name of one of her acquaintances, she

316

gave him some aristocratic-sounding name or at least a double-barrelled name. She called her friends "ladies", not "women" or "girls", as other women might do. Her dress style also suggested a more affluent background than her middle-class accent seemed to betray. Tom came to the conclusion that she was probably a social pretender, a snob.

After a while, he dismissed her from his thoughts and walked to the nearest tube station to catch a train to Victoria Station. He was looking forward to getting out of London and all that noise, looking forward to more peaceful Brighton.

TWENTY

Tom was going through a difficult phase in his life. These days, he spent most of his free time in the pub. For a while, he considered meeting his pals standing around the bar and exchanging their views about the world, politics and women as a very rewarding experience. He really and honestly believed they represented the best thing that had happened to him in his life. They were his saviours, his friends, whom he trusted a hundred per cent.

However, two aspects sometimes crept into his consciousness and threatened to destroy his peace of mind. Women and alcohol consumption. As time was dragging on through the year 2023, it happened more and more often that a woman or two joined the men at the bar, thereby disturbing their peace of mind. Tom had read somewhere that there had been an ancient mathematician and physicist living in Sicily who coined the phrase, "Don't disturb my circles!" He must have been referring to the mathematical constructions he'd been drawing in the sand. This phrase came to Tom's mind on several occasions when a woman brazenly joined the men with their pints in their hands. Usually, these women were holding either a gin-and-tonic or a coke-and-rum. And they had the cheek to contribute their own opinions on whatever the men had been discussing.

This behaviour on the part of the women did not agree with Tom's image of women in general. He considered himself a modern man, but he had his clear ideas as to what women were decently allowed to do. Couldn't they see that the social structures of such male groups were seriously damaged by women's interference?

The second problem creeping into Tom's well-being and threatening his peace of mind was the fact that he often drank too much alcohol. Yes, they only drank beer, which was hardly considered an alcoholic beverage, but when he had more than five pints in one evening, he felt the alcohol giving him a fuzzy mind and sometimes a certain imbalance when he was leaving the pub late at night. How awkward! The alcohol was supposed to make him happy and mellow, not to impede his mental or physical agility.

One evening in early May, they were all discussing the situation in Ukraine. The men agreed that it was a good thing that so many European governments were sending modern battle tanks to support Ukraine in its fight against the aggression of Putin's army of prisoners and slaves condemned to fight a war they had no interest in. Ukraine might eventually succeed in ousting the Russian aggressors from their country. The men were competing in their estimates about how long it would take Ukraine to win the war. Suddenly a woman entered their circle, saying, "I don't think it was a good idea to send battle tanks to Ukraine. This will only prolong the bloody war and cost many more lives."

Several men protested. "But without those tanks, they may not be able to defeat the Russians!"

"Have you ever considered," the woman, whose name appeared to be Chelsea, asked, "why the Russians invaded Ukraine in the first place?"

"Because they wanted to re-establish the Soviet Empire for pure power politics!" answered Tom.

"And NATO never provoked Russia in the past thirty years or so? You must have been blind not to see what a terrible provocation it was when NATO took all those Eastern European states into their treaty

319

organisation, countries like the Baltic states, Poland and others."

"The active part wasn't NATO. All these nations wanted to join because they needed some strategic protection from the aggressor in the Kremlin. NATO has never been set up as an aggressive organisation but as a defence alliance. Defensive strategies are its business."

Chelsea laughed. "How can you believe NATO, but not the Russian population, who have been afraid of another attack from the West ever since the end of the Second World War? Just go to any Russian town and ask the population."

"Of course," Tom explained, "that's what they would tell you because they have been exposed to Russian state propaganda that made sure that they could be governed by fear. The Kremlin fairy-tale that was repeated almost on a daily basis on State TV kept up the idea that Europe – especially Germany – was still governed by Nazis who were only waiting for an opportunity to invade Russia again. On the 9th of May, year after year, those fake stories have been publicly repeated in the context of those enormous military parades on the Red Square in Moscow for the past 78 years. It's no wonder the simple Russian citizen who has no access to critical media will believe the propaganda and honestly nurture this fear of the allegedly aggressive West."

"Oh, you believe everything our politicians are telling us?" she asked in a provocative singsong.

"No," said Tom, "not everything. But what I've just been explaining to you is not just a story invented by our politicians, but a historical fact. What you've just been saying is only a repetition of Putin's propaganda. I think we've got to be careful not to adopt the dictator's mad stories."

Like this, the controversy was evolving mainly between Tom and Chelsea. After they got quite heated for a while, they calmed down again when they both realised they couldn't change each other's opinions. They had to agree to disagree.

"Let's agree at least," Jack, one of the other men, suggested, "that however we see the political situation, war is always bad, whether you want to fight a war or whether you have to defend yourself in a war. In any case, there are always killings involved. And killing people is always a great sin, isn't it?"

"Aye, so it is," some others answered and raised their glasses.

"And in any case," Tom added, "we cannot allow a country to invade a peaceful neighbouring country in such a brutal way. Territorial expansion may have been an objective in the nineteenth century, but definitely no longer these days."

This wasn't taken up by anyone in the group. Chelsea seemed to have had enough and the other men were too tipsy to express a coherent argument that might contribute to the topic at hand.

When Tom left the pub about two hours later, Chelsea followed him.

He only realised she was coming with him after he'd walked some distance. His mind was too fuzzy for him to start an intelligent discussion with her again. From the way she was swaying on her feet, he thought she must have had enough to drink.

She took his arm, which helped both of them to keep their balance and make some real progress along the pavement. After they had covered about three hundred yards, she asked him where he was bound for. "Do you live nearby?"

"Yes, it's only over there in that little street."

"Can I come with you?" she asked.

"What do you want?"

"Just to lie down. I'm so exhausted. Please!"

"Okay, but there won't be any sex. I'm too drunk."

"So am I. But it's too far to my place. I wouldn't make it in the state I'm in."

They soon reached the block of Tom's flat. After some initial difficulties, he managed to insert the key and open the front door. Once they got to the flat, which was on the second floor, they stumbled through the lounge. While Tom shuffled to his bedroom, she reached the sofa at the other end of the lounge and collapsed onto it.

It didn't take them more than ten minutes to fall asleep.

When Tom woke up in the morning, his mind returned to the discussions they'd had in the pub on the previous evening. The dictum that killing was always a bad thing, which had been agreed upon, hit him like a bombshell. He was reminded of his role in that killing all those years ago in that forest. The longer the time elapsed since the crime, the less clear things appeared to him. Did he really take part in the killing? Or was he just imagining it? His youthful exuberance and his boosted ego might have made him believe that he'd been an active part in the killing. The other guy – Andrew, wasn't that his name? – had been the real murderer.

For a few minutes, he felt relieved by his belief that he'd never taken part in a murder. But then the guilt feeling returned with a vengeance. Now, after trying to get out of it in vain, his guilt feeling was even worse than before. It produced a terrible pain in his stomach. He thought he was going to faint. It had never been so bad! He remembered that he'd had such guilt feelings from time to time when he thought of that forest, but they had never been so violent.

He stood up and walked to his bathroom. After he'd washed his face and looked at himself in the mirror for a while, he returned to his bedroom. As he was walking through his lounge, he saw the woman lying on the sofa. Oh yes! She'd come with him last night. Did they have sex? Probably not. At least he couldn't remember any sex. He'd been so tipsy.

Tom looked at the woman. She was lying on her back and had one of her arms across her chest. Her breathing was regular and because her mouth was slightly open, there was a soft snore. She was fully dressed, but he could see that she had a very good figure. Her breasts were lying flat on her chest, but he could guess that they were a very impressive size. He realised she was actually quite a good-looking woman, although she was very pale at the moment. No wonder with all the alcohol she'd had last night!

Suddenly, she stirred. He was afraid she might get the wrong idea if she woke up and found him leering at her. He quietly went back to his bedroom. He grabbed some new clothes and returned to the bathroom where he took a shower, hoping to feel better after that.

While he was rubbing some lotion on his chest and stomach under the shower, the idea that a woman was sleeping on his sofa suddenly gave him an erection. He imagined she was coming to the bathroom naked in order to join him under the shower. He stopped his movements and listened. Was she coming? He only heard the hissing and splashing noise of the water spraying his body from the shower.

She did not appear. His erotic vision was not fulfilled.

He swallowed his disappointment and switched off the water before stepping out of the shower cubicle. Then he picked up his bath towel and dried himself.

When he was dressed, he left the bathroom and went to the lounge where the woman was just about to wake up. She stretched herself, then looked about herself.

"Where am I?" she asked him in a hoarse voice.

"You came to my flat last night. You were too drunk to walk back to your place. I'm Tom if you can't remember." He gave her a friendly smile.

She hesitated, needing some more time to collect herself. But then she seemed to remember. When she stood up from the sofa, he remembered her name. It was Chelsea.

"Would you like to take a shower? The bathroom is over there," he explained, pointing out the way.

"No, thank you. I'll just have a quick wash. I don't want to overstay my welcome. Thanks for the sofa, anyway."

While she was in the bathroom, he prepared some breakfast. Then they had breakfast together.

"Do you have to work on Saturdays?" he asked her while she was spreading some butter on her slice of bread.

She shook her head. "No, my next assignment will be on Monday. So, I've got a free weekend now."

"I see," he replied. "May I ask, what's your job? You have to go on assignments?"

"Yes, I'm a journalist. Freelance but often sent on assignments by the same few papers. I write articles about accidents, crimes, minor court cases, community issues, neighbourhood quarrels, political rallies and so on. It's interesting work."

Tom exhaled, "I'm impressed, I must say."

Then she asked him about his job and he explained the ins and outs of his daily work. While he was going through the more exciting aspects – of which there were only very few – he realised that her work was ever so much more interesting, in fact, very exciting. He told her so while taking another sip of tea from his cup.

"Do you get to write about many spectacular things? For example, about any really bad crimes? And does your work never depress you? I mean when you've got to write about some unfair things or about some great calamity?"

She looked out of the window, trying to decide what to tell him. Could she remember any really exciting cases that she had to write about?

After some hesitation, she said, "Probably the worst case I had to write about was a murder case."

"I see. Were you called to the crime scene and did you see the forensic evidence and the police at work?"

"No, it was about a murder that must have happened in the early 1990s. What I had to write about was the finding of the dead body, which was only a few years ago. It was a dead woman that was found in Bedgebury Forest. That's not far from Hastings, near the A21 between Tunbridge Wells and Hastings. It was quite shocking. I took several weeks to cope with it, having actually seen the skeleton, all that had remained of the poor woman."

Tom felt a pang in his heart. When he tried to say something, his voice failed him at first. But then he managed to ask her why she knew the woman had been murdered, not died a natural death.

"I don't remember all the details. It was the police on the scene and the forensic investigation after the finding. Apparently, they could establish from the injuries to the bones that the woman must have been hit hard, which had killed her. Poor girl, she must have been in her early thirties, far too young to die. Anyway, to die such an awful death!" Chelsea shuddered with horror. Just telling the story gave her the shivers.

Tom was extremely nervous. He asked himself if he ought to ask her any more questions or if that might sound too suspicious. On the other hand, if she had told him such a gruesome story, it would only be natural for him to show more curiosity. Everyone would ask more questions. Such a special story from her professional experience! She must have more to tell and she must expect him to ask her for more. Anyway, she didn't seem to consider his interest suspicious in the slightest.

"Do you know more about the case?"

"As far as I know, the police filed the case under unsolved crimes and they say they'll only re-open the case if there is any new evidence. After all, a murder case never expires. I still hope they're going to catch the murderer one day."

"Do they know if there was only one murderer? Or were there several murderers? Was the murderer a man or a woman?"

"I don't know. But I believe they found the DNA of more than one other person. Whether they had something to do with the murder is not clear. Also, I think they suspected a man who escaped to France or Italy. They can't find him to check his DNA, so everything is still in the dark. Also, they say they found out that the dead woman had been a teacher, so they screened all her colleagues and pupils of the period, but no result."

"So, nothing has been found out so far?" Tom remarked, hoping his relief was not too obvious.

"No, it's an unsolved case, as far as I know."

They were silent for a few moments. Then Chelsea suddenly remembered something.

"I say! There was some new movement in the case only recently, but I wasn't on the case. I was busy writing about a pile-up on the M23, so one of my colleagues covered it."

"Any idea what the new findings were?"

"I read my colleague's article and from what I can remember, it looks as if they found a man who looked suspicious, a poacher trying to get some stuff from the ruins of an old forest hut and he was caught in the act. But then it turned out he had nothing to do with the case. It was just a coincidence he was there. At the time of the crime, in the early 1990s that is, he lived in Spain, so he couldn't be connected with the case. That's all I can remember."

Tom found that enough had been said, so he changed the subject. "Would you like to have more breakfast, or can I put everything away?"

"No, thank you. And thanks again for letting me sleep on your sofa." Saying this, she gave him such a sweet smile that he almost believed she was fancying him. She wouldn't be such a bad woman to be with. A few nights with her wouldn't be amiss. But apart from her big smile, there was no signal to invite him.

Then it hit him that she might be too dangerous to be let into his life. Her knowledge about the murder case disqualified her from a role as a girlfriend. She definitely wasn't for him. He had to admit this to himself with regret. She was so charming. Or was this only an impression born out of her intimate closeness through her presence in his flat and her familiarity with the case which gave him so much pain?

"It has been very nice with you," she said. "Although I needn't go to work today, I have to rush off. It's already eleven o'clock. Sorry."

She stood up from the breakfast table and got ready to leave. "This is my address and phone number," she said, handing him a small business card. The card said, *"Chelsea M. Chapman, Freelance Journalist"* and gave her address, phone number and email. It looked quite impressive.

"Thanks," he only murmured.

"Just in case you want to see me again," she smiled and walked to the door.

Against his inclination, he scribbled his own details on a slip of paper and handed it to her. She thanked him again.

And she was gone.

He heard nothing from her and he didn't try to contact her over the next two weeks. Though he considered her a very fine woman, he knew he couldn't allow her to get to know him too well. It was too dangerous.

However, after about three weeks, it was she who made the next move. One evening she called him on his mobile phone, asking him how he was getting on.

"You don't appear to be so keen. But as for me, well, I'd like us to meet again."

He swallowed. "Really?"

"Yes but look here. If you don't like me, we can leave it..."

"No," he interrupted her, "of course, I like you." Saying this, he knew he was only being polite because, in truth, he had already dismissed her out of his life.

"Or do you have a girlfriend?" she asked. "Are you in a relationship?"

"No, I'm on my own. But… well… I'm not very good with women. If we take this any further, I might disappoint you, you see?"

"Are you gay then?"

"No, not at all."

"So, you like to be on your own, is that it?"

"I don't really know."

They were silent for a while. Tom wondered if she had terminated the call. But then she said, "Listen, Tom. We're both of us no teenagers, we are what's called middle-aged people. Our chances for happiness in life are becoming more limited every year. And yet we seem to be two healthy people. I'm going to be straight with you. I like you and I'd like to spend some more time with you. What do you say?"

Tom was taken aback. Shocked. No woman had ever made such an open offer to him. How could he refuse her now?

"Okay, do you want to go out with me? Would you like to go for a meal in Preston Street on Friday night?"

"Thank you, that would be really nice. Yes, let's do that."

They arranged a time and a spot in town to meet on Friday.

The meal at the restaurant in Preston Street turned out to be a big turning point in Tom's life. It started in quite a relaxed atmosphere. They talked about various topics of the day and also told each other a bit more about their lives. He liked to look into her eyes. They had a magic effect on him. And when, between the main course and the dessert, she reached across the table and gently began to stroke his hand, her touch ran through his entire being like lightning. He'd never felt anything like it. It was so colossal, so gentle and yet so demanding. He turned his gaze away from her eyes and pretended to be interested in something in the restaurant.

"Quite full tonight, this place, isn't it?" he remarked.

She answered, "Is that so?" in a teasingly soft song-song voice with a rising intonation. This was so alluring that he simply had to seek out her eyes again.

"You're so nice," she said. He just swallowed hard.

They remained silent for a while, holding hands across the table. Soon, their desserts arrived and broke the spell.

After the meal, they strolled through the streets of Brighton, Chelsea having her arm through his, clinging to him with passion and they took a taxi to her place. She lived in a nice flat in a good part of the town on the third floor, from where there was still a small section of the sea visible.

When things developed in such a way that the next move would naturally be to go to bed together, Tom suddenly woke up, as it were.

"I know we could make love now," he said, while she was still clinging to him, kissing him and beginning to take off her fine red woollen top, "but I'm not ready for it. I'm sorry. I'm really sorry!"

She stood back. Arranging her clothes, she asked, "What's wrong with you?"

"It's nothing against you. It isn't personal. I like you very much, but I'm not ready for this yet. I just need some more time. Please, don't be offended!"

She looked hard at him. He had the impression she was trying to decide whether to dump him or to allow him some time to find out what he wanted.

"Okay then," she said at last. "You go home now and you think about our relationship. When you're ready, you can call me, but not before."

Tom agreed with relief. It would give him time to breathe, to find out if he could risk such a relationship. He thanked her.

They said goodbye without kissing and he left her flat.

*   *   *

It was a windy afternoon. The weather was still dry enough to risk a walk along the coast, though there were signs in the air that suggested a shower later on. Tom was making headway at a brisk pace. He'd parked his car at the small carpark in Cuckmere Valley and he was now walking along the coast in the direction of Birling Gap through an undulating stretch of protected coastal land that was called the Seven Sisters because its white cliffs looked like seven gentle hills from the sea. His sturdy pace helped him to come to terms with his troubled thoughts. He needed the rejuvenating atmosphere of this scenery to sort out his conflicting emotions, which had been on his mind ever since he'd left Chelsea two days earlier. It was Sunday now and he was hoping to come to some sort of decision as to how to proceed in his relationship with her.

Relationship? Did they already have a relationship?

It was obvious that she wanted them to become an item. In fact, she seemed to fancy him quite desperately. He still wondered at her outspokenness, her direct appeal, her unmistaken offer. And he? He remembered the days when he'd been ever so desperate to find a girl who would come to bed with him. He'd been so frustrated for too

331

long, anyway, as far as he could remember. And now there was this gorgeous woman who openly offered to have sex with him! How could he hesitate?

There was a strange feeling in him, an emotion he'd never felt before. Imagining himself to have sex with her, as he'd done in the shower on Saturday morning, seemed so remote now, so absurd, so unimaginable.

How could it be that he considered her a very attractive woman and yet, at the same time, he wasn't thinking of sex with her but more strongly about something else. Yes, certainly, sex with her would probably be extremely great, but he shirked from the sheer idea of such closeness.

When he arrived at Birling Gap, he was thirsty. The brisk walk had cost him considerable energy. He thought it was a pity the pub and restaurant which used to be here had been closed down. It was probably because of the coastal erosion, which was very marked in this spot. Sooner or later, the few buildings that still stood around here might be destroyed by coastal erosion. They may just drop down the cliff onto the pebble beach and their ruins would only be visible at low tide.

The carpark was filled with cars and buses and tourists were ambling around and stepping onto the steel platform erected above the sea, which allowed them a great view of the coastline to the west with the Seven Sisters. He knew this place looked its best just before sunset, particularly when dusk was introduced by a gorgeous red sky. He'd admired this natural spectacle on several occasions. In fact, this was one of his favourite spots in the area. For this location only, he'd become a member of the National Trust.

Normally, he came here by car, but now he enjoyed the visit even more, not only because it gave him the impression he had to earn this view by walking all that distance, but also because it offered him the right mood to come to terms with his conflicting emotions.

Tom got himself an ice cream from the van parked behind the cars and buses.

When he finished his ice cream, he started his way back in the direction of Cuckmere Valley. The first few hundred yards were all uphill and Tom felt the ice cream churning in his stomach. Why did he feel a bit weak? He still saw himself as a fit person for whom such a hill shouldn't be a problem.

After about half the distance of his walk back to his car, his stomach really started to give him a pain. Also, his breathing was getting more difficult by the minute. He didn't know what was the matter with him. He stopped several times to catch his breath before continuing on his way. At first, he thought it was probably quite normal for him to feel the strain like that, but then he began to worry. Was he going to be sick?

When, at last, he reached his car in the carpark in Cuckmere Valley, he felt really miserable. He was sure he was ill.

He sank into the driver's seat and started the engine.

TWENTY-ONE

Tom was still feeling weak. He took a taxi from the hospital to his flat in Brighton. The driver was chatting, but Tom couldn't listen. He was thinking of Chelsea and what she might be thinking of him.

On his way back from Cuckmere Valley, he'd had to stop in Rottingdean. His breathing had become so hard and he was feeling so miserable that he just couldn't go on driving. He'd called 999 and told them how he was feeling. The ambulance fetched him and took him to the hospital in Brighton, where he'd spent several weeks. He'd received treatment in the ICU. They'd said he had Covid-19. He had been cut off from the world for a good while.

Back in his flat, he first made himself a cup of coffee. He sat down and began to think. He'd had a long time to think at the hospital and it had made a new man of him. He felt that he was starting a new life. He went through all the aspects of his new life in his mind. One of the items very high up on his mental list was Chelsea. During his time at the hospital, he had come to the conclusion that he really needed Chelsea. He felt he couldn't live without her. The solution to the puzzle of his conflicting emotions he had been struggling with before his Covid attack was simple.

Although he considered her a very sexy woman, he felt that it was more important to have her near him as a partner rather than for the sex. He hardly dared imagine sex with her. It would be too overwhelming. He just wanted her near. He was yearning for her good looks, her smell and the aura around her. He wanted to see her every day of his life.

Was this love? He wondered if that was what the poets were writing about. And was this the thing that made people do things they'd never dreamed of before? Was this, at last, the true feeling of love, which he had never known what it could be like?

He decided to call her. She would probably be angry or disappointed. He hadn't contacted her for the past weeks. He had been too weak in the hospital and it would be difficult to make her see his side of things.

He picked up his phone, then put it down again. After a minute, he picked it up again and dialled her number. When the ring tone began, his courage left him again and he pressed the stop button.

His next attempt was more successful. She picked up the phone after a considerable time, during which he needed all his courage not to press the stop button again. But when she did answer his call at last, he felt ever so relieved and all his fears and his initial awkwardness disappeared, evaporated, as it were.

She recognised his voice at once. "Oh, it's you, stranger?"

He stammered. "Yes, it's me. I'm sorry."

"What are you sorry for? For leaving me like that all these past weeks? Or for calling now out of the blue? Or for your ungentlemanly behaviour last time? What is it that you want?"

Tom hesitated before he answered, "What I want is to see you to explain things and to tell you how I feel. Can we get together tonight to talk? I mean, to talk about us and to explain to you why I've neglected you for so long?"

She waited before she said, "Okay, I'll come to your place after eight and your explanation had better be a very good one!" Her voice was clear and almost business-like, but not really angry. He would understand if she was angry, but he couldn't detect any anger even if he tried to replay her words in his mind after the end of their phone call.

After a relaxing nap on his lounge sofa, Tom left his flat to do some shopping in the late afternoon. He had to get some stuff to cook a meal for Chelsea. He decided on something reasonably simple, some pasta with a nice tomato sauce and a green salad. If cooked with expertise, such a meal could be as exciting as a showier meal with expensive meat and exotic side vegetables. With pasta, he always made a point of adding some carrots cut into tiny cubes and some onion and garlic. A good thing that he remembered she liked garlic. Not all women did, but Chelsea adored it.

He began the cooking around seven. He laid the table with a nice mauve tablecloth and yellow napkins and he added a vase with a yellow rose that he had picked up from Sainsbury's. A red rose would be too crass. He completed the decorations with two silver candlesticks with yellow candles.

The sauce and the salad were ready when the doorbell rang.

He opened the door and Chelsea entered his flat. Tom felt this was a historic moment in his life. Here she was! And she looked so gorgeous! She was wearing a pair of dark blue jeans and a dark yellow jumper. No jewellery, but a nicely made-up face. And most important of all, her typical ironic smile!

Tom had to admire her for several seconds before he got out his first words. He stared at her and said, "Here you are."

What a stupid and banal thing to say, he thought. But he couldn't help it, he was so fascinated by her

336

appearance. She was even more beautiful than he remembered.

She handed him the bottle of wine she had brought and asked him, "Won't you give me a kiss?"

He gave her a peck on her cheek and led her to the dining area in the lounge. "Shall we talk first and then eat, or shall we talk while we eat?"

"I think I need to hear your explanation before I can think of food." Then she sat down on one of the dining chairs. "But you can give me a glass of wine."

He got the bottle of red wine he had placed on the sideboard, poured a glass for her and after some hesitation, another glass for himself.

"Here you are. I say, this wine carries the same name as one of the fashionable novelists, as someone explained to me a few years ago."

"But we're not here to discuss wine, are we?" she asked in a provocative but friendly tone.

There was no escape for him. He had to tell her the truth. He told her how he had hesitated to let her into his life because he'd had some very negative experiences with women and he needed some time to come to terms and to find out about his own feelings for her. But then the Covid pandemic had overtaken him. "Look here, I've had the most awful time during the past few weeks. I was in hospital with Covid-19 and I nearly died."

"Oh, is that true? I'm so sorry!"

"Yes, it's true. I was going to think about what you called our relationship the last time, but then I was caught in the pandemic. I'd thought the pandemic was over, but they told me it was still around, only it's no longer a threat to the whole population, but you can still get it." He looked at her, waiting for her comment.

337

"Have you got rid of it now? Or should I be worried about being in the same room with you?"

"Nothing to worry about. They told me I could be with other people now without any danger for me or for them. You are quite safe."

"Okay then. And what conclusion did you reach about our relationship, may I ask?"

"Can't you guess? Would I have called you if I wasn't ready to take things any further? I have found out that… well, I… I think I have fallen in love with you."

The room remained silent for what seemed like an eternity to Tom. At last, Chelsea stood up from her chair and stepped up to him. She put down her glass on the table. Then she bent down to him and kissed him. She kissed him ever so gently, full of affection, on his lips. She held this position, their lips touching, for several seconds before she returned to her chair and sat down again.

"How does this taste?" she asked with an enigmatic smile.

He smiled at her and she smiled back. Then they began to talk about their relationship. He told her how he'd realised that he loved her. He had never known what love could be, he'd always confused it with sex, but suddenly he'd found out. Now he couldn't imagine being without her. He even told her that he now thought true love was more important than just sex. She answered that she had fallen in love with him at first sight. But she'd been extremely hurt and disappointed when he refused her and then when he just disappeared.

She hadn't had the nerve to call him. It had been up to him to contact her. His long silence had crushed her. She had cried through many nights, but then she had blamed herself, thinking she had no right to expect anything from him, they'd only just met at the pub. What right did she have to claim his love?

They talked for more than two hours. Then they remembered their dinner and Tom went to the kitchen to prepare their food. When it was ready, they enjoyed the good things together and emptied the bottle of wine.

Of course, Chelsea stayed the whole night and it was the beginning of a wonderful relationship for both of them. She had forgiven him his long silence and he had forgotten all his previous adventures with women. This was the real thing.

*   *   *

It was three months later. Tom was driving along the A27 and thinking of his good luck. He and Chelsea had made plans for their future together. They were both in their early fifties, so there was no time to lose. They had told each other about their previous attempts with the opposite sex and they had found that they liked the same music styles. She was not so keen on chess as he was, but she allowed him to keep his hobby.

Then there were their political attitudes. They were both not very educated in political science, but they were convinced that only democratic structures could save the world from disaster. They were very sad about the various dictators of the world and they were sorry to observe anti-democratic tendencies in so many otherwise democratic countries. And when their discussions came to Brexit, they both agreed that it had been the worst mistake since the Second World War.

Of course, they both thought the monarchy ought to be questioned. They knew how much revenue it still generated for the tourist industry, but they also knew how antiquated it was and how many problems it created.

Having agreed on issues such as these, they agreed that they were neither of them very political. They were more interested in culture. They both admired beautiful buildings and mainly through Chelsea's initiative, they began to read more literature and to visit art exhibitions. Together, they discovered new artists and new authors.

As Tom was driving along the A27, he had just passed Firle Place when the accident happened.

A blue BMW from the opposite direction was overtaking a slow lorry, misjudging the situation. For Tom, the BMW suddenly appeared right in front, out of the blue. He tried to steer his own car to the kerb to avoid a collision, but there wasn't enough time. It all happened within a few seconds. No chance! The head-on collision was very violent, the kinetic energy annihilated within a fraction of a second was considerable, given that the BMW was doing something like eighty and Tom's small car about fifty-five.

For Tom, it was the end of the world. He saw a film of his life, his young days, his role in the murder, his time with some of his women and his kissing of Chelsea. All within a fraction of a second in slow motion, while he also admired the way the metal bodies of the two cars were getting interlocked and everything was collapsing.

He woke up in the ambulance. He had no idea of the time and he could feel no pain. A paramedic was telling him not to touch his face. But then Tom was gone again.

The next time he woke up was in a hospital room. He felt very sick. A nurse was talking to him. There were lots of wires and tubes attached to his head and his body. He couldn't understand the nurse. He knew he wanted to

340

tell her something, but he kept forgetting the words he needed for his pronouncement.

At last, he dropped off again. When he woke up the next time, there was a different nurse. She looked a bit older than the previous one.

Tom said, "Listen, I want to tell you something."

She told him to save his energy. There was no need for him to talk. She said he should rather concentrate on his well-being and he should try to get better. How did one do that, he wondered?

Tom felt his energy getting weaker. He took all his courage and started again, "Listen, I have to tell you about the murder I committed…"

The nurse only nodded. "Yes, that's quite all right then. Just try to sleep now. You have to relax. Don't think of such absurd ideas. Everything will be all right."

Then a dark shadow overtook him and he felt he was getting very happy and very light. He could fly.

The doctor called by the nurse could only confirm Tom's decease. "Exitus!"

Then they switched off the machines.

It was before Chelsea could reach the hospital.

PART FIVE

TWENTY-TWO

When Philomena called Norman on the phone, he was delighted to hear her voice. He hadn't heard from her for such a long time.

"You're back at last. What was India like?"

"Breathtaking, enlightening, sad…"

"All of these things? Well, I'm looking forward to hearing more details from you. Did you find your old friend?"

"Yes and I stayed until she died."

"Oh, I'm sorry! Was it very bad for you?"

Philomena hesitated. "Listen, these are things I wouldn't like to discuss on the phone."

"Of course, I understand. Probably you want to recover from your jetlag first. Shall we get together when you've recovered?"

"Yes, that's a very good idea. Just give me a few days. I need to get accustomed to life here again, but I'll get in touch with you soon."

After the phone call, she started to unpack her luggage and throw her dirty clothing into the washing machine. Everything had that typical Indian smell. She wanted to get rid of that. But while she was busy with her task, she realised that she might have an aversion when it came to Indian smells, but on the other hand, she cherished her memories of India. She may never go to India again in her life, so this was her only memory of that fascinating culture and its people.

When she had stowed everything away and tidied everything, she went out, got her car from the garage and drove to the supermarket, where she bought all the things she needed for her normal life again. She was relieved to get fresh organic vegetables and some good meat. She was particularly glad to get some good British meat again after the few instances when she had tasted Indian meat, usually mutton, which she didn't really trust for hygienic reasons. Still, she had survived India without a rumbling stomach.

At the supermarket, she heard all the other people around her talking, chatting and negotiating and she had to smile at herself because she missed the Indian singsong in their voices. In a way, she'd learned to like it after spending time over there.

Back at home, she saw her neighbour Lucy near the fence and decided to say hello. Lucy was delighted to see her and was full of questions, but Philomena told her she needed a good sleep first. She would tell her more about her Indian adventure later on.

Then she went to her bedroom, drew the curtains – it was only just six in the evening – and lay down on her bed. It only took her about a quarter of an hour to fall asleep. It wasn't only the jetlag that was responsible for this exhaustion, but also her emotional upheavals in connection with her experiences in India. Sandy's death, her own role in the murder all those years ago, the Indian climate, the monsoon…

She was awakened by the telephone. Rubbing her eyes, she got up and shuffled to her phone. It was Robert.

"Hiya, sister. Have you gone native in India? You must've come home more than twenty-four hours ago, but you didn't think your own brother was important enough to be told you've come back safely."

"Hello, Robbie. It's good to hear your voice. To answer your question, no, I haven't gone native, as you call it – an awfully colonial phrase, if you ask me – but I simply need to sleep off my jetlag before I'm any good at polite conversation. I'll get in touch with you soon."

With this, she just rang off. Let him think of her what he liked, she needed her sleep. Back in bed, she soon fell into a deep slumber.

About four o'clock the following morning, she woke up. It was still dark outside, but she could no longer sleep. She got up, took a shower and brewed herself a nice cup of tea. Then she sat down at her small kitchen table and started to draw up a list of to-dos.

On her long flight back, she'd had enough time to sort out her thoughts. Now she was ready to come to terms with her life on a new level.

She would face the past and her role in it. This meant that she would take Norman into her confidence and tell him everything she knew.

Then she would find an abridged version which she could safely tell her brother, making sure, however, that his wife didn't get any of it.

The next thing she was certain of was her plan for yet another novel. Her writer's gene had raised its head and was now urging her to sit down at her computer and start her next novel. The only problem was that she wasn't so sure if she was going to write another romance – like her fifteen previous novels – or if she should give in to her gut feeling and write a more serious piece of literature.

She went to her computer and started it up. First, she had to get rid of a bunch of junk mail. Then she opened the WORD programme and began to take notes about the things she wanted to write about. Parts of the plot had to be set in India and other parts in Britain. She might consider a third setting, something like France or Italy. Then, there had to be a murder that was too complex to be cleared up and several persons had to be involved.

347

If she wanted the Indian sections to be convincing, she had to draw from her own recent experience. It ought to have the touch of authenticity.

But the main issue was going to be the question of responsibility, of guilt. Was it possible to have several individuals involved in such a way as to make everyone feel guilty? That might be quite a challenge, but she felt she had to write something like this in order to come to terms with what had happened to herself. It would help her to cope with the remaining years of her life.

Why would those individuals want to murder someone? They all had to have different motives, but target the same person. A big question was the victim. Should it be a man or a woman? What difference would that make?

Philomena spent several hours at her desk, drawing up different plots and different characters. She knew how important it was for the credibility of the story to create an even discourse, not to write in an ironical style like Agatha Christie a spectacularly post-modernist style with so many jumps around place and time, but to be factual, to write as if it were a good philosophical essay, but without too complex phrases. Like this, readers would be able to feel empathy and follow her narrative with pleasure.

Then, she ought to avoid too emotional passages in the style she'd employed in her other novels. Let the reader develop his or her own emotions. Let the reader participate in the plot as if he or she were present on the scene of the action.

Having thought of plot, action and emotions, she realised she would have to be extra careful to make things coherent in terms of the characters' inner lives. She would have to proceed with long passages of inner monologue.

The longer she worked for her new project, the more convinced she became that her life as a romance writer was over. That stance had been excellent to create a good income for her, but what she needed now in order to be happy as a writer was to find her true self in the serious genre. Only then would she be a balanced person, she felt.

This meant that she would probably have to publish her new novel under her own name. No more hiding behind a pen name! Probably she would also need a new publisher. She would have to consult her agent.

In the evening, she got a phone call from Henry. He thanked her for being with his sister when she was so ill. He wanted to know more about Sandy's last days in India. Philomena told him what she knew and added how sad her friend's death had made her. They exchanged a few friendly remarks and when Philomena wanted to end their conversation, Henry suggested a meeting. Would she be willing to meet him at their café in Maidstone on Tuesday next? After some initial hesitation, she agreed and they rang off.

Later, after watching the news on TV, Philomena made an attempt to sort her feelings. There were now two men in her life; two men that she liked in a certain way. She asked herself whether she wanted to invite a man into her personal sphere again. Wasn't Henry too old and too closely connected with Sandy? And wasn't Norman almost too young for her? How old was Norman really? Four or five years younger than herself? Did she want to become intimately involved again with another man in her life at all?

The emotional upheaval of her Indian trip had made her uncertain about herself and her life. She was almost fifty and she still had a life expectancy of some thirty years, realistically. In a way, she valued her present situation. She was her own mistress, had more than enough to live on, could organise her days without consulting another person, and was truly independent. On the other hand, when she lay in bed at night, she sometimes felt the absence of someone to love and to hold. After all, she was a normal human being with her desires and dreams. She wasn't sentimental at all, but she felt the absence of a vital aspect in her life. She tossed and turned in her bed, night after night, without coming to a conclusion. Eventually, she arrived at a decision.

If she wanted to get together with a man again – and this was a big IF – she asked herself if she only had the choice between Norman and Henry. Those seemed to be the only men who might be willing to form a sort of partnership with her.

She was too much of a recluse to go out to pubs and clubs in order to find a suitable man. Also, she didn't fancy looking for someone in the Internet through one of those dating platforms. At her age, it would be extremely difficult to find a decent man. They would all have a backpack full of misfired relationships and disappointments. Like herself, really. The Internet would offer her only a very slight chance of finding Mr Right. If both the Internet and real meeting places like clubs were out, there only remained the solution to fall back on the men who might be ready, men she already knew and who presented a smaller risk than total strangers.

But would she be able to love either of them? She was experienced enough to know that she couldn't become intimately involved with Norman or Henry without agreeing to share her bed with them. They were real men of flesh and blood and they would have their physical desires. Would she be willing to have sex with either of them?

She decided to look at Henry with this new possibility in mind when they met a few days later. She arrived at the café sometime after him and she looked at him through the window, judging his looks as he was sitting there at the table waiting for her. He didn't see her, so she got a good view of him. Yes, he was still quite a dashing man in his best years. But going to bed with him? That was another matter.

She entered the café and sat down at his table. At first, they exchanged a few general remarks, mainly small talk. Then she began to tell him about her last days with Sandy. She was careful not to mention anything about the story of Bedgebury Forest. That was a secret between herself and Sandy, none of Henry's business.

She watched his body language and listened carefully to whatever he had to say to her. Could she detect a more intimate interest in her, perhaps? Would he be willing to intensify their friendship if she sent him the right signals? She tried to smile at him with a particularly charming expression, looking deep into his eyes. But she couldn't detect the slightest reaction from him.

They parted after a full hour. He had some business in town and she wanted to get back to her home to digest her experience.

Back in her cottage, she went through the meeting with Henry in her mind. After careful consideration, she realised that she wouldn't want to make love to him. He was too much connected with Sandy, her young days and many memories that were somehow incompatible with a love relationship.

Henry had been her mentor. She had looked up to him, to his better piano-playing and his more extended

351

experience when she was still a child and he appeared so far above her. If she got together with him, he would always be dominating her. He might not want to appear in this role, but in her mind, he occupied such a leading role that would render a balanced relationship too difficult. He would always remain her mentor.

Over the following days, she reviewed her decision several times and she always arrived at the same conclusion. Henry was a darling, but hardly more than a good friend.

So what about Norman?

She called him, still uncertain as to her relationship with him.

"Hello, Philomena," he greeted her cheerfully. "It's so good to hear from you again. Have you fully recovered from your jetlag and your cultural shock?"

It was only now that she realised that he was the only person among her friends and relatives who called her by her full name. A sign of respect. She hated the bad habit of so many people who thought they could change your name. She considered it an infringement.

She remembered how many years ago, she had asked her brother if he preferred to be called Robert or Robbie and he opted for Robbie. So that was all right. But to shorten someone's name without asking if it was acceptable was just rude! Someone had told her that such infringements were more common in the States and in Australia. Not long ago, she had seen on TV how Australians would always find a shorter version of your name. They appeared to be too lazy to pronounce a poly-syllabic name and immediately cut it down to one syllable, thereby cutting down the other person to a smaller size.

Norman invited her for afternoon tea on the same day. She was happy to accept.

In the early afternoon, she checked on herself in her bathroom mirror. Looking at her face and her figure, she had to admit she was still an attractive woman. Perhaps a little too heavy around her bust and her bottom, but nothing to make her an ugly old hag. She thought that her face radiated a friendly attitude. Her blue eyes shone, her nose was straight, her lips were just right and she still had very smooth skin. She was satisfied with her looks. She wondered if Norman could see her charms, given the fact that so far, she had always endeavoured to dismiss sexual attraction from her appearance. She had chosen to adopt the role of a grey mouse and she knew that she had this image in the village. But now she had a different agenda. She wanted to check if Norman might be interested in her as more than just a friend.

When he opened the door for her, she beamed at him and he smiled back, inviting her in. They sat down in his lounge where he had already set the small table for afternoon tea.

While they were talking about India, her friend Sandy, the Covid pandemic and cultural shock, she was observing him. Did he betray any more personal interest in her? Did he take note of her attractions?

Sandy had once told her that men always looked at women and while doing so, they undressed them in their minds. As male animals, they checked the females for their breeding potential. Were their hips too narrow for giving birth to a child? Were their breasts ample enough to produce enough milk for their babies? And more such tests. The result was sexual attraction. For Philomena, such ideas were silly hobby-psychology. But at this moment, she had to think of such opinions. Was Norman weighing the pros and cons of her as a sexual partner?

"Wouldn't you say so?" he asked. She nearly jumped from her seat because he had woken her up from her daydreaming.

"Sorry, what were you asking? I must have drifted off for a moment. I'm really sorry. Please forgive me."

"That's quite okay, my dear. You must still be a bit tired."

"No, no. Please just repeat what you were saying. I'm okay now."

"I was asking you if you'd like to go out for a nice meal with me." He looked at her with an expectant expression.

She decided to take the bull by its horns. "That depends. I have been thinking a lot about our relationship lately."

"And what's your conclusion?"

"I can't say. It takes two people for a relationship. Tell me, Norman, how do you see our relationship? What am I for you? An acquaintance? A friend? A very good friend?" She hesitated before adding. "A potential lover?"

Having said this, she blushed and looked down at the empty cup in her hands.

Norman blushed. He thought for a moment, then he answered. "This comes a bit sudden. You are a very courageous woman. And I admire you for it. I have been thinking about us, too."

"And what?" she begged.

"I'm a man who takes life step by step. My movements are usually very methodical. But when it comes to us and our friendship, I seem to be getting into deep waters, I seem to be unable to switch on my reason.

When I'm with you, when I look at your face, I seem to melt away. I can't help being drawn to you."

After this confession, they looked at each other in silence for a long time. She didn't know if she should take the next step. He also wondered what to do next.

Eventually, she said, "I know it isn't so easy to find each other like this at our advanced age, but are we really too old to form a partnership?"

He didn't answer this dangerous question.

After a moment of silence, she said, "I think I need to tell you more about myself before we allow this to go any further."

He went to the kitchen and fetched two glasses and a bottle of Barolo wine. He poured the wine, then sat down opposite her. They enjoyed the quiet togetherness and the full taste of the red wine before she began with her story.

"You know that I went to India to see my old friend Sandy."

"Yes, she died from Covid, didn't she?"

"Indeed, she did. It was very sad. Even though we hadn't been very close and hadn't seen much of each other after – well, after we quarrelled over a delicate matter more than thirty years ago. But as kids we had been as thick as thieves. She was a year older than I and I admired her. I saw her as a role model in many ways."

She took a sip of wine before she continued.

"And the dark spot in my personal biography lies precisely in that delicate matter that destroyed our friendship."

"What do you mean? A dark spot?"

"Yes, that's what it is." She hesitated. "Before you get involved with me any further, my dear Norman, you

355

have to understand that I might be a murderer. Now, I've said it."

She heaved a heavy sigh and took another sip of wine, looking at him very carefully. She stood on the brink of a precipice. How would he react? Would he blame her and leave her on moral grounds? Would he betray her to the police? Would he play things down? She was on tenterhooks.

He drew a worried expression when he asked, "How do you mean? Why do you say you *might* be a murderer? I don't understand. Is that the same wild story that you told me on the phone from India?"

"Yes, it's the same story, but it's still my dark spot. As I told you on the phone, I really don't know for sure. My gut-feeling tells me I took part in the murder, but then there are some reasonable doubts."

"I know this might be difficult for you, but would you like to tell me everything? Perhaps I can dispel your doubts and allay your guilt feelings."

"I don't know where to start. Before I can tell you what I know about the whole affair, I have to know if you're going to turn me in. If you find that I'm really a cold-blooded murderer, will you go and tell the police? Or will you still be my friend?"

"I am confident that you're not a murderer, but should things look dodgy for you, I'll be on your side. Definitely!"

So Philomena told him everything, thereby also repeating some of the things she had told him before. She told him the story of her friendship with Sandy, their growing up together, their different views on teenage sexuality and their special relationship with their French teacher with the important difference that Sandy totally admired him and often met him alone while she kept her distance.

"What? That teacher took advantage of your friend? And couldn't they see that was an absolute no-go?"

"I believe they were both to blame."

"But he was her teacher and it was his responsibility. She was dependent on him. It wasn't an equal relationship. Well, how far did it go?"

"You see, there was that other thing. Not only did we differ in our opinions of Mr Sullivan, but we also had different views on our sexuality. We were still inexperienced teenagers. I was happy to enjoy my inexperience and let things take their course eventually, but Sandy wanted to shine, to please, to attract men, and she was hoping to become a fashion model one day, something that was far from my own ambitions."

She hesitated for a moment, then continued, "So when Sullivan suggested he'd like to take nude pictures of her – to help her with her career as a model, as he said – she was ever so eager to please him. I could see that for what it was. He just wanted to take advantage of her. But she was so blind in her admiration of him and in her dream of a great career as a model that she agreed to meet him in a secret place in the woods. And she wanted me to come along. I was reluctant to accompany her, but then I thought at least I might be able to talk her out of it if he got too encroaching in his demands. I might be able to stop her from committing some awful stupidity. So I agreed to go along."

Norman looked impressed. His expression was full of compassion. "You don't have to go on if it's too hard for you," he said.

"No, I want to tell you everything. I really do. You see, while this whole development happened between

357

myself and Sandy, there was another scenario that was going on. That Sullivan guy wasn't satisfied with his exploitation of a girl who was his pupil. He needed a sexual relationship with a grown-up woman and he found her in the person of a beautiful young colleague, a science teacher called Christine Mitford. They had their own thing going on while he was cheating on her with Sandy. Well, to tell you the truth, I never learned how far things had gone with Sandy, but at one point Sandy suggested she might be pregnant, which goes to show that there must have been enough reason for such a suspicion."

"So the whole thing blew up and the Mitford woman gave him hell?"

"Not exactly. Things were a bit more complicated and got more dramatic." Philomena looked into Norman's eyes when she prepared him for the worst to come.

"Dramatic? You're making me really curious now."

"Yes. As it happened, we – that's Sandy and I – were at the old forest hut where Sullivan was going to ask Sandy to undress for the photo shoot he had proposed, when suddenly Christine Mitford appeared on the scene. There was a big row, people were shouting at one another, they were fighting with their fists and eventually with implements like saucepans and skillets. I was so furious that I also took part in the great mayhem which followed. And here's where my main problem lies. I fainted. And in the end, I was lying on the ground when I regained consciousness. I panicked. I just ran away."

She stopped, waiting for his reaction.

"What makes you think you murdered someone?" he asked.

"Except for those few days after the fight, when I saw her at school but couldn't talk to her, I never saw Sandy again for several decades after that. A few days after the events at the forest hut, it turned out that Sullivan and Miss Mitford had disappeared. That's what was reported at the school and what the police said on the regional news. Things became quiet after a while. It was believed that the two lovers had eloped to France. Sandy was also absent from England. Nobody knew where she was. But the story suddenly flared up again about twenty-five years later when a dead body was found. The body was identified as the remains of Christine Mitford and there was forensic evidence of a murder. So now it was a murder case. Naturally, I realised I had to be the murderer. I had been on the scene and I had taken part in the chaotic mayhem all those years ago."

Full of expectation, she looked at Norman. She waited for his verdict. What would he say now? How would he react?

He waited a few moments before he said something. He drew a deep breath and sighed.

"My dear Philomena, there's no need for you to feel guilty. No need at all! How could you see yourself as a murderer? As I already told you on the phone to India, there's obviously no evidence that you murdered the poor woman. The other people on the scene had much stronger motives to become violent. You were just a by-stander, a witness at most, but not a murderer."

"That's very kind of you, Norman. But how do you know?"

"I think I know you a little by now. I simply cannot imagine you becoming so violent. It isn't in your nature."

TWENTY-THREE

"Whatever you think of my involvement, promise me, please, that you're not going to tell anyone. This must remain a secret between us!" she insisted.

"I promise!" he replied.

She seemed relieved, so he thought he might risk a change of topic. "I say, our dinner date is still on, isn't it?"

"Of course, if you'll still have me." She hesitated before she went on. "And it's a deal about us. We're good friends, nothing more and nothing less."

"Yes."

They continued with some small talk about the village and its residents. Then Philomena took her leave and went home.

In the evening, they went to have a pleasant dinner at the Wild Mushroom Restaurant in Westfield near Hastings. Once they had placed their orders, they started to talk while waiting for their table to be ready. Soon, their discussion returned to the question of her guilt feelings.

"You know," she said, "I can cope with my daily life, no problem. But in the long run, I want to find some sort of charity activity in order to atone for my possible participation in a crime. I'm sure it would do me a lot of good to know that I can be of some help to people who're in need. Would you have an idea?"

Norman wondered what to suggest. "You know, there are many charities you might consider. You can either donate a large sum of money to one charity, or you can divide your donation into smaller sums and consider several charities. I know how it is. If we give something to one charity, we have a bad feeling about all the others that got nothing from us. You have to make up your mind from the start. Do you want one charity to benefit from a large sum or do you want to spread your donation over several charities?"

"You're quite right. I'd like one charity to get a really large sum from me."

"So you want to know if it should be the Red Cross, Oxfam, Médecins sans Frontières, Unicef, or another large charity?"

"Yes. But I particularly want to help the poor people who suffer because of a criminal dictator. I can't very well find a charity that helps the Uyghur people of China or the oppressed and tortured people of Iran. I've been thinking of the victims of Putin's criminal aggression."

"In that case, I would suggest either the Red Cross or Unicef."

Soon their starters arrived and they devoted their attention to the pleasant task of feeding themselves with good food. After wishing each other *bon appétit*, they began to eat in silence.

"I say," Norman said between two bites after a while, "have you been thinking of a particular sum of money? I'm sorry, this might be too personal, but I just wondered. So far, we've never spoken about money. Oh yes, you told me once that you're really making a lot of money with your romances. So I wondered… But if it's too personal, please just forget my question."

"We agreed that we're good friends, and good friends trust each other, don't they? So I may as well admit to you that I've been thinking of a donation in the region of two million pounds."

Norman dropped his spoon and looked at her with a speechless expression. He only managed to croak. "That's a lot of money."

"Indeed it is," she admitted. "And I want this money to help people who really need it. At first, I had another idea, but that was too unrealistic."

"What was that?"

"I thought that a lot of money would be needed in order to finance the re-education of the Russian people. You know, make them see how badly they'd been cheated, oppressed and brainwashed by Putin and his henchmen in the media. When we hear that something like ninety per cent of the Russian population believe the dictator's absurd lies, it makes us wonder how there can ever be peace between Russia and Ukraine again. So I thought I might finance part of such a re-education programme after the war. But now I've come to the decision that the people who suffer directly under the Russian bombs, the women who got raped by Russian soldiers, the children who got stolen by the Russian occupying forces, the families who lost their dear ones and people who lost their homes and their livelihoods are in more immediate need of financial support. What do you think?"

Norman looked at her with admiration. "You are right!"

Philomena's long speech with her plea for the Ukrainian people had left such a strong impression that they both remained silent during the remaining part of their starters.

Later, in the break between their starters and their main course, Norman took up the conversation again. "In this case," he suggested, "I'd say either the Red Cross or Unicef will be your best bet. With Unicef, you'll target particularly children, whereas, with the Red Cross, you'll help more different sorts of people in need. So it depends."

They discussed the advantages of one or the other solution and they exchanged their views on the Russian war on Ukraine. Soon their main course arrived and they concentrated on their food again.

After the meal, Norman drove her home. When they came to her cottage, she invited him in for a nightcap.

They had the impression that after all that heavy talk about the war during their dinner, they needed something a bit lighter, something more mundane, to talk about.

Philomena had one such topic ready. "I'm going to get a new car and it'll be an electric one. I think I'll go for a Renault Zoe. That's light and small and it'll do me just fine."

He asked, "What about the electricity? Are you planning to install a charging station in your garage and have solar panels set up on your roof?"

"Indeed, that's my plan. Are you going to help me with your advice?"

Norman agreed and promised to support her.

A few days later, they went to the Renault agency in town, planning to order the new car. Philomena was in her gardening clothes. She'd changed from her wellingtons into a nice pair of shoes, tidied up a bit and she'd washed her hands. In her eyes, she looked perfectly presentable. However, once they were in the showroom and standing around a new Zoe model, the salesman who joined them looked at her as if he thought a woman like her could never afford such a car.

This impression was confirmed when Philomena announced her intention to the salesman. She asked how much it would be for a car like that. The salesman answered, "I'm not sure it's a car for your budget."

Norman said, "Come on, my dear. We'll go somewhere else to buy your new car."

The salesman was quick to see his mistake. "Oh, I'm sorry! Of course, I'll be happy to sell you one of our cars. I only thought… You know…"

"I know exactly what you thought," said Norman. "So you better apologise to my good friend here if you don't want her to take her business elsewhere."

The salesman immediately apologised in so many words. Then Norman asked to see the head salesman. When he arrived, Norman told him what the first salesman had said. The head salesman – whose name was Jeremy Whittacker according to the business card that he handed to them – was also full of apologies and sent the other man away. In the end, Philomena managed to place her order. She ordered a blue car for which she would have to wait a few months due to the existing problems with supply chains after Brexit, the impact of the Covid pandemic and the war in Ukraine.

Back in the village, Norman helped her to find the right company for the installation of the solar panels on her roof and the charging station in her garage, as well as the required inverter. He compared several competitors on the Internet and suggested what he believed to be the best offer. Philomena followed his advice.

In the following week, Philomena met her bank manager in London. She wanted to consult him on the procedure in connection with her substantial donation to Unicef. The manager, whose name was James Bolton, tried to dissuade her from such a large donation, but she had already made up her mind. She only wanted to know if there would be any problems with her tax situation and when he informed her that it would actually be advantageous for her in terms of her taxes, she gave her instructions for the payment to be made.

Travelling home afterwards, she felt good about her decision. She knew it wouldn't stop the Russian aggression, but at least some children would be able to profit from her donation. That was something.

The terrible war in Ukraine had another effect on her. In her new novel, which really developed into a novel with a political background – for which she had already delved into serious studies on international affairs, warfare and weaponry – she had her protagonist take an active interest in what was going on in Ukraine.

So, her new novel was taking shape as an anti-war pamphlet in a way. She named her protagonist Frank and, together with a group of like-minded men and women from several different countries, he founded an international network of institutes devoted to what the Americans called civics education designed to educate people in political science, especially in democracy and to teach them about the dangers of emerging dictatorships.

She felt that if she couldn't set up such an organisation herself, at least her protagonist was doing the right thing. She was convinced that such an endeavour was moving things in the right direction. The crumbling of democracies and the emergence of new dictatorships was the most dangerous problem in today's world. So it was absolutely necessary for Frank to do his utmost to fight such evil developments.

This narrative trick gave her an opportunity to show some of these dangers in her novel without becoming too didactic. She wanted her readers to develop through conviction, not to learn by being lectured to.

Embedded in her plot, she managed to show the intricate weavings of some of the dangerous developments for which she gave examples from Turkey, Israel and Hungary. With the introduction of local characters, she showed how would-be dictators oppressed political opponents, began to control the press and managed to abolish the strict division of the powers in the state, like how they gave the executive more influence on the high courts of justice.

She could also demonstrate how the extremist right-wing parties increased their unhealthy influence on the people by using the old tool of fear. Governing by fear was the word of the day! The fairy tales of justified fears from foreign powers and from ethnic minorities were becoming generally acceptable. She knew there would be good examples from other nations, too, but that would turn her novel into a textbook on politics. Of course, her examples from Russia, China and Iran were so blatantly obvious that she had to use them sparsely so as not to shy her readers away. The novel was a good story, not just grey theory.

In a stroke of a genius, her Frank managed to show the obvious parallels between Adolf Hitler and Vladimir Putin. It was such an impudent act of Putin's to use exactly the same methods as Hitler and to get away with it. Just as Hitler claimed that Poland was attacking Germany and he had to defend Germany by invading Poland in 1939, so Putin claimed that Ukraine was attacking Russia and he had to defend Russia by invading Ukraine in 2022. And there were many more parallels.

In the course of her research for the novel, she also went to a refugee camp in Kent where, during her repeated visits, she became quite friendly with a Ukrainian woman. Her name was Natalya. As the two women were becoming friends, Philomena learned that Natalya had lost a child when she was fleeing from Odessa and got attacked by Russian bombing. Her husband, Oleg, was fighting at the front in the Donbass.

Philomena thought of inviting Natalya to come and live in her cottage in the village, but she realised the cottage was too small, with only one bedroom and one bathroom. They would get on each other's nerves in the long run. So she preferred to visit her at the camp very often and from time to time, she invited her to come to the cottage for a day or two. Natalya was very happy with this arrangement. She managed to explain many aspects of the war to Philomena. Also, she showed her lots of pictures of Oleg and the destruction caused by the Russian bombs.

One afternoon, as Philomena was sitting in the lounge with Natalya enjoying a cup of tea, Norman rang her door bell. When he came in, Philomena introduced him to Natalya. She also explained her relationship with the charming Ukrainian woman. Norman was impressed. He asked her guest lots of questions about the situation in her country.

Over the following two hours, the three of them experienced a very pleasant time, but they were also aware of the reason behind their nice get-together. The awful war was never absent from their minds. Norman was intrigued by Natalya's situation, coming to Western Europe and leaving her husband behind.

At first, his impulse was to criticise her actions, fleeing instead of supporting her husband and the other Ukrainian soldiers. But the more he learned about the real situation in her country, the better he understood the fact that there was no shame in being a refugee, especially if one was running away from such brutal criminals who executed every Ukrainian civilian they encountered and raped every woman they fancied. Just like that. He'd seen pictures from the areas the Russians had captured but lost again. Dead bodies were lying in the streets and there were traces of awful war crimes wherever the Russians had been. So he revised his opinion and admired Natalya's courage.

When Norman had left, Natalya asked Philomena, "Why aren't you married?"

"I've never found the right man."

"No, I don't mean any man. I mean your Norman. It is so obvious you two people are in love. I have seen how he looks at you and I have seen how you look at him."

Philomena wondered what to answer. In the end, she came up with, "We just found it wouldn't work. There are many reasons, but they are personal."

"Oh, I'm sorry! I did not mean to pry – pry, is that the word?"

"Yes, that's the right word. Your English is very good."

"I hope it is. I used to work as a teacher of English back in my country."

"Good!" said Philomena. "You told me before. And what was your husband's job before the war, if I may ask?"

"He was a journalist. He wrote for a paper in Odessa. He knew a lot about the Russians. He had warned the readers more than a year before the invasion. He was certain that the Russians would attack our country sooner or later. With Belarus, it was the same thing. Putin made sure Lukashenko remained a disciple of his and when the opposition won the elections in 2020, and Lukashenko didn't leave his post, causing the people to go to the streets in masses to protest against the dictator, Putin supported his disciple and helped him to crush the entire opposition and to put its ringleaders into prison. He even helped to ground an airliner on its way from Turkey to the Baltics as it was flying over Belarus because they wanted to imprison one of the passengers who was an opponent of the regime."

"I understand."

"It is important for the West to recognise that the Russian dictator is absolutely without scruples. He has no moral conscience and he lives in a parallel world of his own imagination. He calls the Western politicians Nazis and he makes sure his own people live in a constant state of fear. The only TV channel that works consists of nothing but state propaganda, lies upon lies, every day. The Russians are being brainwashed all the time. Some of them are being blinded by consumerism in the big cities, while others are being kept in fear from the West. The slogan is 'Don't let the Nazis attack us again. I'm protecting you'."

Philomena sighed.

After she dropped Natalya at the refugee camp, she drove to her brother, Robert's, home. She wondered how much he knew of the war in Ukraine.

Robbie and Maggie were just preparing a light supper and invited Philomena to join them for the meal.

In the course of their conversation over a light meal with rye bread, cold bacon, tomatoes and cheese, Maggie complained that some vegetables were rationed in the supermarket, especially vegetables from Southern Europe. Philomena could explain these shortages. They were an indirect consequence of Brexit. Many traditional producers of Mediterranean vegetables in Spain, Portugal and Italy found that the customs formalities between the EU and Britain were keeping their transports waiting at Calais for too long. This cost money, so they made better profits by exporting their goods to EU countries. The export to the UK wasn't worth it.

Therefore, British supermarkets had to re-negotiate with their supply chains in those countries. All this was taking time. Philomena asked if Maggie didn't read the papers. Maggie replied that she was getting depressed by all the news about the war in Ukraine and about the country's reaction to it. The daily news was so full of warfare and weaponry that she'd given up watching the news on TV or reading the news in the papers. She wanted to have her peace and quiet.

"I hate to think of such awful things," she said.

"I think you're wrong, Maggie," said Robert. "As Philly here has said, this war touches all of us. If Putin cannot be stopped in Ukraine, he will go for other countries in Eastern Europe, Poland, the Baltic States…"

"Yes," said Philomena. "You see, Maggie, by helping Ukraine, we are defending our Western democracies against an evil dictator with an evil government who wants to re-establish the Russian colonial empire of the former Soviet Union."

Maggie put her hands over her ears. "I don't want to hear any more! All this talk about politics makes me sick."

Robert and his sister looked at each other. They saw that it was a hopeless situation. Maggie would never understand.

*   *   *

Philomena was travelling on the London Underground. She was on her way from Waterloo to Tottenham Court Road on the Northern Line because she wanted to look at some of the Egyptian exhibits in the

British Museum. She was sitting with her hands in her lap, lost in daydreaming, as many people are while travelling by tube.

At Embankment station, she registered a passenger who was sitting down opposite her. Lazily looking at the man, she suddenly felt a small shock. The man looked familiar. Who could he be? She racked her brain for such a familiar face in her memory.

The man was about twenty years her senior, an old man, probably some pensioner who was travelling for his pleasure on a weekday like this, like herself. He had a full grey beard that was well trimmed and his straight hair was grey, too. He wore a pair of round glasses. His face was narrow, his eyes looked friendly and he sat upright, seemingly quite fit for his age. His clothes were of good quality and rather chic. He somehow gave the impression of an intellectual Frenchman, which was enhanced by the way he looked round the carriage as if he were in search of someone or something.

She was suddenly sure she knew him, but she couldn't place him. If he opened his mouth and she could hear his voice, she thought, she would immediately recognise him. It was a situation that had occasionally happened to her in a similar fashion when she watched a film on TV and knew the name of one of the actors but just couldn't remember it. It just didn't come to her. She had the feeling she might just catch it in her mind, but it kept eluding her again and again.

Trying to find his name – and thus his identity – she went through the whole alphabet trying out name after name and hoping that the name would connect itself with the man's face. But it didn't work. In such situations, the name usually just jumped up later in her dreams at night or when she was busy doing something completely different.

When the train arrived at Tottenham Court Road, she felt reluctant to get off, convinced that her memory would come back and she would recognise the man if she could only look at him a little longer. But her better judgement prevailed and she made an effort to leave the carriage. She looked back from the platform and watched the train rush off until it disappeared in the tunnel.

Walking from the tube station to the museum, she was still trying to remember who the man could have been. Then she told herself it was no use. He was gone and she wouldn't be able to address him anyway.

At the museum, Philomena took herself to the Egyptian section. She was deeply impressed by some of the exhibits. But soon, her admiration of those mummies and stone slabs was overshadowed by the realisation that all these treasures really belonged to the Egyptian state. They were only here as reminders of the empire that her country had built up in earlier times. She immediately found excuses for her ancestors. What they did – stealing artefacts, enslaving people and killing whoever stood in their way – was common practice in those days. The French, the Dutch and the Spaniards did it and it stemmed from the European peoples' conviction of their own superiority. Besides, the church leaders and the trading interests – mercantilism – stood behind it. So her qualms were really an example of an anachronism. But were they really?

After looking at many more fascinating artefacts, she left the museum and walked along Great Russell Street to St Giles Circus, down Charing Cross Road and down Shaftesbury Avenue. When she saw some of the theatres, she decided to go for a play. She felt she needed a light comedy now after all those heavy thoughts about colonialism and the dark sides of history. A light comedy would be a sort of medicine for her now.

And she was right. Ninety minutes later, she left the playhouse with a light heart full of a joy of life. Some of the scenes of the play she had seen still produced a smile in her face and she even found herself silently humming one of the tunes that had been played in several scenes.

This light mood gave her the courage to turn into China Town. She soon found a suitable little restaurant that looked authentically Chinese enough and she went in for a pleasant early evening meal.

When she arrived back at her cottage in the village, she was in a strange mood. On the one hand, she felt relaxed and happy after an interesting and not unpleasant day out. On the other hand, there remained some hidden feeling of awkwardness in her stomach. Not because of her Chinese meal, no, that had been truly delicious, but because of the strange man on the underground and because of her bad memories of the dark sides of British history.

As she was settling down in her armchair, grabbing the remote control for her TV, she waited a few moments. She wanted to put things in their right perspective. Who was she, criticising the Russians for wanting to rebuild their lost empire? Her own ancestors had done the same thing with Africa and many other regions. The answer was, of course, that it was not the same thing when it was done three hundred years ago vs when it was attempted today, after the historical developments in the modern world. With this solution, Philomena managed to put her dark thought to rest.

She picked up the remote control and began to watch a crime story on BBC One. After that, she went to bed and tried to find some sleep.

As she was about to drift off into the land of dreams, it suddenly hit her. She knew the man! His name was Andrew Sullivan!

TWENTY-FOUR

"How have you been lately?" Maggie asked.

"Oh, I know you want to hear a short comment like 'I'm fine' or something along this line. But I'm sorry, I just get a little depressed with the situation in the world these days. I know you don't want to talk about politics, but we're all affected by the capital crimes that those evil dictators and mass murderers like Putin, Xi Jinping or Ali Khamenei, to name just a few of the worst criminals, are committing day by day." Philomena looked at Maggie with a meaningful expression.

"Come on, Philly," said Robert, "such crimes have been going on all the time. It's only that we get to hear about them more these days, you know, with TV and the Internet. But I don't think we should allow these things to depress us too much."

"The fact that such crimes have always been committed doesn't mean we've got to accept them," said Philomena. "I think we should have compassion and empathy with the victims. It's just a piece of good luck we're born here and not in Iran or China. And if we're not watchful, we might run into similar difficulties in Europe."

"Oh Philly," said Maggie. "You're exaggerating. Such atrocious crimes could never happen in Europe. We're far too civilised."

"People in Russia or Iran go back a long time in cultural history and they achieved lots of good things in the past. But the problem is that in more recent times, they have fallen prey to populist politicians. And as we can see in certain European countries, such tendencies can be found not too far away from us, too."

375

For a few minutes, they were all silent and concentrated on their food. Philomena was here as a dinner guest. It was Maggie's birthday. Robert didn't mind some serious conversation at the dinner table, but Maggie felt that such topics were ruining her birthday party. After those talks about the political threats, Philomena felt she shouldn't spoil the party and held back with her opinions. There was no way to convince Maggie anyway.

Robert took the initiative. "I say, did you know, Philly? You were seen in Hastings last week. And you weren't alone. I saw you with a man!"

"Oh, my dear!" cried Maggie. "You've found a man at last? Tell us, is it serious?"

"I don't know what you mean by 'serious'. He is a good friend and we've known each other for quite some time."

"Oh, but that's wonderful. I'm so happy for you!"

"Maggie, I don't know how the fact that I've been seen walking with a man could make you happy."

"Oh, you sly creature, you! I'm sure there's more to it than meets the eye, as they say." Maggie winked with her left eye.

"Listen," said Philomena. "If I should ever decide to live with a man – which is highly unlikely – I would certainly notify you first of all people. Now, does this satisfy you?"

"All right, point taken." However, Maggie still wanted to know more. "But tell us who the man was, anyway."

"As I said, he's a good friend. His name is Norman and he lives in the same village. I also know his father and they are both very interesting and educated men. Is this enough?"

Robert wanted to put a stop to this pointless discussion. "Let's change the subject. Have you read any interesting books lately?"

So with this change of topic, at last, Philomena could escape her cross-examination. She was glad to talk about other things. She decided to throw a bait to Maggie's eager inquisitiveness. "You remember some months ago you told me you liked the author Giulia Montepulciano? In fact, I happened to meet her the other day. Norman introduced us."

She looked at her sister-in-law, enjoying the little game.

Maggie nearly exploded. "Oh my! They say she is very reclusive, nobody knows her. She doesn't hold any reading events or give interviews. Also, there aren't any pictures of her. You lucky devil, tell me more about her!"

"She is an ugly middle-aged spinster, to tell you the truth. But she has made a handsome packet of money with her novels."

"Oh, I should imagine. Did you have one of her books signed?"

"I'm afraid I didn't have any of her books with me at the time."

Maggie went on questioning her about her favourite author and Philomena made quite a game of it, enjoying Maggie's enthusiasm. After a while, she realised it wasn't very fair on Maggie and tried to change the topic. She asked Robert if he'd heard from their mother or father. She knew that their mother was in a nursing home in Maidstone and their father had left her several years ago.

"She is still mad at Dad for leaving her. Her health is getting worse by the week. I was there last week and found her in a bad way. Her heart is giving her trouble. The doctor says she should really get a new heart, but not only are heart transplantations very difficult because there aren't enough donor organs available, but they are also extremely expensive. The NHS representative said it's not normally attempted at Mum's age."

"Are you saying old people are not worth the effort of a complicated operation?"

"That's what it means, yes."

So we might not have our mother for much longer?" asked Philomena.

"I'm afraid that's true."

"Tell me, have you heard from Dad lately?"

"Not for about two years. Apparently, he's still in Thailand. At least, that's the last I heard from him. He's still with that Thai woman he found in a London massage salon."

"I wonder if we would ever hear from him – or from her – if he should fall seriously ill. After all, he's in his mid-eighties. Do you know if his floozy speaks English at all?"

"I think she does. But what are you thinking?"

"I was just thinking," said Philomena, "if we shouldn't take him back to England and find a nursing home for him. What do you think?"

"Let him rot in Thailand!" cried Robert, quite agitated.

"So you've never forgiven him for leaving Mum, have you?"

Robert didn't answer this question. But she knew the answer. They had both been quite angry at their father when he left their mother and ran off with a young Thai woman, thirty years his junior. That had been nearly twenty years ago now.

"I think we should forget the past and face the facts. Our father is an old man, living in Thailand with the woman he obviously loves and we should worry about his health and his health insurance, which I believe to be somewhat wanting over there."

"I don't mind if you want to do something about it, if you want to spend your good money and throw it down the drain by trying to help him come back."

"That could be expensive!" shouted Maggie. She felt being left out of the discussion and wanted to make her point. "I don't think you could afford to move him back to England. Where would you find the money even just for his airfare?"

Philomena was very careful not to let Maggie think she had a lot of money. So she just said, "I think I could get it from a friend."

"And then be in debt?" asked Maggie.

"Oh, I can sell some of my books," said Philomena.

"Listen, Philly," appealed Robert. "As I said, you can do that if you like, but don't ask me for any help or even financial support."

"Okay, that's settled then. I'll go and make enquiries about getting him back home. I'll let you know of any steps taken, but you don't need to worry about any contributions from your side."

Two days later, Philomena got a phone call from Robert informing her that their mother's health had got worse. The nursing home was asking them to come to see their mother while they still could. Her condition was obviously very critical.

Philomena started her new electric car – which happened to be fully charged – and drove to the nursing home. While driving along the country roads, she was thinking of her mother. She hadn't seen her for nearly six months. She found it difficult to meet her because she still blamed her for the discord between her parents. She had

379

fully understood her father when he left. Her mother had made his life such hell. Indeed, she'd made everybody's life very difficult with her fixed ideas and her bossy ways. Even though she considered the whole affair to be her parents' business, she had taken sides and always found it difficult to talk to her mother in a relaxed way to this day.

As feared by everybody, her mother was very weak. Philomena realised she might see her for the last time when she stood at her bedside. Her mother's weakness didn't prevent her from cursing her husband who had left her in such a shameful way. So, instead of concentrating on her health and keeping the energy that was left to her, she went on and on about her wasted life and the crook who had been her husband. It was difficult for Philomena to remain calm. When she left the nursing home – probably for the last time, she thought – she tried to keep a positive image of her mother in her mind. She wanted to cherish a positive memory of her own mother.

Two days later, the news of her death arrived. Robert, whose relationship with their mother was a little better, offered to look after the arrangements. He only wanted Philomena's promise to help with any financial matters, if needed.

After another few days, the funeral took place. Of course, Philomena attended the ceremony. She found she had to make an effort to keep calm when the priest told the congregation what a wonderful person Linda Webster had been. That was the custom. One never bore any grudge when someone was dead. Philomena remembered a saying they had learned in her Latin class at school so many years ago. *De mortuis nil nisi bene*. When talking about the dead, mention only good things.

Philomena drove home in deep thought. Now that her mother was dead and buried, life took on a different shape, especially because her father was a very old man. Soon enough, she and her brother would be in the front line. Theirs would be the next turn to leave the world. And neither of them had any children. That would be the end of the Webster line.

Was this very bad? She wondered. In what ways did the lives of people with lots of children and grandchildren differ from hers? Their children were leaving their homes anyway, very often there were even quarrels between parents and children. The new generation had to redefine their world, outlooks and interpretations. Even their language. If she remembered some of the words that young people of today were in the habit of using without any qualms, words that had been taboo or even unknown in her young days, she blushed.

When she entered her cottage, there was a letter waiting for her. Her father was the only person she knew who still wrote letters. He hated the Internet, so he didn't know how to send an email message. In his letter, at least, he gave the email address of his lady friend. She called herself Leonie, which was probably her adopted European name, not her polysyllabic Thai name.

The letter gave the details of her father's return to England. He and Leonie had decided to come back and spend the remaining days of their common life somewhere in the south of England. They seemed to have enough money to buy a small bungalow. So Philomena didn't have to worry about the financial side of this plan. In fact, both parts of the letter – her father's and Leonie's – were very friendly, even charming. They asked her if she could have a look around for a suitable property. If possible, not too far away from her place. This might prove to be quite tricky. Did she want to have her father and his lady friend near her? That would probably mean a new burden in her life. She decided to think about this possibility for a while before she would be ready to agree to such a plan.

She discussed the situation with her brother a few days after their mother's funeral. Robert was upset at first. He furiously blamed their father for leaving their mother. When Philomena explained that she would make sure everything would run smoothly and she promised to be financially responsible for their father's accommodation and upkeep, if necessary, he calmed down and agreed. He didn't believe that the old man or his lady friend had the means to buy a property in England, but his sister's promise satisfied him.

"But I don't have to be his good boy again, do I?" he asked. "You know, I don't mind if you want to re-establish friendly relations with him, but please leave me out of it. I'm finished with the old crook."

Philomena consulted Norman on the search for a suitable bungalow for her father and Leonie. Together, they went through the property ads on the Internet. On a platform called RightMove, they found a number of possible properties. So, over the following weeks, they drove around the area looking at some suitable properties. Norman was very helpful not only in navigating them to the locations but also in asking the estate agents the right questions. They knew they had a few weeks before the arrival of the Thai branch of her family, as she liked to think of Dad and Leonie.

*   *   *

When Philomena and Norman were waiting for the arrival of the British Airways flight from Bangkok, they realised that the crowds at Heathrow had returned to their pre-pandemic levels. The terminal was so crowded, they couldn't believe it. Philomena had assumed that more and more people these days were giving up long-distance air travel because of the dangers of the pandemic – which was still around – and because of the environment. Especially in the aftermath of the Russian attack on Ukraine, it had become clear to most people that our natural resources are limited and we all have to do our bit in saving the emission of carbon dioxide into the atmosphere. We are all called upon to save energy and curb the use of internal combustion engines. The news was full of information about the amount of climate-changing gases produced by a single long-distance flight. But what they observed at this Heathrow terminal now spoke a different language. Everybody seemed to be so careless about climate change. Long-distance travel seemed to be the highlight of the day.

Philomena and Norman were patient and waited.

Soon, the arrival of the flight from Bangkok was announced on the great panel of the arrivals hall and after another forty-five minutes, their expected passengers came through the gate. A middle-aged Thai woman was pushing a baggage trolley full of suitcases, while an airport attendant was pushing an old man in a wheelchair. Philomena recognised her father immediately.

Greetings were exchanged and they walked in the direction of the carpark shuttle bus, where the airport attendant left them and Philomena took over while Norman helped Leonie with the bags.

Once settled in Norman's Jaguar, they could all start from square one. Greetings were exchanged again and Philomena asked how everybody was. During the following two hours, driving along the M25 and beyond, the atmosphere relaxed and all four passengers were involved in lively discussions about their health, the situation of the British economy and the problems of the world.

When the talk came to the housing market, Norman, who was at the wheel and had to concentrate on the heavy traffic, explained that since Michael Webster and Leonie had been in England the last time, prices had gone up considerably. For a small bungalow these days, they would have to look at something like the sum for which they would have got a five-bedroom family home in their time.

Norman and his father had invited the new arrivals to live in their house until their new bungalow would be ready. As soon as Michael and Leonie were settled, Norman took them to view the bungalows that he and Philomena had pre-selected for them. They soon decided on a quiet place in the outskirts of Hastings. Their offer was accepted and the long and absurd process of buying a property began at their solicitor's office.

Not only had the property prices gone up over the past thirty years, but the process of buying had been made a lot more complicated; in fact, it had become so absurd that one wondered how anyone still went along with all those stupid questions in the process. Were they planning to build a nuclear power station on the property? Were they planning to breed pigs or poultry on the property? Were they willing to contribute financially if their parish church would ever need to renovate its choir section?

These and more absurd questions had to be answered and then it still took ages until, at last, the contracts could be exchanged and the completion day could be fixed. Everyone was relieved when the day arrived at last.

After a few more renovations, which took another few weeks, Michael and Leonie moved in and Norman and his father had their house to themselves again. The new bungalow in Hastings proved to be ideal for old people. It was suitable for a wheelchair and it wasn't too far from the shops. Leonie would be able to look after Michael very well from a nice and practical spot like this. And Leonie really seemed the perfect companion for him. She even organised a modest house-warming party about two weeks after moving in. Norman and Philomena came, but Robert and Maggie declined.

After they had settled in at last, Philomena regularly came to see them and so she re-established her relations with her father. She began to like Leonie, who was always very friendly and cheerful when Philomena visited.

One day, she was sitting in the lounge of the bungalow with her father. They were talking about the old days.

"I thought you never liked my friend Sandy," Philomena remarked. "At least, that's the impression you gave us."

"You were wrong. Yes, I criticised her. She had her faults, but they were only a consequence of her snobbish upbringing. I could see how much you liked her, so I didn't want to spoil your friendship."

"Yes, she was my best friend."

"But then something happened that put an end to your relationship. Would you like to talk about it?"

"I don't know that talking about it could help. What happened is one of the darkest chapters in my life."

"Well, well!" her father exclaimed. "These are strong words. You don't normally tend to exaggerate things. At least you used to be more balanced in your judgements. I don't know about now. Have you dismissed Sandy from your life?"

"She died, so she took her own leave. I would have liked to mend things with her, but she died before we could really renew our friendship."

"Oh, what did she die of?"

"Covid. It happened in India. She lived there for quite a long time after what had happened, well, all that muddle all those years ago."

"What happened?"

"I don't really know exactly, but it was hard for her," Philomena said in a tone of finality. So her father felt he shouldn't ask any more questions. She wondered if she ought to tell him more, but what would be the point?

When, over the following weeks, she suffered from bad dreams again, she asked herself if it might not be a good idea to tell him everything. As things stood between them now, he seemed a very understanding and wise old man and he was certainly on her side, being her father. He would be full of empathy and he wouldn't blame her.

After putting it off for another two weeks, she came to the conclusion that her dreams were really worrying her very much. Nearly every night, she dreamt that she was about to murder Miss Mitford – she still called her that in her dreams! – and she injured Andrew Sullivan with a skillet from the kitchenette in the hut. Her victim never really died, but she always seemed to be on the point of dying. The poor woman's cries were truly awful, heartbreaking. She usually woke up from those cries, drenched in sweat. This was an unbearable condition. There was some hope that telling her father everything might alleviate her nightly suffering and release her from the nightmare.

She knew that she had already told Norman everything, but there would be a chance that her father's reaction might have a different effect on her peace of mind. For one thing, while Norman was her best friend these days, her father was an authority from her past, someone she also trusted but who was from a different generation. Also, while Norman had never known Sandy except through her own reports, her father had known Sandy personally. He'd even been acquainted with Andrew Sullivan and Christine Mitford from the few parents' meetings he had attended. So things looked somewhat different from his perspective.

She consulted Norman on this point. "Do you think I can risk telling my dad everything about my involvement in the murder case in that forest all those years ago?"

Norman was clear. "Of course, it would do you a lot of good. I don't think there would be any negative effects. He certainly wouldn't report you to the police and he would probably be able to convince you that it wasn't your fault. You might accept the truth at last. The fact that you're not a murderer and it had all been your friend's fault."

This settled it. As soon as the opportunity presented itself – with Leonie out of the house shopping and her father in a relaxed mood sitting in his armchair in the lounge – Philomena carefully approached the delicate subject again.

After some preliminary small talk, she came to the point. "I say, Dad, would you be interested in more details about what happened in the forest all those years ago? I mean, would you like to hear my version of those events? As you might have noticed, it worries me very much and

I think that telling you could perhaps be good for my peace of mind."

"Of course, my dear! You can trust me with your secret. I'll be a well-meaning listener of your story. I'm sure it won't be as bad as you think."

After this assurance, Philomena began to tell him about her one-sided friendship with Sandy, Sandy's more forward activities in her sexual development and her affair with Sullivan.

"She treated me like some naïve schoolgirl, giving herself airs as a prospective fashion model or even movie actress. She ridiculed me when I expressed my doubts about her relationship with Sullivan, who was our teacher, after all."

"How did you find out about her affair with the teacher?"

"Do you remember when I asked you about British car registrations and about Range Rovers?"

"Yes, I do. I was surprised and pleased about your interest in something like that. That wasn't normally something that girls wanted to know."

"Indeed. Well, it was because I had seen a Range Rover like Sullivan's in the forest and it seemed that Sandy had been in the car with him. I wanted to check if my guess was correct."

"Did you challenge your friend?"

"Yes. She didn't deny it. She was ever so proud of her love affair with Sullivan. It made her feel grown-up. I know she was a year older than me, but she was still a teenager and the whole affair was illegal. She laughed at my scruples."

Her father looked hard at her before he went on. "I knew about that affair."

Philomena was surprised and asked him how he knew.

"I saw them. I was walking along Bewl Water with my mate, Brian, checking locations for fishing when I saw them cuddling behind some bushes. I recognised both of them immediately, but they didn't see me."

"Did you do anything about your discovery? Did you tell Mum?"

"No, I didn't tell anyone. Your mother would have made a big scandal out of it and who else could I tell? I only tried to warn you to be a bit more careful about your friend Sandy. But for you, that was only a parent's routine warning."

"I see. I don't know if an intervention from you might have changed things in the long run."

"You're quite right. But my discovery had made me more watchful. Sandy being your best friend meant that you might be drawn into her lifestyle, too. You might suddenly find it attractive to fall in love with a grown-up man. So I watched you more carefully."

"What! You watched me?" she cried.

"Yes, but only for your protection. I saw it as my duty as your father."

After her surprise, she calmed down again. "And did your watch over me lead to any new discoveries?"

"I couldn't watch you all the time. After all, I still had my job. So I had to satisfy myself by select watchfulness. I managed to check on you sometimes when there was absolutely no danger and sometimes when things really were on the brink of danger for you."

"Such as?"

"For example, one day when you were on the beach in Hastings. I saw you on the beach in your bathing things. Sandy was constantly trying to attract men by stretching

389

her body in such an erotic way that I feared she would be seen as a role model by you. She might even have tried to attract a couple of young men and tempted you to team up with one of them."

"And then? Did anything happen?"

"No, it turned out to be a false alarm. But you've got to admit Sandy was trying to convince you to show yourself to the men on the beach like some model."

"Yes, that's true. But I never knew you spied on us. Didn't you feel bad about it?"

"Of course, I felt bad sometimes. But the bottom line of my watchful activities is that I knew pretty well how potentially dangerous your admiration for your friend Sandy was."

Philomena wasn't sure if what her father had been telling her was a good or a bad thing. A father who was spying on his daughter! On the one hand, she found it an inexcusable act of encroachment, but on the other hand, she could understand her father in that special situation and she even felt grateful to him for his watchfulness.

"I could tell you more that you don't know about, but I can hear Leonie coming through the front door."

When Leonie entered the lounge, she said hello to Philomena and said she thought it a wonderful thing for father and daughter to have a heart-to-heart talk from time to time. She would go to the kitchen now. Would Philomena stay for supper?

Philomena thanked her and declined. She said she had to go, but she would be back soon.

"Yes, my dear," said her father. "We've still got a lot of ground to cover in our discussions, don't you think so?"

"Yes, and I'm looking forward to our next chat, Dad."

With these words, Philomena took her leave and drove home. She promised herself she would visit her father again as soon as possible.

When she reached her home, she sat down at the kitchen table with a hot cup of tea and began to sort her thoughts and her conflicting emotions.

Soon, the day had reached the twilight of dusk.

TWENTY-FIVE

Over the following weeks, Philomena mainly occupied herself with her new manuscript. At last, the day arrived when she wrote the last sentence of her new novel. She put the printed version away, planning to come back to it after a week or two and read it again with a critical mind. Like that, she could at least make sure there were no serious flaws, misprints or other errors. She wouldn't send the completed manuscript to her agent before another careful proofreading.

She made herself a nice cup of tea and sat down in her kitchen, looking out through the window and observing the birds.

There was a thumping noise from the floor near her front door. The mail had arrived. Philomena stood up, strolled to the hall and picked up the mail. There were useless flyers from various furniture shops and from new take-away businesses in the area. And there was the paper. She threw the flyers away and sat down in her lounge with the paper.

One of the headlines struck her, "Unsolved murder case reopened."

She read through the entire article. Of course, it was about *her* murder case. There was hardly anything really new about it. The only new development was the fact that a new witness had been questioned by the police. The witness's name wasn't given in full, only his initials and the fact that he was a man. The initials could be Henry's. She wondered what Henry could have to do with the case. Well, he was Sandy's brother, but they didn't know about Sandy's involvement either.

She decided to call him.

He answered his phone after several rings. When he recognised Philomena, he sounded relieved and happy. She asked him about his interview with the police.

"Oh, there wasn't such a big excitement as the press were trying to make out. As you might remember, the police knew about Sandy's friendship with Sullivan and with Sullivan's disappearance, they wanted to make sure again that there was nothing that I, being Sandy's brother, could possibly contribute to the discovery of his whereabouts and to the solution of the case."

"And did you tell them anything they didn't already know?"

"I don't think so. I told them that I only had a vague idea of Sandy's friendship with her French teacher. Also, I confirmed the fact that Sandy had gone to India after the whole affair. In the end, they seemed to be satisfied."

"And is that all you could tell them?" Philomena wanted to know more.

"With you, I can be frank. I didn't tell them that I really knew that she had an illicit affair with the Sullivan guy. I merely called it a friendship. But we both know there was a lot more. That's private, isn't it?"

"But listen, Henry. Have you told me everything that you know about the case?"

This time, she had to wait a bit longer for his answer. When he remained silent, she urged him to tell her everything. After a lot of prevarication, he admitted. "Let's not talk about it on the phone."

So they arranged to meet at their usual café in Maidstone on the same afternoon.

When they were seated opposite each other in the café, she fixed his eyes with hers and asked him to tell her the whole truth.

"She sent me a letter from India," he said.

This really surprised Philomena and she wanted to know everything that stood in the letter. But Henry was more careful.

"Please," she begged, "let me see the letter."

"I'm sorry, I can't."

"Why?"

"Because I destroyed it. It was far too dangerous. It was practically a confession. She wrote that she had murdered the Mitford woman. So I knew."

"And you believed her?"

"Why should she write something like that if it wasn't true?"

"Because she was mentally disturbed and she just imagined she had been the murderer. It was a fixed idea with her. Did she write anything else?"

"Yes. She wrote that you were a witness. She called you one of her witnesses."

Philomena could see how dangerous that letter would have been for her, too. She wanted to know more. "Did she write how many witnesses there were?"

"She mentioned three witnesses. You, Sullivan and a third guy who happened to be present."

Philomena was quite surprised. She remembered how she had also been under the impression that there had been another person involved. But because she had been nearly unconscious with everything that happened, she dismissed that impression, assuming it was just a figment of her own imagination. After all, how could another person have come to the forest hut? And how could he have been involved? But if Sandy had told Henry, there might have been some truth behind it. On the other hand, Sandy had never told her about that other person. Mystery over mystery!

"Tell me, did she write anything about that other witness? Was it a man or a woman? Did she know him or her?"

"She only wrote that it was a young man, but she had no idea who he could've been. Apparently, he was physically attacked by both Sullivan and Miss Mitford. That was all. There was nothing else of interest in her letter."

Philomena and Henry were silent after that. Obviously, he had put this story away in his mind a long time ago and talking about it now upset him almost as much as it disturbed her.

After a period of silence, she said, "And you didn't tell the police anything?"

"Nothing at all."

"Why? I mean, you had nothing to lose."

"Can't you guess? I knew you were with Sandy on most of her exploits, so I thought you might have been part of the action at the forest hut, too. Since she wrote that you were a witness, I knew you were there and though I never believed you to be guilty of murder, I feared that things might become a bit tight for you if the police knew you were there at the time of the crime."

"So you protected me?"

"In a way, yes." He hesitated before he went on. "You know, there was a time when I was actually in love with you. I never told you. I thought you considered me too dry and too old. Although that's a thing of the past now, it still remains in my memory as a very good period. Well, that's why I still want to protect you whenever necessary. You can trust me a hundred per cent. I'll never betray you. And I'm sure you are innocent. Sandy was a lot more aggressive and adventurous than you. You

395

couldn't hurt a fly. I only hope you don't mind my protective attitude."

"Oh, Henry!"

"Yes, let's just leave things as they are. We are just good friends."

"I agree. If you are still protecting me, as you say, I want to thank you, but I also want to release you from your self-imposed duty. Just forget about my involvement in the murder case, but if you want to tell the police, please do so. I don't want you to be under any obligation to me. Besides – well, you never know. I might be the murderer."

"Let me be the judge of this myself."

They agreed to keep silent about the case once and for all. They shook hands on it across the table. And after some more small talk, they left the café and went home.

* * *

When Philomena's new novel – her first serious novel – was published, it was received well by critics. But after an initial interest immediately after the book launch, sales dropped to a very low level. It seemed that the plot was too complicated and the characters were too serious, lacking a sense of humour. Obviously, today's readers demanded characters that they could relate to more easily.

One Sunday, about two months after the book's publication, Philomena was invited for lunch at Robert and Maggie's house. During their pre-dinner drinks, Maggie remarked that she didn't like her book.

"I only managed to read the first fifty pages but then I gave up. Why do you mix the characters like that? Why does the reader never quite know whose perspective we're looking from? It's all beyond me. Then there are all those quotations from other authors that the main character has in mind. Who was that Proust chap? And who were those guys called Locke and Hume?"

"Well, they were – "

"Never mind, my dear. I wouldn't know them even if you told me. I don't believe in name-dropping just to appear clever. But tell me. Why do you make things so complicated for the normal reader?"

Philomena wondered what to say to her sister-in-law. She decided to say something final and then change the topic. "Don't mind if the book is beyond you. Just put it away. I'm not offended if you prefer authors like that Montepulciano woman to me as an author. I say, have you heard the latest news from Brussels? I mean, about their support of Ukraine?"

The tricky situation was circumnavigated like that. Philomena smiled at herself because of the irony in her comparison with Giulia Montepulciano. But she was also touched in a strange way. Could it be, perhaps, that she was being too arrogant? Was there a grain of academic arrogance in her novel? The idea worried her.

After the meal, when Maggie was in the kitchen putting some things away so that he could look after the remaining kitchen chores later, Robert quickly returned to the topic of his sister's new novel.

"Listen, Philly, just one comment about your book, if you allow. I only read the first half and I think it's brilliant. Please ignore Maggie's comments. It must be hard for an author to see their book misunderstood. What an author needs most of all are encouragement and serious critical praise. I'm sorry if you've got to continue your career as a writer without critical success."

She was thinking of her huge success as a romance writer, though that came from different quarters, and it made her smile.

"Don't worry," she answered. "I am satisfied with my success on the whole."

Then Maggie came back from the kitchen and they began to talk about the latest film and about last night's TV programme. Philomena took great care not to say anything about topics closer to her heart, such as literature or politics.

After her meal with Robert and Maggie, when Philomena returned to her cottage, she phoned Norman and discussed her concern about her possible academic arrogance. He took her seriously and discussed the various aspects of this issue.

"One thing is clear to me," he said. "When you want to take up some of the great discussions of our cultural history, you've got to consider what great minds of the past had to say about them. So if we quote from clever books, we're only doing our intellectual duty. For many issues of the world these days, for example, we can hardly contribute a serious idea without quoting from Shakespeare or even some of the ancient Greek and Roman writers. I'm thinking of the modern ideas in Plato or Aristotle, but also of clever minds that made the Age of Enlightenment possible."

"Yes, that's what seems important for me, too," she answered.

"I mean, just look at what's happening in Ukraine these days. Look at the absolute madness of the Russian leader. Doesn't it appear to you that the majority of the Russian leaders – except perhaps Gorbachev – had such absurd ideas that suggest that the whole concept of the Enlightenment has never really reached Russia? It's a frightening thought, but what common ground can we find on which an attempt at peace negotiations could be based? The Russian dictator and his henchmen apparently don't believe in any international laws or humanitarian concepts."

The discussion went on like this for some time. Then they called it a day and decided to continue the discussion at some later opportunity. They rang off, and soon Philomena dropped off to sleep in front of her TV set.

Two days later, she woke up with a strange pain in her stomach. She couldn't imagine what might be wrong with her. She hadn't eaten anything that she would normally have any problems with. For a while, during her morning routine, she managed to put it from her mind. But in the middle of the morning, the pain returned.

Suddenly, she was struck by a frightening thought. She might be seriously ill! So far, her life had been without any serious health issues. She had been so lucky.

Should she see a doctor?

No, she considered it more important to settle her affairs. So she phoned the only solicitor she had ever dealt with, an elderly man by the name of James Holloway. They made an appointment at his chambers. Two days later, she was sitting in the visitor's chair in his office.

"So you want to draw up your last will and testament, as I understand?"

"Yes, that's my intention. I want to write it in such a way that it can't be contested. That's what I need your help for. You know the correct wording."

"Yes, but I must not influence you in any way."

"I know that, but I want things to go my way and no one should be able to change my will later."

"Have you any fears? Is there a danger of anyone from your family or among your friends tampering with your legacy after you've gone? Are there any criminal minds among your acquaintances? Or is your legacy so large that you think somebody might be tempted to interfere?"

"Yes, my fortune is considerable. That's why I've got to be careful."

She mentioned the sum that was printed on her latest bank statement and James Holloway had to swallow hard. "And it's all legal? I mean, have you always paid your taxes, or will there be any problems from that quarter?"

She assured him that it was all above board and gave him the name and address of her business manager. She gave him permission to consult him.

When she left Mr Holloway's office, she went home. There, in the safety of her kitchen, looking out of the window at the birds in her garden, she took the courage needed to call a doctor. She had an appointment in three weeks' time.

This gave her the time needed to write down her last will and testament. Mr Holloway had given her a model will, a sort of blueprint for any type of private will. With its help, she managed to write her own will with the correct jargon, thus making sure it couldn't be contested afterwards.

On Saturday, she was sitting in Norman's lounge. At first, Norman's father was with them and they discussed the war in Ukraine. Philomena told them about her latest exchanges with Natalya.

When his father had left the room to watch his favourite programme on TV, Norman joined Philomena on the sofa.

"Obviously, you have something on your mind, haven't you?" he began.

She said yes and told him about her stomach pains and about her testament. She didn't give him any details, but she conveyed its seriousness to him. Then she asked him if she could name him as her executor in her will.

"Of course. I feel honoured by your trust. But do you really think you need to worry about such things? I mean, you're still quite young and fit. There'll be plenty of time to look after that side of things when you're another ten or twenty years older. Or have you got any other reasons for such a panic reaction?"

She told him about her fears in connection with the pains in her stomach, which just wouldn't go away. He played them down, but when he realised how important and serious this was for her, he apologised and promised that she could rely on him. As he said before, he would be honoured to act as her executor. He urged her to see a doctor. Then she would be relieved.

The following Wednesday, Norman accompanied Philomena to Mr Holloway's office. He signed all the papers he had to and she signed her completed last will and testament. Both men were quite impressed by the large sum of her fortune and also her generosity in her will. She bequeathed large sums of money to charities, her friend Natalya and Norman himself, plus a modest sum to her brother, Robert.

On the way back from the solicitor's chambers, Norman asked Philomena about her health. "Have you still got that irksome stomach ache?"

When she told him how bad it was, he asked her if she'd made an appointment with a doctor. She said yes and she added that she had a really awful foreboding.

"Some nights, I feel this is going to be my undoing."

"What do you mean?" he asked, full of concern. "You don't think this is a fatal disease, do you?"

She was quiet for a few moments, then she answered. "Yes, I do. I'm quite sure this is very bad and I might die from it."

"Oh, come on," he cried. "You are far too young to die. Besides, you can't do this to me. I couldn't cope with it. I don't want to lose you!"

She looked at him from the side.

"Let's wait and see. It's only, well, I just can't help my justified fears. But listen, Norman. If this is going to be the end of me, will you promise to make sure my last will is carried out to the letter, not only in terms of the different legacies but also in terms of the arrangements for my royalties from my romances? Fifty per cent of the royalties are to go to the charities I stated. This is particularly important because I'm afraid my sister-in-law might react with protest when she finds out about my fortune. She'll certainly try to contest the will and steer all my money in her direction. Do you promise to prevent that?"

Norman promised, but he also protested that all her fears were definitely premature. She would live to ninety or a hundred.

When the day came for her doctor's appointment, Philomena was no longer nervous. She had gone through a period of worry and fear over the preceding few days, but now that she was on the way to receive her verdict, she was extremely calm. Whatever the verdict, she had already accepted it.

The doctor made a series of tests. Then he sent her to St. Thomas's Hospital in London for further tests. These took another few days.

When she had her diagnosis, she phoned Norman and asked him to take her to the seaside. She didn't tell him the diagnosis until they were settled in a holiday cottage at Cooden Beach.

It was on the evening of the day of their arrival. Sitting in two armchairs, looking out towards the sea, they were ready for the truth at last.

"It's a case of pancreatic cancer in an advanced stage. I've got a few weeks at most."

Norman asked if there was anything he could do.

"Yes, you can stay here with me for a whole week. You will sleep with me and after the end of the week, you will leave me alone. You will go to your home and I will go to my home, waiting for the end."

"If this is what you wish," he said.

EPILOGUE

When the funeral for Philomena Webster was advertised on the notice-board of the local church and in the paper, nobody but Norman Winslow knew that during the ceremony, the true identity of the well-known romance writer Giulia Montepulciano was going to be announced to the world.

When the priest read out the biography of the deceased, his announcement of her pen name at first had no effect. The congregation didn't quite know what a pen name or a *nom de plume* was. But after a few seconds, a young woman in the congregation stood up and politely but eagerly asked the priest if he could repeat what he'd just said about Giulia Montepulciano.

Having been informed of the enormity of this revelation beforehand by Norman, the priest knew perfectly well that there might be some form of reaction from the congregation. So he complied with the woman's request and made things quite clear.

"My dear friends, what I've just said is true. Philomena Webster *was* Giulia Montepulciano! She used this literary pseudonym to protect herself and her private life."

After this, there was a general murmur in the congregation. One of the parishioners, a regular from the local pub who had always considered Philomena a woman of no importance, but who considered himself to be a particularly sharp observer of people, stood up and left the church, taking his mobile phone from his pocket.

By the time the ceremony was over and people began to file out of the church, there were already two news reporters waiting for whoever could give them more information about the revelation made during the funeral service. It was soon clear that Mr Winslow was the man to give this information. After all, he had been Miss Montepulciano's friend. So he was the man to approach.

The reporters and other people crowded around Norman and in the end, the whole ceremony seemed to be staged for Miss Montepulciano and not for Philomena Webster. Her identity disappeared behind the great news of the day. Like this, she only survived as the great novelist while her true self became a nobody again.

And a dog was barking in the distance.

About the Author

Rudolph Bader studied English and German literature and Near Eastern languages. He got his academic credentials in Switzerland and Germany. In his academic career he worked as a researcher and visiting professor at various universities in Canada, Australia, Germany and Switzerland, publishing widely in the field of postcolonial literatures. He translated Shakespeare, and he was active in teacher training, initiating a number of intercultural projects in education. Having lived and worked in different countries, he speaks several languages. After 2008, he has devoted himself to the writing of novels in English. His previous novels include *The Prison of Perspective* (2010) and *White Lies* (2018), which have also been translated into German. Today, he lives in Switzerland.

Printed in Great Britain
by Amazon

29560038R00229